THE THREADS ⊙F FATE

SEA OF INK PRESS

WAR ON THE GODS

4

THE THREADS OF FATE

A. P. MOBLEY

SEA OF INK PRESS

For Tory, Dillan, Mom, Nikki, and Gabrielle.

If it weren't for you guys dragging me kicking and screaming to the finish line, it would have taken a whole lot longer to finish this book.

CHAPTER ONE

AVATAR

MILLENNIA AGO . . .

Ancient Times

Metis sucked in a sharp breath, bracing herself for the moment her daughter would burst from the dark, warm, stinking prison of Zeus's body. After all, the Titan Goddess of Wisdom and Cunning knew that when it happened, it would be her only chance to escape.

She couldn't say for sure how much time had passed since Zeus had swallowed her. All she knew was that one moment, they'd been in love, happily married. She'd been pregnant with what was sure to be the first of many children. The next, he'd convinced her to turn herself into a fly. Then he'd swallowed her whole, and she'd soon overheard a conversation he'd shared with Poseidon and Hades—all about how he'd betrayed her because their second child was prophesied to overthrow him.

What Metis *could* say was that she'd been trapped inside of Zeus's stomach long enough to give birth to a glowing little goddess with silver irises and a shock of curly hair that matched her eyes. What seemed like years passed, and the babe had developed into a youth.

"Mother, what will I be called when I finally leave this place?" she'd asked Metis only a short while ago. She had many questions regarding the world outside of Zeus, and especially about where she belonged in it.

After some careful thought, Metis answered the question. *"You will be called Athena."* She tenderly stroked Athena's silver ringlets, which had grown so long they tumbled down her back. *"And you will be the wisest, fiercest goddess this world has ever seen."*

Athena smiled, though the expression brought Metis no joy. It was a cruel grin—one of satisfaction, of pride. It reminded the Titan goddess far too much of her treacherous husband. *Even still, Athena is my daughter*, Metis thought. *My beloved girl. I shall do all I can to prepare her for the trials ahead. She is not at fault for her heritage.* And so Metis had set to the task of using her magic to craft armor, a helmet, and a spear for Athena, preparing the youth for the moment she stepped into the outside world.

Now, that time had almost come. Metis allowed the enchantments keeping Athena small to fade away, and she became larger by the second. Before, she'd been as little as an insect, since Metis had ensured they'd both stayed tiny inside of Zeus. Better to remain undetected—to let Zeus believe he'd beaten Metis—than to reveal herself and risk being thrown into Tartarus like Kronos and many of the other Titans.

There was a moist tearing noise as Athena grew, ripping open Zeus's stomach. He bellowed, his innards quaking, and golden ichor spilled like a waterfall toward Metis through the laceration in his gut. Holding her breath, Metis dove into the fluid and swam upward against the strong circulation. *Just a bit longer. We're almost out.*

Zeus kept on yelling. His insides trembled violently, sloshing Metis from side to side. Thankfully, Athena had grown so large that she didn't have to swim. She was submerged within her father, yes, but she managed to press her free hand against his organs and, with a sickening *squelch*, pushed them aside to make room for herself. As she heightened and lengthened even more, the tip of her spear stabbed through one of Zeus's lungs.

Zeus gasped. His uninjured lung expanded and contracted with his breaths, but the punctured organ began to shrivel up. Air bubbles escaped the wound, flittering through his ichor. "It—hurts," he wheezed. The world around Metis tilted sideways. There was a loud *thud*, and the slanting came to a halt. The force sent her somersaulting through ichor. *Zeus must have fallen over.* She waved her arms and kicked her legs to try and find her bearings.

Several deities outside spoke all at once, but Metis couldn't understand them, their words muffled by the liquid trapped in her ears. "Where?" a goddess asked, her regal voice somehow piercing through the rest. "Where does it hurt?" It was Zeus's latest consort, Hera.

The sound of Hera irritated Metis, but as she recalled that Zeus had sired dozens of illegitimate children since marrying Hera, her vexation dissolved. *Perhaps being the lustful fool's last choice is punishment enough for the new Queen of the Gods.*

Athena continued shoving aside and prying apart Zeus's insides, climbing up toward his skull as she grew, and Metis did her best to swim close to Athena's feet. Zeus grunted in pain, still trying to catch his breath. "There's—pressure—everywhere! I—can't—" He didn't finish his sentence, only panted and puffed.

More talking. The next voice Metis made out belonged to one of Zeus's illegitimate children. Hermes, if she remembered correctly. Hermes was a new deity, still a youth but cleverer than most. "If there is pressure, we must relieve it," Hermes said. "Someone break open his body, and hurry!"

"He's clutching his head," Hera added. "Start with his head."

This is it. Metis braced herself. She called on her magic, transformed into a fly, and shrank down to a size impossible to perceive. Any moment now, the light of the world outside would illuminate the dark one she'd inhabited for so long. When that happened, she would shake off the fluids covering her body, take wing, and escape.

Just as Athena reached her full size, her spear arrived at the base of Zeus's skull. He let out a whimper and stilled.

The sounds of bone fracturing and flesh tearing reverberated from Zeus's head. Then there was a wet squishing noise, like the hands of a hunter prodding through the bloody pulp of a fresh kill.

Slowly but surely, light leaked into Metis's surroundings. She tried gazing upon the outside world, only to see brown fingers prying Zeus's skull in two. They dug through the steaming, labyrinthine tissues of his head, steadily pulling it apart.

"What is it, Hephaestus?" Hermes asked, his voice tremoring. "What ails Father?" *Ah, yes. Hephaestus. The hideous babe of Zeus and Hera. The one Hera cast off Olympus.*

When Hephaestus didn't answer right away, Hera barked, "Well, what do you see, you insufferable thing?" Metis flinched at the way Hera spoke to her own child. As much as Metis wished she could strip away the attributes Athena had inherited from Zeus, she'd never talk to her daughter in such a manner.

Before Hephaestus could reply, Athena tossed her spear through the cavity in Zeus's head. The other deities scrambled out of the way, and the weapon clattered to the floor. Using both her hands and feet now, Athena forced herself out the rest of the way, and in her efforts, she practically split Zeus's body in two.

Metis didn't wait to take in the scene before her, didn't wait to listen to the flurry of conversation that followed Athena's emergence, didn't even wait to kiss her beloved daughter goodbye. Athena had not been prophesied to conquer Zeus, and so she would not be in danger. But Metis had yet to bear Zeus a second child—a son to overthrow his father, as the oracle foretold. If Metis were discovered, she'd surely be banished to Tartarus.

She shook off the ichor that covered her body and soared up and out of Zeus's remains, gulping in fresh air for the first time in what felt like forever. *At last, I am free.*

Metis shot through the halls of Zeus's palace, past golden floors and stone statues and marble columns. Soon she reached the farthest edge of the structure and soared into a cloudless blue sky.

For nine days and nine nights, Metis flew. She couldn't risk being discovered; she had to get as far away from Zeus and his minions as possible. Near the end of the ninth night, however, she felt as though her heart might burst, as though she might fall dead. *I need to rest.*

She stopped at the mouth of a cave carved out of a cliff, heavy rain pelting her from all sides. The air here was sweltering, even more so than at home. Exotic trees and plants grew for miles in every direction, the calls of foreign animals echoing across the deep-green terrain.

Exhausted and breathless, Metis buzzed into the cave. She changed back into her normal form and collapsed.

She wasn't sure how long she slept. It could have been days, it could have been months, it could have been years. Her entrapment by Zeus and her eventual escape had weakened her significantly, and she had to replenish the energy she'd lost.

When she did wake, it was because someone was shaking her and calling her name. Metis cried out, her eyes snapping open.

"Shh." A familiar Titan goddess with auburn curls, pale skin, and a midnight-black dress dotted with stars sat before her. The other deity pressed a finger to Metis's lips. "It's all right."

Metis shoved the Titan's hand away, her heart thudding in her chest. "Asteria? What are you doing here? I thought you—you—"

"Would never leave my island?" Asteria finished for her. "As much as I love the protection from Zeus that Delos offers, visions of prophecy lured me away from home. To this place."

"Visions of prophecy brought you here, to the edge of the world?"

"Yes, so I can help you."

"Help me?"

"Of course. If you do not find a better way to conceal yourself, Zeus will discover that you escaped him. He will hunt you down, and if he finds you, the next place he'll send you is Tartarus."

"I thought as much." Metis hung her head. "Where can I go? I've already traveled so far. Where will I be safe from Zeus?"

"I have seen thousands of years into the future, and many great events will come to pass—but only if you accept my help."

Metis raised a brow. "I'm listening."

Asteria leaned in close. "Do you wish to have a second child with Zeus? A child so powerful, he could one day overthrow the King of the Gods?"

"I'm trying to hide from Zeus, not sleep with him."

"He would never know it was you." Asteria chuckled in a way that sent shivers up Metis's spine. The Titan goddess of stars wasn't known as a vengeful goddess, but apparently, her feelings toward Zeus brought out a darker side of her personality. Metis could understand why—she'd been trapped inside Zeus when he'd pursued Asteria. "I've spent many nights conversing with the gods of other pantheons, and Vishnu gave me an idea," Asteria continued. "Metis, have you ever heard of something called an avatar?"

TWENTY-FOUR YEARS AGO . . .

Summer, Year 476 AS

Katarina trudged northwest through Hera City, toward the cemetery located at the edge of the *polis*, her heart heavy with grief. Today was the third anniversary of her mother's and older brother's deaths, and she planned to pay their graves a visit, which she did as often as possible. For libation, she'd prepared wine and honey.

Father had sculpted them new miniature statues, although he couldn't make it today. Katarina had carefully placed the trinkets at the bottom of her basket.

The closer she drew to the cemetery, the gloomier the *polis* around her became. Only minutes ago, there had been children playing around corners, animals scurrying across paths. Birds had been dancing through the air, singing sweet tunes as they twirled round and round, and the sun had been shining high in the blue afternoon sky.

But now there were no giggling children, no scampering beasts. The songs of birds had been replaced with the squawks of crows, and strangely enough, heavy clouds had covered the sun, casting everything in dim gray light.

Katarina rounded one last corner and caught sight of the tall, solid stone gates that led into the cemetery up ahead. Praying to Hera for strength, she stepped through the arched doorway of the gates and into the cemetery.

The burial grounds appeared as they always had—rows of grave markers, lush grass and flowers blooming everywhere, and rock walls towering above it all. There didn't seem to be any processions going on today, but a few people besides Katarina were visiting, shuffling along with their offerings to the dead in hand.

The trek from the entrance of the cemetery to the spot where Mother and Karter had been buried was a long one. Close to the center of the grounds, the graves had been marked with stones Katarina had carved their names into and clay statuettes Father had sculpted for them. Once Katarina got there, she set her basket down and knelt before the graves.

"Apologies, Mother, Karter. Father couldn't make it today." Her lip quivered as she unpacked the wine and honey. "The Master Potter at his shop refused to give him the day off. You understand." She uncorked the bottles of liquid and dumped an equal amount of them on each grave. "He found the time to make you some new presents, though." She rested the empty bottles in her basket and pulled out the statuettes.

On the first anniversary of Mother's passing, Father had made her a figurine of Hera, the patron goddess of their city. On the second anniversary, he'd formed a peacock, one of Hera's sacred creatures. Now, he'd fashioned a little cow, another of Hera's sacred animals.

On the first anniversary of Karter's death, Father had modeled him Hera as well. Probably to appease the goddess. Then, on the second anniversary, he'd made the family dog—Lukas had always loved Karter best. Now, on the third, Father had created a model of Karter and Katarina when they'd been children. They were "sword fighting" with long sticks, smiling wide and laughing uncontrollably. They'd shared many moments like this in childhood, and Katarina couldn't believe the level of detail Father had incorporated into the piece.

She set the statuettes down before their respective graves. The other figurines were already faded and worn, the elements chipping away at them, but that was all right. Father would make more.

Katarina recounted the events of the past year, as she did during each of these "visits." She spoke of how she'd gotten her first job, how she'd had her first kiss, how she'd moved into her first house. "I know you can't hear me," she said, glancing between the gravestones, her vision blurring as tears welled in her eyes. "I know you're not there. But it's still nice to tell you about everything that's going on."

Eventually she ran out of major life events to describe. She gazed out at the cemetery to find no one else around, then looked up at the sky; it appeared the sunset was fast approaching. *Probably won't make it home before curfew*, she thought, gathering her basket and standing up. *I'll need to stay at the inn for the night.*

She waved at Mother's and Karter's gravestones. "I love you." She turned and, to her surprise, was met with a beautiful woman staring at her. The woman had pale skin and curly red hair. Her silver irises glittered, her black dress dotted with constellations and shooting stars.

Katarina's breath caught in her throat. By looks alone, it was clear the woman wasn't human. She had to be a goddess, although she couldn't be Hera—Katarina had only seen Hera once in her life, but from what she remembered, the Queen of the Gods didn't resemble this goddess at all. So, who was she, and what was she doing here?

The mystery goddess smiled warmly and curtsied. "Greetings, Katarina."

Katarina took a step back. "Who are you? How do you know my name?"

"I am Asteria, Titan Goddess of Stars, Prophetic Dreams, and Necromancy. As for how I know your name . . . well, my dear, I knew you long before you were born into this form. I hid you on my island for millennia, then reincarnated you at the very right moment and waited for an equally opportune instant to help you transform into your most powerful self.

That time has come, and so I'm here now. To help you, to guide you."

"You're a Titan?" Asteria—if that was really her name—was speaking nonsense. Katarina clutched her basket to her chest and hurried around the goddess. "No. No thank you. I don't need help. Not from you, and not from anyone else."

There was a flash of white light. Asteria rematerialized in front of Katarina, blocking the path. "Don't you want to know the reason your mother and brother were murdered?"

Katarina stopped in her tracks and glared at Asteria. "I already know the reason they were murdered. A group of people stole weapons from the *astynomia* and broke into my family's house after curfew. They planned to raid our provisions and flee the city, and when we stood up to them, they . . ." She trailed off, her eyes filling with tears as memories of Mother's and Karter's mangled, bloodied bodies flooded her mind. She swallowed hard, forcing the images away as best she could. "The *astynomia* simply couldn't reach us in time. My mother and brother were killed because we were unlucky that night. That's all."

She stomped past Asteria, but once more the Titan goddess materialized in front of her.

"Everything happens for a reason. Bad luck had nothing to do with the killings, I assure you."

Katarina considered Asteria's words. She'd certainly found it odd that when their family had been attacked, the intruders had only seemed to target Mother and Karter. They'd restrained Katarina and Father, then gutted the others like swine. All the while, Katarina and Father had cried out for Hera, had begged the patron goddess of their city to appear and put a stop to the senseless violence.

In the end, Hera never came, and for months after the *kedeia*, Katarina had been furious with the goddess, although she'd rarely said so out loud. Her family had always been pious to the gods, and especially to Hera. For as long as Katarina could remember, they'd offered a portion of all their belongings to the Queen of the Gods—food, drink, money, clothes, animals, everything. They'd praised her, spread word of her good deeds, of her unmatched beauty and power. And what had they received in return? *No, stop thinking like that. Father already said we mustn't question the gods. Questioning them only leads to trouble.*

Still, there was a part of her that wondered why. Why, out of the many homes in the *polis*, their house had been attacked. Why Hera hadn't answered their prayers that night. Why she'd let Mother and Karter die.

Katarina set her jaw and looked Asteria in the eye. "What's the reason, then? Why were my mother and brother murdered?"

"Hera herself ordered their killings," Asteria answered, and Katarina's blood ran cold. "There was an anonymous tip asserting that your mother had been unfaithful to your father in the past, and that Karter could be an illegitimate child. Hera investigated it, and it turned out to be true—you and Karter do not share the same father, and you know how Hera deals with cheating spouses and bastard children in her city. But because so many years had passed, and because Hera was so fond of your family, she didn't feel that a public execution would be right. It would only embarrass you and your father. So, she staged a robbery instead, informing her pawns that the mother and son of the targeted family were to be killed in the struggle."

Katarina pressed a palm to her forehead. The world around her began to spin. "No, no. That can't be right. Karter and I— We can't be half-siblings. We look exactly alike."

"You look exactly as your mother did," Asteria said. "As did Karter when he was still alive. Pale skin, black hair, blue eyes. If the boy had resembled the other man, perhaps your father would have suspected he wasn't legitimate."

"It can't be true." Katarina dropped her basket and fell to her knees. "Who are you, really? Why would you lie about something like this?"

The goddess knelt before her. "I'm not lying about anything, child."

"Of course you are! What do you want from me?" Katarina sniffled, the tears she'd held back earlier returning. They streamed down her cheeks.

"I already told you. I'm here to help you transform into your most powerful self."

"Right." She wiped her face with the hem of her dress. "You said you 'reincarnated' me."

"Because I did, after concealing you for thousands of years."

Katarina scoffed. "I would have had to have been a great hero in my last life to be reincarnated. I would have had to have achieved Elysium, then been given the option to be reborn. And you couldn't have been the one to reincarnate me."

"You'd be right about all that if you were a mortal, and if you were meant to bow to the

Greek pantheon," Asteria said with a shrug. "But you are not a mortal, and you are not meant to bow to them. Not any longer. You are a Chosen One, a goddess reborn into a mortal body, and you are destined to bear a Son of Zeus—a man so powerful he will cast the King of the Gods into the pit of Tartarus."

"You're insane." Katarina shook her head and climbed to her feet. "You're talking nonsense. Blasphemy. I am most certainly mortal, and I am also wholly dedicated to the gods, thank you very much. You're lucky I don't call for any *astynomia* or even Hera herself since you're suggesting otherwise." She started to stomp away, hopefully to escape "Asteria" for good this time. "I'm going now. Please, don't follow me. Leave me alone."

She hadn't gone more than three paces before Asteria blurted out, "Metis, Titan Goddess of Wisdom and Cunning." Katarina stopped dead. Those words meant little to her, yet something twitched at the back of her mind when she heard them.

"That was your name, your title," Asteria went on. "You were Zeus's wife before it was prophesied that one of your children would overthrow him. The first child you bore him was a goddess, and you named her Athena. The second is a son who has yet to be born."

Katarina's nostrils flared, her cheeks heating with fury. She swung around to face Asteria. "Prove it. If you're so confident that what you say is true, then prove it. *All* of it."

Asteria snapped her fingers. In a blink of light, a golden wreath encrusted with sparkling diamonds, rubies, and sapphires appeared in her hands. She held out the crown to Katarina, and as Katarina gazed upon it, a strong buzzing sensation filled her chest. It felt like an assembly of wasps battering against her rib cage. She sucked in a sharp breath and clamped her eyes shut, but even then, she saw the wreath. An image of it flashed across her mind, over and over.

"Metis," Asteria said. "Don't look away."

Katarina opened her eyes, the buzzing in her chest growing stronger. It spread through her arms, her legs, so intense her teeth began to chatter. Once more, she stared at the wreath, and once more, she felt that it belonged to her.

Asteria stepped forward. "Should we see if it still fits?"

Katarina didn't even have to think about it. She gave Asteria a swift nod.

Asteria placed the circlet on Katarina's head. As it touched her, the buzzing feeling subsided, and an electric shock jolted through her body. The hair on her limbs stood straight, goose pimples prickling her skin. *Oh no*, she thought. *This was a trick.*

She tried to reach up, to grab the crown and toss it aside, but found she couldn't move. It was as if she'd looked into the eyes of the gorgon Medusa, her body turned to stone.

She tried to yell for help, to call for Hera or the *astynomia*, but her lips were stuck. The only sound she could utter was a stifled whimper.

Just when she thought things couldn't get worse, black clouds of fog crawled into the corners of her sight. She couldn't even scream as the mist devoured her, body and soul.

ALLEGIANCE

Now . . .

Summer, Year 500 AS

Persephone held her breath as she stepped through Hermes's portal into the throne room on New Mount Olympus.

When she reached the other side of the gateway, she sighed in relief. The chamber was void of other gods—empty aside from the marble pillars and the twelve chairs lining the walls, silent save for the pattering of rain and the howling of wind outside. As always, the ceiling glittered with shooting stars and constellations.

Thunder roared, so close it shook the walls. Persephone flinched and glanced out at the night sky beyond the throne room's arched windows. Clusters of clouds flared between black and green, peridot lightning arcing through the atmosphere. *Zeus must be furious after everything that's happened*, she thought. *Hopefully, so furious with others that he'll pardon my crimes against the Olympians.*

Sandals clacked behind Persephone as the other gods followed her through Hermes's portal out of the Underworld, and she swung around to face them. At first there was only Demeter, Hades, and Poseidon, but then Artemis and Athena appeared behind them. Hephaestus and Ares came next, followed by Hermes, the last of everyone. With a snap of his fingers, the Messenger of the Gods closed the violet portal behind himself.

Persephone flexed her hands, preparing to fight everyone if she had to. She was still on high alert after being dragged out of Tartarus. Especially considering that right after she'd regenerated, she'd discovered that the husband she thought she'd finally rid herself of had been revived—and that her first love, Apollo, had been banished into the fiery pit. Most shocking of all, the other gods had informed her and Hades that the Chosen Two of the Dreaded Prophecy had successfully obtained the Helm of Darkness, Poseidon's Trident, and the Master Lightning Bolt.

For the first time in millennia, the fate of the pantheon hung in the balance. As worst-case scenarios for the Olympians ran through Persephone's head, the hairs on the back of her neck stood straight. Whether the bodily reaction was from terror or glee, she couldn't be sure.

"Where is that insufferable brother of mine?" Hades snarled, stalking farther into the chamber. The remaining gems in his tattered robes shimmered as the dark fabrics swelled behind him. "Zeus! Zeus, get out here! Show yourself!"

Poseidon curled his top lip in disgust as he watched Hades tear across the room. "Hades, please. Compose yourself before the others arrive."

Hades faced Poseidon, a few tufts of his oily hair falling out of place into his eyes. "You're one to talk. Besides, it's because of that buffoon that any of this is happening. He's the one who groomed Karter to become one of us, and he did such a splendid job that now the boy's decided to help the Chosen Two lead a war on the gods instead. He should have slaughtered the wretch when he had the chance. Better yet, he should have never sought out the boy's mother, should have never . . ."

Hades trailed off as footfalls echoed at the entrance of the throne room. At the sounds, Persephone's stomach sank. Was it Zeus? Granted, he'd ordered for Persephone to be rescued from Tartarus, and Poseidon had said the gods needed her in the upcoming battle against the Chosen Two. But she'd still tried to take the Helm of Darkness for herself. She'd still conspired against the Olympians, still betrayed the gods.

"Join me, all of you, and I can assure you you'll live to see another day," she'd said to Karter and Zoey and Andy at the edge of the pit of Tartarus, drunk on the fact that she'd sealed Spencer's and her husband's fates. In that moment, she'd felt giddy and unstoppable. *"We'll steal Poseidon's Trident. We'll steal the Lightning Bolt. Together, we'll take down the Olympians, and I'll rule as your queen. Queen of the world."*

Persephone swallowed hard, shaking away the memories and turning to see who'd entered the chamber. Sure enough, it was Zeus, flanked by Hera, Aphrodite, and Hestia. "Olympians, take your seats," Zeus boomed, electricity whizzing between his fingers and up his arms. "There is much we have to discuss." Everyone did as Zeus said, the only gods left standing Persephone and Hades.

The King of the Underworld huffed and crossed his arms. "Took the lot of you long enough."

Zeus ignored Hades's comment. "First things first. A few minutes ago, we finished slaughtering the last of the nymphs who aided the Chosen Two in invading Olympus. We also captured the traitorous Titans Prometheus and Asteria, and we'll need to toss them into Tartarus straight away."

Hestia threw her hands in the air. "What possessed them to help the Chosen Two in the first place? They knew the consequences for such crimes."

Persephone blinked in surprise. *Prometheus? How did he escape his prison? And Asteria? No one's heard from her in centuries. I was certain she'd faded away or exiled herself in her last years.*

"It is no matter." Hera tapped her fingernails against her armrests. "We'll rid ourselves of them within the hour, and that will be that."

Zeus nodded. "Correct. Secondly"—he gestured at Hephaestus—"your grandchildren. They're not in their cell. It appears Karter, the ungrateful insect, knocked our strongest team unconscious to save the Daughter of Apollo. He must have taken Troy and Marina with him when he, Diana, and the others made their escape. We'll get more details from the team when they wake, but that's what we gathered from a quick inspection of the scene."

Hephaestus's jaw dropped. "What? But then—what will become of—"

"I want them killed on sight," Zeus said. "Along with the Daughter of Apollo and my sorry excuse for a son. Once we cast the Titans into Tartarus, I'll send some of you after the fugitives while the rest of us prepare for war." The King of the Gods let those words hang in the air, then trained his gaze on Persephone. "Finally, I'd like to address you, Queen of the Underworld. It is of the utmost importance you tell the truth when you answer this: What in all the gods' names possessed you to help Spencer, Diana, and the Chosen Two in the Underworld? Then to take the Helm of Darkness for yourself, kill Spencer, and banish Hades to Tartarus?" The sky god leaned forward in his seat. "What could you have hoped to accomplish by doing all that? Didn't you know such a ridiculous scheme would end horribly for you?"

For a long while, Persephone was too stunned to speak. So much had happened in her absence. It was unbelievable. Not only that, but she'd thought her motivations were blatantly obvious. How hadn't Zeus pieced it together yet? Some of the goddesses present already seemed to have caught on. Hera, Artemis, and Aphrodite gazed down at Persephone with knowing, almost smug looks. Demeter obviously knew why Persephone had done what she did, but Persephone could tell the Goddess of Harvest was trying to stay composed. Demeter held her head high, although the corners of her mouth twitched. It was as if her emotions were battling to escape the cage she'd constructed for them.

Finally, Persephone found her voice. "I didn't care how silly my plan was, or whether going through with it would end badly for me. I simply wanted to take revenge on my husband. To slaughter his illegitimate son and free myself of every wrong he's committed against me."

Zeus leaned back. Understanding overtook his expression. He opened his mouth to speak, but before he could say anything, Persephone cut him off. "I wanted to take revenge on the

Olympians, too," she said, knowing full well the gravity of her words. After saving face for so long, she couldn't bear it any longer. They needed to know just how much she hated them. "That's why I stole the Helm of Darkness. I planned to use it to steal Poseidon's Trident and the Lightning Bolt as well. Ultimately, I wanted to uncover the full Descent Spell and combine the objects' powers to destroy you." Many of the Olympians burst into fits of gossipy whispers at Persephone's declaration, and Demeter's lips parted in surprise.

Hera threw her head back and laughed. It was a cold, cruel sound, cutting through the air like a dagger. Everyone quieted and turned to the Queen of the Gods. "Uncover the full Descent Spell? Destroy us? Are you some sort of half-wit?" She gestured at Demeter. "Please, sister, tell me this pathetic daughter of yours is joking."

"I don't think she is," Demeter replied. She took a deep breath as if to calm her nerves. "But perhaps you would do well to remember why Zeus agreed for her to be rescued from Tartarus in the first place, oh great Queen of the Gods." Demeter's words seemed to sober Hera up a bit. Her smile faded. She went silent.

To the right, Aphrodite cleared her throat. "If I may ask, Persephone, why is it that you wanted to destroy us? I understand your anger at Hades. He was unfaithful to you. He sired an illegitimate child. But what did the Olympians ever do to elicit such a—a—*drastic* reaction from you? We gave you a *polis* and many worshippers. What more could you want?" More whispering, though louder this time.

The audacity of Aphrodite's question made Persephone's nostrils flare, a furious frenzy boiling in her blood. She balled her fists at her sides, her flesh growing hot with rage as memories of the day the Olympians condemned her to remain Queen of the Underworld flooded her mind.

"As I mentioned before," Hades had said in this very throne room millennia ago, *"you do not have all the information regarding my wife's stay in our home. While she was there, she consumed food. Pomegranate seeds."*

Demeter had knelt before Zeus. *"Please, great King of the Gods, pardon my daughter's mistake. I beg you."*

"You know that is not possible."

"What does Mother mean, my mistake?" Persephone had asked.

"By consuming food or drink, any food or drink, in the Underworld," Zeus had answered, *"one binds oneself to it. This is a law that has been in place since life*

began. Hades is correct—you belong to the darkness now, Persephone."

"That isn't fair! I didn't want to eat those seeds. Hades ordered me to! I had no choice! Artemis, Apollo"—she'd gestured at her old companions for help—*"you were there when Hades took me! You know I didn't want to be his wife. You watched everything. Tell them you know he must have forced me to eat the seeds!"* But neither of them had stuck up for her, and when Persephone had turned to her mother for help, Demeter had only continued crying and shaken her head with finality.

However, after a rather monstrous reaction from Persephone, Zeus had decided to compromise. The best he'd come up with was that Persephone would be sentenced to an eternity of cycles between the world above and the world below, rather than remaining trapped in the Underworld forever.

Persephone trembled, her body going numb, her vision turning red. In that moment, more than anything, she wanted to hurt Aphrodite. To gash or drown or choke or burn the Goddess of Love and Beauty—whatever made her suffer most—for asking such a ludicrous question.

Persephone spat at the Olympians' feet, and words began to spill from her mouth, though they did not seem like her own. It was as if a malevolent creature had slithered out from the chasms of Tartarus and taken hold of her body. "How *dare* you ask such an imbecilic question," she snarled at Aphrodite. The other goddess shrank back in surprise. "After so many of you allowed Hades to kidnap me. Forced me to be his queen. Stole my birth name, my body, my *life!*"

Electrifying magic burst in her chest and spread through her limbs. Vines and grass twisted out from her form, snaking toward Aphrodite at high speed. *Of all the Olympians, she'll be the first to pay*, Persephone thought.

In the end, she never got the chance to attack Aphrodite. The blade of a sword sliced through her vegetation. Her plants fell limp, Ares standing before them with his sword in hand. Persephone could see his skin growing an angry shade of scarlet in the spots it was visible between his armor, and she wasn't surprised by his outrage—Ares and Aphrodite had been lovers for thousands of years, despite Aphrodite's marriage to Hephaestus and the two's many affairs with mortals.

Ares stalked toward Persephone, weapon raised. "You insolent cow. How dare you attempt an assault on her."

Persephone assumed the best battle stance

she could. Ares was much larger and more powerful than her, but she couldn't care less. She had endured far worse than any punishment he might inflict upon her. "Do your worst, God of War," she replied. "I no longer bow before those who allowed me to suffer as I did."

The other gods cried out, either protesting or encouraging the fight. Artemis, Hephaestus, Hermes, and Poseidon leapt out of their seats. Demeter followed suit and rushed toward Ares, presumably to stop him from going near Persephone. *There's no protecting me from him or anyone else, Mother. I've made my choice.*

Just then, thunder rumbled through the chamber, so loud Persephone's ears began to ring. The floor and walls and ceiling quivered from the force.

"*Silence!*" Zeus bellowed, golden lightning crackling around him as he sat on his throne. "Stand down and be quiet, all of you!"

A hush fell over the gods and goddesses, and they looked up at Zeus. Even as Persephone still pulsed with rage, she did the same, facing the King of the Gods.

Zeus glared down at everyone. "Although it is only through fantastical strokes of luck that the Chosen Two have come this far—that they have stolen our most powerful objects—we must resist the urge to fight each other." He climbed out of his throne and began to pace the chamber. "We must work together to put a stop to this war as soon as possible, or else we could lose precious worshippers who might join the Chosen Two in battle."

"Father, I must tell you that the Chosen Two don't just have our most powerful objects," Artemis piped up. "They've also discovered the Descent Spell's existence." Aphrodite and Hestia gasped, and Hera narrowed her eyes. Artemis went on. "I hunted them down, but before I could capture them, the girl used the Helm and Trident to perform a variation of the spell and sent me to the Underworld. I traveled to Hades's castle so I could transport home with the team coming from Tartarus."

Zeus stopped pacing and stroked his beard at this news, but he didn't look surprised or even fearful. "I see." He seemed to mull over what to say next, and Persephone raised a brow at him. *Does he know something the rest of us don't?*

"Father?" Artemis asked hesitantly.

"Apologies." Zeus strode back to his throne and sat down again. "I'm sure it came as a shock for you to experience that, Artemis. But there's no need to fret over it. It changes nothing."

"How can you say that?" Demeter blurted

out. "The Chosen Two being in possession of all three objects of power, having knowledge of the Descent—it changes everything. You must see that."

"Perhaps if the Chosen Two were powerful and divine, it would frighten me," Zeus scoffed. "But they're not."

"Our king is correct on this," Hestia added. "The Chosen Two might have had enough power to send Artemis to the Underworld when they fought her, but when we battled them here, they could do nothing of the sort. They barely escaped us. If it weren't for Karter, Prometheus, and Asteria, they would be our prisoners now."

Hera pointed at Poseidon. "Lord of the Seas. You, Amphitrite, and Triton insisted that the Chosen Two possessed strong divine essences when they invaded your palace. You even said they resembled the late Calliope and Anteros."

"Which they did *not*," Aphrodite chimed in. "That pig-faced boy with the wings was no more than a cheap imitation of my precious Anteros."

Hera rolled her eyes. "Yes, Aphrodite, you've said that a few times already. As I was saying, when the Chosen Two were here on Olympus, none of us noticed strong divine essences within them. Whatever magical energy they might have had inside them then has since dwindled, and I can't imagine it will grow stronger if it's already begun to fade." She looked at Artemis. "Did you sense divine essences within the Chosen Two when you met them?"

"I did," Artemis answered. "The girl claimed that she was Calliope, and that the boy was Anteros. I don't believe it's true, especially considering that when all of you met them earlier"—she gestured at Zeus, Hera, Aphrodite, and Hestia—"they didn't seem divinely powerful in the slightest."

A satisfied grin spread across Athena's face, and she slammed a fist against her armrest. "Then it's just as our king said before. So long as we work together, we'll easily eradicate them. As a team, we'll end the Dreaded Prophecy once and for all!" Several of the gods whooped at Athena's words, but as Persephone processed what the sentiments meant for her own life, the golden ichor streaming through her veins ran cold, an icy dread settling in her bones.

Yes, the Chosen Two defeating the Olympians was a terrifying thought, unlikely as it was. It meant the hierarchy of the pantheon would crumble. It meant the future of the gods would be uncertain. If that were to happen, what would become of Persephone? Of her mother?

At the same time, the Olympians destroying

the Chosen Two was an equally scary notion. It meant the hierarchy of the pantheon would remain intact. It meant the future of the Greek gods would be certain. If that were to happen, Persephone would still be Hades's wife. She'd still be forced to spend half of every year in the Underworld with him.

Not only that, but if the Olympians eliminated the Chosen Two and won the war, Apollo would probably remain imprisoned in Tartarus forever. And although he and Persephone had barely spoken in thousands of years, although she was still bitter about their past, the thought of his suffering—the thought of his death—made her chest grow tight.

Athena speaks of working together, Persephone thought. *Of acting as a team. But the gods turned their backs on me when I needed them most. Why should I help them? Any of them?*

"Brilliant Athena is correct," Zeus boomed. "We must work together to quickly eliminate this threat to our peaceful reign. Which brings me to my next point: We must make changes to the pantheon if we are to remain in power for all time. We cannot continue operating the way we have for the past millennia and expect things to stay the same." He turned to Persephone. "Persephone, Goddess of Spring, I now realize how much you've suffered over the centuries. So much so that you'd betray your own—you'd throw away your own life, even—to end the pain. I'd like to make you a deal."

This piqued Persephone's interest. "What might that be?"

"If you swear your allegiance to the Olympians once again," Zeus started, "if you fight alongside us, help us to defeat those who oppose us, I will dissolve your marriage to Hades. You'll still be required to spend six months of every year in the Underworld, as you are bound to it, but you will no longer be bound to its king."

Nearly everyone gasped, and Persephone felt as though the air had been sucked from her lungs, her stomach twisting and turning. *I could really, finally be free of Hades. Not of the Underworld, but of him at least.* The floor seemed to tilt beneath her. She staggered to the side, clasping her forehead with a shaking hand.

Hades released a yell of indignation from behind Persephone. He stomped past her toward Zeus and Hera. "You can't do such a thing! Persephone is my wife. She belongs to me! Hera, great Queen of the Gods, you must not allow this. You're the Goddess of Marriage. You understand more than anyone else why this is wrong."

Hera only shrugged. "As much as I might not like the decision, I understand and respect my husband's ruling. He underestimated Persephone's cunning. We all did, and we paid dearly for it. Perhaps she would serve us better in a role other than your queen."

"Besides," Zeus said, "I have something of value to offer you for your cooperation, Hades. The pantheon is short one Olympian. How would you like to fill the position?"

Hades appeared stricken. "W-what? You can't be serious."

Zeus sat back lazily in his seat, his expression one of satisfaction. "I am."

"And would I—would I receive the same privileges as the rest of you? At least, the same ones as Poseidon?"

"Of course." Zeus gestured at Hades dismissively. "We'll also find you another wife. One far less . . . *ambitious* than this one."

A wicked grin distorted Hades's features in a way that made Persephone shiver. "I accept your offer."

"Mother and Father, my queen and king," Ares chimed in, "with all due respect, didn't you hear what Persephone said? She planned to overthrow us. Surely her insubordination is enough to banish her to Tartarus. Can't we just do that, like we did with Apollo?"

Hermes narrowed his eyes. "I thought we already discussed this."

"We did," Hephaestus grumbled. "Apparently, on top of being foolish enough to sleep with my wife, Ares is also so absentminded he forgets details from our plans of strategy."

A low growl escaped Ares's throat. He raised his blade and stalked toward Hephaestus.

Before Ares could reach Hephaestus, Demeter lunged between them. She faced the God of War head-on, glowering at him. "Allow me to refresh your feeble memory, nephew," she said. "There were many times I was forced to stand back and watch my daughter suffer at the hands of others, but I *will not* stand back and watch her be banished to Tartarus. Even if the gods decided that were her fate, I would fight you all to keep it from happening. And then, if you still managed to exile her, I would gather with the rest of my children, and we would use the last of our powers to make the earth go barren. I would starve our worshippers, and the pantheon would fade into oblivion." Ares's dumbfounded expression at Demeter's response was visible despite his helmet, and if Persephone hadn't been so astonished at what was happening, she would have laughed at how foolish he looked.

Poseidon strolled up beside the God of War and rested a blue-tinged hand on the other immortal's shoulder. "This is Persephone's first crime against the gods. If we always punished someone to the greatest extent upon their first offense, Apollo, Hera, Athena, and I would have been banished to Tartarus long ago."

What Poseidon said was true. Persephone remembered a time, thousands of years ago, when Hera had grown tired of Zeus's tyranny and infidelity and had plotted to overthrow him, and Poseidon, Apollo, and Athena had helped her. The gods had drugged their king, bound him to his bed, and stolen his Master Lightning Bolt.

But Thetis, an old goddess of the sea, overheard the four immortals arguing about who should rule in Zeus's place. To save Zeus, Thetis summoned Briareus, one of the three Hekatonkheires—the hundred-handed, fifty-headed Storm Giants. Briareus swiftly retrieved the Lightning Bolt and untied Zeus. Unbound and rearmed with his object of power, Zeus planned to smite the deities opposing him, and because they'd come so close to successfully overthrowing him, he'd even intended on casting them into Tartarus. They'd begged for mercy, promising to never attempt a coup again.

In the end, Zeus chose mercy, but he assured the traitors that if they ever betrayed him again, they wouldn't be so lucky. For a time, Hera hung from the sky by golden chains, and Poseidon and Apollo were sentenced to build walls around the city of Troy. Meanwhile, because of Athena's cleverness (and because she was Zeus's favorite child), she managed to talk herself out of being punished.

Athena smiled at Zeus. "Yes, and we were spared because my father is a great and fair king. He gives second chances, especially when it is in the best interest of the pantheon. I am the Goddess of Wisdom, but the King of the Gods is by far the wisest of us all."

"This is true." Zeus turned back to Persephone. "Now, what say you, Goddess of Spring? Will you once again swear your allegiance to the Olympians? Will you help us destroy our adversaries and have your marriage to Hades dissolved?"

Persephone considered Zeus's offer. As she recalled everything that had happened to her in the past millennia, the path she was meant to take became clear. The Fates were calling her, guiding her toward a grand destiny, and she intended to heed their request.

She composed herself as best she could, climbed to her feet, and gave Zeus her sweetest smile. "King Zeus, I accept your proposal with enormous gratitude. I apologize profusely for my past crimes, and I swear my allegiance to you and the rest of the Olympians"—she glanced over her shoulder at Hades—"in exchange for the end of my farce of a marriage."

CHAPTER THREE

FAULT

Andy wasn't sure how long he and his companions had been flying away from New Mount Olympus. He guessed it had been at least an hour or so because the rush of adrenaline had faded from his body. His wings hurt something fierce; they weighed heavy on his back, like blocks of concrete hanging from his shoulders. His throat was ripped raw from all the wailing he'd done tonight, his eyes dry and puffy from the crying.

But as much as the rest of Andy hurt right now, nothing was more painful than the aching of his broken heart.

He looked down at the red poppy flower he held tightly to his chest, the one Darko's remains had transformed into after the satyr had been crushed by Heracles. *I still can't believe he's really gone*, Andy thought. *He was fine. We were about to escape. And then . . . and then . . .*

Memories rushed through Andy's mind. They'd been in Zeus's palace—him, Zoey, Darko, Diana, and Karter—about to grab Troy and Marina and escape. Heracles had shown up with that broken-off pillar, and he'd raised it above Karter, obviously planning to crush the Son of Zeus.

Andy had wanted to protect Karter. Despite everything the demigod had done to them in the past, he'd finally decided to make the right decision and turn against the gods to save Diana and the twin grandchildren-of-Hephaestus. Andy had used Poseidon's Trident to shake the floor, intending to deter Heracles from hurting Karter.

Andy's plan had worked. The killing blow meant for Karter had been thrown off. Except then it had come for Andy, and before he could move—before he could think, before he could do anything—Darko had shoved him aside, and the marble column had come down upon Darko.

Andy shook his head, suppressing the horrific images, trying to force them out of his mind. *That's not how I wanna remember him. It's not, it's not, it's not.* He focused on Diana and Zoey as they flew ahead of him on the gray pegasus Karter had stolen from New Mount Olympus. Occasionally, he also glanced to the left, at Karter as the demigod soared through the forest with a paralyzed Troy and Marina slung over his shoulders.

Another hour of flying passed before the group reached the spot they'd left the nymphs at. In their absence, the Dryads had erected thirty-foot-tall walls of logs and greenery around an area of forest roughly the size of Deltama Village. They'd done that before when making camp, and Andy guessed it was for protection.

The group descended toward the fortress, and Andy spotted nymphs stationed at the visible corners of the walls, probably to keep guard. He even spotted several familiar faces keeping watch, including Harmony's and Narcissa's as the Dryads sat in a tower made of greenery that was high enough to see outside the fortress.

When Harmony saw the group, her expression lit up with joy. "It's them!" she shouted. "The Chosen Two are back!"

"It appears the Daughter of Apollo is with them," Narcissa said, a rare hint of excitement in her voice. "They did it."

The nymphs clapped and cheered, but Andy felt no joy, no triumph. Yes, he and Zoey had brought back Diana, Troy, and Marina. They'd also managed to steal Zeus's Lightning Bolt. But those victories had come at a great cost. Darko was dead, and because of the chaotic battle in the amphitheater, the group had been given no other choice but to leave behind the twelve nymphs who'd come with them to Olympus. They'd also had to leave behind Prometheus and Asteria.

What had become of those nymphs? The Titans were immortal at least, but the recruits weren't. *If their fates are anything like Darko's, I won't be able to live with myself.*

Karter was the first to stumble to the ground of the campsite, his body shaking. He rested Troy and Marina on the grass with wobbly arms and collapsed. His chest heaved as he tried to catch his breath.

Weak from exhaustion, Andy landed a few feet away from Karter. The gray pegasus Diana and Zoey were riding touched down ahead of them.

The cheering nymphs were already barreling toward the group, Harmony and Narcissa scrambling down from the watchtower, and when Andy looked out at their smiling faces, his stomach fell to his feet. How was he supposed to tell them that he and his companions had been forced to leave behind the Titans and the other nymphs to escape? How was he supposed to tell them that Darko was dead, that the satyr had sacrificed himself to save Andy?

Zoey and Diana climbed off the pegasus, and Diana hurried to Karter's side. Karter gasped for air, steam rolling off his skin as though he was burning from the inside. "I think—I used up—too much power," he said between breaths. "My body—is—"

"Burning up," Diana finished for him. Her hands already glowed with golden light. "Don't worry, I'll heal you."

Diana worked on Karter, and the nymphs reached the group. Their faces went from joyful to confused as they took in the scene, then began to whisper feverishly among themselves. Some even backed away.

Harmony and Narcissa pushed themselves to the front of the crowd. "What is the meaning of this?" Narcissa asked. "What is the Son of Zeus doing here?"

"Where are the other recruits?" Harmony's tone was fearful. "The Titans? Darko?"

This was the moment Andy had been dreading. A lump formed in his throat. He did his best to suppress his tears and held up Darko's flower. "Darko is . . . dead. He sacrificed himself for—for me. He's gone because of me."

The nymphs gasped. A strangled cry escaped Harmony's throat, and she pressed a hand to her heart, tears already trickling down her cheeks. She turned away, and the nymph named Chloe came forward and embraced her.

Narcissa clenched her fists. "What about the others?"

"We don't know," Zoey replied, dabbing her eyes. "They held off the gods while Andy and I stole the Master Lightning Bolt, and then the seven of us—I mean, the *six* of us—barely managed to escape. We had to leave behind almost everyone who helped us on Olympus. I'm so, so sorry. We never wanted to abandon anyone. We were all supposed to get out of there together."

Harmony's cries intensified, and Chloe squeezed her shoulders. Several nymphs in the throng began to sob. Many fell to their knees or into each other's arms.

"There is no—no need to apologize," Narcissa said, her voice strained. "They knew the risks. If they died tonight, they died heroes. Heroes who helped you steal the Lightning Bolt and rescue the Daughter of Apollo."

It seemed Diana had finished healing Karter. Steam no longer rolled off his body, and his breathing had evened out. She stood and helped him to his feet. "If any of the recruits are still alive, I promise to save them," Karter said to Narcissa. "If they've been spared, I swear I'll bring them back to you." This sobered up a few of the nymphs. They started whispering again, glancing between one another and Karter.

From off to the side, Zoey snorted. "Give me a break," she muttered under her breath, and Andy wondered if he'd been the only person to hear her because no one acknowledged her words. Everybody was too transfixed by the scar-faced young man making promises Andy hoped he'd be able to keep.

"Where's Kali?" Diana asked. "I have to see her. Before doing anything else, I need to heal her."

"Of course. Come this way." Narcissa pivoted and walked farther into the campsite.

She gestured for the group to follow. "When you're ready, we'll need you to heal our wounded as well."

Diana hurried after Narcissa, and Andy and Zoey followed. Karter hoisted the twins over his shoulders and trailed behind them.

Several minutes of brisk walking passed before they reached a cabin nestled within the trees, one almost identical to the place the nymphs had previously constructed for Andy and his friends to sleep in. Standing outside the cabin were Kali's pegasi: Luna, Ajax, and Aladdin. The winged horses seemed to watch the building with anxiety.

Narcissa threw open the doors. The group rushed inside. Kali lay on a "bed" of grass, and Andy's stomach lurched at the sight of her. If she'd looked bad the last time he'd seen her, she looked downright awful now. Her once-brown skin had turned gray, and it glistened with sweat even in the night. Her dark eyes fluttered open and closed, as if she were in a drunken daze, her long hair clinging to her face and neck in matted, greasy clumps.

Three nymphs worked in a frenzy around her. They appeared to be changing the bloodied bandages of the wound she'd acquired during the group's fight with Artemis's Huntresses. *The fight where she jumped in front of an arrow to rescue Darko,* Andy recalled, fresh tears springing into his eyes. *How will I ever tell her what happened to him?*

"Kali!" Diana cried. Her hands lit with golden light as she raced to Kali's side. "I'll take care of her from here," she said to the nymphs, and started work on Kali before they even had time to move. The nymphs scrambled out of the way and noticed Troy and Marina. They hastened over to Karter and took the twins from him, then carried them to the opposite end of the cabin, laid them down, and began examining them and asking them questions in hushed voices.

Kali's cracked lips curled up in a small smile as Diana healed her. "Princess, you made it back." Her voice was hoarse, coming out in little more than a whisper. She motioned at Andy, Zoey, and Karter standing in the doorway. "Did you get the Lightning Bolt? What's that jackass doing here? Where are Darko and Prometheus?"

Diana's voice trembled as she responded. "Yes, we got the Bolt, and Karter saved Troy and Marina and me. He's on our side now. As for Darko and Prometheus . . ."

Andy's grip on the soil housing Darko's flower tightened. She wasn't going to break the news to Kali while the other girl was in such a fragile physical state, was she?

"They're outside, talking to the nymphs," Diana said. "Don't worry about them, okay? Just worry about getting better right now. Save your breath."

"I've lost a lot of blood. You probably can't heal me."

"I told you to save your breath!"

"You know, you're really pretty when you're worried. Then again, you're really pretty all the time."

"Please, I need to concentrate."

"I'm just happy I get to see you one last time before I go."

Diana shrieked in frustration. "That's not going to happen! I won't allow it. There have been so many people I loved and couldn't save, and I refuse to let you be one of them."

A raspy chuckle escaped Kali's throat. "Aw, did I hear that right? Are you confessing your undying love for me?"

Diana's cheeks flushed pink. Whether it was from the exertion of healing Karter and Kali or because she was embarrassed, Andy couldn't be sure. "If it means you'll hold on long enough to let me finish healing you, then yes, this is a romantic confession," Diana said. "I love you.

I'm *in love* with you. I don't know how it happened, considering how angry you make me sometimes, but it's the truth. And if you leave me now, I'll never forgive you. Plus, Andy and Zoey need you. Deltama Village needs you. You're going to be their chief someday, remember? Please, stay strong for all of us a little while longer."

Kali's eyes softened as she gazed up at Diana. "While you were gone, I had a lot of time to think about it, and what can I say?" With a shaking hand, she reached up and tucked a golden wave behind Diana's ear. "I think I love you too." She closed her eyes and, after a short time, began to snore softly.

A few more minutes passed before Diana allowed her golden glow to fade. "Since Kali lost so much blood, she'll need extra food and water when she wakes up. It'll take her some time to gain back her strength, but she'll be fine."

Andy allowed his shoulders to relax. "Thank God."

"Will you be all right, Diana?" Karter asked, taking a tentative step forward. "It's been a—a long night, to say the least. You've done so much fighting and healing. Can we get you anything?"

Zoey looked at Karter, a scornful expression

twisting her features. "Would you give the nice-guy act a rest already?"

She stomped out of the cabin, and Andy followed her. "What are you doing?"

"What does it look like I'm doing? I'm trying to get away from that jerk."

Karter jogged after her, Diana not far behind. "Wait!" Karter cried. "Please, don't go. Can't we—can't we talk about this?"

Zoey stopped and swung around. "Sure, let's talk. First, I have a few questions for you: For instance, what's your angle here? What kind of elaborate trap are you trying to set up for us?"

Diana reached Karter's side. "What are you talking about?" she asked.

"You know exactly what I'm talking about." Zoey marched toward Karter, palpable fury rolling off her in droves. She halted only inches from his face. "Since you wanna talk, then answer my question. What are you planning now? Are you trying to lead the gods here, so they can capture Andy and me, slaughter everyone else, and reward you for your 'heroic' deeds?"

A shadow crossed over Karter's face. He hung his head in shame. *Man*, Andy thought. *She's really laying into him.*

"Zoey, stop it. He's on our side now," Diana

said, then looked up at Karter. "Right?"

"Of course!" Karter shouted. "Would I have shot my own father with green lightning and protected you from the gods if I wasn't?"

Zoey huffed. "As if that means anything. Did you forget the time you went against the gods in Hades to help us steal the Helm of Darkness? Then how, not long after, you sold Andy and me out to Violet, Layla, and Xander in Hephaestus City?"

"I helped you in Hades because I wanted to save Spencer," Karter replied in a low voice. "And I betrayed you in Hephaestus City because I thought it was my destiny to become a god. I know now that it was a mistake. I'm truly sorry for everything, and—"

"No need to say sorry," Zoey interrupted. She jabbed him in the chest with her pointer finger. "Because I'm not accepting an apology from you. *Ever.*" She spun around and stomped away from him. Andy wanted to stop her, to try talking some sense into her, but he wasn't sure of what to say. *I don't think I've ever seen her so mad.*

Diana lunged forward and grabbed Zoey's wrist. "You need to calm down and think clearly about this. If it weren't for Karter, so many more people would have died on Olympus."

Zoey yanked herself from Diana's grip.

"Don't tell me *I'm* the one who's not thinking clearly. *You're* the one who's acting insane. You've never defended Karter before, so why the hell are you doing it now? Don't you realize that if it weren't for him, we wouldn't have had to rescue you and Troy and Marina in the first place?" She paused. When she went on, she sounded as if she was on the brink of tears. "Besides, we have no idea how many lives were lost on Olympus. We don't know whether any of the nymphs were killed, whether Prometheus and Asteria escaped. All we can be sure of is that Darko . . ." It was then that she broke down, the hard exterior she'd projected moments ago crumbling away. She put her hand over her mouth and fell to her knees, a fit of anguished sobs racking her body like a hurricane bludgeoning a ship lost at sea.

As Andy watched Zoey suffer, he wanted to take her pain away. He wanted to hug her, to comfort her, but once she'd mentioned Darko, the ache in his chest became too much to bear. Suddenly he could hardly breathe, his body sagging under the weight of his grief. Fresh, hot tears welled in his eyes, and although he'd been sure he couldn't cry anymore tonight, he did. In fact, he did much more than cry: he wept. His surroundings swayed back and forth. Clamping his eyes shut, he clutched Darko's red poppy to his heart for strength.

After Andy managed to quell his tears, he opened his eyes and looked over at Karter. In the dark, Andy couldn't be sure, but Karter appeared . . . sad. Remorseful, even. Maybe his apology to Zoey had been genuine. *Of course it's genuine*, Andy thought. *He regrets what he did, and that's why he saved Diana. That's why he betrayed the gods. That's why he's here, helping us now.*

Hopefully for good this time.

Zoey sniffled and climbed back to her feet. She faced Karter once more. He turned to her with a fearful expression.

They studied one another for a long time. Finally, Zoey, in the most bitter tone Andy had ever heard from her, said, "This is all your fault. Darko is gone because of you." She threw up her hand, yelling now, and Andy spotted a few glistening droplets rolling down Karter's cheeks as he gaped at her. "If what you say is true, if you're really on our side this time, then do us a favor and leave us alone. Get out of here, and don't ever come back!"

"Stop it!" Andy shouted without thinking. Zoey blinked in surprise and turned to him. "I get that you're upset about Darko," he continued. "You're sad, and angry, and your heart hurts so bad you can barely breathe. Trust me, I feel the same way. But you can't blame Karter for Darko's death. Karter didn't kill him. This isn't Karter's fault."

"Of course it's his fault," Zoey retorted.

"No, it's not," Andy said. "It's—it's mine."

"How could it be your fault?"

"Heracles was gonna squish Karter with that column." As Andy explained his reasoning, his voice quivered. "I used the Trident to stop the attack. The attack was redirected at me. Darko saw it coming, and he pushed me out of the way, and it—it killed him instead." The lump in Andy's throat returned. He swallowed hard. "The more I think about it, the more I replay what happened in my head, the more I realize . . . Darko is gone because of *me*."

"No way," Zoey replied. "If anything, what you just said proves my point even more. Heracles was trying to kill Karter, right? And if Heracles hadn't been trying to kill him, you wouldn't have had to protect him."

Diana stamped her foot. "Both of you are being delusional. Darko's death isn't Karter's fault, and it certainly isn't Andy's, either."

Zoey ignored Diana. "Can't you at least admit that if it weren't for Karter betraying us, our situation would have unfolded a lot differently, and Darko might still be here?"

"No, I can't." Andy blinked back new tears. "Because that's—that's not necessarily true, and it's not fair to say. Karter was *helping* us when Darko was killed. Besides, we were gonna have to steal the Lightning Bolt no matter what. In every scenario I can think of, that meant infiltrating Olympus, just like we had to do to save Diana and the twins. Even if Karter had never betrayed us—even if he'd worked with us from the beginning—Darko still could've died on that mission."

Zoey gritted her teeth. "I can't believe this. After everything he's done, you guys are really defending him."

"I'm not defending the messed-up stuff he's done," Andy said, refusing to back down. "If all you were saying was that he's had trouble being a good dude in the past, that we probably can't completely trust him yet, I'd agree with you. But he isn't the reason Darko's gone. And to argue that he is . . . well, it's just not fair. Not to him, and definitely not to Darko."

She sneered at this reply. It was a dark expression, something Andy had never seen on her face before. Something he hadn't known she was capable of. "You know what else isn't fair? The fact that this asshole"—she jutted her index finger in Karter's direction—"couldn't fend off the temptation of glory, or immortality, or whatever other crap his abusive, piece-of-shit dad promised him, and other people suffered because of his poor choices."

Andy opened his mouth to continue arguing with Zoey, but apparently she was done talking to them, because she swung around and stalked off toward a thick wooded area of the campsite without another word. "Zoey!" Andy called. "Stop!" Zoey didn't even give him a backward glance. She disappeared into the trees.

Karter was the first to start after her. "I'll try talking to her again. Explain everything. Maybe—"

"No, dude." Andy put up a hand to stop Karter. "I'm her friend. One of her closest friends. I know her best, so I'll talk to her."

"Neither of you are going to talk to Zoey," Diana snapped. She shoved past Andy and Karter, heading after Zoey. "Karter, if you so much as breathe in her direction, she'll just keep attacking you. It's clear she despises you, and given the circumstances, I can understand why." Karter flinched at these words. "As for you, Andy, you're out of your godsdamned mind if you really believe Darko's death is your fault. Stay here, both of you, before you make things worse."

And just like that, Diana left Andy and Karter standing side by side in awkward silence.

Persephone hadn't visited the rim of the pit of Tartarus many times. In the few instances she had, she'd been accompanied by her husband. A banishment here, a fit of rage there, and then they'd traveled back to Hades's castle and gone about their days. The last time she'd been there, however, she'd been alone—at least, before the Chosen Two and Karter, Son of Zeus arrived to take the Helm of Darkness. That time, of course, had ended a bit differently for her.

Needless to say, the last place Persephone wanted to be was at the edge of the pit. Yet here she was, walking toward it alongside the remaining eleven Olympians and the soon-to-be twelfth one.

After the meeting in the throne room on New Mount Olympus, Zeus had retrieved a "deceased" Prometheus and Asteria. He'd then ordered Hermes to open another portal near Tartarus so the gods could cast them into the pit. The king had wanted to leave Persephone behind with Heracles and Dionysus to look after Olympus while the others tended to the task, but Demeter had insisted that Persephone remain at her side. Before long the gods would reach the rim of the fiery pit, and the two Titans would be banished for all time.

That is, unless the Fates were listening to Persephone's prayers, and the Titans awoke soon.

With every step Persephone took, the black soil surrounding the pit crunched under her feet. Gusts of wind blew into the pit as though it were taking a great, everlasting breath. The gales whipped her hair and skirts forward, threatening to drag her into the cavity's ruthless depths.

As the deities drew closer, Persephone spotted cerulean flames licking the edge like the ocean waves of a beach. Shuddering, she recalled the moment those flames had consumed her. *If I can help it, that will never happen again,* she thought. *Although considering the path I intend to take, I suppose it's a likely end for me.*

Hades stopped. "Don't go any closer, or else the pit could suck you in."

Electricity crackled in Zeus's palms as he and Ares paused, a still-dead Prometheus in their clutches. "If I have to send a team down there to rescue any of you, you won't like the punishments I'll have ready for you when you get back." Everyone halted. "On three we rid ourselves of this cockroach," Zeus continued. Ares nodded in reply, and Persephone held her breath. *Regenerate, Prometheus. Please, regenerate and wake up now so you can escape!* "One, two ... three."

Zeus and Ares grunted, heaving Prometheus toward the flickering blue flames. Combined with the momentum caused by the gods' super-strength, the force of the winds easily pulled the Titan into the pit.

Persephone gulped, her body frozen in fear as the realization that Prometheus would never again regenerate, would never again awaken, hit her. *What should I do now? How will the Chosen Two fight the Olympians without help from the Titans? To properly harness the power of the gods' magical items, they'll need someone with a strong divine essence, and they won't trust me to help with something so important.*

Suddenly, Athena cried, "Asteria has regenerated!" Persephone glanced that way, and sure enough, it seemed a merciful deity had heard her silent pleas. Because as fate would have it, Asteria stirred in Athena's and Artemis's clutches, a soft groan escaping her lips. "Hurry and cast her into the fire before she can fully come to!"

Athena and Artemis shoved Asteria into Zeus's and Ares's hands, and Asteria blinked groggily. She appeared to be registering the situation she'd found herself in; her expression filled with fear as she took in her surroundings.

Persephone began to tremble. She wrung her hands, willing herself to remain calm so the other gods wouldn't grow suspicious. *Fight back!* she thought hard at Asteria. *Get out of here, before it's too late!*

Zeus and Ares tossed the Titan goddess toward the cerulean fire, and Persephone couldn't breathe, positive Asteria wouldn't survive this. *No!*

Before the flames touched Asteria, she disintegrated into millions of miniature shimmering stars and flew fifty feet above the gods. The gales blowing into the pit of Tartarus yanked her stars downward, but after a bit of struggling she found her bearings and soared toward the Fields of Asphodel.

"Don't let her get away!" Zeus bellowed. He leapt into the sky after Asteria.

Hermes's figure blurred as he used his super-speed to dash below Zeus. The rest of the gods released a volley of battle cries, sprinting in Asteria's direction as well.

This isn't ideal, Persephone thought. *I'd hoped both Titans would survive. But perhaps I can still make it work.* She raced behind the other immortals, her heart palpitating as she contemplated her next move.

CHAPTER FOUR

PLEDGE

Zoey tramped along the forest floor, her flesh growing hot and prickly with fury as she allowed the trees to swallow her whole. Anything to get away from Andy, Diana, and Karter.

Especially Karter.

Seriously, though, what was her friends' deal with him? Why were they suddenly all "for" him? Last time she'd checked, Diana hated the guy's guts. In fact, back in Hephaestus City,

Diana had been willing to let him be captured by Violet, Layla, and Xander, while Zoey had been the one to stand up for him. But now, even after *everything* he'd done, Diana was defending him for some deranged reason.

And as for Andy? God, Zoey could barely stomach the fact that Andy was insisting Darko's death wasn't Karter's fault. How couldn't it be? So many of the group's problems would have been solved early on if only Karter weren't so unstable. In fact, if he'd been a good friend to Spencer and Syrena in the first place— if he'd stuck up for Syrena at her execution—he could have been part of the crew all along.

But no, Zoey thought. *He had to go back and forth and royally screw with our heads. And now, near the end of our mission, right before we get ready to have our final showdown with the gods, he wants to act like he's on our side? Like he's changed for good? Like he's a decent person, a legit human being? No way. I'm not buying it. He'll ditch us the moment it's convenient for him.*

"Hey!" Diana yelled from behind Zoey. "Wait!"

Zoey sighed and paused. She turned around to see Diana's tiny form rushing forward. "I need a few minutes alone, okay?"

"No, not okay." Diana stopped in front of

Zoey. "You're acting out of emotion. You're not thinking about the Karter situation logically, and it's keeping you from seeing the big picture."

"I don't need a lecture right now."

"It's strange, too," Diana went on. "Ever since I met you, I've noticed that most of the time, you lean on logic. You do get emotional, but generally it seems you don't let your feelings control you. Even when you and Andy discovered that your old lives were gone, that everyone from the Before Time was dead, you were most concerned with becoming the hero the world needed. You were already mentally preparing to take on the gods, while Andy had a meltdown."

Zoey shrugged. "It was weird finding out all that stuff, but the evidence was right in front of me. I had to accept things and move forward."

Diana laughed. "See? That's what I'm talking about. The world being obliterated by gods? Easy for you to understand, so long as there's evidence. But strangely enough, whenever Karter is involved, you lose the ability to reason. For one, you insisted on saving him back in Hephaestus City despite doing so being incredibly dangerous. Now the notion of him helping us—even after he faced his father to help you and Andy, not to mention save me and

Troy and Marina—is making you lose your mind." Zoey hugged her sides, turning away, and Diana continued. "I'm going to explain something to you, and while I do it, I need you to set aside your personal feelings for Karter. I need you to think about this from a tactical perspective."

"Go ahead, I guess."

"As much as I believe in you and Andy and the Prophecy, and as much as I have faith that the gods can be defeated, that doesn't mean it's going to be easy. Even with the pantheon's three most powerful objects, we could lose this war. We need all the help we can get. We can't be picky about who's willing to do so, especially when they're as strong as Karter. If it means freeing humanity, we might have to fight alongside someone we once considered an enemy."

"Except we can't trust Karter. Back in Hades, he stood by us. Sure, it was so he could save Spencer, but still, he did. Yet after we tried saving him in Hephaestus City, he turned on us. He's too unpredictable. We can't rely on him."

"That was true of him before tonight, but I don't think that's who he is any longer. Again, try to set aside the way you personally feel about him and consider how much he could help if we allow it. I'm not asking you to forgive him and be his friend after everything he's done. Honestly, I don't think I'll be his friend again— not for a while, at least. But I'm going to work with him to fight the gods, because his assistance could be the difference between loss and victory. Can't you try and do the same? Not for him, but for others. For humanity."

As much as I hate to admit it, Zoey thought, *she's making some seriously good points*. Still, she couldn't shake the memory of being trapped with Karter in the Hephaestus City jail. While they'd been locked up, they'd bonded, shared dark parts of their pasts with one another. For a second, she'd believed they could be friends.

And then he'd stabbed her in the back.

"You really believe he's changed?" Zoey asked.

"I don't believe he's changed, necessarily," Diana said. "I think a part of him always knew the gods were the bad guys, like Syrena and Spencer and I did. And just like us, he needed time to find the resolve to defy them."

"You trust he has the guts to stick by us? To not go crawling back to those scumbags?"

"I do." Diana sounded as though she meant it. "He proved it back on Olympus, when he confronted his father and the other gods and fought with us. There's no going back for him after that, and he knows it. In a way, this is all he has left now. *We're* all he has left now."

Zoey couldn't believe what she was about to say. "Okay . . . fine. If it means we have a better chance of winning this war, then I guess I'll try to work with Karter. But I swear, if he turns on us for the gods . . ."

"He won't," Diana asserted. "Not this time." She pivoted and started back toward Andy and Karter. "Now come on. We have work to do."

Once Diana disappeared after Zoey, Karter began to pace the forest floor. He ran shaking hands through his shaggy black hair, his thoughts racing, his stomach sick. How long would they be gone? Should he hurry after them? Go against Diana's orders and try to explain his side of the story to Zoey?

"This is all your fault," Zoey had said to him. *"Darko is gone because of you. If what you say is true, if you're really on our side this time, then do us a favor and leave us alone. Get out of here, and don't ever come back!"* Mere hours ago, he'd wondered whether

he'd be able to make it up to Zoey for betraying her. Now he realized her answer to that question was "no."

Chest aching, he looked at Andy. The boy sat against a fallen tree, his eyes clamped shut. He held the flower that had once been the satyr named Darko to his chest, his newly acquired wings curled around him like a shield.

"Stop it!" Andy had yelled at Zoey after she'd hurled her vitriol at Karter. *"I get that you're upset about Darko. You're sad, and angry, and your heart hurts so bad you can barely breathe. Trust me, I feel the same way. But you can't blame Karter for Darko's death. Karter didn't kill him. This isn't Karter's fault."*

"Of course it's his fault."

"No, it's not. It's—it's mine."

Karter gulped and stepped toward Andy. *Even if I can never make things up to Zoey, perhaps I can still do so for Andy.* "I wanted to thank you," he said.

Andy opened his eyes and glanced up at Karter. "For what?"

"For standing up for me the way you did. Considering everything I've done to you and your companions, I don't deserve it. Still, thank you."

"You're welcome, I guess. It just didn't seem fair of Zoey to say those things to you. It also didn't seem like her. I've never seen her so mad."

"Wonderful." Karter scratched the back of his neck and sat next to Andy. "For what it's worth, I don't believe it's your fault the satyr— I mean, Darko—is gone."

"Yeah?" Andy rested his head on the tree behind him. He wasn't looking at Karter, but Karter saw his eyes growing watery.

"These things, they happen in war," Karter continued. "In the heat of battle, you were protecting me, and then Darko protected you." Andy didn't reply, and Karter wondered whether he'd said the wrong thing. He cleared his throat. "On top of thanking you, I also wanted to apologize to you."

Andy sniffled and wiped his eyes. "For what?"

"For working against you so many times, and especially for what I did to Zoey and Diana in Hephaestus City."

"Listen, as long as you don't run back to the gods and you keep helping us, I don't have a problem with you hanging around. The way I see it, if your apologies are legit, you'll prove it, and we'll have no reason to be suspicious of you anymore. Actions speak louder than words, and all that."

"Trust me, I don't care to align myself with the gods ever again." He sighed. "They're selfish, cruel, and unjust. Besides, even if I wanted to go back, they'd never accept me after what I did tonight. The moment my father sees me next, he'll shoot me with green lightning. In fact, he already tried to back on Olympus."

The faintest trace of merriment flittered across Andy's features. "I guess we're stuck with you, then." Andy's teasing made Karter recall fond moments with Spencer and Syrena, reminded him of the times in which the three of them had poked fun at one another as they watched sunsets on the beach.

"I suppose you're right," Karter said. "I don't plan on going anywhere. Not until I've made up for the wrongs I've committed. Not until I become someone Spencer and Syrena could have been proud of." Grass and twigs cracked from behind them. Karter shot to his feet and spun around. Diana emerged from the trees, followed by Zoey.

Karter's stomach twisted into knots at the sight of Zoey. Had Diana managed to change her opinion of him in the slightest? It hadn't taken them long to return, so it wasn't likely, but he hoped so.

As the girls approached Karter and Andy,

Zoey shot Karter a glare. "You and I are going to have a talk. Now." She walked past him, toward the other side of the cabin, and he trailed after her, his heart in his throat. Sure, she seemed angry, but she was willing to talk to him. That was a good sign, right?

Once the pair was out of earshot of Andy and Diana, Zoey faced Karter, and he clasped his hands. "Please let me explain myself," he said. "Let me apologize and—"

"No, no, no," she interjected, shaking her head. "I don't want to hear it. I don't want explanations, and I definitely don't want any more bullcrap apologies. It doesn't matter to me how sorry you are. What you did to m—*us* . . . it's unforgivable, okay?"

"O—okay. Why did you want to speak with me, then?"

"Well . . ."

"Well?" he repeated, unable to suppress the acidity in his tone.

She narrowed her sky-blue eyes at him. "I wanted to say that despite how little I trust you, I'm willing to look past that and work with you for the greater good."

"The greater good."

"You know what I mean."

"I do. I'd just hoped . . ." He trailed off.

"What?" she snapped. "You'd hoped what?"

"Forget it." He glared down at his sandaled feet, suddenly hyperaware of the grease and grime covering every inch of his body.

"Fine with me, so long as we've reached an understanding. We can work together to save the world, but that doesn't mean I forgive you, and we will never be friends." She shoved past him, bumping his shoulder, and started back toward Diana and Andy.

He spun around. "Wait!" She paused but didn't look at him. He swallowed hard, and his mind went blank. *What was I going to say?* "If you change your mind, I'll be here," he blurted out.

"What the hell is that supposed to mean?"

"Uhh. Umm." He pinched the bridge of his nose. *I'm such an idiot.* "Listen, I know I've made mistakes. Horrible ones."

"I am painfully aware of that fact."

"I've hurt the people I love most. I've harmed them beyond measure. And now that they're gone, I can never truly make up for it. But still, I have to try. Otherwise, I won't be able to live with myself." No response from her. "I should have been a better man for Spencer and Syrena, and . . . and for all of you, too. I promise, from now on I'm going to do my best to be *that* man." Still no reply. "So, if you change your mind and decide there's something I can do for you—something that will help you forgive me—then tell me. I'll be here, and I pledge that no matter what it is, if you ask me to do it, I will."

There was an agonizing stretch of silence. Finally, Zoey said, "Yeah, I don't see that happening." She walked away for good this time, and Karter put his face in his hands, wondering why he'd said anything to her at all.

After Zoey and Karter got back from their talk, she and him and Andy asked Diana what she needed so she could begin treating the injured.

"Just food and water, and for you guys to bring me whoever needs healing," Diana said, and the group headed into the cabin. Diana told Troy and Marina they could go first if they wanted, but they insisted she should start with people who were in the most critical condition.

"We don't have any open wounds," Troy replied. "Save your strength for those who need it most."

"Yeah, we can go last," Marina added. "We're

not dying. Take care of everyone else first."

With that, Zoey and Andy retrieved Narcissa and explained Diana's requests, while Karter stayed behind with Diana and the twins in the cabin. Immediately, Narcissa set everyone who could to work.

The rest of the night dragged on in a dark haze for Zoey. She and Andy spent their time glued to Diana's side, ensuring their friend stayed nourished as she worked tirelessly to heal the wounded one by one, going from those in the most critical condition to those in the least critical condition. Many times, Diana had to rest so she wouldn't burn up, and whenever her skin started steaming, Karter appeared with a bucket of cold freshwater. He'd dump the water on Diana as she lay on the ground taking deep breaths. Coupled with a break in each instance, the technique kept her healing nymph recruits through the night, although it was clear to Zoey she needed sleep more than anything.

When morning came, and sunlight began peeking through the windows of the cabin, Diana could do no more. In the middle of healing a Naiad with a gash in her calf, Diana fainted.

"Oh my God!" Andy cried. "Diana!"

Zoey's heart nearly stopped with worry. She

checked Diana's pulse, breathing, and temperature. Once she determined Diana was okay, she sighed in relief. "She's all right."

"She must have passed out from exhaustion," Karter said.

Narcissa ushered nymphs out of the cabin. "Don't wake her. She's endured enough tonight. Let her sleep before she continues this process. In fact, everyone that fought on Olympus needs to rest while the rest of us move camp."

"How'll you guys move camp if we're asleep?" Andy asked.

"Dryads manipulated nature to build this cabin," Harmony answered. "They can just as easily relocate it, even with you inside."

"Exactly." Narcissa started toward the door. "Harmony, help me gather the others. Half of those with able body can carry our wounded, the cabin, and the weapons and armor, while the other half can keep an eye on the prisoners."

Karter raised a brow. "Who are you keeping captive?"

"Artemis's Huntresses," Narcissa replied coolly.

Karter's eyes widened, and Andy explained to him how the Huntresses had tracked the group down. "There was a massive fight," he said. "We won, and to make sure they can't attack again, the recruits kill them as they regenerate."

Zoey rolled her eyes at Karter for seeming so surprised about the group fighting Artemis's Huntresses and surviving, but before she could snap at him for it, she yawned, her body heavy with exhaustion. If she didn't get some sleep soon, she might faint as Diana had. She offered the remaining nymphs a weak wave, and they exited the cabin.

With the nymphs gone, Zoey and Andy climbed to their feet and shuffled around to find good spots to conk out. When Zoey caught sight of Karter still standing on the other side of the cabin, she froze. Their gazes locked.

Karter coughed. It sounded fake. "Apologies. I was just, uh—just leaving." He lowered his head and hastened toward the door.

"Don't you need sleep?" Andy asked. "You fought on Olympus too."

"Not tired. I can help the nymphs." Karter rushed outside and shut the door.

Andy lay down several feet from Zoey and closed his eyes. "Well, that was awkward. Working with Karter is gonna take some getting used to, isn't it?"

Zoey lay down as well. She didn't want to stray too far from Andy, Diana, Kali, and the twins. Not with Karter around. "Sure, if he doesn't betray us again."

"Do you honestly think he would? After last night?" Andy sounded groggy, as if he was already half-asleep. "I don't know the guy very well, but still. It doesn't seem likely. I'm not saying we should be buddy-buddy with him right away. But I think—maybe—I'm gonna give him the benefit of the doubt." He yawned. "Until he gives me a reason not to."

She turned over to face the wall. "Do whatever you want, I guess. Just don't be surprised if he stabs you in the back." Andy didn't reply, and the last thing she remembered before falling asleep was focusing on the sound of a gushing stream nearby, trying not to think about what would happen if Karter turned on her once more.

For the next few hours, Persephone and the Olympians raced across the black hills and bubbling volcanoes of the rest of Tartarus, barreled through the hordes of confused souls meandering about the dead grassland of Asphodel, and dashed beneath the perfect blue skies and fluffy clouds of Elysium, all in the pursuit of capturing Asteria. And, to Persephone's satisfaction, they could not catch her.

When they'd all but given up, Hermes used his portals to send them to various locations in the Underworld, to every place they thought the Titan goddess might be hiding. Still, they did not find her.

Eventually, Hermes transported them to the throne room of Hades's castle so they could rest and regroup. After the exertion of traveling across the Underworld for so long, they were exhausted.

While the rest of the gods sat around the throne room, panting and covered in sweat, Zeus pounded back and forth across the red rug splayed down the chamber's middle, ripping out chunks of his silver hair. "*Where—is—she?*" he boomed, his voice echoing off the cavernous, skull-and-gem-encrusted walls.

"She couldn't have escaped the Underworld," Hades said, wiping the perspiration from his pale forehead. He slumped back in his throne, which was perched atop the dais at the edge of the chamber. "Few can venture freely between the world above and the world below, and Asteria is not one of them."

"It makes no sense," Poseidon said from his spot on the ground.

Athena rose from where she sat beside Artemis and Hermes. "Actually, it makes perfect sense." She strode over to Zeus and rested a hand on his shoulder. "The Titan goddess must have had help."

Zeus tore away from Athena. "Who? Who would dare?" He pointed an accusatory finger one by one at the deities in the room. Persephone's heart skipped as he landed on her. "Who is the traitor among us now?" Beside Persephone, Demeter grabbed her hand and squeezed it tight.

"Please, Father, calm yourself," Athena said. "It's not any of us."

Artemis sat up. "Athena is right. No one was alone while chasing Asteria. Father and Hermes matched one another's speed, and the rest of us stayed together."

"Exactly." Hermes climbed to his feet and slicked back his hair—he usually wore it neat, but since Persephone had come back from Tartarus, it had been unusually messy. "It must have been one of the Underworld gods. One with the power to travel freely between the world above and the world below."

"But who?" Hera cupped her chin in thought. "And why?"

"Someone with motive," Hephaestus grumbled.

Aphrodite batted her long lashes, fluffing her golden hair. "Motive?"

Athena put her hands on her hips. "Someone who wants to destroy the Olympians, obviously."

"Nyx or Thanatos, perhaps?" Ares suggested. "They seemed quite eager to watch this place in Hades's stead."

Hestia shuffled her feet. "Mm, I don't think so. They have no reason to overthrow us."

"Hestia is right," Poseidon said. "We allowed Nyx and Thanatos to build their own cities long ago, which they've filled with many loyal worshippers, and when they said they wanted to help, they didn't seem to have ulterior motives. Someone else must have helped Asteria. The Furies, perhaps?"

Hera shook her head. "No, I don't believe it was the Furies. They informed us that the Chosen Two had banished Persephone to Tartarus and stolen the Helm of Darkness. If they wanted to help the Chosen Two, they would have tried keeping that information from us for as long as possible. What about Asteria's daughter, Hecate? Could she have helped the Titan?"

"No, I haven't seen Hecate here in a long while," Hades said. "Truthfully, I can't think of a single deity of this realm who would want to help Asteria and the Chosen Two anyway. I'm not sure how the mortals escaped the Underworld in the first place."

The Olympians fell quiet, contemplating Hades's words, and Persephone bit her lip. She had an idea of who could have helped the mortals escape, but she didn't plan on saying anything.

The sinister cackling of a goddess bounced off the walls of the throne room. "My, my. After your visit to Tartarus, you're having trouble finding your head again. Aren't you, Hades?"

Persephone glanced around, trying to locate who'd spoken, but she couldn't see her anywhere. Even still, Persephone didn't need to see the immortal to know who she was. She'd recognize that voice anywhere.

"*Eris!*" Zeus yelled. "What in all the gods' names have you done now?"

There was more laughter, and then tendrils of black smoke curled out from the farthest corner of the chamber. The smoke grew and grew, before finally Persephone's suspicions were confirmed and Eris, Goddess of Chaos appeared from the haze.

Like most of the pantheon, Eris was much taller than Persephone. However, that's where her similarities to the other gods ended. Unlike the rest of them, she wasn't particularly attractive—her skin was paler than a corpse's, her body sunken and skeletal beneath her plum-colored gown. Her lips turned up in a sinister smile as she stepped toward the Olympians, her forked tongue slithering in and out of her mouth.

Hades rose from his throne. "It was you, wasn't it? You're the one who helped the Chosen Two escape. You're the one who aided Asteria as well."

Eris snapped her fingers. In a flash of purple light, a golden apple materialized. She tossed it back and forth between her hands. "Now you're catching on."

"But why?" Poseidon asked, climbing to his feet. "You have a city. Hundreds of thousands of worshippers."

Zeus's face was turning scarlet, the veins in his forehead popping out. "Are you not aware of what we did to Apollo's *polis* for his betrayal of the pantheon? What we did to his loyal worshippers?"

"I never asked for a *polis*," Eris replied flatly. "I never asked for worshippers, either. You only gave me those things because you feared me, but you never stopped to consider whether I wanted them. Truth be told, I didn't. Why would I care what happens to them?"

Hera crinkled her nose. "Because without them, the world will eventually forget you. When that happens, you'll perish. Even as the Goddess of Chaos, you must be frightened of death. It frightens all gods."

"Unlike your pathetic lot, I don't fear fading into nothingness." Eris stopped tossing the apple back and forth. She held it close to her face, examining it. "I imagine death to be an exhilarating experience, really. Something to look forward to at the end of this long, boring existence."

Zeus conjured peridot electricity. "If you're looking forward to death so much, allow me to put you in Tartarus, where you belong." He launched the lightning at Eris. Before it could strike her, she dissolved into black smoke. The bolt shot uselessly into the ground where she'd been standing.

Zeus snarled, and Eris's sinister cackling reverberated across the chamber. "Why would I let you put me in Tartarus, when so many interesting events are about to unfold?" she said. "Don't you see? This will be so much fun to watch." The sound of teeth biting into fruit rang out.

Several seconds passed, and Eris's laughter still echoed along the walls, but she did not reappear.

CHAPTER FIVE

CONNECT

When Andy opened his eyes again, it was dim, and all he could hear were the deep slumbering breaths of his companions. He stretched, sat upright, and glanced through the window. It appeared to be dusk. *Was I out all day? Did the nymphs already find a new place to camp?* He looked around. Zoey, Kali, Troy, and Marina were asleep, and Darko's poppy and the three objects of power were safely tucked away in a far corner of the cabin. However, Diana was gone. *Is she already healing more of the nymphs?* He climbed to his feet and tiptoed toward the door, careful not to disturb his friends.

When he stepped outside, the spicy scent of pine filled his nostrils. Goose bumps prickled his skin as a cool, crisp gust whipped through the forest around him. There was no one here besides Luna, Ajax, and Aladdin—at least not that he could see. Maybe there were nymphs hiding in the woods, or maybe everyone had gathered in another section of the campsite.

"Sorry I didn't say hi to you guys before," Andy told the pegasi. "There was a lot going on. I was worried about Kali. I'm sure you understand." He walked over and hugged each of them, one by one, and Ajax nickered, nuzzling his cheek.

Just as he was about to leave to find Diana, the familiar voice of a girl sounded from behind him. "Good evening," she said, her tone crestfallen. He swung around to find Harmony as she stepped out from a cluster of trees.

Despite the muted light of the evening, Andy could tell how red and puffy Harmony's eyes had become, and his heart sank as he remembered her reaction to the nymphs being left behind, and to Darko being killed. Nibbling on his thumbnail, he averted his gaze from hers.

"Uh, hey. How are you?"

"I've been better. How are you?"

"I've . . . also been better." He paused. "Are we in a new spot? I guess I wasn't really paying attention to what the last one looked like. There was . . . a lot going on. Where's everyone else?"

"Yes, we're in a new spot. We traveled well into the afternoon until we settled here. For now, we're far enough away from Olympus, but we'll need to move again soon. As for everyone else—some of them, like me, are close. We're guarding the cabin. Others are resting or watching for intruders at the perimeter of camp. Diana is healing the wounded over there." She pointed to the right. "It's a bit of a walk from here."

"Right, thanks." He started in that direction, avoiding eye contact with Harmony.

"Wait," she said, and he turned around. "Darko's flower—where is it?"

He tilted his head. "In the cabin. Why?"

"It should be outside," she replied. "It needs water and sunlight."

"Crap." He hurried back into the cabin and retrieved the flower. As he brought it outside, the pegasi eyed it. They pawed the ground, their tails swishing, and he wondered whether they knew it was all the group had left of Darko.

Andy presented the poppy to Harmony. "Where do you think we should put it?"

Her bottom lip quivered. Gently, she took the flower in her hands. "We'll need to plant it somewhere beautiful."

"Not yet," Andy said. "I don't know for sure where his—I mean, *its*—final resting place should be. But I know it can't be here. What about a temporary spot?"

"Very well." She circled around to the back of the cabin. Andy followed her, and soon they found a nice place among a patch of wildflowers for the poppy to sit. "It should get enough sunlight here," she assured Andy. "And I'll water it morning and night."

"I can help with that," Andy said.

A tear trickled down her cheek. "You have enough to attend to already. If you remember to water it, that's fine, but if you don't, I will."

He nodded once. "Okay. Uh, see you."

"Yes," she replied. "See you."

He hastened away, in Diana's direction, and about twenty minutes later, when the sun had disappeared from the sky, he reached a clearing where dozens of injured Dryads and Naiads were lined up to see Diana. She sat on a log at the edge of the clearing, and Karter stood behind her as she healed the nymphs, his bucket of water in hand.

Andy walked toward his companions, and the closer he got, the more he could tell they needed a break. Diana was covered in sweat again, and Karter looked like a straight-up corpse. His pale, sunken face was even more pale and sunken than usual, and dark bags had formed under his eyes.

"You guys look exhausted," Andy said as he approached them.

"Because we are," Diana replied flatly.

Andy held out his hands for Karter's bucket of water. "Why don't you go find a place to crash? And Diana can take a break."

Karter nodded, handed Andy the container, and staggered off into the trees. Diana finished healing the Dryad before her and informed everyone she'd be back after she took a short while to recuperate.

During Diana's break, Andy dumped the remaining water over her, then refilled the bucket at a nearby stream. When he returned, she was scarfing down handfuls of roots and berries and sucking down water from a canteen. "Are you hungry?" she asked. He shook his head, not wanting to take any of Diana's provisions, but his stomach betrayed him by growling. Diana insisted on giving Andy some of her snacks and a couple of swigs of her water, and soon they were ready to get back to work. Around an hour of healing passed before Zoey showed up to help too, and for the rest of the night, the three of them worked together.

By morning, Diana's short breaks were no longer enough, and she had to go back to the cabin to sleep. Initially Andy and Zoey had planned to go with her—to watch over their friends—but Narcissa stopped them on their way back and asked if she could speak with them.

Andy shared a confused look with Zoey; Narcissa seemed more intense than usual. "Yeah, sure, I guess," he said. Zoey told Diana they'd catch up with her later, and they followed Narcissa in the opposite direction through the trees.

Eventually they reached a small gazebo made of branches and vegetation at the edge of camp, and Narcissa ushered them inside. As they stood within the structure, Narcissa waved her arms, and suddenly they were going up, up, up.

Andy and Zoey looked out over the edge of the gazebo. Vines twisted and curled beneath it, carrying them higher and higher. "Are you on watch duty or something?" Andy asked.

"Yes," Narcissa answered. "But this couldn't

wait. I had to abandon my post to retrieve you."

"What's this about?" Andy asked.

Once the gazebo was high above the trees, a view of the clear blue sky and the warm morning sun ahead of them, they came to a stop. Narcissa moved to the edge of the gazebo and scanned the forest. "There's something very important we must discuss."

Zoey raised a brow. "Such as?"

Narcissa turned to them, a grave expression on her face. "You have saved the Daughter of Apollo, preventing Zeus's visions of the gods easily winning this war. Not only that, but you have successfully stolen the Olympians' three most powerful magical objects."

"Yup." Andy crossed his arms, wondering where Narcissa was going with this. "So what's up?"

"I need you to tell me something. How exactly do you plan on winning this war? On defeating the gods?"

"We're going to use the Helm, the Trident, and the Lightning Bolt to defeat them," Andy answered simply.

"Yes," Narcissa replied. "But *how* will you use those items to vanquish the gods?"

Oh shit. I guess I hadn't thought of that. He froze, unsure of what to say. Apparently, Zoey didn't know how to respond either, because neither of them said a word.

Narcissa went on. "I suppose what I'm trying to say is this: Do you know how to use the objects properly? Do you know how to utilize them for the purpose of destroying an immortal?"

"I'm not sure we do," Zoey said. "We know what the objects' general functions are, but we aren't sure how to use them to destroy a god." She cupped her chin. "Circe mentioned something along those lines when we were on her island. I told her she had to do what we asked because we had the Helm and the Trident, but she said that the 'items we spoke of' were useless unless the 'wielders knew how to properly utilize their powers.' It wasn't until after Anteros took over Andy's body that we got rid of her."

Andy snapped his fingers. "Heracles said practically the same thing back on Olympus. I told him to back down, that he didn't stand a chance against us because we had all three items of power, but that didn't scare him. He asked us why we were running away if we were 'so unstoppable' and why didn't we just use the objects to destroy the gods."

"You mentioned that once Anteros took

over Andy's body, you were able to rid yourselves of Circe," Narcissa said. "How? Did Andy send her to the Underworld, as Zoey did to Artemis during our battle against the goddess and her Huntresses?"

"That's exactly what happened," Andy confirmed.

Narcissa returned her gaze to the forest. "Perhaps creating a portal to the Underworld and forcing the gods through it is the way to defeat them."

"No, I don't think so," Zoey said. "From what I understand about the Descent Spell, it opens a portal to the Underworld, but it doesn't trap whoever goes through the portal down there. It's more of a temporary fix rather than a permanent solution."

"Hmm." Narcissa clicked her tongue a few times. "Whatever the case may be, it appears Anteros and Calliope are the key to unlocking the secrets of the gods' magical items. You should contact them for more answers."

Andy and Zoey shared a knowing look. "The thing is, I haven't heard from Anteros since our big fight with Artemis's Huntresses," Andy said, and considering how pushy the god was, he was grateful for their lack of interaction.

"And I haven't heard from Calliope since I

let her take over my body to send Artemis to Hades," Zoey added. "I had a dream with her in it after I passed out, and that was it. She hasn't come around since. I couldn't even channel her and use my voice-powers on Olympus."

Narcissa turned to Andy and Zoey once more. "We must find a way for you to contact them."

"I think we'll be okay," Andy replied. "We'll figure something out."

"No, the Dryad is right." The familiar voice of a goddess rang out all around them. "Anteros and Calliope are the key to winning this war. If you cannot connect with them again, all hope will be lost." Brilliant silver light flashed before them. As it dwindled, a Titan goddess they knew well appeared—Asteria.

The sight of Asteria made Andy's nostrils flare, anger brewing in his gut. Even though Asteria had helped the group flee Circe's island, fight Artemis, and escape Olympus, she also wanted Andy and Zoey to give up their bodies to Anteros and Calliope. Prometheus had told them about her intentions before they'd infiltrated Olympus, and Andy was pretty pissed at her for lying to them about it.

"Asteria?" Zoey cried. "You escaped?"

"Where's Prometheus?" Andy asked.

"The nymph recruits?" Narcissa said.

Asteria closed her eyes. For a moment, her form shimmered at the edges, little stars twinkling where flesh and blood should be, but a second later she looked normal again. Her eyes snapped open. "I'm sorry to say I cannot access Prometheus's location, but I sense the nymph recruits on New Mount Olympus."

"I'm glad the nymphs are on Olympus, at least," Zoey said. "And I bet you can't find Prometheus because of Hephaestus's chains. They weaken his powers, and Troy and Marina said there's even an enchantment on them. Hopefully, he escaped and is on his way here right now."

"It's possible," Asteria replied. "I'm afraid it's also possible that he was banished to Tartarus."

Andy's stomach clenched. "No, we can't think like that. Until we hear otherwise, we have to believe he's okay."

"Very well," Asteria said. "In any case, I barely escaped the gods myself. During the battle, Zeus managed to strike me with a green bolt. When I regenerated, I found myself in Hades. The Olympians were carrying me to the edge of the pit of Tartarus, and they attempted to banish me to the pit. I turned myself into stars and flew away as fast as I could." She briefly glanced over her shoulder, as if to make sure no one had followed her here. "The gods chased after me, but they couldn't catch me. I found Eris just in time, and she agreed to give me one of her golden apples."

The memory of Eris gifting Andy and his friends golden apples on their own trip to Hades slammed into him like a semi going eighty down the interstate. How there had been five of them who'd needed to escape, but the goddess had only given them four apples. Spencer had insisted that Karter take the fourth piece of fruit, while Karter asserted that Spencer should have it. In the end, Spencer had died before the two young men could settle on who would take the last one.

A pained expression came over Zoey's face. Andy guessed she was reliving the memory of Spencer's passing in Hades, too. "Eris just *gave* you one of her apples, huh?" she asked, her tone bitter. "There wasn't a catch or anything?"

"Not that I'm aware of. The Goddess of Chaos seems quite excited to antagonize the Olympians. However, the logistics of my getaway aren't relevant. What matters is that the two of you connect with Anteros and Calliope and complete the convergence, because I fear we're running out of time. I have no doubt Zeus will send a party to hunt you down. And even if you run from them, it won't matter. At some point, the gods will catch you. You'll be forced to face them, and when that happens, you must be ready."

Andy was shaking his head before Asteria could finish. "I'm gonna stop you right there. While you were passed out—you know, before we got to Olympus—Prometheus filled us in on your plan. He told us about how we aren't really Anteros and Calliope, how they're trying to take over our bodies, and how you want that to happen. Sorry, but you're busted, lady."

Asteria's eyes widened. She opened her mouth to reply, but Zoey stopped her. "Thank you for all your help," Zoey said. "Seriously, we couldn't have stolen the Master Lightning Bolt without you. The thing is, we aren't interested in converging with Calliope and Anteros. We aren't interested in letting them take over our bodies. Not permanently, at least. We've gotten this far as ourselves already. Sure, we had help from them, but now that we have all three objects of power, I'm confident we can find a way to win this war without them." She motioned at Narcissa. "Especially because of all the courageous people who are fighting beside us."

"Prometheus, the fool." Asteria huffed. "He promised to let me handle this, but he allowed his fondness for the two of you to cloud his judgment instead, and now he's filled your heads with preposterous notions."

Andy narrowed his eyes at Asteria. "Prometheus told us the truth because he knows we don't deserve to be lied to and manipulated. We had a right to know what was going on, what you were planning for us. Plus, we've already lost and sacrificed so much to defeat the gods. Why would we have to give up our own bodies on top of everything else? Especially to a couple of asshats who can't even respect our personal boundaries?"

"Because this is not about you," Asteria retorted. "Either of you. This is about freeing humanity from the tyranny of the Olympians and ushering the world into a new era."

"We can do that without Calliope and Anteros," Zoey asserted. "We have the objects of power. We just need to figure out how to use them to their full potential."

"You don't understand. How could you?" Asteria sighed. "You're only human."

Andy groaned in frustration. "Why don't you help us understand, then? Because you aren't making sense. Honestly, you never have."

"There's a reason the two of you were chosen by the universe for this task," Asteria said. "There's a reason that after you were killed in the Storm, your life threads turned white and started to glow. A reason the Fates chose not to cut them."

"We already know all that," Zoey snapped. "We figured it out when we were facing off with Poseidon in the middle of the Atlantic. It's because we somehow have Calliope and Anteros inside of us. Having them around gave us an advantage—it gave us powers—and those powers helped us do what we had to."

"Exactly," Andy said, nodding. "Demigods have powers that help them, sure, but they can't touch the gods' magical items without their life forces being sucked away. And even though regular mortals can touch the objects without dying, the gods would massacre them before they'd ever even have the chance to take the items because they're so much weaker than gods and demigods."

"That's right, yes, but you still don't have the full picture," Asteria said.

"Do us a favor and tell it to us straight, then," Andy replied. "*Give* us the full picture."

"I fear that if I simply tell you what your destinies could be, you won't believe me."

Asteria thought for a moment. "No, I think I need to show you instead. Perhaps then you will understand. Perhaps then you will accept the truth." Her form glittered at the edges again. "This will take a great deal of energy. But I believe it is a necessary sacrifice on my part. Flying there will take too long."

Andy and Zoey shared a confused glance. But before another word could be uttered, silver light flared, and Asteria's stars consumed them.

Whole minutes passed before the stars cleared from Zoey's vision. When they did, she found herself in a place she'd only visited twice before. *The lair of the Fates*, she thought, the scent of dewy grass flooding her nostrils.

The lair appeared to be outside, but Zoey knew it wasn't. High above her, where the sky should have been, there was a cave ceiling. Around her stood tall walls of vines and white-petaled flowers, and along the ground, grass grew. Millions of blue strings were woven throughout the turf and vine-and-flower walls, the threads so tangled and twisted and knotted that Zoey couldn't be sure where any of them began or ended. In the center of the cavern, candles flickered around a wooden spinning wheel.

Andy stepped up beside Zoey, gazing at her in bewilderment, and Zoey gasped at his appearance. He looked like a ghost, his form as blue as the strings in the chamber, his edges as hazy as mist on a cold fall morning. Zoey held up her hand to see if she looked the same. Sure enough, she did.

In a blaze of silver, Asteria manifested before them. She appeared as blue and foggy as they did. "Why'd you bring us here?" Andy asked. "Last time we came, the Fates told us they can't help us anymore. They said they'd already helped us too much."

"We're not here to request help from the Fates," Asteria said. "We're here so that I can show you what will happen if you finish the convergence, and what will happen if you don't. Come, this way." They followed Asteria to one of the walls, and she began digging through the vines, searching for something.

Zoey looked around nervously. "Where are Lachesis, Clotho, and Atropos?"

"They're weaving and cutting life threads in another one of their chambers," Asteria said.

Andy's jaw dropped. "There are more rooms like this one?"

"Of course. You don't expect the Fates to keep the destinies of everyone who's ever existed in a single cavern, do you? Not to mention mortals are born every day. The Fates create new strings all the time." She tugged on something in the wall. "No need to worry, though. Even if the Fates were in this chamber, they wouldn't be able to see us. Our bodies aren't here, which is why we appear the way we do. Our physical forms are at the nymph camp, while our spirits are here. This spell is easier for me rather than physical teleportation because of my dominion over necromancy."

"But I thought the Fates were all-powerful and all-knowing?" Zoey said. "Even if we're only here in spirit, won't they figure out what we're doing?"

"Perhaps." Asteria pulled something out of the wall, and Zoey recognized her and Andy's life threads. She remembered the Fates showing them the strings the first time they'd come to this place.

The threads were white and glowing, snarled together as if one string and not two. But something was different about them this time: a blue string had entangled itself with them.

"Whose thread is that?" Andy asked. "It wasn't there last time."

"It's Karter's." Asteria held up the knotted threads. "Because of the path he's chosen, your destinies have become entwined."

Zoey rolled her eyes. "Our destinies weren't 'entwined' with his before? You know, when he was trying to capture Diana, or when he was kidnapping me? How about when he stabbed us all in the back?"

"Yes, ever since your resurrections, your threads of fate have had a great influence on Karter's," Asteria said. "But they have never been so closely linked, and you will soon understand why." She offered them the knotted strings. "Go ahead. Touch the threads, and you will see."

Zoey and Andy looked at each other. "Ready?" Andy asked her. She wasn't, but she nodded anyway.

Together, they reached forward. Their fingers brushed the strings at the same time, and in the blink of an eye, they were no longer in the lair of the Fates.

Instead, they were floating hundreds of feet in the air, the sky black with a rainstorm, green lightning bolts shooting from the clouds. Far below them was a struggle of epic proportions, gods and monsters and mortals alike fighting among what appeared to be the ruins of New Mount Olympus. It seemed the boulder holding Zeus's palace had fallen from the heavens, all the way down to Earth. Now it served as a muddied, bloodied battlefield. Thunder rumbled, wind whistled, and the sounds of war cries and clashing weapons rang through the air.

Asteria materialized in front of them. "I have seen this exact scenario in my dreams," she yelled over the storm. "It is the version of the future in which you converge with Anteros and Calliope. Although there are many outcomes to every situation, it is my understanding that unless this vision—or a close variation of it—comes to fruition, the two of you will not win the war on the gods." She spun around and floated down toward the battle. She twirled her hands, and clusters of stars carried Zoey and Andy behind her.

"After the destruction of New Mount Olympus, a great confrontation will occur," Asteria explained as they grew closer to the fight. "Hundreds of friends and foes will perish, but there is a chance you may still rise victorious . . . all because you will have fully converged with Anteros and Calliope."

Asteria paused about thirty feet above the

center of the conflict. Zoey and Andy stopped when they reached her side, and she gestured at the brawl below. Zoey and Andy looked down. Even in the dark, even in the heavy rain, Zoey spotted Andy and herself. "Zoey" used Poseidon's Trident to make earthquakes and stab their opponents, a pack that presumably held the Helm of Darkness slung over her shoulder, while "Andy" electrocuted their adversaries using Zeus's massive Master Lightning Bolt.

However, something was off about the "Zoey and Andy" Asteria was showing them. At first glance, and from so far away, they looked like themselves, although they were wearing unfamiliar, gladiator-like armor. But as Zoey squinted through the rain, peering closer at the pair, she realized they weren't quite right. For one, "Zoey" had her right hand back, and they appeared taller than Zoey and Andy did now. They also looked more muscular and classically beautiful.

After the versions of Zoey and Andy below finished off nearly everyone around them, "Andy" pulled the Helm from "Zoey's" pack and slipped it over her head. She disappeared, and then he did too.

"Together, using the Helm, Trident, and

Bolt, Anteros and Calliope will cast the more powerful form of the Descent Spell," Asteria said. "Because all they had were the Helm and Trident before, they could only perform the weaker variation, which opens a portal to the Underworld. Now that they have all three objects, they'll be able to open a portal to the pit of Tartarus."

Zoey's breath hitched. "Tartarus? Wait a second, does that mean— Is *that* how the gods are supposed to be defeated? They're killed, and before they can regenerate, they're thrown into the pit?"

"Yes," Asteria answered. "Banishing the Olympians to Tartarus is the only way to ensure they can't terrorize humanity any longer. Ironically, it's also how Zeus imprisoned his tyrannical predecessors at the end of the Titanomachy. An immortal's powers are neutralized in the pit of Tartarus, so if they're 'dead' at the time of being sent there, or if they die after being sent there, they can't regenerate. And if they can't regenerate, they can't escape the pit.

"Sure, those loyal to the gods could go in after them and attempt to bring them back to be restored in the land above, but it's very difficult to free someone from the pit. It's only been done a handful of times by the Olympians themselves. If any of Zeus's followers *do* try it, it isn't likely they'll return."

Below, "Zoey and Andy" must have finished the spell because the ground started to quake. It split open to reveal a giant dark pit crackling and popping with blue flames. *The pit of Tartarus,* Zoey thought. With a shudder, she recalled the moment in Hades when she'd almost met her demise at the edge of it. How Persephone had dragged her toward the abyss, how Karter had saved her at the last second.

Gusts of wind swirled into Tartarus's fiery depths. Those closest to it screamed, trying to scramble away, but they couldn't escape. Gales carried them into the inferno.

Zoey blinked, and she was back in the lair of the Fates. Before her and Andy, Asteria held out the threads again. "Go on," Asteria said. "There is more."

Zoey and Andy touched the strings, and a new sequence revealed itself. They hovered above the ruins of New Mount Olympus once more, but the portal to Tartarus was gone, the sky peaceful as the sun rose in the distance. Rubble surrounded a kneeling Zoey and Andy below.

At first, the moment appeared peaceful, but

Zoey's heart sank when she noticed something disturbing about it. The scar-faced Son of Zeus lay before "Zoey" and "Andy." Karter's jaw was slack, his golden eyes wide and unblinking. One of his legs had been charred to the bone, reduced to scorched flesh and gore.

At the sight of Karter dead on the ground, Zoey gasped. Her eyes filled with tears. She didn't trust Karter, but seeing him like that . . . well, it made her regret the nasty things she'd said to him the other night, made her regret yelling in his face and blaming him for Darko's death.

The Zoey below gently closed Karter's eyes, propped his head in her lap, and cradled his face in her hands. Even from up here, Zoey could hear her as she wailed. "Andy" wrapped his arms around her shoulders and pulled her close.

As the strange scene continued, Andy gave Zoey a curious side-glance. "It's not me down there," she said quickly, wiping her eyes. "Not really. It's Calliope, remember?"

"How would Calliope know Karter, though?" he asked. "He wasn't born until centuries after she'd disappeared." Zoey tried to think of a good explanation, but nothing came to mind.

Asteria floated in front of them. "The

Dreaded Prophecy has not been the only time Zeus's authority has been challenged. Millennia ago, the King of the Gods' first wife—Metis, a Titan goddess—was prophesied to give birth to two children-of-Zeus. The first child was a daughter, Athena. The second child was going to be a son, and the son was supposed to be powerful enough to overthrow Zeus. Fearing rebellion, Zeus knew he couldn't sire more children with Metis, so he convinced her to temporarily turn herself into a fly, then swallowed her. She gave birth to Athena inside of him and, unbeknownst to him, when Hephaestus burst open his head and Athena emerged from his body, Metis also escaped."

Andy raised a brow. "What does this have to do with anything?"

"I helped Metis after she escaped Zeus. I hid her on my island and waited for the perfect opportunity to release her so she could bear Zeus a son who would overthrow him and help usher the world into a new cycle." Asteria's face fell in sorrow. "That son is Karter."

"No way," Andy said. "Karter isn't a god. He's a demigod. Half human, half god."

Zoey nodded. "That's right, and he already has Zeus for a father, so his mother can't be immortal too."

"Karter is only a demigod, but Metis is also his mother," Asteria said. "Both of these things can be true, and soon you'll understand why. For now, just know this is why Karter's life thread has become entangled with yours. If the two of you converge with Anteros and Calliope and manage to destroy the Olympians, it's likely that Karter will be the one to exile Zeus to Tartarus—but Zeus will kill him in the process." She smiled sadly. "His destined greatness, finally realized."

"Zeus ends up killing Karter in this version of the future?" Andy cried. "Like, for real? I mean, I know the guy's crazy, but . . . I thought he'd maybe decide to have mercy on his own kid at the last minute. You know, parental instincts or whatever."

"No, Zeus wouldn't have mercy on anyone, not even his own son, unless it was beneficial to him somehow." Zoey pointed to the right side of her face and neck. "Zeus is the one who gave Karter that awful scar. The gods were going to punish Spencer and Syrena for trying to leave Olympus, and Karter told Zeus that if he didn't hurt them, Karter would make sure they never tried to leave again. Zeus said that since Karter took responsibility for their crimes, he'd be punished in their place. The result was a lightning bolt to the face."

Andy winced. "That's psychotic."

"And very much the truth." Asteria focused on Zoey. "Who told you about that?"

"Karter did," Zoey answered with a shrug. "Back when we were trapped together in Hephaestus City."

Asteria cocked her head at Zoey. For some reason, it made Zoey feel as though the goddess were looking straight through her. She shrank back, wishing she hadn't said anything.

Suddenly they were in the lair of the Fates again. Asteria offered their life threads to them a third time, and they touched the strings.

The scene they were transported to next was far different from the last two. This time "Zoey" and "Andy" sat serenely on thrones located within a large, pillared chamber that appeared to be constructed from gold and marble. Sunlight poured in from arched windows, illuminating the raw precious gems arranged in swirling patterns along the walls. A painting that depicted the battle in which Zoey, Andy, and Karter had banished the Olympians to Tartarus covered the curved ceiling.

"Shortly after Anteros and Calliope defeat the gods, they will wed," Asteria said, and Zoey was pretty sure if she weren't in "spirit" right now, she would have gotten sick to her stomach. She didn't want to give up her body to Calliope, let alone be forced to marry Andy. "Together, as husband and wife, they will right the wrongs of the Olympians, and many humans will worship them. After their deaths, their children will continue their legacy, and after their children pass, their children's children will do the same, and so on and so forth. This marks the beginning of a new cycle. The cycle of the avatars."

"Avatars?" Andy asked. "Do you mean like the blue guy in the James Cameron movie? Or Aang in *Avatar: The Last Airbender*?"

"No. Avatars are a concept that stems from the Hindu gods, although other pantheons have adopted similar ideas."

Zoey pursed her lips. "The Hindu gods? Are you saying they're real, like the Greek gods are?"

"Yes, Hindu deities are as real as Greek ones," Asteria said. "Many pantheons of gods exist in other dimensions or planes of existence. Some are aware of what the Greeks have done to this world, although they remain complicit because they fear what will happen if a war breaks out among the pantheons. The rest have no idea what's happened because of the tricks and enchantments the Greeks cast on them long ago."

"That makes sense, actually." Zoey motioned at Andy. "We couldn't see our loved ones' souls in Hades, and we figured they were in another underworld, with other gods. Hopefully better ones."

Andy shifted his weight. "Also, when I touched the statue of Anteros and got a vision of Zeus telling the rest of the gods about how he wanted to destroy the modern world and force humanity to worship them, someone asked what the 'other pantheons' would say if they found out what he was planning. I remember them mentioning the Norse and Egyptians, but I didn't give it much thought because of everything else that was happening at the time."

"Yes, the Norse and Egyptians were once the Greeks' closest allies," Asteria said. "They aren't any longer, but that is a story for another day."

"Ohhh-kay," Andy said. "Seriously, though, if avatars aren't related to the blue people or *The Last Airbender*, what even are they?"

"Every pantheon defines the concept of avatars a bit differently," Asteria began. "This is because the rules for the various pantheons differ. For instance, the Greek gods can't be permanently killed. They can only fade away from lack of worship. But while the Norse and Egyptian gods can fade away from lack of worship, they can also be permanently killed. In the old days of Egypt, Set murdered Osiris, and Osiris would have stayed dead had Isis not used magic to resurrect him. Not only that, but the Norse deities must consume the apples of Idun to maintain their youth.

"In short, the fundamental idea of an avatar is that they're a god confined within a mortal body. Some of the most well-known avatars are the ones of Vishnu, the Hindu God of Preservation. It's said that Vishnu descends to Earth as an avatar when his people are in desperate need of help. Other pantheons have avatar-like figures, such as the Egyptians with the pharaohs. Some believe that pharaohs hosted gods within their bodies, or that the pharaohs were gods in human form."

Zoey fiddled with one of her stray curls. "Okay, I think I see what you're getting at. Calliope and Anteros are gods trapped in our bodies . . . somehow. I'm still murky on how that happened, so maybe you can fill in the details later. Anyway, you believe that they're the Greek version of the avatar idea, and that they're the ones who are supposed to overthrow the Olympians. That's why you said the next cycle for the Greek pantheon is the cycle of the avatars."

"Yes. Just as the Olympian gods ended the tyranny of the Titan gods, and the Titan gods ended the tyranny of their father, Uranus, it is the destiny of Anteros and Calliope to end the tyranny of the Olympian gods. It is the never-ending cycle of life and death, of conception and destruction. The Olympians have been in a state of decay for centuries, and a thirst for their old power has corrupted whatever small bit of goodness might have once resided within them. The time has come for new saviors to cut out the rot and burn it to ashes, as is the natural progression of the universe."

Andy pointed at Asteria. "Wait a second! That's how Karter is a demigod, but also the son of Metis and Zeus, isn't it? You said you hid Metis on your island, and then you released her at the right time. You turned her into an avatar at the perfect moment, all so she'd conceive a son with Zeus, didn't you?"

"Yes," Asteria said. "I proposed the idea to Metis thousands of years in advance, as I'd seen visions of her possible futures, and I explained what we must do for the favorable outcomes to come to fruition. She wanted revenge on Zeus for what he'd done to her, so she readily agreed to the idea. It wasn't until centuries after Apollo had foretold the Dreaded Prophecy and I received visions of what Zeus had done to Anteros and Calliope—and of how they would one day return—that I was given the opportune moment to reincarnate Metis into the body of a mortal. Naturally, I thought the chances of her son overcoming Zeus would be higher if he fought alongside the two of you."

"Okay, so you didn't make Calliope and Anteros avatars, right?" Zoey asked. "Zeus is the one who did that."

Asteria nodded. "Correct. It's my understanding that he needed a way to rid himself of them without anyone discovering what he'd done. That meant Tartarus was out of the question because he would have had to consult the other gods about it. He could have been inspired by the Hindus or Egyptians to create the first Greek avatars, just as I was long ago, but in the end, it doesn't really matter. The outcome remains the same: Anteros and Calliope were made into avatars, just as Metis was."

In yet another blink of an eye, the three of them reappeared in the lair of the Fates. Asteria's expression hardened as she stared at Zoey and Andy. "Now it's time you see what will happen if you choose not to converge with Anteros and Calliope—if you don't allow them to become full avatars."

The Titan goddess held out their threads of fate one last time. Zoey gulped and reached for the strings. Andy reached for them, too. Their fingers touched the threads at the same time.

In an instant, they were floating over the ruins of New Mount Olympus, a battle raging below and a thunderstorm blazing above.

Zoey scanned the destruction, soon spotting Andy, Karter, and herself standing back-to-back. She and Karter looked pretty much the same, but Andy no longer had his wings, and he wore glasses again. What was most concerning, though, was that the versions of her and Andy below didn't seem to be in possession of the Helm, Trident, or Lightning Bolt. To fight, Zoey had a spear, Andy had a sword, and Karter had green electricity. Three formidable figures closed in on them; Zoey recognized the figures as Zeus, Poseidon, and Hades. The trio of gods brandished their respective objects of power.

"What's Hades doing down there?" Andy cried. "I thought Persephone banished him to Tartarus!"

"She did," Asteria said. "However, the Olympians must have rescued him because he's in this vision now. Interesting, as he wasn't before. I thought I saw him when I finished regenerating outside of Tartarus. I would have investigated further, but I couldn't risk being captured."

Hades slipped the Helm over his head and disappeared. Zeus and Poseidon raised their weapons. Together, they began to chant.

Karter's eyes went wide with panic. He screamed something, though Zoey couldn't hear what, and spun around to grab Zoey and Andy. He yanked them into his arms and leapt into the sky.

The ground began to tremble. It split open, revealing the pit of Tartarus. Blue flames licked up toward Zoey, Andy, and Karter, gusts of wind tugging on them. Karter bared his teeth, straining against the gales, but it was no use. The gusts pulled them down.

The three of them held onto one another for dear life, screaming as wind and fire jerked them into Tartarus's depths.

Zoey, Andy, and Asteria transported back to the lair of the Fates. Andy appeared horrified, and Asteria's expression was grave. Zoey imagined she didn't look much better, her heart racing.

"I hope you understand now why you must

converge with Anteros and Calliope." Asteria returned Zoey's, Andy's, and Karter's life threads to the wall she'd retrieved them from. "They are gods descended to Earth, confined within your mortal forms, and you need to allow them to become the strongest possible versions of themselves to save humanity. You two and Karter are the only people in millennia that have posed a real threat to the Olympians, and if you're sucked into the pit, you'll be lost forever."

Asteria waved her arms, and stars swept over the three of them. After the stars dissipated, they were back at the nymph camp, standing with Narcissa in the gazebo, and they no longer looked like ghosts.

Asteria gasped for air, sweat seeping from her pores. She leaned against the vegetation that made up the railing, and the edges of her form glistened, as if stardust swirled around her.

Narcissa rushed toward Zoey and Andy. "What did you see? What did the Titan goddess show you?"

The pair stayed quiet for a long time. It seemed neither of them could bring themselves to answer Narcissa, and Zoey wondered if Andy was thinking the same thing as she was: that some of Asteria's logic didn't make sense.

For instance, Zoey didn't understand how

she and Andy not converging with Calliope and Anteros automatically equaled humanity losing the war against the gods. Although the possible futures Asteria had shown them were compelling, Asteria had also said there were many possible outcomes to any given situation.

Why did saving humanity *have* to fall on Calliope's and Anteros's shoulders? Why couldn't Zoey and Andy be the ones to do it? They'd already gotten this far with the help of their friends. Why did they have to converge with gods to finish the job?

Eventually, Zoey decided to speak up. "Asteria, I don't think you're right about me and Andy and Calliope and Anteros."

"Neither do I," Andy said, and Zoey let out a sigh of relief. *Glad I'm not the only one.* "It makes zero sense that we'd have to give up our bodies to them to do this," he continued. "We already have the gods' three objects of power, so all there is to do now is figure out the words to the Descent Spell, cast the version of the spell that opens a portal to Tartarus, temporarily kill the gods, and banish them so they can't regenerate."

"Exactly," Zoey said. "It'll be the hardest thing we've ever done, and there's no telling whether we'll make it out alive, but we have to try. You said it yourself—there are many possible outcomes to any given situation, and it looks like the second version of the future you showed us has already changed because Hades was there when he wasn't before. With everyone's help, there's a chance we can change our fates and do this on our own. We'd still be leading the world into a new cycle, too. It might not be the cycle of the avatars, but it would be the cycle of humanity."

Asteria panted, pressing a palm to her damp forehead. "It is clear—that I haven't—explained this—well enough. Or perhaps you—refuse to hear—what I'm saying."

"Oh, we hear you," Andy argued. "*You're* the one refusing to hear what *we're* saying. We'll figure out how to open a portal to Tartarus and banish the gods by ourselves, no convergence and avatar-ness required."

"No—you will—not." Asteria lowered her head, gulping in several deep breaths before going on. "Regular mortals can't use the Helm, Trident, and Lightning Bolt to full capacity. This is because they don't possess a divine essence. Even if mortals had a divine essence, it wouldn't be strong enough to open a portal to Tartarus. A portal to another part of the Underworld, maybe. But not to Tartarus."

Zoey knit her brow. "Are you saying the only

ones who can cast the spell are—are gods? Or, I guess, anyone with a strong divine essence?"

"That's precisely what I'm saying," Asteria replied. "Unfortunately for you two, the divine essences inside of you are rapidly fading because you broke your connections with Anteros and Calliope." She gestured at Zoey. "Why do you think your voice-powers weren't working on New Mount Olympus?" She motioned at Andy next. "Why do you think it's growing difficult for you to fly? Why, in the version of the future where you don't converge with Anteros, you no longer have wings, and you must wear glasses? Anteros and Calliope are once again trapped in the labyrinth of your minds. There, they're powerless. They can't help you. It won't matter if you discover the words to the Descent Spell, because without Anteros and Calliope, you won't be able to cast it."

Goose bumps rose on Zoey's skin. She shared a frightened glance with Andy. "But that means . . ." Andy trailed off.

"Finally, you're catching on," Asteria said. "You must connect with Anteros and Calliope again, Chosen Two. And when you do, you must finish the convergence with them. You must hand over your bodies to them. Because if you don't, they'll never become full avatars, and we'll never win this war on the gods."

CHAPTER SIX

SOULS

Andy couldn't believe what he was hearing. Not that anything else he'd been told over the past couple of weeks had been easy to swallow. But what Asteria was saying about Tartarus and convergences and avatars and just . . . *everything*? It had to be the most insane stuff anyone had said yet. He bit the tip of his thumb, trying to stop the anxiety from rising in his chest.

"No, no," Zoey started from beside him. "There's still more that doesn't make sense. In my dream—"

"What dream?" Asteria interjected.

Zoey opened and closed her mouth several times. When she didn't answer, Andy replied to Asteria for her. "It's the same dream you woke me up from. I had it after you transported us from Circe's island to the mainland. The one in the garden where we're running from either Anteros or Calliope—we've both been having it."

"I see."

"Y-yeah." Zoey's voice shook. "In my dream, I ran away from Calliope, jumped off a cliff, and was reunited with my dad and Spencer and Syrena. They told me that—that once I complete the convergence with Calliope, Calliope will no longer be Calliope, and I'll no longer be me. They said the same thing about Andy and Anteros. Once those two join, Anteros won't be Anteros, and Andy won't be Andy. We'll all be something else, something new. Not gods, but not humans. Divine but not immortal. It just . . . It doesn't add up with what you're saying about Calliope and Anteros being the Greek version of avatars, and us having to give up our bodies to them."

"Doesn't it, though?" Asteria countered. "'Not gods but not humans, divine but not immortal'—I couldn't think of a better description for avatars, what with them possessing the spirit of a god and the body of a mortal all at once. Then there's the 'something else, something new' bit. To my knowledge, Anteros and Calliope have never been avatars, and you've never fully converged with gods before. Once the convergence is complete, you'll all have become brand-new beings."

"Except it won't really be the four of us, will it?" Zoey said. "It'll be Calliope and Anteros wearing our bodies like meatsuits."

Andy shivered, his stomach turning at the imagery of Zoey's comment. "And what about our souls?"

"Your souls?" Asteria repeated.

"Yeah, you know, the things that make us *us*. Our ghosts, our spirits, whatever you wanna call 'em."

"I know what a soul is. I meant, what about your souls?"

"What happens to them if we go through with the convergence?" he asked. "Will they get to leave our bodies so we can be reunited with everyone we've lost? So we can, you know, die? Or will they be trapped in our minds while Anteros and Calliope are gallivanting around in our bodies?"

"I'm afraid your human spirits will be locked away in the labyrinth of your minds, as the spirits of Anteros and Calliope have been since your births. That's what happened to Katarina when Metis took her over—her human soul was not set free until Hera sent Ladon to murder her. Once her body died, the Fates separated Metis's and Katarina's life threads and cut Katarina's."

Andy's head was spinning. He rubbed his temples. "Gods have life threads?"

"All living beings do. The difference is that mortals' threads can be cut, while gods' can't. They can only fade away."

"Wait a second," Zoey began. "You said anyone with a strong divine essence can cast the spell that opens a portal to Tartarus. You're a Titan goddess, which I'm assuming comes with a super-strong divine essence, so why can't you just open the portal with the objects of power?"

Asteria's figure drooped with something that looked like sadness, exhaustion, or maybe both. "I don't know all the words to the spell. Only Zeus, Poseidon, and Hades know the Descent in its entirety, and only the Olympians and a select few of their minions even know of its existence."

"Then how did Calliope find out about it?" Andy asked. "I remember Anteros telling Circe that Calliope is the one who taught it to him, or something like that."

"I believe Calliope uncovered the spell's secrets and passed them on to Anteros before Zeus sent her away," Asteria answered. "Although there's much I don't know, there's one thing I can be certain of: the universe wants Anteros and Calliope leading this war on the gods. No one else. The two of them just so happen to be trapped within the two of you."

"It could have been any of the other billions of people on the planet, but it ended up being us," Zoey whispered. "We were never special. We aren't part of the Prophecy because we're magical, or gifted, or anything like that. The only difference between us and every other regular person on Earth is that gods got randomly stuffed into our bodies. It happened by pure chance."

Andy had so many questions, so many objections, he didn't know where to start. "How do we know you're not lying? You've tried tricking us before. How do we know there aren't other likely versions of the future? Ones where we get to live?"

"All I want is for the gods to be defeated, for the new cycle to begin," Asteria replied. "If I were lying to you, what good would it bring?

How would it help the world?"

Andy shook his head. "I have no idea what your motive for lying would be. But that doesn't mean we should trust you. You told us we were *for sure* Anteros and Calliope in human form, but then you told Prometheus something totally different. So yeah, sorry if I don't automatically trust everything you tell us."

"Andy's right," Zoey said. "There could be other possible futures you didn't show us, different ways for us to defeat the gods. Maybe there's another god who knows the words to the Descent Spell, even. Maybe they'd be willing to help us."

For a long time, Asteria studied Andy and Zoey, and Narcissa watched the three of them in shock.

Finally, Asteria spoke. "I admit that I lied to you before, and I apologize for doing so. You're upset with me for good reason. What I did was wrong, but you must understand that I only lied because we're running out of time. You needed to do this quickly, so that the gods wouldn't have as much of a chance to stop you. The convergence process is not an easy one, and now that you know the truth about it, the heaviest burden of all has been placed upon your shoulders: the burden of choice." She clasped her hands. "I'm begging you. Please, choose to connect with Anteros and Calliope. Choose to finish the convergence. Choose to allow them to use your bodies and become full avatars. I swear on the heavens and underworlds that all I've told you today is true.

"If there were any other way, do you believe I'd be here? Do you believe I'd be pursuing you in such a manner? Zoey said it herself—this happened by chance. You weren't chosen for magical ability or physical prowess. Do you honestly think I would beg two powerless mortals to trust me if I thought there was an easier way to do this?"

At this, Andy gave pause. Even though Asteria had lied to them before, even though he knew she couldn't be completely trusted, something told him that right here, right now, she was being honest with them. He wanted to believe she was lying, that there was a way out of this situation and that she was keeping it from them. But as she'd already pointed out, if there were a better way, why would she be here, begging them to listen to her?

"That's why we had the dreams in the first place, isn't it?" Andy said. "Our friends and families are really out there somewhere, and they wanted to warn us about what's going on. They know what we have to do to save the world, but they wanted us to have a choice before going through with it. They wanted us to have all the facts so we wouldn't blindly follow whatever you told us to do."

Asteria let her hands fall to her sides. "I believe that's within the realm of possibility, yes. I've sensed your loved ones' presences around you a few times now. Guiding you, protecting you. Warning you." That bit of information should have comforted Andy, but it made him feel as if someone had socked him in the gut. "Do the two of you now understand what it is you must do?" Asteria asked. "Or do you have more questions for me?"

Andy looked at Zoey, but she wouldn't meet his eyes. "I don't—I don't think I have more questions," he said.

"Me neither." Zoey hugged her sides, turning to Narcissa. "Can you please let us down? I need out of here."

Persephone sprinted along one of the golden paths that wound toward the edge of the

Garden of Olympus, her palms slippery with sweat, her heart pounding in her chest. *There's so little time. I must escape before anyone realizes I'm gone.*

Ever since Persephone and the other immortals had returned from the Underworld, the Olympians had been formulating a plan of attack. They assembled a team to hunt down Diana, Karter, the grandchildren-of-Hephaestus, and the Chosen Two. The prospective team's assignment was simple: kill the traitorous descendants, retrieve the objects of power, and bring the regular mortals back to Zeus alive.

Right away, Demeter had insisted that Persephone go with her wherever she went, and Zeus had agreed to this, so long as she kept close watch of Persephone. But the moment Demeter and everyone else had become distracted, Persephone had bolted out of the palace and into the Garden of Olympus. She planned to flee from here, to turn her back on the pantheon and never return unless it was to destroy the gods alongside the Chosen Two.

The Chosen Two, she thought, remembering the shocked expressions on their pathetic faces when she'd betrayed them in Hades. *Who knows if they'll allow me to join their little group. They'll certainly need my help, but the question is whether they'll accept it after I killed their precious Spencer.*

The truth was, Persephone didn't regret murdering Spencer, nor did she regret betraying her husband. The only thing she regretted was the fact that she'd underestimated those mortals when she'd fought them in Hades. She'd allowed her giddiness for obliterating Spencer and her husband to cloud her senses, and it had cost her the Helm and her life.

Even still, if she had to pick between the mortals and the Olympians winning this war, she'd select the mortals every time. If they prevailed, the future was uncertain, but their victory meant everyone who had wronged her would no longer be in power, and that's all she'd ever wanted.

Soon she reached the edge of the garden—a jagged cliff overlooking the forest below. The sun was rising in the distance, its splendid yellow rays slicing through the trees and making the water droplets atop the greenery around her glisten.

She smirked, opened her hands to the sky, and focused on conjuring the longest, strongest vines possible. *All that's left is to climb down from this cursed hunk of rock and—*

Her thoughts were cut short when a familiar voice rang through the air. "Persephone," her mother called. The goddess didn't sound far from here. "Persephone, where have you gone? What are you doing?"

Damn it all to Tartarus. Persephone clenched her fists, and the vegetation curling out from her palms disintegrated. *I won't be able to climb down. Mother will catch me and make me go back. I could teleport away, but I'd rather not weaken myself unnecessarily.*

She glanced around frantically, searching for a suitable place to conceal herself. If she found a good enough hiding spot, perhaps she could form another plan of escape before being discovered.

"Persephone!" Her mother was even closer now, her voice shrill. Panicking, Persephone leapt into a tall, thick bush on the left and willed the foliage to still. "Please, sweet daughter, don't do this to me. I've lost you twice now. I can't bear to lose you a third time."

A pang of guilt shot through Persephone's chest. Millennia ago, when Hades had kidnapped her, her mother had searched for her for years. Demeter had been so grief-stricken that she'd abandoned her duties and allowed the pantheon's worshippers to die so that Zeus would tell her the truth about where Persephone had gone.

If Persephone went through with this—if she betrayed the Olympians once more and helped the Chosen Two defeat them—what would become of her mother? Was it possible for gods to fade away from a broken heart? If it was, that's certainly what would happen to Demeter. *Unless I explain myself. But if I reveal my plans, will Mother force me to go back with her? Force me to obey the gods?*

There was a noise like feet striding through grass just outside Persephone's hiding spot. "Persephone?" her mother said, then whispered, "Kore?"

A lump formed in Persephone's throat when Demeter uttered her old name, the name Hades had stolen from her long ago. Since then, the only deity who'd called Persephone "Kore" was Demeter, and it had always been in secret. At the last summer solstice party, Persephone had asked her mother to call her Persephone from now on, because she was no longer a maiden, as the title "Kore" suggested. Over time, she'd become what the name Persephone meant: "bringer of destruction."

It's time to let go of what I was and embrace what I am. While Kore might have fretted over her mother's fate, Persephone never would. She'd only do what she must to ensure the Olympian gods and everything they've built are torn down for good.

With that thought, resolve came over Persephone. She called upon her magic. Pulsing, hot power burst in her chest and spread through her limbs. A rope of vines slithered from her palms, and she readied herself to vault from the bush. To pounce onto Demeter's back, wrap her plants around her mother's throat, and squeeze until the goddess dropped dead.

As Persephone prepared to lunge from the greenery and attack, Demeter let out an anguished cry. Persephone paused and listened closely; all she could hear now were her mother's quiet sobs.

Persephone willed the bush to part slightly so she could look upon her mother. The goddess had her back to Persephone. She knelt at the edge of the garden, her face in her hands. "Please, my darling Kore," she whispered. "Come back."

Persephone couldn't help herself. No matter how merciless she'd become over the years, the sight of her mother weeping on the ground was too much to bear. She allowed her vines to fall and stepped out of the bush. "I haven't gone anywhere."

Demeter swung around, her expression shifting from sorrow to relief. "Oh my gods, you didn't leave."

"Not yet."

"Then you *do* plan on betraying the Olympians." Demeter hung her head. "Just as I suspected."

Persephone wrung her hands. "Before you try to convince me otherwise, you must know, there's nothing you can do to stop me. I've made up my mind."

Demeter stared down at the grass for what felt like an eternity before she spoke again. "If you leave, I'm not sure whether I can protect you from them."

"I know." Persephone forced a smile. "But you mustn't worry. I've tasted sorrow and heartbreak and hatred in all their bitter glory. I've been swallowed by the flames of Tartarus and experienced true death. Even if I stayed here on Olympus, even if I remained by your side for all time, it wouldn't change what I've become. There's nothing left for you to protect me from."

A choking noise escaped Demeter's throat, and she fell into a new fit of sobs.

Persephone's chest grew tight. "Mother, no." She knelt beside the goddess and hugged her. "I didn't mean to upset you. I only wanted to assure you—"

"Assure me? Of *what*? That I've failed you? That because I couldn't protect you, you're broken, and there's nothing I can do to fix it?"

"No." She gave her mother a squeeze. "I wanted to assure you that I'm not afraid. That there's nothing left for me to fear. That I'm no longer Kore. I'm Persephone." Demeter pulled out of their hug, and Persephone cupped her mother's cheeks. "The Olympians took everything from me. They made me suffer for thousands of years and turned me into the goddess I am today. Zeus is finally willing to set me free from Hades, but it's too little, too late. He doesn't deserve to be King of the Gods any longer, and Hades doesn't deserve a spot among the Olympians either. That's why I must go. I must find the Chosen Two and help them in their war on the gods. Not because I believe in them or their cause, but because Zeus, Poseidon, and Hades are no longer fit to rule the world."

Demeter lifted her hands and curled her fingers around Persephone's wrists. "I told you once that I wouldn't take your agency from you." Her voice held a slight tremor, and Persephone could tell she was holding back more tears. "After all these years, I still don't plan on doing so. Not even now, as you tell me you intend to embark on such a perilous journey, as you tell me you're no longer my little Kore, but instead my—my fierce Persephone. I'd hoped you'd stay with me, especially after Zeus promised to dissolve your marriage to Hades, but . . ." She took a shaky breath, then closed her eyes and pressed her forehead against Persephone's. "I understand your life is your own." Relief flooded Persephone, tears welling in her eyes. "And whether you're Kore or Persephone, you'll always be my child. I'll always love you."

Persephone threw her arms around her mother's neck. "I'll always love you, too."

"We'll see each other again—when the time comes. For now, though, I need to stay with Corinna. To protect her and find somewhere safe to hide her."

Persephone nodded. Corinna was her mother's only mortal child, so it stood to reason that Demeter should remain close to her for now. There had been a few other demigod children-of-Demeter in the old days—such as Plutus and Philomelus—but they'd been elevated to godhood and lived in their cities full of worshippers on the other side of the world.

Demeter had given birth to other deities, such as Persephone's half-sister Despoina, but

Despoina was located across the Atlantic, and she'd always been immortal. Not only was Corinna mortal, but she lived right here on New Mount Olympus. Out of all Demeter's offspring, Corinna would be in the most danger if Zeus discovered Demeter had let Persephone go.

Persephone wasn't sure how long she and her mother sat there, holding one another. All she knew was that eventually the moment had to end. That they had to let go, stand up, and part ways.

They bid each other farewell. Demeter started back toward Zeus's palace, and Persephone conjured her vines and descended from Olympus to Earth. *Now to find the Chosen Two, and hopefully stay out of Zeus's clutches.*

CHAPTER SEVEN

PUPPETS

As exhausted as Karter was, he hadn't gotten much rest since Andy had relieved him from helping Diana. He'd walked farther into the trees, though not so far he wouldn't be able to hear if there was trouble, and collapsed to the forest floor. He'd closed his eyes, rolled onto his side, and tried to relax, but it was no use. He couldn't get the last conversation he'd had with Zoey out of his head.

"So, if you change your mind and decide there's something I can do for you—something that will help you

forgive me—then tell me. I'll be here, and I pledge that no matter what it is, if you ask me to do it, I will."

"Yeah, I don't see that happening."

He groaned at the memory, at how stupid he must have sounded to her. *Why is it so hard to think of something—anything—besides how angry she is with me?* It wasn't as if her bitterness wasn't justified. He knew it was. He just wanted the chance to make things better.

Fortunately, fatigue overtook his racing mind once or twice that night, and he managed to sleep a bit. It wasn't enough, but it was better than nothing.

When morning came, Karter couldn't lie there any longer. His body ached, his head pounding, yet he knew his new companions needed his help. *If I want to make things up to them, I have to put in the work.* He climbed to his feet and hobbled over to a nearby stream for a drink, then started back to where Diana had been healing nymphs.

It didn't take long to reach the spot, and he found that Diana, Andy, and the nymphs were gone. Assuming Diana had needed sleep, he shuffled toward the cabin she and Andy and Zoey were staying in. *Hopefully when I show up at the door, Zoey doesn't slam it in my face.*

A while of walking passed before the cabin

appeared up ahead. Three pegasi—two with chestnut coats and amber eyes, and one with a black coat and green eyes—stood in the forest a ways outside of the building. The creatures had flown above the cabin as the nymphs carried it while moving camp, and Karter suspected they belonged to Kali.

The pegasi seemed to glare at Karter as he approached. The black one even huffed at him. He did his best to ignore the creatures, plodding past them.

He reached the front door, paused, and knocked, but no one answered. He knocked again. Still no answer. He inched open the door and peeked inside.

Zoey and Andy were nowhere to be seen, but Kali lay unconscious on her bed of grass, and Diana was sleeping too, snuggled up in the crook of Kali's left arm. *Are they together?* The thought brought a small smile to Karter's lips. He knew Pearl would have wanted Diana to be happy, to fall in love again.

At the opposite end of the cabin, a pair of Dryads were hunched over Troy and Marina; it appeared they were asking the twin grandchildren-of-Hephaestus some questions. Karter crept inside and shut the door behind him. *I should check on them. See if there's anything I can do.* He tiptoed across the cabin toward Troy and Marina, careful not to wake Diana and Kali.

The twins caught sight of Karter, stopped whispering, and nodded at him. The nymphs paused as well. They stood straight and turned around. The moment they saw Karter they frowned, looking him up and down with scrutiny. "What do *you* want?" one of them snapped, her tone hushed. Her short blonde hair stuck out in spikes, and like the other Dryads in the camp, she stood at about the same height as Diana and wore a forest-green dress.

Karter winced a little, averting his gaze from them. *You're a Son of Zeus,* he thought. *You've done some awful things throughout your life, and you came back from Olympus when twelve of their friends have not. They're not going to like you.* "I wanted to ask if there's anything I can get for Troy and Marina," he said. "To make sure they're as comfortable as possible until Diana heals them."

The second Dryad—this one with tan skin and bright-blue irises like Zoey's—got in Karter's face, screwing up her eyes at him. "Their paralysis isn't likely to be cured, as irreversible damage has been done to their bodies. Your father made sure of that." She shoved past him and started toward the entrance. The other nymph followed suit. They exited the cabin, leaving him standing before Troy and Marina in uncomfortable silence.

Karter closed his eyes and pinched the bridge of his nose. That was *not* the news he wanted to hear. "I'm so sorry. For everything. It's my fault this happened to you."

Marina chuckled, though there wasn't a shred of joviality in the air. "Kind of, yeah. But mostly Zeus's."

"Nothing is set in stone." Troy sounded hopeful despite the grim prognosis. "The Daughter of Apollo might still manage to help us."

Karter mustered his courage and focused on the twins. "I made a promise. Back on Olympus, I told you that if Diana can't help you, I will. I plan to keep my word. In case she can't heal your paralysis, what's something I can do for you? I'll start right now."

Troy and Marina shared a somber glance. "I doubt there's enough metal around here for them, if any," Marina said.

"There's always woodworking," Troy replied. "I'm not the best at it, but it might have to do until we have access to better materials."

Marina faced Karter. "If you want to help us, start gathering wood. As much as you can. We'll need a lot."

"We'll need tools as well," Troy added. "Get us rocks. Sharp ones, flat ones, round ones. All sizes. Bring whatever you find and leave it outside the cabin. Then you can take us out there and help us build."

"I won't be long." With new purpose coursing through him, Karter rushed out of the cabin.

As he stepped outside, he caught sight of three figures walking toward the cabin. He recognized Zoey and Andy right away, and when he realized who the third person was—a familiar Titan goddess with red hair and silver eyes—his heart leapt with joy.

"Asteria!" He jogged toward them, unable to mask how happy he was to see her. "You're okay!"

The Titan goddess smiled and gave him a quick hug. "I am. It's good to see you, Karter."

Karter's grin widened. After the last time he'd talked to Asteria—when she'd tried to convince him not to listen to his father's manipulations and he'd rejected her advice—he thought she'd hate him forever. But it seemed she didn't. "It's good to see you too. I'm so glad you made it here." He looked around, trying to spot Prometheus and the nymph recruits who'd helped Zoey and Andy on Olympus. "Where are the others? They escaped too, right?"

Asteria's face fell. "I don't know where Prometheus is, but I sense the nymphs on Olympus. Unfortunately, I had to come here alone."

"Oh." He frowned. "Hopefully, they'll reach us soon."

"Hopefully," she agreed, her tone crestfallen.

For some reason, Zoey shot Asteria a scowl and began to stomp away.

"Where are you going?" Andy asked, trailing after Zoey.

She paused to glance over her shoulder at him. "Don't follow me." He stopped in his tracks.

"We don't have time for this," Asteria said. "We need to leave. Now. Must I remind you of the urgency of the situation?" *What's going on?* Karter wondered. *What happened?*

"All that back there—that was a lot." Zoey's voice cracked as she spoke. "I—I need to be by myself for a bit. To think things over. You can't expect us to be okay with this right away. You have to give us some time." Asteria didn't reply; she only stared at Zoey with exasperation.

When Zoey turned around to continue her trek, her eyes briefly met Karter's, the grief in them so palpable his heart clenched. What was wrong? How could he help? But before he could work up the nerve to ask, she tore her gaze from his and disappeared into the trees.

Karter realized he was staring at the section of forest Zoey had vanished into. He blinked hard and shook his head. *Don't get distracted. You're helping Troy and Marina right now.*

Easier said than done. Andy also watched the trees, an anguished expression plastered on the other boy's features. Seriously, what was wrong? *Perhaps I'll gather whatever wood and rocks I can find around the cabin first. See if Andy says anything.* With that, Karter began his search. He glanced over at Andy and Asteria periodically, waiting for one of them to break the silence.

Whole minutes later, Andy spoke. He balled his fists at his sides. "How are we supposed to reconnect with Anteros and Calliope, anyway? You know, to finish the convergence."

"I'll answer that with another question. How did you connect with them in the first place?"

Karter raised a brow as he plucked stones from the dirt. What did Anteros and Calliope have to do with anything? Those old gods had faded away over five hundred years ago. Also, what did Andy mean when he said "convergence"?

"I have to go back to Aphrodite City," Andy

said. "Back to that temple. I need to touch the statue of Anteros like I did before, and we'll reconnect. Then I'll touch Zoey, and she'll reconnect with Calliope."

"That should work, yes," Asteria replied.

As Karter pieced together what Andy and Asteria seemed to be saying, he dropped the rocks he'd found. *Are Zoey and Andy harboring gods within their bodies?*

Had Calliope and Anteros never actually faded away from lack of worship? Instead, had something occurred that forced them to be reborn into mortal bodies? It was crazy to consider, but it would explain why Andy had grown wings, why Zoey and Andy had been chosen by prophecy to lead a war on the gods, how they'd survived a trip to Poseidon's palace and stolen his Trident without the assistance of gods or demigods . . .

Does that have something to do with why Father needs them left alive? It had struck Karter as odd that Zeus didn't want the Chosen Two killed the moment they were discovered. The King of the Gods had always asserted that they must be captured and banished to Tartarus.

"We should leave for Aphrodite City as soon as possible," Asteria said. "Ideally, once Zoey returns."

Karter couldn't contain his curiosity any longer. He turned to them. "Pardon my intrusion. If I may ask, what are you talking about? What's going on?"

Andy looked at Karter. "Oh, right. I forgot you don't know about the Anteros-Calliope stuff that's been going down. Don't worry, Diana doesn't know about all of it either. Why don't I fill you both in when she wakes up?" Karter nodded in response.

"As I've already said," Asteria began, "we must make haste. I'm afraid there won't be time to 'fill everyone in.'"

"Listen, if Zoey and me are gonna permanently give up our bodies to gods, you're gonna have to let us tell our friends about everything that's happening, no matter how much time it takes." Andy crossed his arms. "They deserve the truth, and they need to hear it from us. Plus, Zoey's right. You can't rush us into this. We need some time."

Asteria opened her mouth to reply. Karter beat her to it. "Permanently give up your bodies to gods?" he blurted out. "Why would you have to do *that*?"

"So we can open a portal to Tartarus, I guess." Andy shrugged nonchalantly, but the panic lacing his tone told Karter he was far from calm. "It's the best way to keep the gods from terrorizing humanity, and me and Zoey—I mean, Anteros and Calliope—are apparently the only people who can do it. Basically, Zeus stuffed Anteros and Calliope into our bodies in the Before Time and lied to everyone about them fading away because they knew how to defeat the gods. Now if we let them take control of us, they'll become full avatars—gods confined within mortal forms—and save humanity."

Karter's jaw dropped, his stomach churning. It wasn't that this didn't make sense. It shed light on why Zoey and Andy were the Chosen Two of the Dreaded Prophecy, after all. But the idea of the two of them being forced to sacrifice themselves in such a way . . . it made him ill. *It's a fate worse than death.* He bent down to pick up the stones he'd dropped.

"I'll tell you more about it later," Andy said. "After Zoey comes back and Diana gets up. Also, after you finish . . . whatever it is you're doing."

"Right." Karter swallowed down the bile rising in his throat.

Asteria sighed. "I suppose it was unfair of me to expect the two of you to reconnect with Anteros and Calliope straight away."

Andy threw his hands in the air. "Ya think?"

"You're only human," she went on, ignoring his outburst. "You're also quite young. You don't see the world the same way immortals do. You must understand, my intention was never to harm either of you. Only to help the rest of the world." She transformed into millions of miniature shimmering stars, and as she uttered her next words, her voice echoed all around them. "Take time to process your destinies and inform your companions about what's going to happen. A few days at most—not so long that the Olympians discover your location and capture you. I'll be around, conserving my energy, watching for the gods, and plotting for the final battle." She disappeared into the sky.

"Wow, thanks," Andy muttered under his breath. "You're the best ever."

Karter couldn't blame Andy for being frustrated with Asteria. More than once, he'd been in a similar position. "I'm sure everything will work itself out," he said without thinking. "Asteria is . . . just that way."

Andy tilted his head. "Just what way?"

"You know."

"I don't think I do. I've only met her a handful of times."

Karter hauled his stones over to the side of

the cabin, let them fall in a heap on the ground, and resumed his search for more. "Um. Well. She swoops in. Says something vague. Leaves. Sometimes she saves you, but mostly she just tries to give you advice. It can be infuriating, I know."

"No offense, but you're not helping *at all*."

"Sorry. I'm not the best at, uhh—this."

Andy plopped down and put his face in his hands. "I need Asteria to be wrong. Dead freaking wrong. Please, please, *please*."

Would it be best if I went somewhere else? Karter turned away. He could tap into his strength to knock down some trees, since Marina said they'd need a lot of timber. Still, he didn't know how he'd keep his mind from wandering back to what Andy had said about Anteros and Calliope.

Glancing in the direction Zoey had gone, Karter wondered how long it would be until she came back. *I should stay by the cabin a bit longer.*

For the next few minutes, Karter gathered a dozen more stones in the area and tossed them into his pile. As they clattered against one another, Andy looked up at Karter. "Seriously, man, what are you doing?"

"Collecting wood and rocks for the grandchildren-of-Hephaestus," Karter answered. "I asked them what I could do for them in case Diana can't heal their paralysis, and this is what they requested."

"Huh. I bet they're gonna build something."

"I would assume so."

"They're really good at that kinda stuff. They built a Pocket-Sized Submarine and gave it to us. It's how we escaped Poseidon's palace, but then it broke down. Want some help?"

Karter paused. "What?"

"You." Andy pointed at Karter. "Do you want help? With what you're doing?"

"Um, sure. I mean, please."

Andy stood and plodded to Karter's side. Together, they gathered supplies.

Zoey couldn't remember the last time she'd cried this much for herself.

Had she done so when Persephone cut off her hand? How about when she'd discovered Jet had been cheating on her and she'd broken up with him, only for him to tell everyone at school she'd slept with guys for money to pay her mom's rent? Or perhaps when her parents got divorced and she never saw her father and their dog again?

No, she thought. *Because somehow, none of those times felt as bad as this one does. At least in those instances, I had hope for the future. There was always a chance for things to get better. But now there's no hope for me, no hope for Andy, and apparently no hope for Karter. As much as I don't like him, I don't want Zeus to kill him.*

The truth is, none of us have control over our futures anymore. We're all just puppets.

Sobs racked Zoey's body as she lay on her side, curled up beneath a pine tree. Snot dribbled down her face, tears blurring her vision. She hadn't wanted anyone to see or hear how upset she was, so she'd walked far from the cabin before breaking down.

She'd always been embarrassed to show this kind of emotion in front of others. What made it worse was that she was crying for herself. She was upset over being forced into a position she desperately didn't want to be forced into, and that made her feel as if she was being selfish. Because what about everyone else the gods had thrust into this messed-up world? Those people hadn't gotten to choose how their lives panned out. What gave her the right to want autonomy when no one else had it?

Shouldn't she be thankful that now the only

thing she had to do to save the world was sit back and let a goddess take over her body? All she'd ever wanted was to do something amazing with her life. To make her mark. That's what she'd thought, at least. Wouldn't sacrificing herself to end the tyrannical rule of the Greek pantheon be enough of a triumph for her? Surely people would remember her name forever, would be grateful to her for all time. Right?

Yes, they would, she answered herself. *Except there's one problem. The whole reason I wanted to "be" someone in the first place was so that my life would finally be my own. But now that'll never happen. Even if I manage to survive the war and beat the gods, I'll be trapped inside my own mind, while Calliope is out there, using my body to do whatever she wants.*

By the way, universe, how is that setup even remotely fair? Calliope lived for thousands of years before I was born. I only got to live a measly eighteen, and they majorly sucked.

Zoey sniffled and blew her nose on the hem of her tattered dress, her cries subsiding slightly. *This isn't like me. Not at all. I've got to get it together. I've got to find a way to come to grips with what's happening.*

What would Spencer say if he were here? What would he want me to do?

Why had she even asked herself that question? She already knew the answer. As much as Spencer cared for her and Andy and Karter, he'd always loved Syrena way more. She was why he'd turned on the gods in the first place. If he was watching over Zoey and Andy, he probably sympathized with their predicament, but Zoey was positive he also wanted them to be brave. He surely wanted them to think about the greater good, to set aside their personal hang-ups and do the right thing. In the end, what was more important: her own life, or the future of the world?

The future of the world, she thought. *That's what this has always been about. Saving everyone from the gods. Winning back people's freedom so they can lead better lives.*

Even if it's at the cost of my own happiness.

As Zoey continued to rationalize the situation, she managed to somewhat calm herself down. Although she was trembling, she wiped the tears and snot from her face and climbed to her feet. Terror pulsed through her in anticipation of what was to come, but still she turned around and headed back toward her companions.

CHAPTER EIGHT

NEWS

Andy wasn't sure how long he and Karter wandered around picking up stones and logs. Karter had even knocked down some trees, and then they'd piled up their findings outside the cabin. They had to have been at it for an hour or two, because they'd accumulated quite the mound: the heap was wide and stood almost as tall as them. But maybe the task had only felt like a long time because Andy didn't want to spend another second away from his friends.

Seriously, if Asteria was telling the truth, he

wanted to be with Zoey, Diana, and Kali until the bitter end. Because despite how horrific this journey had been, he couldn't help but be grateful for the three of them—especially Zoey. If it weren't for her, he'd have never agreed to go on this quest in the first place. For that reason, and for so many others, he knew that he loved her. That he was *in love* with her.

Hopefully, she'll tell me whether she feels the same before our big convergence, he thought. *Because if she does and she never says so, it'll suck more than anything to never get to be with her, even if it's just for a short time.*

Karter flung another tree into the pile. "That should be enough, don't you think?"

"Jeez, I hope so." Andy wiped the perspiration from his forehead.

"Thanks for helping."

Andy stuck out his hand for a high five. Karter hesitated to give him one at first, then gave in. The force stung Andy's palm, but it wasn't too bad. Karter must not have used his superhuman strength for it. "I thought you were gonna make that hurt way worse," Andy said, wiggling out his arm.

Karter snorted. "If you thought that, why'd you ask for it?"

"Probably to prove how manly I am, or something like that."

Karter let out a laugh. Not a snicker, but a happy, honest-to-God laugh. The noise was so unexpected it took Andy aback. For a second, he didn't know how to react, but then he chuckled a little. "Dude, I didn't know you could smile, let alone laugh."

"Probably because I haven't in a while." Karter's smile faded. "Not since the night Syrena ran away. I wish I'd have gone with her instead of lying to the gods for her."

"Wait, you covered for Syrena when she left Olympus?"

"Yes. Syrena and Diana both. It was the night of the annual summer solstice party, and I caught them sneaking away. I should have gotten Spencer, and we should have all escaped together, but I . . . I just told them to go. The last thing I wanted was for the gods to discover them. For them to be killed. My father asked me when I'd last seen them, and I said I hadn't since the festivities. If I'd have gone with them instead, maybe—maybe Syrena and Spencer would still be here. Maybe I could have sacrificed myself in Syrena's place to resurrect you and Zoey, and maybe Spencer wouldn't have died in Hades."

"Maybe." Andy bit the tip of his thumb. "Maybe not." He recalled what Asteria had told him and Zoey about Karter's fate—about how it was highly possible that Karter would die in the final battle against the gods. He wondered if maybe, just maybe, that's why it had taken Karter so long to join the good guys. Maybe everything had unfolded this way because God, or the universe, or whoever was up there pulling the strings, had made it so. Maybe the choices that Karter had made and the events that had happened to him were supposed to lead him to this moment right here, right now, so he could throw Zeus into Tartarus.

Andy recalled the image of Karter's lifeless form and shuddered. Should he tell Karter about what Asteria had revealed to them? Maybe if Karter was prepared for his potential future, the outcome would change.

And if that were the case, could Andy and Zoey change their destinies? Could the threads of fate be wrong—could there be another way to win this war on the gods?

Footfalls sounded from the direction Zoey had gone in, yanking Andy from his thoughts. He and Karter jumped to attention. Zoey appeared, and Andy sighed in relief. "Zoey," he said. She offered him the tiniest of smiles, her eyes so red and puffy it looked as if she'd been punched in the face. *She's been crying*, he realized.

He wanted to wrap her in his arms and never let go.

"Andy." She reached his side. "I needed time to think. To process what's happening. If I hurt your feelings, I'm sorry."

"There's nothing to apologize for."

Bottom lip quivering, she threw her arms around his shoulders and hugged him tight. He hugged her tighter. "This isn't how I imagined things ending for us," she said. "I thought that even if we died fighting, it would be on our own terms. I thought it would have been *us* trying to save humanity."

Tears welled in his eyes. "I know."

The door to the cabin creaked open. Zoey pulled away from Andy, and he caught sight of Diana stepping outside. Her shoulder-length yellow hair stuck out in all directions, dark circles under her green eyes. She closed the door behind herself and plodded over to them. "Hey, guys."

"How are you feeling?" Karter asked.

"Not so great." She faced Andy and Zoey, her expression solemn. "Kali woke up. She's wondering where everyone is. I got her to eat and drink some, but she's asking for you. She's asking for Darko too. I think it's time."

Andy's stomach dropped to his feet. The

moment he'd been dreading since they'd reached camp had come.

"I'll bring Troy and Marina outside," Karter said, heading toward the cabin. "Give the four of you some privacy."

When Karter came back, he had Troy and Marina slung over his shoulders. He carried them over to the pile of stones and logs he and Andy had made. The twins started ordering him around, telling him where they wanted to sit and what they needed him to bring them first.

"Ready?" Diana asked.

"No." Andy was just trying to stay upright. He felt as though the ground had been ripped out from under him. "But we have to tell her, one way or another."

Diana grabbed his hands in hers. "It's not your fault."

Zoey rested her hand on his shoulder. "Diana's right. You're not responsible for what happened."

Yes, I am! he wanted to scream, but he didn't.

"Kali will be devastated," Diana said. "We all are. But she's not going to blame you, so don't blame yourself."

Andy tried to swallow the lump in his throat.

"Let's get this over with."

He leaned on Zoey and Diana for strength, and the three of them walked to the cabin.

Zoey had known that breaking the news to Kali was going to be hard. She just hadn't realized *how* hard.

When Zoey, Andy, and Diana had only begun to explain what had happened to Darko, Kali's expression crumpled in anguish. It was as though she already knew what they were going to tell her. By the time they reached the end of the story, she was weeping, her face buried in Diana's shoulder. Diana sniffled and rested her cheek against Kali's head, stroking her long dark hair.

"I'm—s-so—s-sorry," Andy whimpered. He sat next to Kali, his hand on her back.

"We—we also had to leave behind Prometheus and the nymphs," Zoey said, doing her best to keep it together as she sat in front of Kali. "Asteria too, but she escaped, and we talked to her today. She says she can sense the nymphs on Olympus, but she can't locate

Prometheus. We have no idea where he is." Kali's crying intensified, and Zoey choked back a sob. She took one of Kali's hands and gave it a squeeze.

For a long while the four of them stayed like that, crying and holding onto each other, but eventually there was a knock at the door, and Diana cleared her throat. "Who is it?"

"Narcissa. May I come in?"

Diana looked at Kali, as if asking whether Narcissa coming in was okay. Kali nodded. "Yeah, that's all right," Diana said.

The Dryad opened the door and stepped inside. Her lips parted slightly when she saw Zoey and Andy, and she shifted her weight from one foot to the other. "Apologies, I didn't mean to disturb you."

"It's okay," Zoey said.

"We're better," Andy added. "Sort of."

Diana cocked her head at their exchange. "Did I miss something important?"

Andy exhaled sharply. "You have no idea."

"We'll fill you in later," Zoey assured Diana. "What can we do for you, Narcissa?"

"Many of the nymph recruits are still wounded," Narcissa began. "If the Daughter of Apollo is feeling well-rested enough, they need her care."

"Right." Diana let go of Kali and climbed to her feet. "I think Karter is busy with the twins, so Andy, you come help me, and Zoey, you stay here with Kali."

"I'm not sitting around any longer," Kali said. "I've been passed out forever. It's time I make myself useful." She shot into a standing position, then promptly collapsed.

"Kali!" Zoey and Diana cried in unison.

"Are you okay?" Andy asked.

Kali pressed a palm against her forehead, her face growing ashen. "I'm not sure."

Diana knelt next to Kali. "You lost a lot of blood. I healed you, but I can't replace what's gone. Especially because it took me so long to reach you, it will take a while for you to get your strength back. All I want you to do until then is eat, drink, and sleep."

"Anything for you, Princess." Kali smiled weakly.

Usually, Diana would have huffed at Kali for calling her "Princess," but this time, she pecked Kali on the cheek for it. Zoey figured it had something to do with the fact that they'd just told Kali about Darko's death; Diana and Kali would probably be gentler with each other until things started looking up.

Some color returned to Kali's cheeks. "I'll be

back later," Diana said. She exited the cabin alongside Andy and Narcissa, leaving Zoey and Kali by themselves.

For the next couple of hours, Zoey ensured that Kali followed Diana's instructions, and the two of them discussed what had happened on New Mount Olympus. How Zoey had stolen the Lightning Bolt from Zeus's robes, how a great battle had ensued, and how they'd escaped the amphitheater by the skin of their teeth.

"What kind of flower did Darko's body turn into?" Kali asked, her eyes watery.

Zoey bit her lip, trying not to cry. She'd done enough of that today. "The most beautiful red poppy you'll ever see."

"After you and Andy defeat the gods, where do you want to plant it?"

Zoey's breath caught in her throat. She and Andy wouldn't be in control of their own bodies by the time the war was over. She doubted Calliope and Anteros would care what happened to Darko's flower, but she couldn't tell Kali that yet. She needed to wait until she and Andy could explain what was going on to everyone as a group. For now, how should she reply? "Maybe you decide."

"I'll ask Andy what he thinks. Can I see it?"

Zoey stood. "Yeah, of course. It's behind the

cabin. Andy said he and Harmony put it out there. I'll, uh—I'll go get it."

"Thank you."

Zoey headed out the door and walked toward the back side of the cabin. On her way there, she spotted Karter, Troy, Marina, and three Naiads. The twins were tinkering with wood and rocks and fire, and the Naiads had streams of freshwater hovering above everyone's heads, presumably in case something that shouldn't be set ablaze was. It appeared Troy and Marina had fashioned sharp tools out of some of the stones, most notably what looked like a kind of saw. Karter was holding the saw, and Troy was bossing him around.

"I need you to cut off all the branches, then chop it into four equal sections," Troy explained, pointing at a massive pine that lay before them.

"The sections don't have to be exact, right?" Karter asked.

"Maybe not exact, but very close to exact."

"But I don't have a measuring tool."

"He's only a Son of Zeus," Marina said. "His talents obviously don't lie in craftsmanship. Why don't you tell him where to saw, Troy?"

The Naiads smirked, clearly enjoying themselves as they watched Karter struggle with some of the twins' directions. Zoey was sure that if she'd passed the scene before Asteria had informed them of Karter's fate earlier today, she would have done the same. But now all she could manage was to bow her head and look away.

When she reached the back of the cabin, she picked up the clump of dirt housing Darko's flower. The plant had perked up since she'd seen it last, the soil beneath its stem soft and moist. She looped around the building and went inside.

Seeing the poppy understandably made Kali cry more, but holding it seemed to be therapeutic for her. After eating a snack and guzzling down the rest of her water, she drifted off to sleep, the flower nestled in her lap.

Kali slumbered for the rest of the day while Zoey hung out. She would have napped as well, but her mind was racing. She couldn't stop thinking about all the things she wanted to do before she and Andy converged with Calliope and Anteros.

For one, she wanted to ensure that Darko's flower would be planted in a nice spot when this was all over. *I'll have to make Diana and Kali promise to take care of it.* She also wanted to tell those two how much they meant to her, to thank them for everything they'd done for her and Andy. She hadn't been able to tell Spencer and Darko how much she cared for them before they'd died, and she regretted it now.

Most of all, though, Zoey wanted to talk to Andy. He'd told her that he was in love with her, and he seemed to *really* want to know what her feelings toward him were. She wanted to tell him that she loved him very much, that he was one of her best friends in the whole world, but that she wasn't *in love* with him.

It was going to break his heart, but he deserved to know the truth before they sacrificed themselves to Calliope and Anteros. He deserved not to wonder for the rest of his life about what could have been. *Telling Andy how I feel about him will be the first thing I do*, she decided. *It's time I rip off that Band-Aid.*

When evening came, Andy and Diana returned. Sweat seeped from Diana's pores, her freckled complexion so pale it was almost gray, and Andy didn't look much better. They both could have used Kali's afternoon of napping.

"It's—done," Diana said between breaths. "All the—nymphs are—healed. Tomorrow I'll—try to heal—Troy and Marina."

"Since you're back, why don't you stay with Kali while I find us something for dinner?" Zoey suggested. Andy and Diana agreed, collapsing into their grass "beds," and Kali gave Zoey Darko's poppy so she could put it back outside. Once Zoey finished returning the flower to its spot, she started her search for their meal.

The sun was setting. Pretty soon it would be dark, and Zoey wasn't sure what to bring back. *Probably the same old same old*, she thought, a cool breeze tickling her skin. *Roots and berries. No rabbit until Diana's feeling better, though. There's no way I could catch one. Ooh, maybe I'll get lucky and find some mushrooms.* She walked farther into the trees, watching out for edible things.

Eventually she stumbled into a familiar Dryad. Harmony. "Hey there," Harmony greeted her with a weak smile.

Zoey returned the smile, although she was sure it was as feeble of an attempt as Harmony's. "What's up?"

"My sentry duty is over for today. I was about to check on Darko's flower." As Harmony spoke, she sounded despondent. A far cry from the bubbly, exuberant nymph she'd been before the deaths of Eugenia and Darko. "What about you? What are you doing out here all by yourself?"

"Oh, you know. Trying to find dinner. Andy and Diana are way too tired to come with, so I figured I'd do it myself."

"Do you need my help? I planned on going to bed after watering the poppy, but I could find something for you before it gets too dark."

Zoey shook her head. "That's kind of you to ask, but you must be tired."

"Are you sure? Do you know what you're looking for?"

Before Zoey could say she did, a young man cleared his throat in the trees behind Harmony. Zoey and Harmony turned that way, and Zoey caught sight of shaggy black hair and glowing golden irises. "I can help her," Karter said. "I've been on missions in this area of the forest. I know which plants are edible and which aren't."

Harmony gave Karter a skeptical look. She opened her mouth to speak, but Zoey beat her to it. "It's fine, Harmony. I've got this."

"If you say so." Harmony shot one more wary glance in Karter's direction, then trailed off into the trees toward a nearby stream.

Once Harmony disappeared, Zoey crossed her arms and turned to Karter. "It's rude to eavesdrop."

He avoided her stare, examining the greenery around them. "I wasn't eavesdropping. I mean, I wasn't trying to. Troy and Marina told me they were hungry, so I offered to find them dinner. I came this way, overheard you, and thought you could use assistance."

Visions of Karter's electrocuted corpse flashed through Zoey's mind. If he was likely to die for her and Andy's cause, did that mean he was sincere in his intentions—that he was truly on Zoey and Andy's side—despite the decisions he'd made in the past?

"I guess you can help," she said. "You know, since you're kind of a part of our group now." He stopped to look at her, his expression brightening. "Listen," she went on. "I wanted to apologize to you."

"Wait, really? For what?"

She couldn't believe what she was about to say. She couldn't believe she actually meant it, either. "I'm sorry for blaming you for Darko's death. It's not your fault. He isn't gone because of you. He's gone because—because he sacrificed his life for Andy's."

"You have nothing to be sorry for," Karter replied, and their gazes locked. "I deserved everything you said to me and more. Even if Darko's death wasn't my fault, I still caused you pain. All of you. You have every right to be angry with me."

She nodded slowly, unsure how to respond, then pivoted to continue her search.

As Zoey worked alongside Karter in silence, she realized there might be one last thing she wanted to do before converging with Calliope. *"I should have been a better man for Spencer and Syrena, and . . . and for all of you, too. I promise, from now on I'm going to do my best to be* that *man. So, if you change your mind and decide there's something I can do for you—something that will help you forgive me—then tell me. I'll be here, and I pledge that no matter what it is, if you ask me to do it, I will."*

"Yeah, I don't see that happening," she'd replied.

But maybe there is *something. And if I can think of that something, maybe it would feel good to forgive him. Maybe it would make my last days as "me" a bit less . . . painful.*

She looked over her shoulder at him, catching a glimpse of his scarred profile as he stood hunched over a bush. Brow knit, he picked through the clusters of berries growing from the shrub, inspecting the fruit with laser focus. He was so deep in concentration, he could have been cramming for the ACT.

Zoey suddenly imagined Karter living in the Before Time, wearing normal clothes and worrying about something like an exam. The mental picture made her giggle.

Karter glanced up at her. "What?" He smiled nervously. "What's so amusing?"

"Just the—the, umm . . ." She pointed at the bush. "The way you were studying the berries. It was, you know . . . funny."

He chuckled, bowing his head. "Laugh away, I suppose. I'm not done."

She gave him a thumbs-up. "Will do." She cringed at how weird she must have seemed just now—seriously, a thumbs-up?—then swung around and kept on foraging.

For the rest of their search, Zoey and Karter didn't speak, but Zoey didn't mind. She spent that time brainstorming what she could ask him to do for her, something that would help her forgive him.

When Karter and Zoey returned to the cabin with dinner, the sun had yet to dip below the horizon. Because they'd worked together, it had taken less than an hour to locate enough food for everyone. They stepped inside the building and went to work—washing, chopping, and plating the roots, berries, and mushrooms they'd gathered.

After Andy, Diana, Kali, Troy, and Marina

had been served, Karter and Zoey grabbed their own plates. Karter leaned against a wall away from everyone else while Zoey took a seat next to Andy, and they ate.

Andy finished scarfing down his meal and set his plate aside. "So, uhh, me and Zoey have something to tell all of you. It's kind of important."

Karter stopped chewing. *Is this regarding their discussion with Asteria earlier today?*

"I wouldn't say it's just 'kind of' important," Zoey said. "It's a really big deal. Asteria told us about it, but before we go through with it, everyone deserves to know what's going to happen to me and Andy." Her words were answer enough for Karter. This did, in fact, pertain to the Calliope-Anteros situation.

"I don't like how this sounds," Diana said.

"Neither do we," the twins added in unison.

Kali gulped, concern etched upon her features. "What's going on?"

Zoey shared a look with Andy. "We should start from the beginning," she said, and start from the beginning they did. From the gods' patron cities to Poseidon's palace, from Circe's island to a section of forest infested with Artemis's Huntresses, Zoey and Andy relayed their story in the greatest of detail. They explained that after gaining powers because Andy touched a statue of Anteros in Aphrodite City, they'd concluded they were Calliope and Anteros incarnate. However, they'd later realized that Calliope and Anteros were just trapped within them, and they even said the gods periodically took over their bodies.

At one point, Andy recounted an instance in which Calliope and Anteros had possessed Zoey and Andy for a fight with Artemis. He said that before the battle, the gods had forced them to passionately kiss each other.

As Andy described the event, Karter tensed. For a reason he hadn't yet come to understand he leaned forward, curious to see Zoey's expression, but she shielded her face with her hand.

Karter relaxed slightly once Andy finished that part of the story, and Zoey relayed how her and Andy's powers had begun to dwindle since they'd severed their "connections" with Calliope and Anteros.

"Now that we had our talk with Asteria, we know the reason all of this has been happening," Andy said.

Diana tucked some hair behind her ears.

"Which is?"

"We were never special," Zoey started. "We were never 'chosen' to lead a war on the gods."

Troy's and Marina's jaws dropped, and Kali threw her hands in the air. "What are you talking about?" she cried.

"Of course you were chosen to lead a war on the gods," Diana insisted. "When Syrena was executed, her blood sacrifice brought *you* back to life, not anyone else. I've watched you grow so much. I've watched you learn and train and—"

"None of that matters anymore," Andy interrupted. Diana gaped at him, but he wouldn't meet her eyes.

"Andy's right," Zoey said. "Despite how much training we've had, despite how much we've grown, none of it matters because we'll never be able to harness the full powers of the gods' magical items. Not as we are now, anyway."

"Why can't you harness the objects' full powers as you are now?" Marina asked.

"Because we're only regular humans," Andy answered. "We don't have divine essences, like gods or their descendants."

Marina furrowed her brow. "Who can harness the objects' full powers and defeat them, then?"

"It can't be descendants of the gods," Troy said. "None of us are able to touch their magical items without getting our life forces sucked away."

Diana shook her head. "Oh my gods, no. No no no. It can't be."

"What is it?" Kali asked.

"For Andy and Zoey to defeat the Olympians, they have to give up their bodies to Calliope and Anteros." Diana turned to them. "Please tell me I'm wrong."

Andy hung his head. "You're not. After they take us over, they'll become full avatars, and we'll be trapped in the 'labyrinth of our minds.' Only then will they be strong enough to harness the full power of the Helm, Trident, and Bolt. Using the objects, they'll cast a spell that opens a portal to Tartarus and banish the gods there."

"Avatars?" Troy said. "What are those?"

"Gods in mortal form," Kali answered. "Such as the avatars of Vishnu. He's one of the deities my people worship. He's from the Hindu pantheon."

"I didn't realize you and the rest of Deltama Village worship the Hindu gods," Zoey said.

Kali pressed her lips into a thin line. "I don't worship them. Actually, I don't believe they're real, because if they were, why didn't they stop the Greeks? They're just another outdated ideology of my people—like arranged marriages."

She added that last detail with a great deal of bitterness. Diana's expression became even more distressed than before, and Zoey and Andy winced. *Was Kali betrothed before meeting Diana?* Karter wondered. *This seems like a sensitive subject.*

"Anyway, yes," Kali continued. "Many citizens of my village believe in the Hindu gods, hoping and praying that one day they'll save us. My mother even named me after one of them. Kali, Goddess of Destruction."

"Asteria says they exist," Andy replied. "She says all the different pantheons of gods do, like the Norse and Egyptians and stuff."

"That doesn't bring me comfort." Kali massaged her temples. "I can't believe this is happening."

Silence fell over the group, and Karter did his best to process Zoey's and Andy's words and deliberate upon possible solutions. He hadn't known them for very long, and during most of that time, he'd been in opposition to them. But the thought of Calliope and Anteros taking over their bodies made his stomach sick.

He'd begun to see why Spencer and Diana had grown so fond of them. In the instances that Karter had battled with and against them, they'd possessed a certain bravery, a certain selflessness, that he didn't often witness. If there was a way to win this war and keep them intact, he wanted to find it.

He cleared his throat. "The future isn't set in stone. Asteria doesn't know how situations will unfold—not for certain. She's a goddess of prophecy, yes, but she's said herself that there are many possible outcomes to everyone's destiny."

"I also said that the universe sometimes allows certain things to happen in order for others to take place." Asteria's voice echoed around them. A cluster of stars soared into the cabin through one of the windows, and then the Titan goddess materialized before Karter. "Did you plan on leaving out that little detail?"

Karter stood as straight as he could. "I just wanted to point out that things can always change. There might be another way."

"There isn't," Asteria said. "I've looked into all possible futures, and the only ones in which the Olympians are defeated involve Anteros and Calliope taking control of Andy and Zoey." Her gaze softened as she looked at Karter, a knowing expression that made him squirm coming over her face. "I know it's not what you want to hear, but this is what the universe has in store. Some things simply can't be changed."

Diana hopped to her feet and started pacing. "No, Karter's right. The Tartarus spell will work if the person casting it has all three objects of power and a strong divine essence, right? No matter who they are?"

"Correct," Asteria said.

"Okay, then Andy and Zoey can just have another god cast the spell," Diana replied. "Problem solved."

Zoey shook her head. "No, it doesn't work like that. The only other gods who know the full spell besides Calliope and Anteros are Zeus, Poseidon, and Hades, and I don't see any of them agreeing to casting it so we can banish *them* to Tartarus."

"If that's the case, you and Andy could reconnect with Calliope and Anteros for the sole purpose of getting the words of the spell from them," Diana argued. "You can promise them something in return, like investigating ways to free them from your bodies. But when we get the words of the spell from them, we'll just need to find a god who will use the objects of power and cast the spell for us. After the portal is opened, all that will be left to do is banish the Olympians to Tartarus. Easier said than done, but if we can find more people to help us, and if we work together, anything is possible."

Asteria's form glimmered, almost as if she were going to transform into thousands of little stars and fly away, but then she quickly returned to normal. "No, I'm afraid that won't work. Just any god overthrowing the other gods won't bring about change. It won't lead the world into a new cycle because the pantheon has been in a state of decay for too long. The gods are selfish, selfish creatures—unable to think of anyone but themselves. If one of them got ahold of the Helm, Trident, and Lightning Bolt, they wouldn't return the objects, even after banishing the Olympians. Humanity still wouldn't be free."

"You just contradicted yourself," Diana said. "You say a god overthrowing the other gods won't 'bring about change,' but you seem to be forgetting that Anteros and Calliope are gods. Why can they bring about change, but the other gods can't?"

"Anteros and Calliope will never be as they once were. By binding them to Andy and Zoey, Zeus disposed of their immortal bodies. Essentially, they're ghosts, and through this process, their spirits have been forced out of stagnation. Once they become avatars, they can usher the world into a new cycle. Long ago, the Titans overthrew Uranus. Later, the Olympians overthrew the Titans. Now, it's time for the avatars to overthrow the gods. This is the natural progression of the universe."

"What about Prometheus?" Diana asked. "You escaped the gods. Who's to say he didn't? Who's to say he isn't on his way now? If we're reunited with him, he could cast the spell. He's selfless enough to give the objects of power back."

"Even if Prometheus finds his way here, he's been weakened by Hephaestus's chains," Asteria replied. "Unless we can free him of them, his divine essence won't be strong enough to cast the spell."

"Why can't it be you, Asteria?" Karter asked, and everyone faced him. "You have a divine essence, and you're far from selfish. You've risked your freedom time and time again to help me, and I'm guessing to help Zoey and Andy as well. Why can't you be the one to cast the spell, so long as Zoey and Andy get the words from Calliope and Anteros? When you finish, you can return the objects to Zoey and Andy, and rather than avatars leading the world into a new age, humans can be the ones to do it. That would bring about change, don't you think?"

Asteria's face fell. But before she could reply, shouts sounded from outside the cabin. "Goddess!" someone screamed. "A goddess has infiltrated the camp!" Karter's stomach turned. He dropped everything, swung around, and sprinted outside.

The forest around him would have been pitch black if not for the faint light of the moon and stars above. He conjured two green lightning bolts, the electricity crackling and popping in his palms. Focusing on his gift of flight, he shot into the sky and soared toward the yells. Beside him, Asteria appeared. She transformed into a cluster of stars and flew toward the conflict as well.

It didn't take long for them to reach the source of the commotion. In a clearing not far from the cabin, Dryads and Naiads alike stood in a circular formation. They manipulated their plants and water or thrust their swords and spears at someone located in the center of the clearing—presumably the goddess who'd invaded camp. However, Karter couldn't see the goddess very well. He caught glimpses of milky skin and long chestnut curls, barely visible in the night, but the features kept disappearing beneath the horde of nymphs.

It can't be one of the Olympian goddesses, Karter thought. *They're so tall they'd tower over these nymphs. So if she isn't an Olympian, who is she? Which minor goddess decided to go out on her own and search for us?*

Karter soon received the answers to his questions. As he hovered above the fight, lightning arcing in his hands, he saw which goddess had found them, and his bolts fizzled out. He couldn't believe who it was. *Am I seeing things? Can I trust my eyes, or is the darkness playing tricks on my vision?*

"Stop!" Persephone, Goddess of Spring and Queen of the Underworld, cried from down below. "Stop attacking me! I'm not here to hurt anyone!"

CHAPTER NINE

FEELINGS

Andy grasped the Master Lightning Bolt as he and Zoey dashed after Karter and Asteria through the dark forest. Zoey had the Helm and Trident, but she was wearing the Helm, so she was invisible.

The Bolt should have weighed a ton. The golden zigzag contraption was so massive Andy couldn't wrap his hands all the way around it, and yet it couldn't have been more than thirty pounds. Its smooth metal was hot against his hands, and it vibrated lightly, a low humming sound emanating from it.

Back at the cabin, when Andy had seized the object from its pack, Zoey had questioned his decision to grab it. *"We have no idea how to work that thing,"* she'd said. *"Do you really think it's a good idea to take it?"*

"I figured out how the Trident works," Andy had countered. *"And how to drive Troy and Marina's submarine. I got this."* With that, they'd sped outside, leaving Diana with Kali, Troy, and Marina.

Before long, Andy and Zoey lost sight of Karter and Asteria. The pair simply flew too fast, and honestly, they seemed so hyper-focused on finding whichever goddess had infiltrated camp that they likely hadn't noticed Andy and Zoey running behind them.

"Which way'd they go?" Andy asked, searching the sky for them.

"Doesn't matter," Zoey replied. "The yells are coming from the right. Go that way!"

Sure enough, within another minute or two Andy and Zoey barreled into a clearing full of shouting nymphs. Karter and Asteria hovered high above them, a rageful expression on Karter's face.

"Stop!" a feminine and weirdly familiar voice cried from somewhere up ahead of Andy and

Zoey. "Stop attacking me! I'm not here to hurt anyone!"

Beside Andy, Zoey gasped. "Is that . . . ?"

"Persephone!" Karter screamed. "All of you, out of the way!" The nymphs didn't have to be told twice. Karter raised two green bolts, and they hurried back.

While they scattered, Andy rushed forward, shoving through the panicked, dispersing nymphs and trying not to whack them with Zeus's weapon. *This has to be a trick, right?* he thought. *Persephone got sucked into the pit of Tartarus when we were in Hades. How could she have escaped? And, even if it's actually her, why did she come here, and how can she expect us to believe she doesn't want to hurt anyone? She stabbed me, cut off Zoey's hand, and murdered Spencer in cold blood!*

The nymphs must have gotten far enough out of the way because Karter chucked one of his bolts down. There was a yelp, then a sizzling sound like veggies roasting on a grill. Karter snarled and pitched more lightning.

Andy pushed through the last couple of Dryads and Naiads blocking his view, and when he laid his eyes on the goddess standing before him, his jaw dropped. He readjusted his grip on the Lightning Bolt, his palms growing slippery with sweat.

Even in the night he could tell it was Persephone, with her tiny stature, pale skin, and curly brown hair. She wore a black dress, and she had multiple thick, thorny vines twisting and curling around her in a dome shape—a shield of vegetation. A few of her vines had fallen to the forest floor, completely fried. As fumes coiled up from them, the smell of smoke permeated the air.

Karter landed beside Andy, new green electricity sparking in his hands. "How did you escape Tartarus?" He kept his stare trained on her, his voice quiet and menacing.

"I didn't." Her vines grew stockier, obscuring Andy's view of her. "The Olympians were going to rescue Hades, and my mother demanded they save me as well. Had they left Hades and me in the pit, we'd still be dead."

"What are you doing here?" Andy barked. The Bolt hummed louder in his hands, as if it was responding to his anger. "Are you working with the gods? You know what, don't answer that. Of course you are. You're pure evil."

"You know nothing about me, mortal boy," Persephone bit back. "Nothing about my life, about my experiences. Perhaps I'm evil, perhaps I'm not, but you can be sure of one thing: I didn't come here to help the gods. I came here to help *you* destroy them."

A noise like feet crunching against dry grass sounded next to Andy. He looked over but saw no one. It must have been Zoey. "Yeah, right," she said. "I distinctly remember what happened the last time you claimed to be on our side."

Karter let out a battle cry and hurled lightning at Persephone. The electricity blasted her barrier of greenery, and the vines it touched shriveled and blackened, falling to the forest floor. Persephone swiftly replaced the scorched plants with new ones.

"I understand why you wouldn't trust me," Persephone said. "But I promise you, I swear to the Fates themselves, I don't intend to trick any of you. Not this time. I'm here to help."

"Your promises are empty," Zoey snapped. "I think it'd be best for everyone if you just waltz down to the Underworld and throw yourself back into Tartarus."

"Wait," Asteria interjected from Andy's left. He looked over to see the Titan, no longer a cluster of stars. "Consider this: Persephone is a goddess. If she's telling the truth, if she truly wants to help, she could make winning this war that much easier."

Behind Andy, some of the nymphs began whispering to one another. He thought he heard someone suggest that they should hear Persephone out, since Andy and Zoey were working with Karter.

"No way!" Andy waved the Lightning Bolt at Asteria. As he yelled, it vibrated so much he almost dropped it. It grew warmer, and he swore he saw golden electricity dancing around it. "Persephone's a liar. For all we know, she could be notifying the gods of our location right now."

More whispers from the nymphs—this time they sounded fearful. *As they should.*

"If Persephone were notifying the gods of our location, they would have already arrived," Asteria said. "The moment Persephone saw Karter, she could have called on Hermes, and Hermes would have easily transported everyone here through a portal."

Andy looked to Karter. "Is that true?"

Karter clenched his fists. "Yes. But just because she hasn't called on the gods doesn't mean she can be trusted. She could be here for another reason, perhaps to steal the objects of power so she can defeat the Olympians herself and become the queen of everything. Perhaps she's here to finish what she started."

"Oh, that does sound fun," Persephone chirped. "But no, it's not part of my plan. I don't intend on taking the objects of power from you.

Sure, having them would be nice. But what I want most is for the Olympians to pay for everything they've done to me."

Andy snorted. "You're not inspiring confidence, lady."

"That's no kidding," Zoey said. More crunching grass, and then the ground around Persephone's shield of vines shook. Karter soared past Asteria, conjuring red bolts instead of gold or green. Andy assumed he didn't conjure any other color because Zoey was invisible, and he didn't want to accidentally hit her with something that would seriously hurt or instantly kill her.

Andy pivoted to face the nymphs, raising the Lightning Bolt above his head. "Everyone, listen up. Pack your stuff and gather the others as fast as you can. We have to leave, now. If Persephone found us this easily, then I bet Artemis or the other gods are bound to find us soon, too. We've gotta move camp before anyone else tracks us here!" At the mention of Artemis, the nymphs leapt into action.

Andy swung around to help Zoey and Karter take down Persephone, but Asteria blocked his way, raising her hands in surrender. "Trust me when I say it could be pivotal that we hear Persephone out," she said. "It could make the difference between failure and victory. The final battle against the gods will be your most difficult yet, even after you and Zoey finish the convergence with Anteros and Calliope. We need as much help as possible."

"Not from someone like Persephone," Andy replied. "Maybe *you* should trust *us* when we say she's evil. We're not gonna work with her, and you can't force us to."

Asteria transformed into a cluster of stars. "I suppose if you feel that strongly about her, there's nothing I can do to sway your decision. While you carry on, I'll inform those at the cabin that it's time to leave."

Andy narrowed his eyes. "You're not gonna make sure Persephone doesn't kill one of us? Or steal the magical objects?"

"There's no need." Asteria soared away, and Andy's nostrils flared. Man, all she did was make him mad. He knew she was a goddess of prophecy—he knew she saw a bunch of possible futures or whatever—but there was no way she could be positive about what Persephone's intentions were.

Readjusting his hands around the Bolt, Andy focused on the scene ahead. Karter flew over Persephone's shield; he'd ditched the red lightning, and it appeared he was trying to infiltrate the barrier by prying the vines apart. All the while, Zoey must be causing earthquakes with the Trident, because the ground around Persephone tremored.

"Now you've caused a panic," Persephone said, her voice muffled from within the greenery. "That was entirely unnecessary. I already told you, I'm here to help."

"We'd be stupid to believe anything you say," Andy shouted, racing forward. The Bolt buzzed in his grip, and this time he was sure he saw it right—yes, little sparks of electricity crackled around the weapon. The closer Andy got to Persephone, the hotter the object grew. "Zoey, Karter, get outta the way!" The quakes stopped, and Karter veered backward through the air.

Andy halted ten feet in front of Persephone's shield and focused on the Bolt. He focused on its heat, on the electricity hissing and popping around it. Most importantly, he focused on how much he hated Persephone.

Something gold flashed in the clouds. It disappeared in an instant, and thunder rumbled over their heads, Andy's heart palpitating. *Did more of the gods find us?*

A second later, he got his answer. The Master Lightning Bolt went from buzzing slightly to throbbing like a racing pulse in his hands. It made a high-pitched squealing sound that reminded him of an alarm, and there was another flash in the clouds. This time, Andy knew it wasn't a god.

A massive lightning bolt—like something a thunderstorm would produce—whizzed out of the sky. It shot toward the clearing, straight for Persephone's shield. It zapped the vines in an instant, arcing through them in half a second.

As quick as the lightning came it dissipated, Persephone's plants charred black. Thunder rumbled again, and what was left of the plants crumbled away in the breeze, reduced to ash, leaving the goddess fully exposed.

Karter barreled toward Persephone. She yelped, conjuring more thorny vines. They snaked out of her palms and slithered around her in defense.

Andy blinked, hardly able to process what had just happened. He gazed down at the Bolt as it stopped squealing and returned to a softer vibration. *There's no way that just happened.*

"Watch out, Zoey," Karter said. He shot gold electricity at Persephone's new vines. Persephone shrieked as some of the plants fell out of line, revealing her face. Karter chucked more gold electricity through the opening. Persephone vaulted to the side, the lightning missing her by inches. With a wave of her hand, she manipulated the vines to close the gap.

"Don't you understand?" Persephone cried. "I don't want to fight! Please, just listen to me!"

Her pleading snapped Andy back to reality. "How about instead, you let us kill you? That way, if we get outta here fast enough, you can't follow us to the next place we go." He looked at the Bolt again. Thought about bringing another zap of electricity down upon the goddess.

"You made me an ally by calling on me for help on your way to Hades, half-wit," Persephone said. "The protection spell the Fates cast on you won't keep me from finding you. Even if you kill me, I can access your location once I regenerate."

"Then maybe we should keep you as a prisoner," Zoey suggested, still invisible. "Just like how we're keeping Artemis's Huntresses as prisoners. All we'd have to do is kill you every time you regenerate."

"You'd be making a grave mistake," Persephone replied.

Just as the Bolt began to pulse in Andy's hands again, Karter seized some of Persephone's vines. Andy stopped focusing on the weapon and allowed its charge to peter out so he wouldn't hit Karter.

Karter grunted in effort, prying Persephone's plants apart. Persephone lifted a hand, surely to conjure more. Before she could, Karter snatched her by the wrist and jerked her arm at an unnatural angle. She screeched in pain. He heaved her out of her barrier and tossed her onto the open grass. Behind her, the shelter of plants collapsed in a heap.

Persephone scrambled to her feet. There was a sickening *slice*, like something sharp spearing through flesh, and she froze, gasping. Golden liquid began to dribble from three spots in her abdomen; Zoey must have stabbed her with the Trident. A choking noise escaped her throat.

Despite her new wounds, Persephone waved her arms. More vines shot from her palms. She manipulated the plants to wrap around something in front of her, then wrenched it outward and upward. The Trident appeared, tumbling to the ground. Zoey and the Helm appeared next, thirty feet in the air.

Andy cast the Bolt aside and tried flapping his wings, but it was no use. They barely moved. They definitely couldn't lift him off the ground. *No*, he thought. *No no no!*

Zoey plummeted toward the forest floor. Karter shot toward her and caught her in his arms before she hit the grass.

With Zoey safe, Andy reached down to pick up the Bolt, but Persephone manipulated her vines to wrap around the weapon. She yanked it away before Andy could grab it. He cursed and dove toward the Trident. Again, Persephone seized it and jerked it away with her plants.

Karter soared down and landed in front of the Helm. He stomped on Persephone's vines before she could use them to steal it next. Zoey clambered out of Karter's arms and grabbed the object.

Coughing up golden liquid, her wounds still seeping, Persephone stumbled toward Zoey and Karter. Her vegetation wriggled around her like the tentacles of an octopus.

Karter stepped in front of Zoey, shielding her from Persephone. Andy raced to their sides. "I knew it," Karter said. "I knew you couldn't be trusted. I knew you wanted to take the objects for yourself."

Persephone paused, looking up at the vines that held Poseidon's Trident and the Master Lightning Bolt. Then she did something Andy never expected.

She flicked her hands, and her vines tossed the weapons in Andy's direction. The items clattered to the forest floor by his feet. He snatched up the Bolt and kicked the Trident toward Zoey.

"I don't want the objects of power," Persephone said. Her wounds started to close. Pretty soon she wasn't bleeding anymore. "I don't want to lead the Olympians to you. I hate them just as much as all of you do. More than anything, I want to see them fall. I want their reign to end so they can never torture anyone else the way they've tortured me."

Zoey dropped the Helm, picked up the Trident, and walked around Karter toward Persephone. "If that's how you feel, you should have helped us back in the Underworld, like you told Spencer you were going to. How could you ever expect us to work with you after what you did to him?"

At the mention of Spencer, Persephone scowled. "From the moment I discovered Spencer's existence, he was fated to die. He was the result of my husband's infidelity. He represented every wrong the gods have committed against me."

"He shouldn't have," Karter said. "It wasn't his fault Hades was unfaithful to you, and he truly loved you. He saw you as his mother. If he were still alive, I imagine he would never recover from the way you betrayed him. It would devastate him every day."

Persephone threw her head back and laughed, an unnaturally airy and tinkle-y sound for someone so wicked. "That's interesting coming from you, Son of Zeus. Especially because you're the one who held Spencer back from saving Syrena at her execution." As she continued, her tone dripped with sarcasm. "I'm sure, if he were still alive, he'd never recover from the way you allowed the love of his life to die. It would devastate him every day."

Karter shrank back, Zoey glared at Persephone, and rage pulsed through Andy's body at her words. "That's not fair," Andy snapped. The Bolt heated and buzzed in his hands. "You can't compare yourself to Karter. He's not like you, not at all." Electricity danced up and down the object. "You just admitted to murdering Spencer out of spite, but Karter never wanted anyone to die." A high-pitched squealing noise like an alarm blared from the Bolt. "Sure, he's made mistakes, but you're evil, lady. Pure evil!" Golden light flashed in the clouds above them, and Persephone looked up, her eyes going wide.

A massive lightning bolt shot from the sky and zapped Persephone. She screamed, her body convulsing as electricity hissed through her.

As quickly as the lightning came, it disappeared. Persephone fell to the forest floor. Her hair was gone, her skin as black as her dress. The scent of scorched flesh assaulted Andy's nostrils, and he knew the strike had "killed" her. Thunder rumbled high above them, wind whipping through the clearing, and what was left of Persephone crumbled to pieces and blew away.

Zoey and Karter turned to Andy, their eyes wide with horror. "Was that . . . ?" Zoey trailed off.

"The Lightning Bolt," Andy said. "Second time I've used it tonight. I told you I'd figure out how it works."

"I've seen it used on people many times, and in each instance, it's never easier to witness," Karter remarked.

Andy smirked. "Well, good thing she's not a person. She's a homicidal goddess, and she'll recover."

Zoey picked up the Helm and slipped it over her head. She disappeared, and then the Trident vanished with her. "I wish you would've done that earlier."

"I didn't wanna incinerate either of you," Andy said. "Now c'mon. We gotta get outta here."

They ran in the direction of the cabin. When they got back, they worked alongside everyone else to get stuff packed so they could move camp again. With everyone accounted for, they checked the clearing and the surrounding area to ensure Persephone hadn't regenerated, then headed out.

Narcissa and Harmony led the pack, while Karter and Asteria flew high above to watch out for any gods, demigods, or monsters who might threaten the group. Down below, Luna, Ajax, Aladdin, and the gray pegasus Karter had stolen hauled Diana, Kali, Troy, and Marina on their backs. Andy and Zoey trod close to the four of them, carrying the gods' objects of power, all of them surrounded by Dryads and Naiads. Some of the previously wounded nymphs were now strong enough to walk, but many of them were still recovering, so they had to be transported by their peers' vegetation. Yet another set of nymphs had been entrusted with the task of lugging along Artemis's Huntresses and ensuring they stayed "dead."

By afternoon the next day, the group had passed through the destruction of two entire cities from the Before Time. Finally, they found a spot in the surrounding forest they deemed safe. The Dryads set up camp once more, and

Narcissa and Harmony directed recruits to their new posts. Some slept, while others watched the Huntresses or guarded the perimeter of the area.

As everyone got settled, Karter approached Andy and asked whether he could talk to him.

"Sure, man," Andy said. "What's up?"

Karter rubbed the back of his neck. "Last night, when you said I'm not like Persephone—did you really mean that?"

"Of course I did," Andy replied. "And it's true. Sure, you've made mistakes, but you're not an outright psycho-murderer." Karter didn't seem convinced, so Andy went on. "Seriously, man. Don't let what she said get under your skin. You're trying your best to become a better person, and in my opinion, you're on the right track."

Karter gave Andy a smile—a genuine, honest-to-God smile. "Thank you. You have no idea how much that means to hear."

Andy smiled back. "You're welcome." He held out his hand for a high five, and this time, Karter didn't hesitate to give him one.

A short time later, Andy, Zoey, Diana, Kali, Karter, Troy, and Marina had lunch in a newly constructed cabin. Afterward, Diana affirmed she felt well enough to try healing Troy and Marina. "I'll focus on them one at a time and give it everything I have," she said. She knelt before Marina and lit her hands with golden light. Marina closed her eyes, and the light spread through her body.

Whole minutes passed before Diana allowed the light to fade. She sat back, her breathing labored, her skin soaked with sweat. "How—do you—feel?" she asked, wheezing.

Marina grunted and groaned, clearly trying to stand, or to even move her legs the tiniest bit, but they wouldn't budge.

"Damn it—all to—Tartarus." Diana scooted over to Troy. "Let's try—you next."

The same thing happened with Troy. Despite Diana's attempt to heal him, he couldn't move his legs, no matter how hard he tried.

Diana insisted that maybe they just needed repeat healings. And so, for the next several hours, she lit their bodies with golden light and poured every bit of strength she had into them. Andy, Zoey, and Karter stayed close to her, dumping cold water on her and getting her snacks when she needed.

When evening came, and the sun began to set, Diana could do no more. She nearly passed out, toppling sideways onto the grassy floor. Her skin had turned a sickly shade of gray, and she looked as if she needed a week of sleep before she'd be back to normal.

"Diana!" Kali cried. She scrambled to Diana and brushed some hair off her face.

Diana groaned, reaching up to take Kali's hand. "I'm—okay."

"How about now?" Karter asked Troy and Marina. "How do you feel? Can you move your legs?"

They tried to do so one last time, but nothing happened.

"I'm—sorry," Diana said between breaths, her expression despondent. "Some injuries—are simply—beyond repair."

"You did everything you could," Troy said. "I—I'd suspected this is what would happen, although I'd hoped not."

Understandably, Marina didn't take the news half as well as her brother. She covered her face with her hands and started to cry.

Troy's expression crumpled as he watched Marina. He wrapped an arm around her shoulders and pulled her close. "It's going to be okay," he assured her. "This is another obstacle we'll have to overcome, but it's not the end."

"I know." Marina rested her head against his. "It's just difficult to accept." She fell into another fit of sobs.

Troy gave her a squeeze. "Let's finish

building our wheelchairs. Maybe we can craft special additions for them, ones that will help us fight the gods."

Zoey stepped forward. "You guys don't have to do that. You've done so much already."

Troy looked up at her, a fiery determination in his eyes. "I won't stop fighting. Not until the Olympians are in Tartarus or I'm dead and gone."

Marina nodded. "Me too. I'll do whatever I can to help. If you and Andy are willing to sacrifice your lives for humanity, then so am I." After everything the twins had lost, their resolve took Andy aback. He blinked in surprise. Zoey put her hand on her heart.

Karter motioned at the twins. "I know it's getting dark, but we can work on the wheelchairs if you'd like. I won't sleep until they're finished." His eyes grew watery. He wiped them with the back of his hand. "I'm so, so sorry I let this happen to you."

"We know you are," Marina replied.

"And we'll take you up on your offer," Troy said. "Let's finish the project."

Karter picked up the twins, carried them outside, and shut the door behind them.

Andy released a heavy sigh and flopped down onto the grass floor of the cabin. "Man, that sucks about Troy and Marina."

"Seriously." Zoey sat next to him. "I wish there was more we could do."

Diana took a swig from her canteen, then set it aside and lay on her back. When she spoke, it sounded as though she'd finally caught her breath. "Like I said before, some injuries can't be healed." She gestured at Zoey. "You know that better than anyone."

"Yeah, I guess so," Zoey replied, gazing at the stump where her right hand used to be.

"It's awful, but my powers can only do so much." Diana yawned and closed her eyes, and Kali curled up next to her.

Andy and Zoey turned to one another, and Zoey whispered, "Want to go talk outside? Just you and me?"

His heart skipped at the thought, but he needed to act cool. "Sounds good," he whispered back. They stood up and tiptoed to the door.

Once outside, Zoey crept around the cabin, and Andy trailed behind her. "What's up?" he asked.

She glanced over her shoulder at him. "I, um—I don't know when we'll have another chance to talk alone. Or *if* we'll have another chance to talk alone. Before we ... well, you know."

His stomach flip-flopped. He recalled the last couple of times he'd been the one to ask whether *he* could talk to *her* alone, and what that had entailed. *Me telling her how I feel about her*, he thought. *Or apologizing for the way I've acted about stuff that happened in her past. Or assuring her she doesn't have to say how she feels about me until she's ready.*

Is this that time? Is she ready to tell me whether she loves me back?

They walked through the trees until they reached a small clearing with three boulders perched at the far edge. A view of the sunset as it painted the sky with oranges and purples and pinks was perfectly visible here, and Andy figured the sight would have taken his breath away if he weren't so mesmerized by how gorgeous Zoey looked.

Seriously, how did she do that? Her dress was stained and torn, her curly brown hair sticking out in every direction, dirt smudged all over her face. But still, she was a vision of beauty. *Maybe that's what happens when you love someone. Maybe they're always perfect to you, no matter what.*

He coughed. "This looks like a great spot for two people to talk. You know, alone."

"It sure does." She started toward the

boulders. "Let's sit down?"

He followed her. "Sure." They took a seat on the shortest of the boulders. "So, what do you wanna talk about?"

"Just how this whole Calliope-Anteros thing is really freaking me out." The words spilled rapidly from her lips, as if she'd been holding them in since yesterday. "I can't begin to imagine what it's going to be like to be 'lost in the labyrinth of my mind.' You know?"

He gulped. "I do. I—I've actually been trying *not* to think about it. I hope we have a few more days together—all of us—before it has to happen. I'm not ready."

"I'm not either. It feels like we're being sent to our deaths. I know we'll technically be alive, but we won't be living. I don't think I've ever been so afraid." Her hand began to tremble, and before Andy could stop himself, he cupped it in both of his. They locked eyes. She didn't pull away from him.

He leaned closer. "Zoey, I—"

"There's something I have to tell you," she blurted out, and his heart nearly stopped. *She's gonna say what her feelings for me are.* "Something I don't know how to put into words. I thought that we'd have more time. I thought that after this war, we'd have the whole rest of our lives to hang out. I wanted to find the perfect way to explain this, because I love you so much, but . . ."

His stomach clenched. "But what?" She'd said *"I love you so much,"* and he loved her too. That meant this should be a happy moment, right? So why did he feel sick? "What's going on?" Her hand shook even more, and he tightened his grip on it, trying to calm her. "Zoey, it's okay. I'm right here. I'm right here and I love you. No matter how little time we have left together, I love you."

She whimpered, shutting her eyes. Tears trickled out from them, down her cheeks. "Do you remember when we were locked in the Hephaestus City jail?" she asked. "When that Daughter of Aphrodite tried to make me fall in love with her, but I didn't?"

How could he forget? *"Is she the reason you didn't fall for me, little boy?"* Violet had taunted him. *"Why you were able to evade my love spell? Oh, you're in luck. She must feel the same. Otherwise, she'd have fallen desperately for me and wouldn't have turned away like that. Unless she cares for someone else. That's always awful. For the one whose feelings go unrequited, anyway."*

"Yes, I remember," he said, doing his best not to sound bitter.

Zoey opened her eyes to look at him, still crying. "The reason I didn't fall for her . . ." Andy held his breath. *This is it.* "The reason I didn't fall for her isn't because I have feelings for you—because I don't. I love you so much, Andy, but I don't love you the way you love me."

He sat there, stunned.

Finally, he let go of her. His hands fell limp against the boulder beneath him. He suddenly felt very, very heavy, as though his bones had alchemized into lead.

"I wanted to wait to tell you," she said. "Not only because I didn't know how to say it, but also because I didn't want to hurt you. Especially while we're in the middle of the fight of our lives. But now . . ."

"But now that we know what's gonna happen to us in the end, you wanted to tell me the truth." It was hard for Andy to get the words out, his tongue feeling as cumbersome as the rest of him. "You didn't want to leave me wondering about what could have been."

"Yes."

He stared at her, astounded that they'd finally had this conversation, that she'd finally given him her answer. She stared back at him, her face fearful. It almost seemed as if she was waiting for a response.

What did she want him to say? It wasn't okay. He wasn't going to be okay, not after this. He'd had a crush on her since the first time he saw her. For years, he'd admired her from afar. She'd stood up to Jet for him, and they'd become friends. When the world had ended, she'd been the last piece of home he'd had left.

After he'd discovered his family and best friend were gone, she'd been the reason he hadn't given up. He'd wanted to die so badly, to be with his loved ones again, but she'd pulled him back to the land of the living and made him see what was important.

If it weren't for her, he never would have gone on this insane quest to steal the gods' magical items and save humanity. He loved her in a way he'd never loved someone before, for more reasons than he could count. But she didn't feel the same.

Of course she doesn't, he thought. *Why would she? She's the most amazing person alive, and I'm . . . me.*

"Andy?" Zoey reached for him, but he pulled away and stepped off the boulder. She bit her lip. "Please, you have to understand. I never wanted to hurt you. If I could make myself fall in love with you, I would, because you mean that much to me."

"I'm a screwup," he said with a shrug. "I understand why you feel the way you do. You don't have to sugarcoat it."

"Don't say that. You're not a screwup."

"Darko is *gone* because of me. I'm the biggest screwup on the planet."

"Darko is *not* gone because of you," she cried. "Will you stop being so hard on yourself? You're brave, and adorable, and funny and sweet."

"If I'm so great, and if you care about me so much, then why don't you love me?"

"I do love you. I'm just not *in love* with you."

"I think I get it now." Before he could stop himself, he said, "It's because of Spencer, isn't it?" Her eyes went wide, her frown deepening. "That's why you don't have feelings for me, right? That's why you didn't fall for Violet when she made you look into her eyes. It's also why you didn't want to work with Karter, even after he helped us on Olympus—because you're so in love with Spencer, you couldn't bring yourself to give Karter a chance. You blame Karter for Spencer's death, just like you blame Karter for Darko's death."

"No. The reason I'm not in love with you is because you're one of my best friends, and I don't see you that way. And I'm not in love with

Spencer, either."

Andy chuckled, shaking his head. "Seriously? Do you think I'm stupid? I saw the way you looked at him. You were completely crazy for him."

She threw her hand in the air. "Okay, fine. I *liked* Spencer. Good job, you figured it out. But liking someone and being in love with someone are two different things." She sighed. "It doesn't matter anyway. It's not like he would have ever reciprocated my feelings after losing Syrena. He thought of me as a friend, and I knew that. I wouldn't have pushed for more unless he gave me some indication that he wanted me to."

"Then why didn't Violet's spell work on you?" Andy knew he was taking this too far, that he should drop the subject, but he couldn't bring himself to stop. "She said the only time it doesn't work on a person is if they're in love with someone else."

Zoey thought for a moment. "I felt connected to Spencer. I felt like we understood each other. Maybe that's why Violet's spell didn't work—because I was attracted to him for reasons that weren't only skin-deep."

Andy rolled his eyes. "Sounds like love to me."

"It wasn't."

"Well, I don't believe you."

"Well, I don't care if you do." She stood up, scowling at him.

There were a few moments of silence where they just glared at each other. Andy considered ending the discussion, sensing that if he took it any further, it wouldn't end well for him. But he still felt as if he didn't have the whole story, and an uncomfortable sensation tugged at his gut. If he didn't get to the bottom of this, he might go crazy.

As he held Zoey's stare, he replayed the events of the last several days through his mind. He thought about the distaste Zoey harbored toward Karter, about the way she'd treated him when he'd joined their group, about how upset she'd been after she'd tried saving him in Hephaestus City and, instead of helping them, he went home to the gods.

Diana has way more to be mad at Karter for than Zoey does, he thought. *He kept Spencer from saving Syrena, and he tried to capture Diana while we were traveling to Hades. Diana also tried to save him in Hephaestus City, just like Zoey did, and after that, he dragged her back to Olympus with the intention of executing her. Yet after we escaped Olympus, Diana stood up for him. She wanted to work with him, while Zoey refused.*

The only explanation is that Zoey must not realize she's in love with Spencer. She can't get over him. That's what all the signs point to. Unless . . .

Suddenly, Andy understood why he felt as though he didn't have the full story. *It's Karter she's in love with*, he realized with agonizing clarity. *That would explain why she's angrier with him than the rest of us are.*

Zoey had mentioned something yesterday, when Asteria showed them the aftermath of what was supposed to be Karter's death by Zeus. *"Zeus ends up killing Karter in this version of the future?"* Andy had asked. *"I thought he'd maybe decide to have mercy on his own kid at the last minute."*

"No, Zeus wouldn't have mercy on anyone, not even his own son, unless it was beneficial to him somehow," Zoey had replied. *"Zeus is the one who gave Karter that awful scar."* She'd then recounted the tale accurately, according to Asteria.

"Who told you about that?" Asteria had asked.

"Karter did," Zoey had answered, as if it were obvious. *"Back when we were trapped together in Hephaestus City."*

Back when we were trapped together in Hephaestus City.

Something happened between them that day. She just never told anyone about it.

Andy balled his fists at his sides. "It's not

Spencer, is it? You couldn't have him, so you decided on the next best thing. His closest friend. Karter. You were trapped together in the Hephaestus City jail. What happened while you were alone?"

Zoey furrowed her brow. "What the hell are you talking about?"

"I get it now. Man, I didn't understand why you were so hung up on the guy long after he'd picked the gods over us. I mean, I didn't like what he did either, but I also didn't get as mad as you did whenever someone mentioned his name."

"Because he didn't screw you over like he did me," she said. "He made me think that we had something in common—that we could be friends. And then he betrayed me."

Andy laughed once. "Except he didn't really 'betray' you, Zoey. He couldn't have because he was never on your side. Not until recently. He even said it the other day. Before now, he was looking out for either Spencer or himself. But you're still taking what he did personally, and it's because something went on between you. What is it? What happened?"

Her cheeks flushed a furious shade of red. "Absolutely nothing happened between us."

"Then why'd he tell you about how he got his

scar?" Andy asked. "That seems like a personal thing to tell someone. Pretty intimate if you ask me."

"Good thing I didn't ask you," she retorted. "Like I said before, nothing happened between us, and nothing ever will. I'm just now starting to accept that Karter is part of our group. I hated him before."

"Really? You hated him? I don't think you'd risk your life, and Diana's life, and Prometheus's freedom, and our *entire mission*, to try and rescue someone you hated."

"I wanted to help him because he was Spencer's best friend."

"And there it is, ladies and gents." Andy slow-clapped. "We've come full circle. Zoey just proved my point. She couldn't have Spencer, so she decided she wanted his best friend."

Zoey's nostrils flared. "I can't believe I was ever worried about breaking your heart. Seriously, thank you for showing your true colors. You are an *asshole*."

She shoved past him, back toward the cabin, and considering how irate he was about whatever was going on between her and Karter, he should have been relieved by her absence.

But as he watched her stomp away, it was as if someone were hacking open his chest and carving out his insides. He'd been so heavy earlier, but now that Zoey was leaving like this, he felt empty.

He paced back and forth, holding his hands behind his head and trying to breathe. She disappeared into the trees.

After she left, he wanted to call out to her. He wanted to ask her to come back. He needed to say that he was sorry, that he'd reacted poorly, that he'd been unfair. The truth was, he'd heard the cruelty in his voice as he spewed his venomous words, but he hadn't been able to stop himself from saying them.

No, that's not true, he thought. *It's not that I couldn't stop myself. It's that I chose not to stop myself. Because I'm mad at her. So, so mad at her.*

But why was he mad? She hadn't done anything wrong. In fact, she'd done exactly what he'd asked her to do: tell him how she felt about him when she was ready. He'd assured her she didn't need to express her true feelings toward him until she was comfortable doing so. She hadn't exactly been comfortable during their conversation, but she'd been honest. *And all I did was yell at her.*

He stopped pacing. "Zoey?"

No response.

The empty feeling in his chest subsided,

replaced with a searing pain that shot through his body. The only other times he'd felt this bad had been when his loved ones had passed away. *Except Zoey's not gone. She's not dead.*

But maybe he'd lost her all the same.

He focused on putting a foot forward, on going after her. He couldn't let their friendship end, not like this. Not right before they were pretty much going to die.

He had to make this right.

Unfortunately, his legs failed him. They trembled so violently he could barely stay upright.

Incapable of following Zoey, Andy toppled to the forest floor and put his face in his hands. And as he lay there, thinking about the people he'd lost, the future stolen from him, and his breaking heart, he wept.

CHAPTER TEN

RESTART

Hot anger coursed through Zoey's body as she stomped through the trees toward the cabin.

She couldn't believe how poorly that had gone. How immaturely Andy had reacted to her confession. *I knew it was going to hurt him, but I didn't think he'd act like such a jerk about it. I figured he was better than that.*

I was so afraid to tell him. I just wanted him to know the truth before both of us are gone.

Seriously though, who did he think he was, asking her such intrusive questions? Demanding answers from her? She didn't owe him an explanation for why she felt the way she did. Overanalyzing it and grilling her about it wasn't going to change things.

And the *nerve*. The *nerve* he had to accuse her of being romantically interested in Karter, of all people, just because she didn't want to be with Andy. Sure, it would be nice if she could find a way to forgive Karter for what he'd done and be his friend. When they were locked up together, she'd even thought they might have made a connection.

But that didn't mean she *liked* him.

Shaking her head, Zoey cursed under her breath. Andy was hurt. He was lashing out and acting crazy. He didn't know anything about her love life, or lack thereof. He was just trying to cope with his own heartbreak. Pain was making him see things between her and Karter that weren't there. That would never be there.

With that thought, some of the fury in her body dissipated, although the hurtful words she and Andy had exchanged kept replaying in her head. *Maybe I shouldn't have cussed at him and left like that. Yeah, he was being a jerk, but there's been so much going on. Maybe, on top of everything else, this was too much for him. It's definitely too much for me.*

As she continued her walk to the cabin, another thought entered her mind: this was probably Andy's first real romantic rejection. He'd told her before that he'd never even kissed a girl, and he'd convinced himself that he was in love with Zoey. Her turning him down might not just sting. Because he'd never experienced romance before, it might feel like the end of the world.

I know from experience, she thought, remembering how she'd felt when she'd found out Jet was cheating on her. She'd integrated that stupid boy into every aspect of her life, practically made him her whole identity, and her foolishness had almost caused her to stay with him even after discovering his betrayal.

He'd begged her forgiveness, and when she'd told him it would take a lot more than words to prove that he was sorry, that he was going to have to prove it through his actions, he'd brought up what she'd done when she was fourteen to pay her mom's apartment rent. *"Let me get this straight,"* he'd said. *"You whore yourself out and expect a pass from me, but I make a mistake and you can't let it go?"*

His words had wounded her in a way nothing else could. *"We weren't together when that happened.*

You can't hold that against me."

Except he had. After she'd ended their relationship, he'd used that information to make her life a living hell. On top of losing the first person she'd ever been in love with, she'd become the designated slut of the city almost overnight.

Jet's disloyalty had shattered her. Losing him had been like a knife to the heart, and when he'd disclosed her darkest secret to their classmates, it had been like someone wrenching the blade through her body.

If Andy felt even a portion of the distress she'd experienced back then, perhaps she shouldn't hold this against him. However, she wasn't going to let him disrespect her again, so maybe the best course of action was to give him time alone. "Time," she whispered to herself. "Something we don't have. We're probably going to spend our last few days together fighting. I should have kept my feelings to myself."

But would never knowing the truth have been more torturous for Andy? She'd thought the right thing to do was to tell him. Now she wasn't sure.

When she finally reached the cabin, the sky was dark. Karter, Troy, and Marina were still working on the wheelchairs outside. She crept past them, hoping they wouldn't notice her. Once inside, she could hear Diana's and Kali's soft snores as they slept beside one another. *I know they need rest, but I'm not sure how much time we have left together. I have to talk to them now.*

She tiptoed over to them and shook Diana's arm. "Diana? Hey, Diana?"

Diana yawned, her eyes barely opening. "What is it?"

"I need to talk to you. Well, actually, I need to talk to both of you." Zoey shook Kali next. "Kali, wake up."

Kali's eyes fluttered wide open, and she shot into a seated position. "What's going on? What's wrong?"

"Nothing's wrong. Not exactly. I just wanted to talk."

Diana sat up and stretched. "Yeah, you said that already. Go ahead."

"Okay." Zoey's eyes grew watery again. She sniffled, holding back tears. She did *not* want to cry any more tonight. "First of all, I need the two of you to make me a promise."

"Anything," Kali said without hesitation.

"Anteros and Calliope probably aren't going to care whether Darko's flower is planted somewhere, or whether it's a pretty place," she started. "After they take over Andy and me, after this war is over, I need you two to find an amazing spot for that flower, the most beautiful one you can find, and I need you to plant it there. Can you promise me you'll do that?"

Diana and Kali shared a look, then turned back to her. "Zoey," Diana began, a reassuring smile on her lips, "we don't need to make you a promise like that, because we're going to find a way to cast the Descent Spell without Andy and you having to converge with Anteros and Calliope. If you can just get the words to the spell from them, we think Asteria could cast the spell. You have nothing to worry about. Both of you will be able to find the best place for Darko, you'll see."

"But what if we can't?" Zoey hated the way her voice was cracking. "Will you promise me that if we're not around anymore, you'll find him the perfect spot?"

Diana took Zoey's hand in one of her own. "Of course."

Kali gave Zoey a side hug. "We promise."

Zoey squeezed Diana's hand and hugged Kali back. "Thank you. There's one other thing. Something I wanted to tell you in case I don't get another chance." When they didn't say anything, she went on. "Before Darko died, before Spencer died, I—I didn't get to tell them how much they meant to me. I didn't get to thank them for everything they did for me and Andy. I didn't get to thank them for being our friends. I just wanted to tell both of you—thank you for everything. I wanted to tell you that I love you, that you mean the world to me. That you always will."

Diana pressed her free hand against her heart, and Kali squeezed Zoey's shoulders. "Aww. We love you too, Sweet Stuff."

Zoey laughed. "Sweet Stuff? Are you giving all of us nicknames now? Not just Diana?"

"Might as well," Kali said with a shrug. "I'm not sure what to call Andy yet, though. I'll have to think about it."

Diana smirked. "This is how I know you're starting to feel better."

For a while, the three of them talked about nothing in particular. Zoey kept looking at the doorway, hoping Andy would show up, but he didn't. Eventually, they had to go to bed. *Maybe he'll come back while we're sleeping.*

Zoey awoke with a start early the next morning. The sun had barely begun to rise, but enough light peeked through the windows that she could make out her surroundings. She glanced around—Diana and Kali were cuddled up, snoozing, but other than them, there was no one else in the cabin. *Andy must not have come back last night, and Troy and Marina must be working.* Sure enough, when she headed outside and looked around the corner, she spotted Karter and the twins building away. *I wonder where Andy is.*

A cluster of stars appeared in Zoey's peripheral, and she turned to face it. A moment later, there was a flash of silver light, and Asteria appeared before her. "Morning," Asteria said, smoothing out a nonexistent wrinkle in her star-dotted dress. "I assume you're looking for Andy?"

"I am."

"He's just where you left him last night."

Zoey's cheeks heated. "Have you been watching us?"

"Not always, but often enough. I have to ensure that you remain safe, and that you aren't led astray."

"Led astray? From what?"

"Your destinies."

"Yeah, yeah. We're resigned to our terrible ends, okay?"

"Good. Because if you want to defeat the gods, this is the path you must take. Your threads of fate demand it."

Footsteps sounded ahead of them, and

Zoey's stomach sank when she saw who was approaching. *Oh, great. Just the person I want to see after what Andy accused me of last night.*

"Asteria, I'm so glad you're here." Karter stopped beside Zoey. "I haven't managed to catch a free moment with you so we can finish our conversation."

Asteria tilted her head. "What conversation?"

"The one about Zoey and Andy, and Calliope and Anteros." He held his head a bit higher, as if trying to muster his confidence. "You say the only way for Zoey and Andy to win this war is if they sacrifice themselves to Calliope and Anteros. Your reasoning for why it has to be them is that gods are too selfish—that if any god who hasn't been forced to grow uses the Helm, Trident, and Bolt to overthrow the gods, they'll essentially become drunk with power and the world won't change for the better. But I asked why it can't be you who uses the objects and casts the spell.

"You're far from selfish, and you're a Titan goddess, so you have a strong enough divine essence to do it. Zoey and Andy could get the words from Calliope and Anteros, and after you've finished, you can give the objects back to Zoey and Andy. Rather than avatars leading the world into a new age, humans—worthy heroes—can be the ones to do it. That would bring about the change we desperately need. What do you think?"

Zoey already knew where this was going. Asteria would come up with some convoluted explanation as to why Karter's suggestion wasn't worth considering, and then she'd insist they had to do things her way, or the plan wouldn't work at all.

To Zoey's surprise, Asteria said, "I've considered your suggestion a few times already, Karter."

Zoey's heart leapt with hope. Was there a way for her and Andy to get out of this? "And?" she said.

"It won't work," Asteria replied.

Zoey could practically feel herself deflating. "Why not?"

Asteria held out her hands. "Look." Zoey and Karter shared a glance, then did as the Titan goddess requested.

For what seemed like whole minutes, nothing happened. "What are we supposed to be looking at, exactly?" Zoey asked.

"Watch and be patient," Asteria said.

A second later, something *did* happen. Asteria's hands sparkled as if they'd been replaced with luminescent glitter, converting from pale flesh to silver stars in an instant. They didn't stay that way for long, but even when they returned to "normal," they glimmered around the edges. It was as if Asteria were a fairy plucked from a children's story, pixie dust pouring from her skin.

"Oh no," Karter murmured. "It can't be. You're—you're fading away?"

"I am." She lowered her hands to her sides, and Zoey studied the rest of her form. All of her was twinkling now, not just her hands. Soon the shimmering stopped.

Zoey wrapped a stray curl around her index finger. "After the big fight with Artemis, Prometheus said you'd overtaxed yourself. Even then you were fading away, and that's why you can't be the one to perform the Descent Spell. Your divine essence isn't strong enough because you're dying."

"Yes."

Karter stepped forward and rested a hand on Asteria's shoulder. "I'm so sorry, Asteria."

"It is the fate of all gods, eventually." She stated it as she would any other fact. "It happens a bit differently for everyone, depending on our domains and where we draw our power from."

"You're a goddess of stars," Karter remarked. "And you're turning into stardust."

"It could be worse," Asteria said, and Zoey was surprised she didn't sound sorrier for herself. Weren't gods supposed to be terrified of death? "There comes a point when our worshippers die out, our names forgotten, lost to time. New gods are born, and the cycle repeats itself. I'm a Titan goddess, so I've had a full life. I'm very old, and very tired."

"You're ready to go, aren't you?" Zoey asked.

"Correct."

Karter pulled away from Asteria. "There's something I don't understand. All of us know you exist. We're looking at you right now, and I'm sure there are some who still pray and make sacrifices to you. So how is it possible that you're fading away? You haven't truly been forgotten yet."

Asteria smiled at Karter the way a loving mother would smile at her inquisitive child. "You're right, but gods don't only fade away because our names are forgotten. The more power we expend, the weaker we become, and I have expended an immense amount of power over the years. Hiding Metis, turning her into an avatar, helping all of you ... The Olympians have been weakened from their feats as well, I can assure you, although they were stronger than me to begin with, so it hasn't affected them as much."

Zoey unwound the hair from her finger. "They've been weakened? But I thought they were all-powerful."

"They're powerful, yes," Asteria replied. "But not all-powerful. Not anymore. There was a time in the old days when the gods' true forms were so overwhelming, they had to disguise themselves when they interacted with mortals. Back then, a single glance at their true forms would kill a human." She motioned at Karter. "I'm sure you were never told this story, but it's true, nonetheless. Long ago, Zeus had a lover named Semele, and he promised to grant her anything she wished for. Hera found out about Semele, and about the promise Zeus had made her. Furious, Hera disguised herself as an old woman and went to Semele. She convinced the mortal woman to request that Zeus reveal himself in the same way he'd reveal himself to Hera—in his true form. Semele did just that, and Zeus was forced to grant the wish. His true form incinerated Semele."

Karter's brow furrowed. "No, I was never told that story, and as far as I know, neither were the other demigods. But I believe it happened. I didn't realize the gods were even more powerful in the old days than they are now."

"I bet they didn't tell you about it because they didn't want you to know they've been getting weaker over time," Zoey said. "The more scared you are of them, the easier you are to control."

"They have no problem controlling their offspring," Karter replied. "Most of the time, anyway. But if mortals were still incinerated simply by looking at their true forms, none of us would stand a chance. Not that we stand much of a chance as it is." He gestured at Asteria. "All right. You're fading away, and Prometheus has been weakened by Hephaestus's chains—not to mention, he's not here. Neither of you can cast the Descent Spell. But maybe there's another god who can."

"I know none selfless enough to hand over the objects of power to Andy and Zoey afterward," Asteria asserted. "I'm truly sorry. They'll have to make the ultimate sacrifice to save humanity. If there were another way, I would pursue it."

Karter pressed a fist against his mouth, thinking, and Zoey narrowed her eyes at him. Why did he care so much about what happened to her and Andy?

"Speaking of," Asteria continued, looking at Zoey. "It's been a few days. Two, to be exact.

Are you and Andy ready to reconnect with Anteros and Calliope?"

"You want us to do it now?" Zoey's stomach turned. She still had loose ends to tie up. She'd talked to Andy last night, but now that he was so upset, she needed to make peace with him. She'd also chatted with Diana and Kali about Darko's flower and about how much they meant to her, but she hadn't yet thought of something Karter could do so she could forgive him.

"Time is of the essence, my dear. Once you reconnect with them, the convergence process will have to restart. I have no idea how long it will take for them to grow strong enough to take over your bodies, and the gods have surely sent a search party after you already. We must make haste."

Zoey bit her lip. If they had a couple of days or even a week before completing the convergence, maybe she'd be able to wrap everything up. "Okay," she said. "I'll talk to Andy. If he's ready, we can go."

It was early morning, the sun's brilliant rays

shining on the destruction around Persephone. She marched through a city from the Before Time, gorgeous green overgrowth peeking through the collapsed buildings and rusted shells of automobiles, the spicy smell of pine invigorating her senses. She'd always hated the way humans ravaged so much of nature to create their inferior towns and cities, so at least the gods had done one good thing in the last five hundred years: they'd reverted the planet to a beautiful, untamed state.

She swiveled her head from side to side, keeping her eyes peeled for any sign of other gods or monsters. *I'm positive Zeus has already sent a search party after the Chosen Two*, she thought. *Probably after me, too.*

She huffed in irritation, recalling how poorly she'd been received at the nymph camp. She'd known she wouldn't be welcomed with open arms, but she certainly hadn't expected the chaos that had ensued. Nor had she expected to be reduced to ash with the Master Lightning Bolt, only to awake in desolate wilderness a few hours later.

At least tracking the Chosen Two was simple and used a minimal amount of her power. When she'd awoken, she'd traced their location immediately, and she was headed toward them now. They were safe, so she didn't need to use a great amount of effort to transport herself directly to them, but if she sensed they were in danger, she'd happily do so. For now, though, she planned to travel on foot. *They should have listened to me. Allowed me to join them. I'd be with them now, helping them with whatever it is they plan to do next.*

They must not realize how useful I would be to them. Perhaps they think I'm weak because I underestimated them while we fought in the Underworld, or maybe because I held back while fighting them at the nymph camp.

But deep down, Persephone knew the real reason they wouldn't work with her. *"From the moment I discovered Spencer's existence, he was fated to die,"* she'd told them. *"He was the result of my husband's infidelity. He represented every wrong the gods have committed against me."*

"He shouldn't have," Karter had replied. *"It wasn't his fault Hades was unfaithful to you, and he truly loved you. He saw you as his mother. If he were still alive, I imagine he would never recover from the way you betrayed him. It would devastate him every day."* A strange ache twinged in Persephone's chest as she repeated that word in her head: *mother.*

She thought of her own mother, of the last interaction they'd shared before Persephone abandoned the gods forever. For a moment, she wondered how it would feel if, instead of supporting Persephone, Demeter had betrayed her in the same way she'd betrayed Spencer.

Persephone swallowed the lump in her throat. How she would feel in that situation didn't matter, because she wasn't Spencer's mother, and she never had been his mother. Spencer was her idiot husband's illegitimate child by that whore, Aisha. Because of what Spencer was—because of the pain he'd caused Persephone—he'd deserved everything she'd done to him. Right?

Of course, Persephone thought. *Besides, what does Karter know? He has no idea what the last millennia have been like for me. What I've been forced to endure. How could he? He's only mortal. He hasn't the slightest clue what it's like to exist in misery for thousands of years, and he hurt Spencer just as much as I did, if not more.*

She trudged on after the Chosen Two, hoping that the next time she spoke with them, they'd listen to her and allow her to help them.

After Karter and Zoey finished their discussion with Asteria, Zoey and Asteria went off into the forest to retrieve Andy. For some reason, Andy hadn't slept in the cabin last night. He'd instead spent his time out in the trees. While Karter waited for them to return, he helped Troy and Marina complete their wheelchairs.

It didn't take long to finish the chairs, and thankfully, they didn't look as though they'd been thrown together in only a few days. They appeared as nice as ones crafted by professional wood- or metalworkers in the cities. *Troy and Marina are the Master Blacksmiths of the Hephaestus City Forges*, Karter thought. *Should the fact that the chairs look great come as a surprise?*

Troy and Marina tested them out, and they worked perfectly. Marina still seemed sad that Diana couldn't heal their paralysis, but Troy was doing his best to get her excited about the special additions they planned to make for the chairs. "Imagine the possibilities!" he kept saying. His enthusiasm alone was enough to brighten her mood, and Karter's heart warmed as he watched them interact. Their support for each other reminded him of the days when he'd been especially close with Syrena and Spencer.

Even though the twins had stayed up all night, they didn't seem tired, and they decided to begin adding on to their chairs. "If it's all right with you, I need to speak with Diana about something," Karter said to them.

Troy nodded. "That's fine. We'll take it from here."

"If we need help and you're not around, we'll find one of the nymphs," Marina added.

"Thank you." Karter walked into the cabin to see if Diana and Kali were up yet. He figured it would be best to fill them in on the latest development in Zoey and Andy's situation—about how Asteria wanted them to reconnect with Calliope and Anteros today. The two girls were asleep, so Karter woke them and proceeded to tell them everything he and Zoey had discussed with Asteria earlier today.

"I'm not giving up hope," Diana said after he finished. "Prometheus could still be out there. He and Asteria might not be strong enough individually to open a portal to Tartarus, but maybe there's a way for them to combine their powers to do so. Andy and Zoey can still reconnect with Anteros and Calliope today. In fact, they need to so they can get the words to the Descent Spell. Then we can track down Prometheus, and he and Asteria can cast the spell together."

"And if we can't find Prometheus in time,

maybe we could strengthen Asteria instead," Kali said. "Make a bunch of sacrifices to her before she does the spell, or something like that."

"I hope you're right," Karter replied.

A while later Zoey, Andy, and Asteria returned. The six of them swiftly discussed a plan of action, deciding it would be best for Diana and Kali to stay at camp to continue building their strength. Since Diana wouldn't be coming, she appointed Karter to go so he could protect Zoey and Andy. Asteria said that they probably wouldn't reach Aphrodite City until after night fell because it was so far south, but that Zoey and Andy needed to reconnect with Calliope and Anteros as soon as possible, so they'd just have to sneak in while citizens slept and *astynomia* prowled the streets.

"When will you come back?" Diana asked.

"Sometime tomorrow," Asteria answered.

Kali said, "And what if we have to move camp before you return?"

"If that's the case, just make a sacrifice to me and notify me of your new location."

With that, they let Troy, Marina, and the nymphs know where they were going and what for. Andy grabbed the bag holding the Helm of Darkness, Poseidon's Trident, and the Master

Lightning Bolt—they decided the objects of power would be safest with their group, considering that a lot of the nymphs were still recovering, that Asteria was a goddess, and that Karter was a child-of-Zeus—and then they left.

Now they soared above miles of forest, Karter sitting beside Zoey and Andy as Asteria flew them south toward Aphrodite City by way of stars. They could have taken pegasi, but Asteria's method of travel was faster. Aphrodite City was a long distance from camp, and it would have taken days to reach their destination if they utilized pegasi, whereas it would only take about a day if they used Asteria's stars. Also, it wouldn't be safe to leave pegasi alone in the forest outside of the city.

Throughout the day, Karter, Zoey, and Andy napped on and off, and Asteria stopped a few times to rest. While she recuperated, the others ate and drank.

By evening, no one was sleeping, and no one was talking either. Andy seemed especially upset, and Karter couldn't blame him. *It feels like we're leading Zoey and Andy to their deaths*, he thought. He could tell by the anxious expressions on their faces that they probably felt the same.

After night fell, they finally neared Aphrodite

City. The stars shone down on the *polis* in the distance, illuminating the sparkling gold-and-ivory statues and pillared buildings erected in the center of the city. Fanned out around the center and making up the outer rim were hundreds of thousands of stone-and-wood houses and acres upon acres of farmland.

Asteria landed in the thicker part of the forest outside the *polis* and allowed Karter, Zoey, and Andy to step onto the ground, then changed back into her normal form. She was covered in sweat, her breathing labored. Zoey had notified Andy on the trip here that Asteria was fading away, and he'd already told her he was "sorry to hear about it" and that it was "a bummer."

Since Karter had discovered she was dying, he noticed the moments when her body appeared to be converting from flesh to stardust—one of which was right now. She twinkled around the edges, and if he squinted, he could see specks of glitter flecking her skin. "Just give me—a few moments," she said, leaning against a tree and gasping for air.

It took a decent amount of time for Asteria to recover. While they waited, Zoey and Andy picked who would use which objects of power while in the city. They decided that for now, Zoey would use the Trident, Andy would use the Bolt, and they'd keep the Helm in the bag until they needed it.

Once Asteria was ready, Karter lit his hands with red electricity to light their way, and they started through the dark trees toward the *polis*.

A bit of time passed before Karter looked over at Zoey and Andy. "You said the two of you have visited Aphrodite City before, correct?"

"Duh." Andy readjusted his grip on the Bolt. "How else do you think I touched the statue of Anteros that's in the temple there?"

Zoey shot Andy a glare, and Karter paused, surprised at the boy's hostile tone. *I suppose if I were the one who had no choice but to sacrifice myself to a god, I'd be upset and lashing out too.* "Good," Karter said. "That means you already have an idea of how the city works. Remember, sundown is curfew, so the *astynomia* will be patrolling the streets. We must remain vigilant."

Andy rolled his eyes. "Yeah, we're aware. We've been to a couple different cities, including *Hephaestus* City. Remember?"

Karter didn't know what that was supposed to mean, so he figured he'd better be quiet unless someone else spoke first. Andy was clearly distressed about what they had to do and was taking it out on others.

"You remember where the temple is, right?" Zoey asked Andy.

"Nope," Andy said.

Zoey's jaw dropped. "How can you not remember? You walked there all by yourself after you ditched me and Prometheus in Jasmine's bakery!"

"I was in a trance when it happened. I'm guessing Anteros sort of took over my body to get me there. One minute, I was in the bakery. The next, I was at the temple. I figured that's what he'll do again."

Zoey huffed in reply, and Asteria shook her head at them. "Calm down, both of you. I know the temple's location."

"I've been to Aphrodite City more than once," Karter said. "I think I know where it is, too."

"Of course you do," Andy muttered.

It felt like forever before the four of them reached the outer rim of the city. They crept through its acres of farmland, hiding in the tall grass to stay out of sight of any *astynomia* who might be close. Before long they reached the first few neighborhoods of wood-and-stone houses. As they tiptoed through the communities, they nearly ran into a few *astynomia*, but they managed to dodge behind corners and into alleyways before the satyrs and centaurs could spot them.

Finally, they reached the *Agora*. A massive fountain with a statue of Aphrodite bursting from her clamshell towered over them as they entered the area. With its miles-long rows of pillared shops, cobblestone paths, and dirt roads, the *Agora* made up a decent portion of the *polis*. Unfortunately, the temple of Anteros was positioned near the other side of the *Agora*, close to the nicest area of the city, which was where the aristocrats lived and most of the temples could be found.

"Don't walk in the middle of the streets," Karter whispered to his companions. "Stay on the sidewalks near the shops in case any *astynomia* show up and we need to hide."

"Obviously," Andy hissed.

Karter allowed his red bolts to dim slightly, enough so he could see but they'd be less likely to detect, and the four of them crept as quickly and quietly as they could through the *Agora*. In several instances, Karter heard the clopping of hooves approaching them, and they were forced to conceal themselves within the shadows of vacant shops. They'd wait until the satyr or centaur *astynomia* passed, then sneak out of the buildings and hurry on their way.

Soon Andy had to stop. He leaned over and groaned, hugging the Bolt to his chest. "Are you okay?" Zoey whispered, concern lacing her tone.

He gritted his teeth. "The buzzing feeling. It's back."

"What does that mean?" Karter asked.

"It's Anteros," Asteria said.

Andy grunted. "Yup. Told you he'd help. He'll lead me to the temple." Andy stumbled forward. Karter, Zoey, and Asteria chased after him.

With Andy in an Anteros-induced trance, hiding from *astynomia* wasn't as easy. On the way to the temple, Karter had to drag Andy into the shadows to hide from several small groups of centaurs and satyrs.

Hours after arriving in the city, the group reached the temple at the far end of the *Agora*. Karter had only ever seen it in passing, but he knew they were in the right place. The temple was white and pillared and sat on a small hill. Thankfully, its location was in a more remote part of the *Agora*.

Andy halted. He groaned and pressed a palm against his forehead. He seemed to be coming to. "Andy?" Zoey touched his arm. "Are you okay?"

"Yes," he murmured. "Let's go in."

Asteria motioned at the temple. "Hurry inside. I'll wait here and keep watch."

Karter, Zoey, and Andy ran up the stairs and hastened through the entrance. Karter allowed his red electricity to brighten, illuminating the temple's interior, which was covered in a thick layer of dust. It looked as if it had been fashioned from gold, swirling designs carved into the floor, walls, and ceiling. Unlit torches lined the walls, leading all the way to the back of the building, where a statue of Anteros stood tall on a golden base. Like most depictions of Anteros that Karter had seen, the statue had feathered, butterfly-shaped wings identical to Andy's, a bow and arrow in hand.

"Whoa," Zoey said. "He kinda looks like you, Andy. Or you look like him, I guess."

Karter caught sight of something black on the floor in front of the statue and paced toward it. As he got closer, he realized it was a familiar pair of square-shaped eyeglasses. "Andy, aren't these yours?"

Andy walked forward tentatively. As he did so, the torches on the walls began to light with crackling flames, one by one and in sync with the boy's steps, as if they'd been anticipating his arrival. When he reached the glasses, he knelt and picked them up. "Yeah, these are mine. I shouldn't have left them, but I was so freaked out, I just kinda dipped. Doesn't look like anyone's been in here since then, though."

"No one has reason to be," Karter said. "The citizens don't worship gods who aren't around anymore. This place is for Aphrodite more than anything."

"You'd think she'd do a better job of keeping up with the place," Zoey remarked. She set the Trident aside and stepped up next to Andy. "Okay, what happens now? You just have to touch the statue, right?"

Andy stuffed his glasses into the pack holding the Helm, then rested the bag and Bolt before the statue. "Yeah, there shouldn't be much to it. Last time I froze and had some weird visions, though. If that happens again, don't freak out. I'm not sure you're supposed to wake me up, either. I think the visions start the convergence process."

He reached out to touch the statue's plaque, but Zoey grabbed his wrist before he could. "Wait." Andy paused, turning to her, and for several moments, they stared at one another. "I'm so sorry, Andy," she said, her voice shaking. "For . . . well, you know. Please, don't be mad anymore. I don't want to spend our last days fighting."

Andy frowned, and Karter swore he saw a tear trickling down the boy's cheek. He looked away, feeling as though he'd intruded on a private moment between them.

A pained cry sounded from outside, followed by a *thump*, like someone striking the ground. Karter spun toward the entrance.

"My, my, Zeus was right to send us here first," said the familiar, seductive voice of a young woman. Karter caught sight of long blonde hair and flashing opalescent irises as Violet, Daughter of Aphrodite sashayed into the temple. *Where is Asteria? Did Violet sneak up on her and kill her?* "I mean, I knew we were going to find you," Violet went on. "I just didn't realize how easy it was going to be, or that you were going to have all three objects of power ready for us to take, too."

Karter positioned himself in front of Zoey and Andy. "Don't make eye contact with her."

"We know the drill," Andy replied.

"Good." Karter summoned peridot electricity in his hands. "Andy, touch the statue. Zoey, stand back. I'll take care of this." Andy touched the plaque. He cried out, his body jerking as if by electric shock. Then he froze, still as a corpse.

Zoey, on the other hand, didn't follow Karter's instruction. She snatched the Helm from the bag and pulled it over her head, disappearing, and then the Trident vanished with her. Footfalls sounded all the way up to Karter's side. *I suppose I should have expected that,* he thought, refocusing on Violet. *She seems to have a knack for risking her own life for others'.*

Violet's eyes blazed in the dim light, and she glared at the spot where Zoey might have been. "Hmm. Is *that* girl the reason you didn't fall for me while you were on Olympus last?"

Karter's cheeks went hot. He had yet to determine why Violet's spell no longer worked on him, but he hadn't considered his feelings for Zoey to be the reason why.

Come to think of it, he hadn't considered *what* his feelings for Zoey were. He admired her courageousness, and he appreciated how she'd acted so selflessly when she'd tried saving him in Hephaestus City. The great kindness she'd shown him while they were locked up in jail, when he'd told her how he got his scar, had also touched him.

When it came to her, he wanted nothing more than to prove himself. To show her that he was sorry for hurting her, that he truly cared for her.

Dammit, he thought. *Maybe there's something to Violet's accusation.* But even if there was, he couldn't worry about it. There were more pressing matters at hand. "For someone who claims to despise me so much, you seem quite invested in my personal life," he said.

Violet strolled closer. "I know she's the reason the cheap imitation of Anteros didn't fall for me, but I thought you had better taste. Honestly, I don't see the appeal." She reached into her robes—presumably to grab one of her poisonous darts—and Karter hurled a bolt at her. She dodged the attack with ease.

"Try that again and I'll kill you, Son of Zeus," said another familiar voice. A young man's. "Although I suppose that's why we're here in the first place. To kill you. How fun that will be." Xander, Son of Hermes, with his smooth black hair and crooked smile, walked through the entrance, and Karter wondered where Layla, Daughter of Ares was. Had the gods discovered she'd helped him and Diana?

Two more figures appeared in the temple opening next, and Karter's heart dropped to his feet. *No*, he thought. *No, no, no.*

Impossibly tall and inhumanly formidable, Ares and Athena sauntered into the building. Ares didn't hold a weapon, as the super-strength he'd inherited from Zeus was usually enough for him to overcome his opponents in battle, but Athena brandished a spear and the special shield she shared with Zeus: the aegis.

At one time, Medusa's severed head had decorated the aegis, turning mortal opponents to stone with a single glance, but when the gods destroyed the world five hundred years ago, Zeus and Athena had decided to resurrect Medusa alongside the rest of the monsters slain in the old days. Consequently, they'd removed Medusa's head from the golden shield, then brought the gorgon back to life, and to this day, the aegis was bare.

Athena smiled wolfishly. "Where did Calliope's copycat go? I was really looking forward to meeting her." She jerked her head in Andy's direction. "This must be the boy who thinks he's Anteros." She studied him for a moment. "What's wrong with him? Why isn't he speaking or moving?"

"None of your business," Zoey said from beside Karter.

"I suppose we'll discover it for ourselves soon enough." Athena gestured at Ares with her spear. "This is Ares, God of War, and I am Athena, Goddess of Wisdom. Pleased to make your acquaintance."

"Hey, you're the one who turned Medusa into a gorgon because Poseidon assaulted her in your temple," Zoey said. "She could have lived and died as a normal person, but you stole that away from her. You made her a monster for a crime she didn't commit. Some 'goddess of wisdom' you are."

Athena's smile widened despite Zoey's insult. "Show your face if you're going to speak to me in such a manner, insolent girl. How do you know Medusa, anyway? Or have you only heard of her? I ask because a rumor has spread that she was slain, her head chopped clean from her body."

"The rumor's true," Zoey said. "She *was* slain. By me and Andy. She turned our friend's brother to stone, and he was determined to stop her from doing it to anyone else ever again, so we helped him find her, and we killed her." Karter's lips parted in surprise. He didn't know Zoey and Andy had encountered Medusa and lived to tell the tale.

"And where, perchance, might her severed head be? You must understand, now that she's dead again, I'd like it back." Athena tapped her shield with the tip of her spear. "It made such a fearsome ornamentation for my beloved aegis."

"As if I'd ever tell you," Zoey retorted.

Athena's smile faded, and she pointed her spear at Karter. "I was disappointed when Father informed us of the path you chose, little brother. I expected so much more from you. I'd hoped that after executing Diana, you would have stepped into Apollo's role, replacing him as our new twelfth Olympian."

"I'd hoped the same," Ares said. "But now we're stuck with the slimy King of the Underworld. Thanks a lot."

Karter conjured more green bolts, preparing to strike, although he did want to try one thing before engaging in a fight. Considering Athena's and Ares's reputations in battle, it was unlikely he'd make it out of a clash with them alive. But maybe, just maybe, he wouldn't die tonight, if only he could manage to sway them to join his side—at least for the time being. If not, perhaps he could stall them until Andy came to. Then they'd make their escape.

"You don't have to be stuck with Hades," Karter began. "You don't have to be stuck with any of the other gods or continue to deal with their corruption either." He motioned at Ares. "I know you hate the way Father is constantly unfaithful to your mother, Ares. He's made Hera cry more times than you can count because of his affairs. If you turn on Father, you could finally make him pay for all he's done to Hera. You could finally avenge her heartbreak."

He motioned at Athena next. "And Athena, I know you're the wisest god in the pantheon. Not Father, as he likes to believe. I know you'd make a far better leader than him, and I also know you crave his title, because you tried to overthrow him in the old days with some of the other Olympians. The only reason all of you didn't succeed is because Thetis overheard you arguing about who should rule in Zeus's place and summoned Briareus to save him. But if you tried to overthrow him again—if you worked with me and the Chosen Two—you could become the pantheon's new ruler." He took a deep breath. "Join us. Fight on our side. In return, you'll both get something you want."

Athena and Ares shared a look, then threw their heads back and howled with laughter.

They chortled for a long while, before finally Ares wiped a tear from his eye. "What we want is to stay alive. To not fade away."

"I'd love to lead the pantheon," Athena added. "But what I'd love even more is to not succumb to eternal sleep. Enough nonsense, now. We have a proposition for you."

Karter glanced over his shoulder at Andy. The boy was frozen, his hand on the plaque.

Since they won't entertain the idea of joining us, I'll have to continue stalling for as long as possible. He faced them again. "What is it?"

"To come quietly," Ares said. "To give us the Helm, Trident, and Lightning Bolt, and to let us take the Chosen Two without a struggle. Then, to let us kill you. Despite how angry everyone is with you, we'll make your end swift and painless. But only if you surrender now."

Karter bared his teeth, the electricity crackling in his palms. He looked back at Andy one last time—still motionless—then turned to his godly half-siblings and shook his head. "No. Never."

Athena's expression hardened. "You must know, I take no pleasure in this. I've always cared for you, more than I do for any of the other demigods." She stepped back. "Go ahead, Ares."

Zoey must have slammed the Trident against the ground. A quake rumbled through the floor, sending Violet and Xander flailing backward. Athena barely budged, and the force didn't affect Ares at all. The God of War barreled straight toward Karter.

Karter chucked a bolt at Ares, and Ares raised a hand and blocked the attack with his forearm cuff. The lightning deflected and blasted through the ceiling. Karter threw his other bolt, but Ares redirected it.

The god slammed into Karter, armor colliding with his skull. He stumbled backward to the floor. Pain pounded through his head and neck. For a moment, his vision went black.

"Karter!" Zoey cried.

As Zoey said his name, his sight returned, but it was blurry. Ares and Athena loomed over him. At the entrance, Violet and Xander climbed to their feet. While Karter fought Ares and Athena, the demigods would surely go after Zoey and Andy.

Skull throbbing, Karter reached toward Violet and Xander. Electricity sparked in his fingers. If he could just strike one or both of them with lightning, Zoey and Andy would be—

Ares seized Karter by the arms and thrust him into the right-side wall of the temple. Instead of hitting the wall, Karter smashed through it spine-first. The sound of rocks fragmenting and crashing against each other exploded all around him, sharp pain searing through him. His vision went black again as he tumbled to the ground outside.

He came to a stop in the grass and blinked hard. Slowly, his sight returned. His eyelashes were coated with dust, and blurry stars twinkled in the night sky above.

He tried to breathe but couldn't, the wind knocked out of him. A few more tries, and he managed to inhale a bit of air. With it came grime and chunks of stone. He coughed up the debris and wiped the filth from his face.

Gasping, Karter forced himself to roll over and face the temple. Ares's giant red hands poked out of a hole in the wall—presumably the one he'd made when he'd flung Karter outside—and he tore at it, making it bigger and bigger until it was roughly the size of the building's entrance. He and Athena stalked through it toward Karter.

Karter clambered to his feet, his head spinning. Ares and Athena reached him. Ares balled a fist and punched him in the ribs. The force stole the air from his lungs, his ribs *craaack*ing. He flew backward.

He crashed into the grass at the bottom of the hill. His vision faded between red and black. "Too bad, it looks like he's still breathing," Ares said as he and Athena gazed down at Karter from the top of the hill. "I thought for sure that would kill the little pest. Would you like to finish him off?"

Athena sighed. "Would I like to? No. Will I?

Yes." She raised her spear and headed down.

Karter forced himself to stand, blinding pain shooting through his body from his shoulders, spine, and ribs. *I'm sure I've broken something*, he thought, groaning as he clutched his side. *Probably multiple things.* He glanced up at Athena. She drew near. *I need to go where they can't touch me. My strength is no match for Ares's.*

Focusing on his gift of flight, Karter leapt into the air. It's what he should have done in the first place since neither Ares nor Athena could fly; he just hadn't wanted to abandon Zoey and Andy. His bones ached, agony racking his body, but he managed to get high enough that Ares and Athena couldn't grab him.

Athena narrowed her eyes into slits up at Karter. She reared back her spear and launched it at him. He lurched to the side. The weapon grazed his shin and plunged toward a dirt road below. Pinpricks of pain stung from where the spear broke skin, blood dribbling out of the scrape.

Athena whistled, and dread flooded Karter's senses. *A pegasus signal. They must have flown here.* Sure enough, two snow-white pegasi neighed in the distance, soaring toward Ares and Athena. They swooped down, and the gods mounted them.

Karter conjured green lightning in his hands. He hurled one bolt at Athena, the other at Ares. Athena deflected the attack with the aegis, while Ares used an arm cuff to do the same. The bolts shot into the sky and sputtered out. *I'm going to have to kill the pegasi, or Ares and Athena are going to kill me.* The gods steered the pegasi into the air toward Karter.

Heart pounding, gut turning, Karter created more electricity and pitched the bolts at the charging pegasi. Athena directed her pegasus out of the way in time, but Ares was a second too slow. The peridot bolt hit Ares's pegasus.

The lightning crackled and popped around the winged creature. It cried out, and Ares did too as the electricity traveled up from the pegasus to his body. The scent of scorched hair and skin filled the sky. Ares and his pegasus plummeted toward the ground.

Three centaur and two satyr *astynomia* clopped out from a nearby building. "What's going on?" one of the centaurs shouted at Athena. They must have realized she was a goddess, their eyes going big. They bowed their heads in respect.

"The treacherous Son of Zeus has infiltrated your city," Athena said, pointing at Karter. "We've come to kill him, but he's resisting.

Shoot him down."

Somewhere in the temple, a girl screamed, and Karter's stomach clenched. Was that Zoey? What were Violet and Xander doing to her? Were they hurting Andy, too?

Two of the centaurs and one of the satyrs began shooting arrows at him. He weaved between the projectiles as they careened toward him, narrowly avoiding the sharp tips.

Another scream. This time, there was no doubt who it belonged to. *Zoey.* Karter summoned more peridot lightning and shot it at Athena's pegasus, but he didn't wait to see if he'd hit the creature. Ignoring the excruciating pain that seared through him, he streaked toward the temple. More arrows whistled through the air, missing him by a hair's breadth, and he barreled into the building through the hole in the wall.

What he saw next made his blood boil. Andy was still frozen, his hand on the statue's plaque, the Helm and Trident on the floor behind him; Xander must have used his super-speed to knock Zoey's weapons away, as he often did to opponents. Zoey lay on the floor, on her back. Her feet were twisted at odd angles, her ankles clearly broken, and Xander straddled her, dagger raised. Violet stood a short distance from them, a sneer on her lips as she watched Zoey squirm.

Zoey tried hitting Xander and wriggling away from him, but he held firm. "Andy, wake up!" she shrieked. "Please, wake up!"

Xander laughed with deranged glee, slashing his blade across Zoey's cheeks in a few swift motions. She yelled in pain. "Aw, did that hurt, too?" he said. "Just wait until I gouge out your eyes and cut off the hand you have left, you disfigured bitch. For whatever reason, Zeus says we can't kill you, but that doesn't mean we can't torture you."

Suddenly, Karter didn't hurt anymore. The pain in his shoulders, his spine, his ribs, his shin, all gone, replaced with white-hot rage that numbed him to the core.

No one, *no one* was going to harm her like that and get away with it.

In a flash Karter was upon Xander, tackling him to the ground. Xander lost his hold on the dagger, and they slid across the floor, away from Zoey.

Karter grasped Xander by the throat and trapped him in a straddle, then slammed the back of his skull against the floor. "Do it for real this time, coward," Xander rasped. "Kill me. Snap my neck, you spineless son of a—"

Karter snarled. He summoned peridot

electricity in his palms.

Xander convulsed as green lightning crackled through him. A second later it dissipated, and he stilled. His jaw went slack, the light leaving his eyes, smoke curling up from his lifeless form.

Karter stared down at the dead young man beneath him. The stench of cooked flesh assaulted his nostrils, and the gravity of what he'd done washed over him. *This is the first time I've ever killed a person with green lightning.*

It probably won't be the last.

Zoey yelling his name over and over snapped him from his thoughts. "Karter! KarterKarterKarter! Look out!"

He glanced back and was met with a dart careening toward him. He ducked beneath it, and it whizzed through the air above his head.

"*You killed him!*" Violet screamed. She grabbed another dart and charged toward Karter, tears streaming down her cheeks. "*You killed Xander!*"

She brought the dart down like a knife. Karter scrambled to the side, narrowly avoiding the attack. He raised a hand and, before he could think of which color electricity to summon, conjured some and shot it at her.

There was a flash of gold, then a sizzling noise. Violet crashed backward to the floor and howled in pain—a horrible, animalistic sound. Heart pounding, Karter lowered his hand, stood up, and stepped toward her.

She lay sprawled on the ground, shaking and crying, and Karter's scar throbbed with the memory of old pain as he realized what he'd done to her. Her face and neck were charred, blackened with lightning burns. *She's unrecognizable.* Still trembling, she let out a hoarse whimper and closed her eyes. *Is she dead?*

He didn't have time to check. Zoey needed him. He rushed to her side. A mixture of blood and tears spilled down her cheeks, and her ankles were definitely broken. She used her hand and elbows to try and sit up, but there was no way she was going to be able to stand, let alone walk. Karter would have to carry her, because they had to get out of here. *Now.*

"Are you all right?" she asked him.

He almost laughed. Had she seriously just asked him whether he was all right? When Xander had forced her to the floor? Begun mutilating her? "Don't worry about me."

"Ares put you through a wall."

"And Xander broke your ankles. Here, let me help you." As gently as possible, he circled his arms around her waist and pulled her to his chest. She wrapped her arms around his neck and rested a cheek against his shoulder. As he climbed to his feet, she sucked in a sharp breath, and his brow furrowed. "Am I hurting you?"

"No," she said, but her nails digging into his back suggested otherwise.

Doing his best not to aggravate Zoey's injuries, Karter hastened toward Andy. Whether the boy's "visions" had finished didn't matter. Karter was going to yank him away from that statue, and they were going to leave. If they had to, they'd find another way for Andy to reconnect with Anteros.

Karter readjusted himself so he could hold Zoey with one arm. He reached toward Andy with the other, then snatched the boy by the back of his robes and jerked him away from the statue of Anteros. He thought for sure that would wake Andy up, since he wasn't touching the statue anymore, but the boy didn't even blink. He just stood there, staring forward blankly.

"Andy," Zoey said. "Wake. Up." Nothing happened.

"I'll have to grab the objects of power myself," Karter said. "I'll carry Andy, too."

Zoey stiffened in his grip. "You can't do that. Touching them will suck away your life force."

"I briefly touched the Helm when I was

fighting you outside Hephaestus City," he replied. "It hurt, but I'm still here, and it probably only took off a few years of my life. Maybe, if the objects are in the bag, it won't be so—"

"No. You could die. We can't risk it."

"Then what do you suggest?"

"Set me down," she said. "I'll pack them up, and I'll do my best to make sure the bag doesn't touch you." He did as she asked, and despite her limited mobility, she stuffed the objects into the bag surprisingly quickly. The Trident and Bolt stuck out of the pack, but it would have to do.

With one arm Karter scooped her up by the waist. The top of the Bolt grazed his neck momentarily, his flesh stinging as though hundreds of needles were pricking his flesh, and he hissed in pain.

Zoey gasped, yanking the bag as far from him as she could. "I'm fine," he insisted. With his free hand, he hoisted Andy over his shoulder next, on the side of his body Zoey wasn't pressed against, then pivoted to run out of the temple.

Arrows *whoosh*ed in front of Karter and his companions, and he staggered backward. The three centaur and two satyr *astynomia* from earlier stood in the jagged hole in the wall. Some of them nocked more arrows, while the rest brandished other weapons.

"Stop, all of you." Athena's voice echoed from the entrance.

Karter looked that way. Athena appeared in the opening. Either Karter hadn't hit her with his lightning, or she'd regenerated almost immediately. She had her spear again; it dripped with golden ichor, and Karter spotted Asteria's unmoving figure sprawled out on the steps behind her. *Asteria must have regenerated and tried defending us, but Athena killed her once more. How are we going to escape?*

"Don't shoot the Son of Zeus," Athena said. "He's holding the Chosen Two of the Dreaded Prophecy. We can't risk killing them."

"Why not?" one of the centaurs asked, baffled. "If we simply kill them, they'll no longer be a threat to—"

"You will do as I command." Athena pointed her spear at the *astynomia*. "You will not question the gods." They lowered their weapons, and she stepped forward. "Put down the Chosen Two and the objects of power, Karter. It's over."

Karter glanced back and forth between Athena and the *astynomia*, tightening his grip on Zoey and Andy. He wasn't going to let them go—not a chance in Tartarus. But no matter which way he ran, the three of them were trapped. *What are we supposed to do?*

"The ceiling," Zoey whispered. "Can you use your strength to break through it? Or is it too much, with me and Andy and your injuries?"

Karter set his jaw. It didn't matter if he was on the brink of death. He was going to get Zoey and Andy out of here. He'd have to leave Asteria behind, but he was sure she'd understand. After all, they had to ensure Zoey, Andy, and the objects of power were safe above everything else.

"Hold on," he told Zoey, and leapt into the air, flying toward the ceiling as fast as he could. Once he knew Andy wasn't going to fall off his shoulder, he raised that arm above his head and balled his fist, summoning every bit of strength he had left.

"Karter!" Athena screeched. "Get back here, before I tear you limb from limb!"

Karter reached the ceiling, his fist colliding with stone, and time seemed to slow. He watched his knuckles compress, the bones fracturing beneath his skin as his hand broke through the roof.

Cracks spiderwebbed from the hole Karter had created. He shoved his fist through more rock, creating an opening large enough for them to fly through, and debris began to crumble around them.

Zoey buried her face in Karter's shoulder. He coughed up rubble as bits of it pelted his head, his eyes watering as dust rained down.

Finally, the hole looked big enough, and Karter blinked hard. His vision was blurry, tears gushing down his face as his eyes tried to clear themselves of debris, but still he pressed on. He soared through the opening, out into the clear night sky.

Something seized Karter by the foot, stopping him from flying any higher. He glanced back, caught sight of silver curls. *Athena.* She'd climbed up onto the roof.

Karter kicked at Athena, tried to wriggle free, but she had an iron grip. She dragged Karter down. The force made him lose his hold of Zoey and Andy. They tumbled away—Zoey crying out as the bag of objects flew from her hand, Andy not reacting at all. The Helm, Trident, and Bolt clattered onto the rooftop, scattering in different directions, and Athena yanked Karter down again. He nose-dived into stone.

Head spinning, he clambered around to face Athena, conjuring peridot electricity in his palms. However, he was met with the golden metal of the aegis. The shield slammed into the side of his skull, and then he knew no more.

REALIZE

Zoey watched in horror as Athena hit Karter over the head with her shield, as he fell still on the rooftop.

"Karter!" She tried to army crawl toward him. The stabbing pain in her ankles was almost too much to bear. It reverberated through her legs and feet, but she couldn't sit back and watch Athena hurt him. "Karter, wake up!"

He didn't wake up. Athena raised her shield and struck him again. *She's going to kill him*, Zoey thought. *She's going to bash his brains in, and there's nothing I can do. I can't walk, my voice-powers stopped working . . .*

When Karter had betrayed Zoey in Hephaestus City, she'd honestly believed she no longer cared whether he lived or died.

But now, as he lay helpless on the roof of this temple, as death itself loomed over him, Zoey realized she did, in fact, care whether he lived or died. She realized she cared very much.

Athena brought down the shield once more, surely to make the killing blow. "*No!*" Zoey screamed.

Something snaked out from behind Athena—something long and green and thorny—and looped itself around the goddess's throat.

Athena's eyes went wide. She dropped the shield, and it clattered to the side.

The goddess clawed at whatever was around her neck, but more of them slithered out of the darkness to reinforce the choke hold. Some of them even wrapped around her wrists, her arms, her waist, wrenching her backward. Where the thorns met her flesh, golden liquid blossomed, dribbling out from her new cuts.

Athena struggled, then went limp.

A new goddess rose out from the hole Karter

had punched through the ceiling, dozens of twisting, curling vines carrying her up into the air. Her skin glistened with sweat, her breaths ragged, her face stone cold as she gazed down at Athena's body.

"Persephone," Zoey said in a daze. She could hardly believe the Queen of the Underworld was here. "You—you followed us."

Persephone's hard expression softened ever so slightly. She gulped down several breaths. "I told you I would. It's a good thing I was keeping an eye on you, too." She motioned at Karter. "If I hadn't been—if I hadn't known you were in danger and teleported to your location—he'd be dead. You and Andy would be captured, and the gods would have the Helm, Trident, and Lightning Bolt again."

A few feet ahead of Zoey, Karter groaned, and her pulse quickened. He raised the hand he hadn't used to punch through a ceiling and cupped the side of his head, and she said his name, crawling the rest of the way to him.

She tried to sit up, as she needed to turn herself around and properly examine him. Athena had hit him *hard*. He had to have a concussion at least, and head injuries were no joke. But the sharp, stabbing pain in her ankles grew worse, shooting up and down her legs and feet. She lost her balance, her cheek smacking against the rooftop.

Because of how Karter was lying, and because of how Zoey had fallen, she had an upside-down view of his face. It wasn't perfect, but it was going to have to do.

He rubbed his head, groaning again, and opened his eyes. They locked on hers right away, his expression drawn in concern. "What happened?" he asked. "Are you all right?"

"Athena's dead for now, and I'm fine." She inched closer to him, to make sure he was okay, and he blinked in surprise, scooting back a bit. "Hold still," she snapped. "I need to look at your eyes, to check for signs of a brain injury. If you have one, it could be really serious." She reached over to hold his cheek steady, gently resting her fingers on the mottled flesh of the lightning scar on the right side of his face, and leaned in to study him.

Oh, yeah. He was out of it. His pupils were crazy dilated, which could have been because it was nighttime, but his eyelids were droopy too. He *had* to have a concussion. Maybe something worse. They needed to get him to Diana, and fast.

She pulled her hand away from his face. Their gazes locked once more, and she realized just how close they were. So close, if she moved only a couple of inches forward, their noses might touch.

Her heart skipped as she recalled what Violet had asked him before Xander, Athena, and Ares had shown up. *"Is that girl the reason you didn't fall for me while you were on Olympus last?"*

What are the odds that Andy accuses me of having feelings for Karter, and one night later, Violet accuses Karter of having feelings for me?

Zoey wiggled backward to put more space between them. *It's probably just a weird coincidence. I shouldn't worry about it, especially not at a time like this, when Andy and I are about to be trapped in our own minds and Karter will be dead.*

He doesn't even know he's supposed to die. When we get out of here, I should tell him.

"We need to leave," she said.

Slowly, Karter began climbing to his feet, but when he spotted Persephone standing before them, he yelped and tumbled backward.

"It's okay," Zoey assured him. "At least, for now it is. Persephone—she followed us here, and she took down Athena. She saved you. She saved all of us."

"As I told you before, I want to help you," Persephone said. "And I'm going to continue following you until you understand that I'm on your side. I know you hate me for what I did to Spencer, and your opinion of me doesn't have to change. In fact, I'm not exactly fond of any of you, but I still hope we can work together to defeat the Olympians." She stared at something off to the side of the temple. "No matter your decision, though, you really should be on your way. The *astynomia* I knocked unconscious are stirring, and I'm sure more will be coming soon. It also won't take long for Athena and Ares to regenerate."

Karter stood, rubbing the side of his head with his good hand some more. The other was undoubtedly broken.

He knelt and placed his arm with the unbroken hand around Zoey's waist, and she wrapped her arms around his neck. Grunting in effort, he pulled her to his chest. The pain in her ankles flared, and she winced, biting back a cry. "You're sure you're okay?" he said.

"I'm sure, yes." If she hadn't been hurting so bad, she would have laughed at him. Seriously, what was his deal?

Someone gasped behind them, and Karter swung around. Zoey craned her head and saw Andy had finally awoken. He sat up quickly, taking in their surroundings, his chest heaving.

Relief flooded Zoey. "Andy!" She had to

resist the urge to hop out of Karter's grasp and run over to hug him. When he'd been out of it for all that time and she'd been stuck on the floor, she'd been so scared. So afraid that something was going to happen to him while she couldn't protect him and he couldn't protect himself.

"What happened?" Andy asked. "I reconnected with Anteros, but why are we up here? Karter, you look like shit. Zoey, your face, your ankles . . ." He trailed off, staring at the space behind them, then leapt to his feet and seized the Lightning Bolt. "Persephone! What the hell? Did you follow us?"

"I told you I would," Persephone replied. Andy brandished the weapon and stalked toward the goddess.

"Andy, stop," Zoey said. "It's okay, sort of. Persephone saved Karter's life, and she saved us from being captured." There was commotion to the left, up in the nicer part of the city past the *Agora*, and she looked over. A bunch of satyrs and centaurs were galloping toward the temple. "I'll explain more later, but right now, we have to go."

"Asteria hasn't regenerated, so we'll have to travel on foot," Karter said.

"Unless Persephone can transport us out of

the city," she replied.

Persephone shook her head. "I'm afraid not. It takes a great deal of power for a god to teleport such long distances. Unless you make me a hefty sacrifice right now, I need more time to recuperate."

"There's nothing suitable for an offering close to us," Karter said. "Can you at least carry Asteria with your vines?"

"Yes. I can carry Zoey too, if you'd like."

Karter tensed. "No, I've got her. Andy, you grab the objects of power."

Andy shot Persephone a suspicious look. He gathered up the items, stuffed them into the bag, and slung it over his shoulder. "Let's go."

Karter readjusted his grip on Zoey and flew to the ground, and Persephone manipulated her vines to lower herself and Andy down. Then she picked up Asteria with the vegetation and, together, everyone ran. Karter led the way through the *Agora*, Zoey kept her eyes peeled for any *astynomia* that might be creeping in the shadows, and Andy and Persephone sprinted close behind them.

For several minutes, the coast was clear. Zoey thought they might escape without any more trouble. But the hope she had for an easy escape was dashed as they rounded a corner to start down another street. Brilliant white light flared before them, and Karter stopped dead. "It's a god!" he yelled.

As the light blazed, Persephone rested Asteria on the road, and Karter and Andy hastened over to one of the shops on the side of the street. Karter set Zoey down on the cobblestone path while Andy dropped the bag of magical objects next to her.

Snatching up the Bolt, Andy briefly glanced at Zoey. She opened her mouth to speak, but before she could say anything, he pivoted and ran toward Persephone.

Karter followed Andy, and Zoey retrieved the Helm from their bag and pulled it over her head. Chills charged through her as it turned her invisible. She grabbed the Trident too, just to be safe.

The white light faded, revealing Ares. His breathing was labored, though not nearly as heavy as Persephone's had been when she'd arrived. Probably because he hadn't teleported as far as she had to reach them. Zoey guessed he'd woken up, seen them running, and anticipated which direction they'd go, then transported there in a flash.

Andy raised the Bolt, Karter conjured green lightning in his good palm, and Persephone summoned more vines. Zoey's hand twitched, and she flexed her fingers around the handle of the Trident. The worst part about her broken ankles was that she was stuck on the sidelines, unable to help her companions.

"I knew you couldn't be trusted," Ares said to Persephone. "We should have left you in Tartarus where you belong. Let you rot with Apollo and Prometheus forever."

Zoey gasped. *Prometheus is in Tartarus?*

"You put Prometheus in that hellscape?" Andy shook with fury. Electricity sizzled up and down the Bolt, and clouds began to form in the sky above them.

Ares laughed. "What did you expect us to do with him? That's where we're going to put you and the girl, after all."

Zoey's bottom lip quivered, her eyes filling with tears as she imagined Prometheus suffering for eternity in the fiery pit. Prometheus, who had a great-great-granddaughter right here in Aphrodite City. Jasmine was counting on him to return from this war victorious so they could spend their days together—so she'd have a family again.

Now that would never happen.

The Bolt looked as though it was vibrating in Andy's hands, a high-pitched squeal sounding from it. *"I'll kill you for that!"*

Golden light flashed in the clouds. Ares raised an arm above his head. Lightning shot from the sky, straight toward the god.

In an instant, the electricity zapped Ares, but rather than incinerating him, it only hit him—no, it hit his arm cuff—and rebounded into the sky.

Andy's jaw dropped, and Ares smirked. "Don't you know I'm a Son of Zeus, Chosen One? I might not be able to create lightning, like Karter can, but when given the right tools, I can deflect it."

He stomped toward Andy. Persephone lunged into Ares's path, launching her vines toward him. As the greenery neared him, he grabbed it in his burly hands and thrust it aside, sending Persephone and her vines somersaulting across the street.

Karter shot his peridot bolts at Ares. As Ares redirected them into the sky, Karter soared toward the god. Karter prepared to kick Ares, but the immortal grabbed Karter's foot and flung him into the dirt. All the while, Zoey watched, helpless. If she shook the ground with the Trident, she'd knock Andy over too.

Andy raised the Bolt again, surely trying to conjure more lightning, but Ares backhanded the object from Andy's hands and seized the boy by the collar.

Narrowing his eyes, Ares dragged Andy toward himself. Andy struggled in his grasp, kicking and punching him, but he didn't even flinch.

Zoey brought the Trident down, sending quakes through the earth. She hoped to at least knock Ares off balance, but the tremors did nothing. Ares widened his stance, still examining Andy. Was Zoey seeing things, or had his expression morphed from fury to confusion?

"Let him go, Ares." Karter struggled to stand. "You need to kill me, remember?"

The god ignored Karter to continue staring at Andy. "What're you lookin' at?" Andy said. "Are we gonna fight or what?"

Persephone jumped to her feet and hurried toward Andy and Ares, conjuring more vines. She manipulated the plants to wrap around Ares's neck.

Golden blood trickled from where the thorns dug into Ares's skin, his lips parting as the vines tightened around his throat, but he remained focused on Andy. "Anteros, my—my son," he choked out. "I thought you'd—faded away. What is—the meaning of this?"

"No, no. I'm Andy, not Anteros. I'm not

your so—"

"Nonsense." The muscles in Ares's neck bulged as Persephone continued strangling him. "Your divine essence—it's dim. But I—I see it now."

"Listen to me," Andy said frantically. "I'm not your son, but you're right. Your son is here. His divine essence is inside of me. And he's inside of me because Zeus put him there. Anteros found out about something Zeus did to Calliope, and Zeus banished him into my body 516 years ago! Sixteen years before the Storm! That's why I'm part of the Prophecy. Syrena, her blood sacrifice brought me back to life. You should be mad at Zeus, not me! You should help me!"

Ares bared his teeth, his body flaring with brilliant white light. Persephone's eyes went wide, and she allowed her vines to fall as the glow spread into Andy. "We're getting to—the bottom of this—immediately," Ares said.

"No!" Karter hurtled toward them, but it was too late. He stumbled straight through the blaze.

The light dwindled, and Zoey blinked in disbelief. Andy and Ares were gone.

When the white glare eventually faded from Andy's vision, he found himself in the largest, most luxurious bedroom he'd ever seen.

Andy tried flapping his wings and grimaced at how they ached. They'd been sore since he'd reconnected with Anteros, but even if they were working again, he couldn't fly away. Ares had him in custody.

He took in his surroundings. The room appeared exactly how he would imagine an ancient-Greek-themed suite in Vegas to look, complete with polished white-and-gold columns and walls. Stars shimmered outside the wide, arched windows, illuminating the scarlet blankets and pillows arranged just so atop the perfectly placed marble furniture.

On the left side of the room, there was something that looked like a giant Jacuzzi. Stairs led down into a bubbling pool of glowing blue water, and splashing around in that pool was . . .

Oh, God. It was a woman. An absolutely

stunning and very naked woman. Her wavy golden hair fanned out in the water around her, her opalescent irises flashing when her gaze fell on Andy. *Wait a second. Violet kinda looks like her, and Violet's a Daughter of Aphrodite. Is she Aphrodite? Anteros's mom?*

Just then, the familiar voice of a god sounded in his mind. *"Of course she's our mother, you fool. How could you not recognize her?"*

Anteros! Andy thought. *How'd you show up so fast?*

"I can't be sure," Anteros replied. *"But I suppose it could have something to do with the fact that Father is touching us. Since he's done so, I've felt stronger, similarly to when Circe used her magic on us and it strengthened me."*

I guess that makes sense. Do you know where he brought me?

"Yes. We're on Olympus, in his bedchamber."

Crap. I gotta get outta here.

"No! Listen to me. You must stay here. If you let me take over, I can explain to Mother and Father all that's happened, and they'll help us however they can. They're the most selfless, loving parents in the universe, and—"

Are you insane? They helped decimate humanity. There's no way they'd wanna join our side for the right reasons. I have to get back to Zoey, anyway. She still needs to reconnect with Calliope.

Anteros kept talking, saying something about how they could awaken Calliope later, but Andy tuned the god out. He glanced around the bedchamber, plotting out his escape route.

"Ares," Aphrodite said. "Glad to see you back so soon. Why don't you drop off the cheap imitation of our son at the dungeons, and we can have a little fun before we summon Zeus to let him know you and Athena were the ones to succeed? I imagine she's already imprisoned the copy of Calliope. Does she also have the Helm, Trident, and Lightning Bolt?"

"I haven't the slightest clue what Athena is doing," Ares spat. "For now, just forget about the girl and the magical objects. We don't have them."

"Why did you come back, then? No one was supposed to return until one of the parties completed the mission."

"I'm afraid we have a far more pressing matter at hand, my love. One we need to address immediately."

Aphrodite knit her brow. She stood in the pool—she had to be over six feet tall—and climbed up the stairs. "What are you talking about?"

"Come here. Look at this. Look at *him*."

Aphrodite gave Ares a suspicious look, then

fetched a towel, wrapped it around her body, and flounced toward them. As she drew closer, Andy's heart raced. He knew he was the "pressing matter" Ares was talking about, but how the god planned to "address" him, he couldn't be sure.

When Aphrodite was just a few feet away from them, she halted in her tracks. "How—how can this be?"

"What I want to know is how you missed this?" Ares released his hold on Andy, and Andy tumbled to the floor. "You said he wasn't our son, but he obviously is. The divine essence is practically seeping through his pores, growing stronger every second."

"He didn't resemble Anteros when I saw him. I would have told you if he had."

They continued bickering, and Andy climbed to his feet and began flapping his wings. *Now's my chance to escape. Hopefully this works.* Despite the pain, Andy flapped harder, then leapt into the air. By some miracle, he stayed aloft.

"Hey!" Ares cried. "Get back here!"

Aphrodite wagged a finger up at him. "We aren't finished discussing this!"

"We need to stay with Mother and Father!" Anteros insisted. *"Don't do this, please!"*

The three of them kept on yelling at Andy,

but he wasn't listening to a word they said. He reached the nearest window, then soared out into the open night sky.

CHAPTER TWELVE

GONE

Zoey leaned forward where she sat, unable to believe what she'd just witnessed. Ares had called Andy his son, had said that they were going to "get to the bottom of this." They'd lit up like an atomic bomb, and then they'd disappeared.

In the middle of the road, where Andy and Ares had been, Karter knelt, punching the ground with his good hand. "No!" he yelled, his fist colliding with the dirt again and again. "No no no!"

He's gone, Zoey thought. *Andy's really gone. Ares teleported him away.*

Persephone manipulated her vines, making them gather up Asteria's body and the Master Lightning Bolt, then plodded toward Karter. "Don't hurt yourself further. Striking the ground won't bring him back. What we need to do is leave this place, return to your companions, and formulate a plan to retrieve him."

"They're going to put him in Tartarus," Karter said.

"No," Persephone replied. "Ares seemed to believe Andy was truly Anteros. Luckily, Anteros is a child-of-Ares by Aphrodite, and the offspring they share are their favorites because they've been lovers for so long. Until Zeus discovers Ares is harboring Andy, he shouldn't be in danger."

Karter stopped hitting the ground and looked up at Persephone. "Do you know where Ares took him? Since you tracked his location before?"

"I'll try to see where he is, but if Ares is using enchantments to cloak him, I won't be able to find him." She raised her hands and closed her eyes, and Zoey held her breath. "I can't see him.

Like I said, we need to get to your camp and compose a plan to retrieve him."

Zoey released her breath and swallowed hard. She felt like vomiting. She dropped the Trident and pulled off the Helm, then covered her mouth with her hand and choked back a sob. She wanted to break down, to let her emotions run wild, but she had to keep herself together. Losing her mind wasn't going to bring Andy back.

Karter stood up. "Persephone, give the Bolt to Zoey so she can pack up and carry the magical items. You'll carry Asteria, and I'll carry Zoey. Let's get out of here."

"Wouldn't it be easier for you if I carried everyone, everything?" Persephone asked. "You're awfully hurt."

"You might have saved my life, but that doesn't mean I trust you," he said.

Clopping hooves sounded in the distance, and Zoey snapped to attention. "More *astynomia*. They probably saw the light and heard the commotion. Let's go."

Persephone gave Zoey the Bolt, and she packed up the magical objects. Karter picked her up with his unbroken hand and hastened farther into the *Agora*. Persephone followed them with Asteria secure in her vines.

As they ran through the city, no one said a word. Rage rolled off Karter in droves, his body tense, and Zoey couldn't shake the sick feeling in her stomach. She prayed that Persephone was right, that Andy was safe for now. If he were put in Tartarus, Zoey wasn't sure she'd be able to go on.

Not only that, but Andy was her link to Calliope. The only reason she'd connected with the goddess in the first place was because after he'd touched the statue of Anteros, he'd touched Zoey, sending an electric shock through her and "awakening" Calliope. How in the world was she supposed to connect with Calliope now? Maybe she could touch a statue or relic related to the goddess, but that meant they'd probably have to sneak into another city.

Soon Asteria regenerated. At first, the Titan goddess misunderstood the situation, thinking that Persephone had taken her captive and was chasing Zoey and Karter. She tried to attack Persephone, and they had to stop and catch her up on everything that had happened while she was out. As they recounted the events to her, she glittered around the edges.

"How could I have let this happen?" she said. "I was supposed to keep you safe while we infiltrated the city. I've become so weak in such a short time." She turned to Persephone with tears in her eyes. "Thank you for helping them." She offered to fly them the rest of the way, but Karter insisted she needed to conserve her energy. Instead, Zoey handed her the bag holding the Helm, Trident, and Bolt, and they continued running.

It took what felt like hours to reach the forest outside Aphrodite City. By then, Karter was hot to the touch. He panted, steam curling off his skin. "I have to—lie down," he said between breaths. "My body is—starting to—burn up." He set Zoey against a tree and collapsed beside her.

"We must get back to camp," Asteria began. "We need to get you to Diana so she can heal you, and then we'll go after Andy. I'm just not sure whether I have enough power to teleport us straight there, even with a sacrifice. Persephone, would you be able to? Do you know where the nymph camp is?"

"If these two"—Persephone gestured at Zoey and Karter—"make an offering to me, and so long as the Daughter of Apollo is at the camp, then yes, I'll be able to teleport you."

Asteria gathered roots and berries for a proper offering for Persephone, and Zoey couldn't help but reflect on how strange it felt to be working alongside the goddess who'd murdered Spencer. How she could have stolen the objects of power from the group back when they fought her at camp, but how she hadn't. Also, how she'd saved them from Athena and handed over the Bolt without question when Karter asked her to.

Maybe Persephone was telling the truth. Maybe she really was on their side. She wasn't a good person—she didn't seem to want to change for the better, nor did she seem to regret her past decisions—but maybe whether she was good or bad didn't matter at this point. Maybe they should accept her help all the same.

Once Asteria had collected the necessary supplies, she helped Zoey start a fire, and Zoey made the sacrifice by herself since Karter had yet to fully recover.

When the offering was complete, Persephone's pale skin became luminous. It looked as if she was glowing from the inside out, and her long chestnut curls fanned out in the air around her. "Everyone, hold hands. We have to be touching for this to work correctly." They did as she said.

A white glow overcame Zoey's vision, and she clamped her eyes shut, bracing herself for what was sure to be hell on her already upset stomach.

However, nothing seemed to happen. For what felt like entire minutes, they sat as still as ever, and Zoey wondered if she'd been wrong to think that Persephone could have been on their side.

"We're here," Persephone suddenly said. Zoey opened her eyes. Sure enough, they were in the cabin at the nymph camp. "The Daughter of Apollo is outside." Asteria hurried to fetch Diana. Moments later, Diana and Kali came running into the cabin, followed by Troy and Marina in their new wheelchairs.

Everyone was confused as to why Persephone was there, and Zoey recounted what had happened, detailing the ways in which Persephone had helped them, and how Ares had kidnapped Andy. While Zoey explained, Diana healed her and Karter.

After Diana finished healing them, she wiped the sweat from her brow. "I bet Ares took Andy to New Mount Olympus."

"That, or his *polis*," Karter said.

Zoey snapped her fingers. "Wait a second. I think I know where you could go to find out for sure." She looked at Asteria. "Can you travel to the lair of the Fates? In spirit, like before, so you don't overtax yourself. Maybe, if you touch

Andy's life thread, you can see where he went."

"Yes, that's perfect," Asteria said. "The past doesn't change, and Andy has already been kidnapped. I'm sure I can manipulate the threads to show me where he is now." She seemed to remember something, and her shoulders sagged, the edges of her figure shimmering.

"What's wrong?" Karter asked.

"Considering how close I am to fading away altogether, I'm afraid I might not have the power to go. Not even in spirit."

Zoey climbed to her feet. "What if we made you a sacrifice, like we did for Persephone? Would that give you the strength you need?"

Asteria mulled it over. "An offering should suffice. What's most important is that we discover Andy's location, no matter how much of my energy it expends. All I need is to get there and back."

They headed outside, gathered an offering, and built a fire. Once they finished the sacrifice, Asteria even looked better than she had before. Not so sparkly.

Asteria waved a hand, and little galaxies flashed in her eyes. She stiffened, her jaw going slack. Zoey assumed that's what she and Andy had looked like when Asteria had taken them to the lair of the Fates in spirit.

It couldn't have been more than five minutes before Asteria returned. When she did, she keeled over, panting and puffing and clutching her chest. "Asteria!" Karter knelt beside her and took her hand. "You're far too warm. Do you need water?"

Breaths heaving, she shook her head. "Andy—is—on—Olympus. Ares—and—Aphrodite—pursue—him. He—has—six—days. You—must—go—now—before . . ." She trailed off, her form shifting between flesh and glitter, just as it had when she'd told Zoey and Karter she was fading away. But this time it was happening at a rapid pace, and it didn't seem to be getting any better.

"Asteria?" Karter said.

She wheezed as if in reply, then smiled at him one last time before disintegrating into silver stardust.

Asteria's remains slipped through Karter's fingers like tiny grains of sand. As they hit the ground, they made tinkling sounds, like crystals chiming in the wind.

"Holy shit," Zoey whispered from behind him. "Is she . . . ?"

"Gone," Karter said. "She faded away. She used up what strength she had left to get Andy's location." A gust whipped through the trees, blowing Asteria's stardust away, and he felt so light, so empty, he was surprised he hadn't been carried with it.

He stared at the space where Asteria once lay, clutching the air where her hand had once been. He wiped his eyes, a few tears leaking out from them.

"I don't know what to say." Kali's voice sliced through the silence. "It's horrible what happened to Asteria, but . . . she got to live for thousands of years, and—"

"Kali!" Diana chided.

"Let me finish," Kali said. "What I'm trying to say is I'm more worried about Andy and Zoey right now. Since Asteria is gone, and since no other god is selfless enough to cast the Descent Spell, will they *have* to converge with Anteros and Calliope?"

Karter hadn't thought of that. Diana and Kali's plan to save Zoey and Andy hinged on help from Asteria and Prometheus, but the Titans were gone. He turned around to look at everyone else.

"I don't know," Diana replied. "Maybe Asteria was wrong. Maybe Hephaestus's chains haven't weakened Prometheus to the point that he can't cast the spell, or maybe there's a way to break them that we couldn't think of before."

At the mention of Prometheus, Karter and Zoey shared a knowing glance. Zoey's lip quivered, and Karter wondered if he needed to be the one to tell the group what had happened to Prometheus.

In the end, Persephone beat him to it. "Prometheus can't help the Chosen Two. The Olympians banished him to Tartarus."

Diana blanched, Kali gasped, and Troy and Marina covered their mouths with their hands. "How do you know that?" Diana asked.

"I know because I was there," Persephone said. "I saw it with my own eyes."

"Wait, you were there?" Diana cried. "Did you—did you at least try to stop it?"

"What could I have done to stop it?"

Diana's nostrils flared. "Let me get this straight. You just *let* the gods banish Prometheus to Tartarus?"

"I prayed to the Fates to wake him, so he'd have a chance to escape," Persephone said. "But he didn't regenerate in time. There was nothing else I could have done. If I had fought the Olympians then, they would have banished me too, and I wouldn't be helping you now."

"If you'd have tried helping him, he might be here." Diana narrowed her eyes. "There could have been a chance to save Andy and Zoey. You know, he has a great-great-granddaughter. Jasmine. She's counting on him to make it back to her. Because of the gods, she's all alone. She has no family left!"

Something that almost looked like shame flittered across Persephone's features, but then her expression morphed into that of rage. "This 'Jasmine' is none of my concern. All I want is to ensure the gods pay for everything they've done to me, and I can't do that if I'm imprisoned in Tartarus."

"No, but you could have worked with Prometheus so that both of you escaped," Diana countered. "That *might* have been enough to convince me you're on our side. It would have meant you were looking out for someone besides yourself. But you're not, because you're just as self-serving as the Olympians."

Persephone let out a cry of indignation. Greenery snaked out from her palms toward Diana. "You really are as insolent as your father, Daughter of Apollo."

Diana conjured spheres of blazing sunlight in her hands. "And you really are as slimy as your husband, Queen of the Underworld."

Karter jumped to his feet. He and Zoey rushed between Diana and Persephone. "Stop!" Zoey yelled. "Just stop it, both of you! Fighting isn't going to help anything. It's not going to bring Prometheus back, and it's not going to rescue Andy. We have a common goal here: to defeat the gods. We need to work together. Yes, Persephone was our enemy, and it's crummy she didn't try to save Prometheus. But with the only other immortals on our side dead or in Tartarus, we need her help more than ever, and she needs us too."

Diana and Persephone glared at each other, but they lowered their attacks.

"Fine," Diana said. "We should probably round up the nymphs and come up with a plan of action, anyway. Asteria said Andy was on Olympus, and that he has six days. I'm not sure what that means, but I'm guessing it's the amount of time he has before Zeus discovers him. We have to get him back before then."

Kali marched toward the trees. "We don't have any time to lose. Let's go!" Troy and Marina wheeled after her, and Diana and Persephone followed them, shooting each other suspicious glances as they walked.

Karter should have followed as well, but he could only bring himself to turn back toward the space where Asteria had once been. He stared hard at it, a knot forming in his throat.

Zoey stepped up beside him. "Are you okay?"

"I . . ." He paused. "Yes, I think I am. It's just that Asteria, she—she did a lot to help me."

"I'm sorry." She reached out as if to touch him, then yanked her hand back to her side. "It happened so fast. It isn't fair."

A few tears slipped out of Karter's eyes. *This can't be happening,* he thought. *First Mother. Then Syrena and Spencer. Now Asteria.*

"Are you sure you're okay?" Zoey asked.

He faced her, and the care and concern in her sky-blue eyes struck him. *I can't fall apart right now. I have to be strong for her and help her save Andy. There will be time to grieve later.* "I will be," he replied, and after a last glance at where Asteria had once lain, he and Zoey headed after Diana, Kali, Persephone, and the twins.

It took about an hour to gather everyone up. The group explained to Narcissa and Harmony what had happened to Andy and Asteria, and what they'd discovered about Prometheus, and then everyone congregated around the Dryad leaders in the middle of camp. Karter was sure the nymphs farthest away wouldn't be able to hear everything that was said, but hopefully, the people closest would spread the message along.

"Asteria has faded away, Prometheus has been banished to Tartarus, and Andy has been taken captive by Ares, God of War," Narcissa shouted. "He's on Olympus, and he has six days before he'll presumably be locked away in Tartarus. We must assemble a team to save him. Once the team goes after him, a second group will have to continue gathering more recruits—whether they be nymph, human, centaur, or satyr. I fear this war on the gods will soon be coming to a head, and if we are to rise victorious, we need as many soldiers as possible."

"Obviously, Zoey, Diana, Karter, Kali, and Persephone will be going after Andy," Harmony yelled. "So will Narcissa and I. We'll need many more recruits with us, though. Especially because while we're saving Andy, we're going to try saving the other recruits. Any volunteers?"

Dryads and Naiads began shouting and coming forward, and Persephone manipulated vines to carry herself high above their heads. "Stop and listen for just a moment, all of you," Persephone said. Everyone went quiet, looking up at the goddess. "After I was rescued from

Tartarus, Zeus held a meeting in the throne room. During the meeting, he confirmed that the nymphs who aided the Chosen Two in infiltrating Olympus had been slaughtered in battle."

"No, that can't be," Harmony said. "Asteria said she sensed them on New Mount Olympus."

Persephone hung her head. "Perhaps she sensed the plants they transformed into after death. I'm sorry. Your companions are gone."

Harmony and many other nymphs began to cry, falling into each other's arms, and Karter's stomach sank to his feet. He'd sworn to the nymphs that if their friends were still alive, he'd save them from the gods. He'd hoped to make good on that promise, but now he couldn't.

"They knew the risks." Although Narcissa's voice shook, she held her chin high, her shoulders back. "All of us do. Those who have died in this war are heroes. We'll never forget their names. We'll always be grateful for their sacrifice. Now, who is willing to go with Zoey and the rest of us to Olympus to save Andy, who is willing to go out and gather more recruits, and who is willing to continue guarding the prisoners?"

Zoey raised her hand. "Wait. Before you guys start dividing people up, there's something I need to say." The focus shifted to her. "While we were in Aphrodite City, Andy was supposed to touch me after he connected with Anteros so that I could connect with Calliope. He didn't get the chance, and I haven't been able to reconnect with her yet. I think . . . I think that maybe I need to go off with a group of my own so I can connect with Calliope. Just in case we—we can't reach Andy in time."

"Nonsense," Narcissa said. "We aren't too far from Olympus. We'll easily reach him within the six-day period Asteria gave us."

"Except fate isn't a fixed thing," Zoey replied. "There're lots of different possibilities for the future. What if something goes wrong, and it changes the course of events, and Andy is discovered before his original six days are up? What if he's banished to Tartarus, and I have no way of connecting with Calliope then? If that happens, we won't be able to get the words to the Descent Spell, and even if we had them at that point, I wouldn't be able to cast it because I wouldn't have Calliope's divine essence handy. We'd be totally screwed."

Harmony sniffled and wiped her eyes. "Considering that Andy was taken while the both of you were out with a team of your own, I don't think it would be wise to separate yourself from the rest of us. We need to stay together. Besides, if the way you originally connected with Calliope was by touching Andy, then who's to say you'd be able to connect with her on your own at all?"

"Harmony is right," Narcissa said. "We must reach Andy as quickly as possible so you can touch him. That will be the safest way for you to restart the convergence process."

"But Asteria said the convergence process could take whole days," Zoey argued. "What if by the time we reach Andy, there isn't enough time for me to fully converge with Calliope, and the gods annihilate us because I couldn't get her goddess-powers back fast enough?" She looked to Diana and Kali. "A little help here, guys?" They wouldn't meet her eyes. She turned to Karter next, but all he could manage was a defeated shrug. He wasn't sure of the best course of action. While he could see where Zoey was coming from, he could also see the nymphs' point.

"It's settled, then." Narcissa gestured at the crowd. "Let us decide who will go where and gather our things."

Zoey rolled her eyes. "Fine. Don't listen to what I have to say." She weaved between nymphs, back toward the cabin. "I'll grab my stuff so we can leave, I guess." As she passed Karter, she seemed to deliberately bump him in the shoulder, and she whispered, "Follow me."

He cocked his head, confused. Had he heard her right? Had she really asked him to follow her? *Better safe than sorry*, he thought. *It seems she's just now warming up to me, and I don't want her mad again.* He made sure Narcissa and Harmony weren't paying attention, then chased Zoey through the horde.

They made it through the crowd and into the trees, and Karter hurried up to her side. "What's going on?" he asked.

She looked back as if to confirm no one was following them. "I wanna talk to you. I'll explain more when we get to the cabin." For the rest of the walk back to the building, they didn't say a word.

Once they arrived and stepped inside, Karter shut the door and turned to Zoey. "What is it you want to talk to me about?"

She swallowed hard. "Do you remember when you told me that if I thought of something you could do, something that would help me forgive you, to tell you about it? How you promised that no matter what it was, if I asked you to do it, you would?"

His heart nearly leapt out of his chest. A few

days ago, he'd thought Zoey would never give him another chance. Had she decided to let him prove himself to her? "I remember."

"Well, I thought of something you could do," she said. "I want you to leave camp with me and help me reconnect with Calliope on my own."

CHAPTER THIRTEEN

ASK

"You want me to . . ." Karter pinched the bridge of his nose. "Do you realize how dangerous that is? Just you and me leaving camp? It's practically suicide. No, it *is* suicide."

So much for doing anything I ask, Zoey thought. "No, it's not. At least, not after I reconnect with Calliope. If I'd have been connected with her while we were in Aphrodite City, things would have gone down a lot differently. She has those voice-powers, remember? She can manipulate people into thinking and doing what she wants."

"Except her voice-powers don't work on everyone the same way," Karter countered. "You and Andy mentioned it when you told us the story of how Calliope and Anteros began to manifest within you. You said that although the voice-powers took care of Amphitrite and the Trojan Cetus, they didn't affect Circe at all, and Andy said they only influenced Artemis for a moment. They aren't consistent enough to be relied upon. Not when your life is at stake."

"Well, maybe if I stopped fighting Calliope so much, they'd be more reliable. Maybe if I gave her more control, she'd be unstoppable. She could protect both of us that way."

"So you *want* to give up your body? You *want* to complete the convergence and let her take over?"

The bitterness in his tone surprised Zoey. "What else am I supposed to do? Asteria's gone, Prometheus is in Tartarus, and I don't know about you, but if Persephone were to cast the Descent, I wouldn't trust her to give us the objects of power afterward. It's not fair, but at this point, I've accepted it. Like I already said, what if something happens to Andy before we get there, and I have no way of connecting with Calliope?"

Karter's expression softened. He ran a hand through his hair. "Okay. If this is really what you want, I'll take you."

She perked up. "Wait, really?"

"Yes. Grab whatever you might need, and I'll snag one of the pegasi so I don't have to fly us everywhere. We need to go quickly. We don't want anyone to see us leaving in case they try to stop us."

Elation washed over Zoey, and she couldn't help but grin. Without thinking, she raced to Karter and threw her arms around his neck, nearly tackling him. He staggered back, then gained his footing, his hands raised in surprise. "Thank you thank you *thank you*," she said, squeezing him tight. "You have no idea how much this means to me."

For a second, they stood like that, Zoey hugging Karter, Karter standing awkwardly with his hands in the air.

Then, hesitantly, Karter hugged her back, resting his head against hers. A warm, almost soothing sensation flooded Zoey as he embraced her, and in that moment, she realized something, although she could hardly believe it: She'd already forgiven him. He hadn't held up his end of the deal yet, but as far as she was concerned, he was absolved of his past crimes.

Since joining their group, he'd done everything he could to prove he was on their side. He'd protected Zoey and Andy with his life, and he would continue to do so, right up until the bitter end. *Which I still need to tell him about*, she thought.

She pulled away but kept her hand on his shoulder, unable to stop smiling. "I'm serious, you know. I'm really, really grateful."

He chuckled, releasing his hold on her waist. "I can tell." His cheeks flushed a faint shade of pink. Was he embarrassed? Didn't demigods hug their friends? *Of course they do. I hug Diana all the time, and I hugged Spencer too.*

No, he wasn't embarrassed. He looked . . . happy. The happiest she'd ever seen him. Did her forgiveness really mean that much to him?

Zoey cleared her throat and dropped her hand to her side. "I'll, uhh—go get my stuff."

She gathered her things, and Karter started toward the door to grab a pegasus. But before he could leave, the door swung open, and Diana, Kali, Troy, and Marina barged in.

Diana balled her fists at her sides. "We know what you're up to."

"And we don't approve," Kali said, frowning.

Zoey's stomach dropped. She'd been as discreet as possible when asking Karter to come with her, but apparently, they'd noticed the pair leaving. "You can't stop me," she said. "I have to do this. I have to reconnect with Calliope myself."

"We already know we can't stop you." Diana sighed. "You've made up your mind."

Kali crossed her arms. "But if you're going off on your own, you're going to need backup, so we're coming with you."

"Well, Diana and Kali are," Troy said.

"Troy and I will continue making modifications to our wheelchairs as we help gather more recruits," Marina added.

"I already told Persephone not to follow us, and to lie and tell the nymphs she can't access our location anymore," Diana explained. "She thinks it's a good idea for you to reconnect with Calliope on your own, so it wasn't hard to get her to agree to the plan. I'm not sure whether that makes me trust her more or less."

"Seriously?" Zoey asked. "But what about Andy? Aren't you worried about him? Don't you want to go after him?"

"Obviously I'm worried about him," Diana snapped. "But Persephone and a bunch of the recruits are going to save him, and you and Karter were going to be alone."

Even though Diana and Kali were frustrated

with Zoey, her heart swelled with gratitude for them. She'd been confident that Karter would be able to help her—otherwise, she wouldn't have asked him—but it was comforting to know that Diana and Kali would be there too.

"Troy and Marina, go cover for us," Diana went on. "Zoey, grab the objects of power and some weapons. Karter and Kali, help me get the pegasi." Diana and Kali headed out the door, and Troy and Marina wheeled behind them. "It's time to leave."

When Andy had flown out of Ares's bedroom, he'd expected to simply go outside, soar off the edge of New Mount Olympus, and start his journey back toward the nymph camp. Sure, he didn't know exactly how to get there, but with Asteria (and possibly Persephone) working alongside his companions, he'd been confident that if he didn't stumble upon the camp anytime soon, he'd be tracked down.

Sadly, he hadn't found his way off this stupid hunk of rock yet, and Anteros wouldn't give him directions, either. He'd flown above the palace for a bit, lost and confused, Anteros rambling on in his head about how he'd "made a mistake" and "needed to let Mother and Father help."

"No way, man," he'd whispered to the god.

Zeus's palace alone seemed bigger than Andy's town from the Before Time, with all sorts of add-ons and extra corridors that led to massive courtyards and parks. Not to mention every time he'd been going in one direction for a while, a god or demigod or nymph or *someone* would poke a head out a dumb window or come walking out a dumb door, and he'd have to flutter away as quick as he could before they saw him. It totally screwed up his idea that if he went in one direction long enough, he'd eventually get out of here.

Worst of all, his wings were killing him. Like, seriously, they felt almost as bad as they had when they'd been breaking through his skin.

But he didn't feel safe walking out in the open. If he did that, it would be a lot easier for someone to catch him. So when he spotted a dense garden with trees as tall as the clouds, he decided to take cover there. *"The Garden of Olympus,"* Anteros said. *"We spent so many romantic nights with Calliope here."*

"You spent so many romantic nights with Calliope here," Andy retorted. "Asteria

confirmed we aren't the same person, remember? You're an avatar. A god trapped inside a mortal body. *My* body."

"Asteria has made many conflicting assertions," Anteros replied. *"And you and Zoey aren't the only ones she's discussed this avatar business with. She's visited me in dreams to tell me about it, and I'm assuming she's talked to Calliope about it at some point as well."*

"What did she say to you?"

"That you and I are the same being, and that Zoey and Calliope are the same being. Personally, I'd like an explanation as to why she's suddenly so certain none of that is true. She's not an avatar, so how would she know?"

"Uh, maybe because she's a friggin' goddess of prophetic dreams? Also, she made Metis an avatar, and I'm assuming she was there for Metis's convergence."

No response from Anteros this time.

Hours passed. The sun was rising, and Andy was still resting his wings by going on foot in search of an exit. Since Anteros refused to help him, he'd decided to use the sun as his guide to travel west—that way he shouldn't get lost again.

As he walked through the garden, glancing at his surroundings, he couldn't help but feel uneasy. Although he'd never been here in person, this was a place he'd seen multiple times in visions and dreams. It was beautifully designed, full of statues and paths and fountains and ponds. Thankfully, it wasn't just the trees that were large; there was also an abundance of thick bushes that made for the perfect hiding places.

Unfortunately, the garden also appeared to be a favorite hangout spot among the residents of New Mount Olympus.

Since entering it, Andy had been forced to pause his sneaking on multiple occasions to dart behind vegetation so he wouldn't get caught. And, as if by some cruel act of God, he'd only ever had to do so because some couple was slinking away from the palace to hook up.

It was mortifying enough to be forced to hear what they were saying and doing (although he always snuck away at the first possible opportunity). But what made things worse was that every time it occurred, he was reminded of the fact that the girl he loved didn't love him back. That what could be the last conversation he'd ever have with her had been a fight, and he'd acted like a total jerk. That the few times they'd kissed, it had been nonconsensual because a god and goddess had forced them on each other.

Yes, he had more "important" things to worry about, like escaping Olympus and saving the world. But he'd be lying if he said he could get Zoey—and the thought of her having feelings for Spencer, or Karter, or anyone but him—off his mind. And trying to find his way through this endless garden all by himself, practically surrounded by young lovers whispering sweet nothings to each other, didn't make him feel any better about the situation.

"I guess if there's one good thing about you taking over my body soon," he said bitterly to Anteros, "it's that I won't have to deal with the bullshit of life anymore."

"What do you mean by that?" Anteros asked. *"Life is beautiful."*

"No, it's not. Ever since I got brought back, it's been one bad thing after another. But if you take me over, that'll change. I won't have to deal with the fact that the people I love were killed by gods, or that it's my fault Darko was crushed by a column, or that I had to leave Prometheus behind and he got thrown into Tartarus, or that Zoey doesn't love me back. You can deal with all of that while I sit around and wait to die." It didn't sound like a great existence, but it had to be better than crippling heartbreak.

"It pains me to hear you speak this way." To Andy's surprise, Anteros sounded sincere. *"Don't lose hope, child. Calliope and I are destined to be together. Therefore, you and Zoey are destined to be together. This isn't the end for either of you. You'll see."*

Andy snorted. "Yeah, right."

To Andy's dismay, he walked the entire day without reaching the edge of Olympus. Evening was fast approaching, the sun dipping in the sky, and he fell into a fit of coughing, his throat parched, his stomach grumbling. *Is there any good drinking water around here? Anything to eat?*

"You know, Mother and Father would provide sustenance if you went back to them."

No thanks.

He wandered over to the next fountain he saw and peered down into the water. It was crystal clear. Should he risk it?

"Don't do it," Anteros warned him.

"Buzz off." He dipped his hands into the fountain, cupped some of the cool liquid, and brought it to his lips.

"I wouldn't drink that if I were you," a young woman said from behind him. He yelped and swung around, the fluid swashing out of his hands.

A familiar girl appeared from behind a cluster of trees, and at the sight of her, his stomach sank. She was about his height, with medium-brown skin and a mop of tight burgundy coils piled atop her head.

It was Layla, Daughter of Ares.

CHAPTER FOURTEEN

HELP

"**M**ost of the gods and demigods left on missions to find you and the girl." Layla stepped closer to Andy. "But for some reason, you're in the Garden of Olympus. Is Diana here too?"

Pulse quickening, Andy leapt into the air. He had to get away from her, had to escape before—

"Wait!" Layla cried. Against his better judgment, Andy paused midair and turned to look at her. "How is she?"

"How is who?" he replied.

"Diana."

"What do you care? Didn't you help capture her? Didn't you bring her here to be executed?"

"I did." She glanced down at her hands, fidgeting. "I was afraid of what the gods would do to me if I didn't. But . . ."

He raised a brow. "But?"

"Karter," she began. "He betrayed the gods for the people he loves, and in doing so he—he inspired me to do the same. When you and the girl infiltrated Olympus, I knocked out Xander so Diana could escape more easily. I just—I needed her to live. Please, tell me whether she's all right, and I'll leave you alone."

"All things considered, Diana's okay," Andy said. "Oh, and no, she's not here with me."

"Good." Layla pivoted, as if preparing to walk away. "In that case, I'll leave you to . . . whatever you're doing. Try not to run into anyone else."

"Hey, hold on a sec," he called, and she stopped. "I'm, um—I'm not supposed to be here."

"Well, obviously."

"Don't you dare ask for her help," Anteros said in his head.

Don't you dare tell me what to do, Andy thought back. "What I meant is I'm lost, sort of," he said. "This place is huge. I've been walking west all day, and I still haven't reached the edge. I need to get out of here."

"Are you trying to give us away?" Anteros cried.

No, I'm trying to get back to Zoey.

Layla put her hands up. "Wait, you don't know where you are? You didn't come to Olympus on purpose?"

Andy shook his head. "No and no."

"How'd you get here, then?"

"I was kidnapped last night."

"Who kidnapped you?" she asked.

"If you tell her, you'll be putting Father at risk! You can't do that! Not after everything he risked for us!"

"Ares," he answered, and Layla's eyes went big.

Anteros groaned. *"You're hopeless."*

Glad you finally figured it out. Maybe now you'll shut up about Ares and Aphrodite and let me do my thing.

"My father brought you here?" Layla asked. "He's back? But then why . . . why hasn't he summoned everyone else? Once one of the teams captured you and the girl and retrieved the objects of power, they were supposed to send for the others and convene in the throne room."

"Ares didn't capture Zoey, and he didn't get any of the objects of power. He just grabbed me and teleported me here." Andy left out as many details as possible. He couldn't be sure whether Layla knew about the Anteros-Calliope deal, or whether he wanted her to know about it.

"Oh gods." She covered her mouth with her hand. "He must be planning something. I don't know why he'd bring you here without notifying everyone else."

Andy forced a shrug. "Yeah, I don't know either. It's pretty suspicious, huh?"

"Did he try to kill you?"

"Yeah, totally," he lied. "He definitely did that. But I, uh—I flew away."

"No one is supposed to kill you or the girl. Zeus made that *very* clear. My father is up to something."

"For sure. Which is why I really, really need to leave. My friends are gonna be looking for me. Diana's gonna be looking for me." At another mention of Diana, Layla perked up. "Could you show me the quickest way out? So I can get back to her?"

Layla nibbled on her bottom lip. After thinking for a while, she nodded. "Follow me."

For the rest of the day, Zoey, Karter, Diana, and Kali flew Luna, Aladdin, and Ajax, putting a good amount of distance between themselves and the nymph camp. As night fell, the air cooled significantly, and even though Zoey was sitting behind Diana on Aladdin, she shivered from the crisp wind biting her face and making her hair blow about wildly.

The group landed by a stream in the forest. While their pegasi ate and drank, they worked together to prepare dinner. Diana hunted rabbits, Zoey and Karter collected roots and mushrooms, and Kali cooked everything. Soon it was time to eat, and they gathered in a circle around their campfire.

Karter swallowed his first bite. "This is . . . surprisingly good."

"Did you expect anything less, jackass?" Kali smirked at him.

"Oh, it's just— I wasn't expecting it to be seasoned so well, and . . ." He trailed off, his cheeks flushing pink.

"To be fair, I was shocked at how excellent of a cook you are too, Kali," Zoey chimed in. "And I had no excuse, considering how delicious the food in your village was."

Kali's expression darkened. "My village. Right."

"What's wrong?" Diana asked.

"Well . . ." Kali paused, setting her food down. "The closer we get to ending this war, the more I can't stop thinking about going home. In all honesty, I don't want to."

Diana frowned and looked away, and Zoey's stomach sank. She knew Kali was thinking about Deltama Village's tradition of arranged marriages for their leaders, which included Kali, since she was supposed to be chief someday.

"Maybe you won't have to go back," Zoey said. "Or maybe, since you're supposed to be your village's next chief, you'll have a chance to change the customs you don't agree with."

"Maybe." Kali picked up her food and popped a few mushrooms into her mouth. "Anyway, who wants to watch for monsters first?"

"I'll do it," Karter said. "I don't think I'll be able to rest, anyway. Not after—not after what happened to Asteria."

The look on his face almost made Zoey want to give him another hug. "I'm sorry," she said, and he offered her a sad smile.

Diana finished inhaling her rabbit and gave Karter a stern look. "You need to try to sleep. You were up all last night, and all today. Same goes for Zoey. I'll take first watch."

"What I'm most concerned about is a plan," Zoey said. "I have no idea who Calliope really is, or how to reconnect with her. I'd hoped one of you would have some suggestions."

Karter nibbled on a root. "I know Calliope is a Daughter of Zeus and Mnemosyne, and she's one of the nine Muses. If I remember correctly, she's also the Goddess of Eloquence."

"You *did* remember correctly," Zoey said. "That's her official title. Question is, how do I reconnect with her?"

They sat quietly for a while, mulling it over as they ate.

Eventually, Kali spoke up. "Hey, what about Calliope's mom?"

Karter raised a brow. "Mnemosyne?"

"Yeah, her," Kali said. "Would she know a way for Zoey to reconnect with Calliope?"

"Mnemosyne was one of the oldest Titans," Diana started. "She was a goddess of memory. Specifically of the memorization of history and old stories before writing was invented. But no one has heard from her since even before the Storm. As far as anyone knows, she faded away, lost to time. I don't think we'll be able to get ahold of her."

"Crap, that sucks." Zoey bit her lip. "What about the nine Muses? Who are they? You said Calliope was one of them. Are any of them still around?"

"The other eight Muses are Calliope's little sisters by Zeus and Mnemosyne, and yes, they're still around," Diana replied. "In the old days, they spent a lot of time with my father because they're so closely linked to the arts. Now, they have cities full of worshippers on the other side of the world."

"From what I understand, Calliope's sisters aren't very outspoken toward Zeus," Karter said. "Calliope seems to be the most headstrong of the bunch, so I'm not sure they'd be willing to help."

Zoey tilted her head. "Maybe they're just afraid of Zeus because Calliope disappeared right after she pointed out how much of a tyrant he was."

"Or maybe they're fearful of fading away, like they believe she did," Kali pointed out.

"I don't think asking the other eight Muses is

the way to go," Diana said. "Calliope was influential enough that we could probably find a relic related to her. Not only was she the Goddess of Eloquence, but she was also the Muse of Epic Poetry. It's said that epic poets throughout history called on her to help inspire them—writers like Homer and Virgil."

Karter's eyes brightened. "That's it! The cities—all of them have libraries in the *Agora*. I'm sure at least some of the gods require copies of the epic poems to be stocked. Perhaps if Zoey touches the verses where Calliope is mentioned or called upon, they'll reconnect."

Diana tapped her chin. "You know what? That just might work."

"Which gods would most likely have copies of the poems, though?" Kali asked. "We need to go to a city that's close and that would have the poems readily available. We only have five days left before Andy's supposedly going to be discovered and thrown into Tartarus."

"The closest cities to our location are Hera's and Zeus's," Karter said. "And considering how much Hera hates children of Zeus by other women—even women who came before her, like Mnemosyne—I wouldn't be surprised if, even if she had the poems in her library, she had the passages calling upon Calliope removed."

"Does that mean Zeus City is our best bet?" Zoey asked.

Diana nodded. "I'm afraid so."

Zoey gulped, trying to process the fact that she was going to have to sneak into yet another one of the gods' cities, and that it was the city belonging to the literal king of the pantheon.

"How about after dinner, all of you get some rest?" Diana suggested. "And try not to think about, you know, everything that's going on."

Later that evening, once the group had finished eating, Diana started circling the perimeter of the camp. Kali curled up in front of the fire and fell asleep, snoring almost immediately, and Karter lay with his back facing the flames. Zoey sighed, flopped down, and stared at the stars.

For what felt like hours she sat there, restless. She tossed and turned, unable to drift off or even relax. She couldn't stop thinking about Andy, about the way Ares had grabbed him and how they'd disappeared. Would she see him again? And, if she did, would he still be Andy? Or would he be Anteros? Would the last real conversation they'd had before giving up their bodies to the gods inside of them be a horrible fight?

Someone else she couldn't get off her mind

was Karter. She and Andy were doomed to spend the rest of their lives trapped in the labyrinth of their minds, but was there a way to change Karter's fate? Did he really have to be the person to banish Zeus to Tartarus, all because of a prophecy foretold millennia ago? And, if he did, did he also have to die in the process?

Maybe if I tell him about it, he'll be able to change his destiny, she thought. *Maybe he'll be able to save himself, and live a long, happy life after this is over.*

She sat up to look at him. Because of the way he was positioned, she couldn't see his face. Hopefully, he wasn't asleep. If he was, she'd have to wake him. "Karter?" she whispered.

He rolled over, his eyes droopy. Dark bags had formed under them. "What is it?"

"I need to talk to you about something. Well, actually—I need to ask you something first."

He offered her a teasing grin. "Don't tell me you've decided you want me to take you on another suicide mission."

"No, not at all," she said, laughing a little.

He sat up. "Then ask away."

"Um, so—do you believe in fate? In destiny?"

He took some time to think before responding. "I do believe in fate, but not in the way you might think. My half-brother Heracles—he said something to me while I was training for Diana's execution, and I'll never forget it. He said that destiny is the result of a series of decisions we make throughout our lives, from when our threads of fate are spun all the way to when they're finally cut. He helped me understand that even if I can't control what happens to and around me, I can control myself. After that, I realized I didn't want to execute Diana. I wanted to save her, and I wanted to make up for the wrongs I'd committed against Syrena, Spencer, and all of you."

"You and I are on the same page, then," Zoey replied. "Our fates don't have to be set in stone, not entirely. We have some control over them."

"Why'd you ask, anyway?"

She paused, working up the courage to continue. "When Andy and I touched our threads of fate, and we saw two of our possible futures, you died in both. You died helping us."

Karter barely blinked. Her words should have horrified him, should have struck fear into his heart, but he didn't seem afraid. "How did I die?"

Zoey tucked a curl behind her ear. She didn't want to recall anything from what she and Andy had seen, but Karter deserved the truth. "In the first one, you didn't make it because you banished Zeus to Tartarus, and he killed you in the process. In the second one, you were sucked into the pit with me and Andy while trying to fly us away."

"I see."

A long pause. Finally, she went on, the words spilling from her mouth in rapid succession. "There's something else, though," she said. "Asteria says your destiny is entwined with mine and Andy's now, and we saw the proof. Your life thread is tangled up with ours. Asteria claims it happened because of the choices you've made, but also because your mother was a goddess— the Titan Metis, apparently. Metis escaped from your father after Athena burst from his body. I guess she became an avatar, like Calliope and Anteros, and there was this old prophecy about how she would give birth to a child-of-Zeus who would be powerful enough to overthrow him, and that child is you."

"Yes, I know of that prophecy." Karter knit his brow. "But I'm not sure Asteria is right in saying my mother was Metis. For one, my mother named me after her late brother, Karter. Don't you think that if my mother had been Metis, she would have given me the name of a great hero from the old days, like Theseus or

Achilles? Also, my father would have recognized Metis's divine essence within the mortal's body she was possessing if she'd been an avatar, just as Ares recognized Anteros's divine essence within Andy, and when I was on Olympus, Metis came up in a conversation between my father and me. I asked him how he knew she hadn't escaped him, and he assured me she was still trapped inside of him."

Zoey shrugged. "Yeah, I don't know. Those are good points. I just wanted you to know what Asteria told us."

"I suppose it doesn't matter anyway. Whether Metis was my mother, I mean. She's dead and gone, and it seems I'll be joining her soon."

"I didn't bring this up to you so you could be all doom and gloom about it. I wanted to tell you because you have a right to know what we saw. I also want to believe that maybe it doesn't have to happen that way. Maybe you can protect us, and banish Zeus, *and* not die. Or maybe someone else can banish Zeus, and you can be left out of the equation entirely."

"You don't need to worry about me." He chuckled wryly. "I would gladly die locking Zeus away in Tartarus forever. I would gladly die saving you and Andy as well."

Zoey's throat went dry. "You'd *gladly* die?"

He sighed. "That's not what I meant. I look forward to my prophesied death as much as you look forward to your prophesied convergence with Calliope. It's not that I'm excited for it to happen. It's just that I've accepted it's what must be done."

"So much for having control over your fate," Zoey muttered.

"If you really believe I can live through the final battle with the gods," Karter started, "then you should also believe you can save the world without sacrificing yourself to Calliope."

Zoey narrowed her eyes at him. "Why do you care so much about that, anyway? Shouldn't you be encouraging me and Andy to finish the convergence, since it will help us destroy the gods? That's why you joined us, isn't it? Because you want revenge on them for what they did to Spencer and Syrena?"

"That's one of the reasons I joined you, yes," Karter replied. "And, at first, it might have been the main reason. But it isn't the only one. Believe it or not, the thought of gods possessing your bodies makes me sick. After everything that's happened . . ." He looked down, scratching the back of his neck. "The point is, Spencer and Syrena aren't the only reason I'm here. I care about you. You and Andy."

From across the fire, Kali released an especially noisy snore, one so loud Zoey was surprised she didn't wake herself up. Zoey and Karter jumped in surprise, then shared a glance and stifled their laughter.

"If I couldn't sleep before, I really don't think I'll be able to now," Karter said.

Zoey giggled as Kali snored some more. "Same here."

"Maybe we could just talk until we fall asleep, then," he suggested.

She liked that idea. "Sure. What about this time?"

He lay back down and rested his hands on his stomach. "Something other than destiny and death. For instance, what's something you do for fun?"

Zoey blinked in surprise. She couldn't remember the last time someone had asked her a question like that, in this life or the last. "To be honest, it's been so long since I got to do anything fun. Even in the Before Time, I went to school all day, and in the evenings, I either worked or did homework. Or both."

"There must have been something, even if it was in an earlier part of your life. Something you'd like to do again."

She thought about it, and soon recalled a time before her parents' divorce. "I loved playing with my old dog, Daisy. I always dreamed of getting another dog and taking her on hikes in the mountains. That still sounds like a blast."

"It does sound nice. Dogs are wonderful creatures."

"They are." She lay down as well, facing the stars now. "What about you? What's something you do for fun?"

"Spencer and Syrena and I used to watch sunsets together. We never grew tired of it. There's a beach not far from New Mount Olympus, and when the gods would send us on missions, we always made it a point to stop there and watch the sky until night fell."

"Aw, that's really sweet." Zoey tried to imagine the three of them lounging on a beach and watching the sunset together. As she pictured Spencer's face, her heart fell. "I wish Spencer were still here."

"So do I," Karter replied. "And Syrena, too. You would have liked her."

"I already like her. If it weren't for her, I'd still be dead. But to be honest, I don't think she would have liked me very much."

"Why do you say that? You never met her."

Zoey rolled over to face him. "Well, she and

Spencer were boyfriend and girlfriend. They were totally in love, right?"

Karter looked at her, his brow furrowed. "Yes. What does that have to do with how she would have felt toward you?"

"Well . . ." Was she seriously going to tell Karter about her crush on his late best friend? The only other person she'd talked to about it was Andy, and the only reason she'd admitted to it was because he'd been grilling her.

But maybe, if she told Karter about how she'd been into Spencer, it would put the weird stuff about Andy and Violet accusing them of liking each other to rest.

"Man, you won't believe this," she started. "It's so awkward, and I know he would have never felt the same about me. But I, umm—I kind of had feelings for Spencer."

Karter averted his gaze. "Oh."

"Yeah. I think that could be the reason Violet's love spell didn't work on me when I met her."

"It didn't work on you when we fought her the other night, either." He sounded as though he was stating a fact, not asking a question. "Unless you didn't make eye contact with her."

"Yeah, no. I didn't. Just in case. Anyway, I can't imagine Syrena would have appreciated me having feelings for her boyfriend. If the roles were reversed, I'm sure I wouldn't have been happy with her either."

"Syrena wasn't like that. She loved Spencer with all her heart. She would have wanted him to move on, to be happy and find someone again. I don't think she would have been mad at you. I'm sure Spencer would have fallen for you too, eventually. Why wouldn't he have?"

The way he said it made Zoey feel worse, and she decided that telling him about her crush on Spencer had *not* put what Andy and Violet said to rest. A part of her even began to wonder if maybe, just maybe, there could be some truth to the accusations.

"So, how come Violet's spell didn't work on *you*?" she asked, trying to sound upbeat, casual. "Is there someone special you haven't told us about?"

He turned to her once more, and they locked eyes. "I'm beginning to believe there might be." Her breath caught in her throat. She looked down, focusing on the grass instead of him, and he continued. "You said you 'had feelings' for Spencer. If I may ask . . . do you think you were in love with him?"

"No," she answered quickly, still staring at the ground. "I mean, I felt like I had a connection with him, but it wasn't full-on love. Not yet."

"Have you ever been in love before?"

"I—I think so, yeah. Have you?"

"Yes. With Violet."

"Violet? Seriously? She's a horrible person."

"She is, but she was my girlfriend a long time ago. She used her powers on me, and after I received my lightning scar, she broke up with me. It shattered my heart, so I think I really did love her, because usually once she breaks her love spell, the feelings wear off. But mine didn't. Not for a while. She tried to use her powers on me again the last time I was on Olympus, and she—she was unsuccessful."

"Maybe that's why her spell doesn't work on you anymore," Zoey suggested. "Because she really hurt you, I mean."

"That's what I thought at first, but she claims it's not possible. Apparently, a person has to have strong feelings for someone else for her powers to have no effect."

Zoey hugged her sides, unsure of how to respond. "Well, that's—that's just stupid. You know what? Her powers are stupid." *So articulate, Zoey*, she thought, cringing at the way she'd sounded. *He must think you have such a way with words.*

"You're not wrong," Karter said with a chuckle. He hesitated before going on. "I think the worst part about it all is that while I was back on Olympus, I still hoped Violet truly cared for me. Before I discovered the truth about what she was doing, I wanted her feelings to be real, for us to be together. Not because I loved her, but because I didn't want to feel so alone anymore. A part of me probably always knew she was wrong for me, but I refused to face it until I had no other choice."

Zoey mustered the courage to look at him again. "I get that. I get what it's like to hope someone is something they're not because you need the company."

"Really?" He sat up. "You don't strike me as someone who would be attracted to the wrong type of person. You were attracted to Spencer, and he's one of the best people I know."

"Yeah, Spencer was a great guy. But trust me, I had a Violet of my own back in the Before Time. Jet might not have been a child-of-Aphrodite, but he was manipulative enough to be one. He acted like he was this amazing person, that the girls before me were just 'crazy' and 'misunderstood' him, and I completely fell for it. Then one day, I told him something I'd *never* told anyone else. It was a secret, one I thought I'd keep to myself forever. I just felt so close to him, you know? I thought I could trust him with it, and I didn't want to carry the burden of it by myself anymore. It used to keep me up at night, and I thought telling someone else would help.

"So, I told him about it. Almost right after I did, he cheated on me, and when I got upset with him over it, he used my secret against me. He said I shouldn't be mad about his actions because of something I did before we'd ever started dating. I dumped him, and to get back at me, he told my secret to everyone at school. Pretty soon it spread through the whole town, and I was more alone than ever after that."

An expression of sad realization came over Karter's face. "When we were trapped together, after I said I would be known forever as a disgrace, you mentioned you'd been through something similar. This is what you were referring to, isn't it? He's the one who made you feel like a disgrace."

Her throat felt as if it were closing up. "No. I did it to myself. I've learned to live with my— my secret. I've accepted it. But I still regret it, and I especially regret telling him about it."

He opened his mouth to reply, but before he could, Diana emerged from the trees and stomped toward them. "I thought I heard talking." She wagged a disapproving finger at them. "What do you two think you're doing? You need to be sleeping!"

Kali let out another ridiculously loud snore, and Karter motioned at her. "We can't. Your girlfriend's being too loud." Diana tramped over to Kali, shook her awake, and began scolding her. All the while, Zoey and Karter stifled their laughter.

Diana finished chiding Kali. By the time she returned to watch duty, Kali had already fallen back asleep. All the while, Zoey and Karter decided they'd better try and rest. "Good night," Karter said with a yawn. He lay down on his side and closed his eyes.

"Night," Zoey whispered, and she must have been more tired than she thought, because even though her mind was reeling with everything she and Karter had discussed tonight, she was out the moment her head hit the ground.

"Why aren't you out searching for me and Zoey with the other gods and demigods?" Andy asked

Layla as he followed her through the garden. The sun had finished setting a while ago, their only light that of the stars above, and they'd been quiet since leaving the spot Layla had found him at. Things were getting super awkward, but on the bright side, Anteros hadn't bothered Andy in a while. "You said a bunch of them are out looking for us. Aren't you in a group with Violet and Xander? Violet was with Ares, so I saw her before he kidnapped me, but I didn't see you or Xander. Were you guys there?"

"Xander was, but I wasn't," she said. "I'm being reassigned."

"What does that mean?"

"It means the gods have decided I'm the weak link of the team, and they're in the process of finding somewhere else to place me. A less crucial spot."

Andy pursed his lips. "That's weird. I mean, I don't really know you, but when we fought you, you seemed super strong."

"They believe I was too cowardly to fight Karter on the night of Diana's execution. That's the story I fed them, anyway, so they wouldn't discover I was helping him and Diana. Since we're asking questions, I'd like to know something. When did you grow those wings?"

Andy had forgotten that the one time he and Layla had crossed paths, Anteros's wings hadn't appeared yet. "Right before my friends and I traveled to Poseidon's palace to steal the Trident."

"And where did they come from?"

"No idea," he lied.

"Hmm. Yet another mystery of the Dreaded Prophecy."

"Oh, for sure." He quickened his pace so he could walk beside her. "My turn. If Karter 'inspired' you to save Diana, then why are you still here on Olympus? Why didn't you leave with us on the night of her execution?" He thought of Darko, and his eyes burned with tears. "We could have really used the extra help."

She kept on staring forward, but her frown softened at yet another mention of Diana. Andy remembered from Spencer's visions of the past—memories saturated with death—that Layla had once been on Diana's warrior team. He was starting to think there was some serious history between them, considering the way Layla was acting about her.

"I care for Diana," Layla said. "But I fear my father's wrath."

"If you're so afraid of him, then why are you

helping me now?"

"Helping you leave Olympus is not the same as leaving it myself."

"Wouldn't Ares be upset either way?"

"Yes." Her scowl returned. "My whole life, he's taught me to honor the gods, but especially him. If he discovers that I helped Diana and Karter, or that I'm helping you, he'll kill me."

"Really?" Andy was legitimately curious as to whether Layla was being serious or just exaggerating. It seemed as if all the gods had anger issues, but Ares had disobeyed Zeus's orders to bring Andy here because he sensed Anteros's divine essence. That had to mean he loved his children in some capacity, right?

Layla clenched her fists, the shade of her skin shifting into the same red color as her hair. "These days, the only children my father gives leniency to are the ones he shares with Aphrodite."

Andy gulped. *Oh boy. She wouldn't be happy to find out who's trapped inside of me, would she?* "So, you have a lot of demigod siblings?" he asked.

"Demigods are rare." She didn't sound less angry, but her skin began to change back to brown. "The only reason there're so many of us today is because there are hundreds of living gods who have free rein to do whatever they'd like to humanity. Right now, I'm the only known mortal child-of-Ares, although there have been others, mostly in the old days."

"Got it."

A twig *crack*ed from somewhere behind the pair. They snapped to attention. Andy leapt into the air, and Layla raised her fists. "Who's there?" she said.

Out of the trees stepped a feminine figure standing over six feet tall. She was dressed like a gladiator, her wavy golden hair tumbling out from her helmet down her back. She held a blazing torch, and what looked like a lasso hung from her belt.

Anteros piped up in Andy's head. *"Mother! It took her long enough."*

"Layla," Aphrodite drawled, sashaying forward. "It's so nice to see you bonding with your long-lost half-brother, Anteros."

Layla's jaw dropped. "A-Anteros?" She glanced back and forth between Andy and Aphrodite in disbelief.

"Don't listen to that psycho," Andy said. "I'm not Anteros. Now run!" He spun around and soared farther into the garden.

Layla sprinted after him. "What exactly is going on here?"

"I'll explain later. Right now, you gotta get

me to the edge of Olympus. You gotta help me reach Diana!"

Layla caught up to him, running below him now. "Fine. But I'm not doing it for you. I'm doing it for her."

At her words, relief flooded Andy. "Thank you so much."

"Don't thank me until we've escaped."

There was a glint of gold up ahead. Andy's stomach clenched. Fearing the worst, he veered right. Layla followed.

Just when he thought they were in the clear, a massive man clad in battle armor leapt out of the shadows before them.

"Oh, excellent. Father was tracking us as well," Anteros said.

Ares seized Layla by the hair. She shrieked as he jerked her to the ground. "Let her go!" Andy shouted, flapping toward her. He grabbed her hands and pulled and—

Thick rope looped around Andy's waist and yanked him backward. He lost grip of Layla and toppled wings-first to the ground. Sharp pain shot through them.

Groaning, he reached down to loosen the cord, when more of it coiled around his neck, then his wrists and ankles. He grappled against the bindings, but it was no use. They'd been pulled tight. He couldn't move.

He cursed and struggled, the rope cutting into his flesh, and Aphrodite stepped into view above him. "My beloved son," she said. "After all these years, it's so good to have you back."

CHAPTER FIFTEEN

ALONE

When Karter awoke the next morning, Zoey and Diana were fast asleep, and Kali was the one on watch duty. After Zoey and Diana woke up, they all had breakfast, mounted their pegasi, and soared northeast toward Zeus City.

Despite how close they were to the *polis*, it still took several hours to fly there. They landed in the surrounding forest, and once they did, Zoey washed up in a stream and changed into the brown dress Karter remembered her wearing in Hephaestus City, as Diana had insisted that she could no longer wear her blue gown.

"It's filthy," Diana had said, pointing at the dress. *"Ragged. When people see you, they'll know you're a fugitive."*

"Thanks, Diana," Zoey had replied sarcastically. *"'Ragged' is just the way every girl wants to be described."*

Kali had laughed at the exchange. *"Princess here is strictly referring to the dress. We all know you're gorgeous, Sweet Stuff."*

Even though Karter couldn't help but agree with Kali—he'd always thought Zoey was pretty, he'd have had to be blind not to—he'd kept his mouth shut. Zoey had rolled her eyes and headed off to clean up.

Zoey returned, and they began to form a plan. Since they had pegasi, and since the creatures were their most reliable way to reach Andy before his time was up, someone needed to stay outside the city to ensure they didn't fly away or get attacked.

"Obviously, one of us will still have to go in with Zoey," Diana said.

Kali raised a hand. "I'll do it. That way, we can use the Helm to stay invisible. We'll be in and out in no time."

Diana cupped her chin. "That's true."

"The problem is that neither of you have been to Zeus City, and it's extremely large and crowded," Karter pointed out. "You don't know where the library is—or where anything else is, for that matter. Even if we gave you directions, it could take you days to find what you need. Also, despite being invisible, you could still be detected. Someone could catch sight of your footprints if you're walking on a dirt road, or someone could bump into you and realize who you are because you can't be seen."

"What do you suggest we do, then?" Zoey asked.

He contemplated the question. "Someone who's been to Zeus City needs to go with you. That way, you can head straight to the library, so no time is wasted. And if for some reason finding literature that calls on Calliope takes the rest of today, or even some of tomorrow, whoever goes would need to be familiar with the city so they can check you into an inn for the night."

"Wait, did you say 'inn'?" Zoey asked. "Do you mean like a motel? Why would the people in the cities need one of those if they aren't allowed to leave? Wouldn't they just stay at their own house every night?"

"Sometimes the aristocrats travel from city to city, but only if they have permission from the gods," Karter explained. "Occasionally, there are also regular citizens who are out too late during the day, or they're made to work later than they should be, and they can't get home before sundown. When that happens, they stay at an inn for the night to ensure they aren't arrested."

Kali shook her head. "That's such a strange law. Unless it's unsafe, they should be able to go outside whenever they please."

"It's yet another way the gods control people," Karter said to Kali, then turned back to Zoey. "As I was saying, you might need to stay at an inn overnight if your mission is taking too long. It wouldn't be wise to sneak into Zeus City today, only to sneak out later tonight, and then sneak back in tomorrow. It wouldn't be a good idea to hide in the streets until sunrise either. We can't risk you being taken by a god like Andy was."

"I completely agree," Diana said. "Especially because the gods are out looking for you, Zoey. If there are any searching for you in there, they'll be more likely to catch you if you're out while everyone is inside and the streets are clear. I also think Karter is right—you need to go with someone who knows how to navigate the city. Unfortunately, that person isn't me. I've been to Zeus City once, a long time ago, and I don't remember much from the trip."

Karter had figured he'd have to be the one to take Zoey into the *polis*, but he didn't mind. Since she'd warmed up to him, he'd been enjoying her company, even when their conversations were less than lighthearted.

Speaking of—she'd really taken him by surprise last night. First by telling him that he was destined to die, and then by sharing that she'd had feelings for Spencer.

Oddly enough, dying didn't scare Karter anymore. Ever since he'd betrayed the gods, he'd known there was a good chance he wouldn't survive this war. He'd made peace with the possibility of it, and now with the inevitability of it.

But every time he thought about the fact that Zoey had liked his late best friend—which, since she'd broken the news, had been often—his chest grew tight. And although he thought he might be starting to understand why he felt that way, he wasn't sure if he was ready to confront it, or if he should tell Zoey about it at all.

He'd *almost* brought it up to her last night,

after she'd asked him why Violet's spell hadn't worked on him, but he'd decided against it. *We're in the middle of a war*, he thought. *This isn't the time.*

"In that case, it has to be me," Karter said. "I have to be the one to go in with you, Zoey."

"All right," she replied, unfazed at the prospect. "What should we do with the objects of power? I don't think it would be smart for us to take them after what happened in Aphrodite City, but I don't think it would be smart to leave them outside, either."

"Only take what looks inconspicuous in your bag," Kali said. "So, just the Helm, and probably one of the daggers you brought. Leave the Trident and Lightning Bolt out here."

Diana shook her head. "I don't know if that's a good idea. What if we're attacked by gods or *astynomia* or something, and they get ahold of the Trident or Bolt? What if Zoey and Karter are discovered, and during a fight they lose the Helm?"

"We could bury the objects," Karter said. "As deeply in the ground as possible. Then, if you're attacked while Zoey and I are in the city, whoever's found you won't have as much of a chance at discovering the objects. They might figure out that they were buried, but it would take time to uncover them."

Kali narrowed her eyes at him. "That's not a bad idea. Maybe you're not as much of a jackass as I thought." He shrugged sheepishly.

They decided Karter's idea was their best bet and crafted a digging stick out of the wood of fallen trees nearby. Over the next hour, Karter used his super-strength to dig three holes far from one another, each nearly six feet deep, in spots where the grass was sparse so it wouldn't be as obvious that the earth had been disturbed. Zoey and Kali dropped the objects of power into the holes, and then everyone helped to replace the soil.

As Karter and Zoey prepared to enter the city, Diana gave Zoey a hug. "Be careful in there," Diana said, squeezing her tight.

Zoey squeezed her back. "Of course, and you be careful out here."

"We will."

Kali hugged Zoey next. "Don't give yourself up to Calliope too quickly. We'll brainstorm new possible ways to cast the Descent without her and Anteros. Maybe, if Persephone proves she's changed, we could even ask her to do it."

"I don't think that's a good idea." Zoey pulled away from Kali. "After what Persephone's done, it would take years—and a lot of good deeds—for me to trust her with something this important."

Kali's shoulders slumped. "You're right not to trust her. I think I'm just getting desperate for a solution."

"We'll come up with something," Diana said.

Zoey frowned in a way that told Karter she wasn't hopeful they'd be successful in their efforts. "Okay."

Karter shook Diana's hand and offered Kali a curt nod of farewell. "I'll keep her safe," he assured them, and then he and Zoey were off.

For a long while they walked in silence, and Karter found himself glancing at Zoey often: at her delicate facial features, at the curves of her figure, at her damp brown curls bouncing against her back, drying in the summer sun.

He didn't mean to do it, and each time it happened, he grew angrier with himself. *Focus, focus, focus. We're in the middle of a war, remember?*

Hoping to keep himself from staring more, he decided to speak. "I might have to steal a cloak once we reach the houses on the outer rim."

"Oh, yeah," Zoey said. "The citizens will probably recognize you right away, huh?"

The lightning scar on the right side of his face throbbed with the memory of old pain. He brushed his fingers against the mottled flesh. "Yes. They probably will."

"Oh, uh . . ." She fiddled with a stray curl. "That's, umm—I didn't mean it like that. I meant they'd recognize you because you're Zeus's son."

Karter dropped his hand to his side. "That's true, but I also have a distinct mark. My irises are recognizable as well. They were brown before my father struck me with lightning. I'll need something to cover my face, or we'll be discovered immediately."

"A hooded cloak, maybe? I bet that would look mysterious."

"Mysterious?"

"Yeah, you know, in a good way."

He snorted. "Let's hope you're right."

They both kept the conversation going, and within an hour or so they arrived at the outer rim of the *polis*. They crept through acres of farmland, then finally approached the first neighborhood. There were a lot of people around, but thankfully, enough clothing had been strung between the houses that it was easy to hide as they entered the area, and Karter made sure to snatch a cloak as they passed the initial few houses.

He put it on and tugged it over his face, and

Zoey put her hand on her hip, smirking at him. "Just like I said, mysterious in a good way."

"Glad you think so."

They snuck through the neighborhoods, dashing behind houses and into alleyways to avoid being spotted until they reached the *Agora*. Like the rest of the cities, Zeus's consisted of miles and miles of streets and buildings, and since it was the middle of the day, the *Agora* bustled with thousands of citizens. Some rode in horse-drawn carts down the roads, while others hurried along the cobblestone paths, baskets of goods in hand. The citizens were crammed together, packed so closely it was difficult for everyone to keep from bumping into each other.

"Wow, you were right. It's really crowded here," Zoey yelled at Karter over the roar of chatter.

"As King of the Gods, Zeus has the most citizens in his *polis*," Karter shouted back. "It's the biggest in the world."

"Of course it is."

Karter tugged his hood as far as he could over his face and held it in place, then offered his free arm to Zoey. "Hold onto me so we don't get separated." Was it just him, or had she blushed at his suggestion?

After a second's deliberation, she laced her arm with his, and his heart palpitated. Guiding her forward, he hoped she wouldn't notice how anxious he'd become.

They hastened through the *Agora*, doing their best not to be trampled, and every so often, impolite people were bold enough to shove the pair. "Hey, watch where you're going!" Karter would snap at the citizens, and as they stalked away, they'd shout something imperceptible over their shoulders.

It took what felt like forever to reach the section of the *Agora* where the library was located, and evening already drew near. Worried about what they'd do for tonight, Karter let go of his hood and purposely bumped into a few people to pick their pockets for silver drachmas.

"What are you doing?" Zoey asked, panic in her voice.

"Getting money in case we need to stay at an inn tonight," he said simply.

They arrived before the library, which sat atop a grassy hill. It was a massive gold-and-white pillared building with multiple levels. Citizens hurried up and down the tall staircase leading up to it, and in and out of its arched entryway.

Karter jerked his head at the structure. "This

is it."

Zoey let go of his arm, staring at the library with wonder. "It's huge."

"What did you expect?"

"Not this. Libraries in the Before Time were *not* this enormous. Well, the one where I lived wasn't. Maybe the ones in big cities were, but I didn't get to travel much." She stared at the building a bit longer, and then her face fell.

He reached out to put a hand on her shoulder but decided he'd better not at the last moment. "Is something wrong?"

"Both times we were in Aphrodite City, Andy had that strong buzzing feeling in his chest," she replied. "It was Anteros guiding him toward the statue, so he'd touch it and they'd connect or whatever. But I don't feel anything like that. Not at all."

"I'm sure the buzzing sensation occurred because a statue can indicate a strong form of worship. There isn't a statue of Calliope in here, just some epic poetry that references her, so your pull to this place might not be as strong as Andy's was to the statue."

"That's fair, I guess. It would also explain why I wasn't drawn to the library in Aphrodite City, assuming it has poetry where Calliope is referenced."

"Exactly." Karter motioned at the staircase leading up to the library. "If we walk around and browse for a bit, perhaps you'll start to feel a similar draw, and it will lead you to something before the evening's over."

"Here's hoping." Zoey laced her arm with his once more and practically dragged him up the steps. As they walked inside, she gasped.

"Do you feel a pull?" he asked.

"Unfortunately, no," she answered. "I just can't believe how beautiful it is in here."

He was about to say he agreed, then realized he was staring at her again. He tore his gaze from her and shifted it toward the library's interior to find they stood on the bottom floor, and that alone was larger than the dining chambers on New Mount Olympus. Marble statues of the Olympians lined the walls, and everywhere Karter looked, there were long, rectangular tables with people reading at them and stone shelves filled to the brim with leather-bound tomes. Three more levels overlooked this one, closed off by balconies embellished with geometric swirls, and Karter assumed more books were stored on those floors.

Zoey released her hold on Karter. "I don't even know where to begin."

"Look for the 'epics' section." He started

farther into the library, his sandals clacking against the golden tiles of the floor. "That's where we'll find what we need."

She followed him. "Do you have any specific titles in mind?"

He combed through memories of old history lessons with Apollo. "I don't. It's been so long."

"Didn't Diana mention that Homer and Virgil were inspired by Calliope?"

"She did. It wouldn't hurt to investigate their works first."

It took some searching, but eventually they found the epics section, which had hundreds of translations in every spoken language of this part of the world stocked along its lengthy shelves.

Zoey's eyes widened as she absorbed the sheer volume of books before them. "Uh, how many of these did Homer and Virgil write, exactly?"

"Don't worry," Karter said. "Many are the same poem but in different languages."

"Huh." Zoey grabbed the nearest English-translation copy of the *Aeneid* from its shelf and flipped through the pages. "I guess that makes sense. The originals would have been written in ancient Greek or Latin, right?"

"That's right," he replied.

"If the originals were written in ancient Greek or Latin, then I'm assuming one of those is the gods' first language, but everyone Andy and I have come across so far speaks English. Why haven't the gods forced everyone to learn their first language?"

Karter scanned the shelves for a copy of the *Iliad*. "Because the gods are such transcendent beings, and because they've existed for thousands upon thousands of years, they already knew how to read, write, and speak every major language in the world. Consequently, they didn't *need* to force anyone to learn something new; they focused their energy elsewhere and allowed people to continue using whatever tongues were most familiar to them. The reason everyone you've met so far speaks English is because, before the gods took over, it was the most spoken language in this part of the world."

"Ah, okay. Got it."

Over the next several hours, Karter and Zoey scanned the poems written by Homer and Virgil as quickly as they could, but Zoey wasn't drawn to any of the verses, and the tomes seemed to be missing several pages, white sheets torn jaggedly from the bindings.

Zoey placed a book back on the shelf. "This is so weird. I can't find anything about Calliope or even the Muses. You'd think they'd be named at least once, since all these other gods are." She thought for a moment. "You don't think Zeus ripped out passages where Calliope was mentioned, do you?"

"He might have done that, especially if he feared her return," Karter said. "But citizens could have torn out the pages too, and there are still a lot of books to look through."

Just as they started to investigate another author's work, a bell rang at the entrance, and a man's voice echoed across the chamber. "Sun is setting! Library closes in ten minutes! Everyone out in ten minutes!"

Zoey slammed her book shut. "Crap."

"We'll just have to stay in the city for the night and come back tomorrow," Karter said, and they put the books away. "There's an inn with an eatery not far from here. We'll go there."

They hastened out of the building and down the stairs, back out onto the cobblestone paths with everyone else, and Karter led Zoey down the path on the left. If he remembered correctly, the inn was only about a fifteen-minute stroll away, but they couldn't waste any time, so they speed-walked. As they hurried in the direction of the inn, satyr and centaur *astynomia* began to patrol the streets, their mere presence urging people to get indoors as soon as possible.

Soon they neared the inn, which was a building similar in structure to the citizens' houses, although it had to be twenty times larger than any regular home.

"Here it is," Karter said as they approached it. "Do you want dinner before we request rooms, or—"

"Did you say 'rooms,' like, *plural?*" Zoey interrupted, her grip on his arm tightening. "Because I'm *not* staying in a hotel in friggin' Zeus City by myself."

"You're right, sorry. I only wanted to be respectful of you. I wasn't sure . . . well, I wasn't sure whether it would be, uhh . . . appropriate. For us to stay here alone together . . . if you know what I mean." He chanced a glance at her and saw her face had turned scarlet.

"I wasn't worried about whether it was 'appropriate' before, but now I am," she said. "There are rooms with more than one bed, right?"

"Of course, and even if one isn't available, I can sleep on the floor."

"Then I don't know why your mind went there in the first place."

"Neither do I," he lied. "Apologies."

"Hey, are you okay? You're getting all

sweaty."

He kept his focus on the inn entrance ahead. "Must be the cloak."

"You were fine all day. You know, when it was way hotter outside. Are you sure you're okay?"

"Mm-hmm."

They entered the building, which was illuminated by flaming sconces hanging from the walls, and the smell of cooking meat and freshly baked bread tickled Karter's nostrils. His mouth watered, his stomach grumbling, but he decided they should request a place to stay before going to the eatery. He asked the innkeeper—a hunched-over old bald man with a silver beard—for a two-bed room for one night, and paid using some of the drachmas he'd stolen.

The innkeeper gave them a bronze key and directions to their room, and they headed toward the right-hand side of the building, then up a winding staircase. Three flights and a few hallways later, they found the room, confirmed it had two beds, and went back downstairs to have dinner.

They opted for a table at a far corner of the eatery, where there weren't as many sconces and they'd be partially hidden by shadows. Like the rest of the building, the eatery was crafted with stone, wood, and clay. A server brought them cups and a pitcher of wine, then menus and a basket of bread with seasoned olive oil for dipping. He started back toward the kitchen, which was closed-off behind a wall.

"Is there alcohol in this?" Zoey asked, pointing at her cup of wine.

"Yes, but it's watered down," Karter said. "It's customary in the cities to have wine with every meal, but you can ask for something else if you'd like."

"You know what? No. I've never had alcohol, and if someone else is going to be taking over my body soon, I'm going to try it while I can." She grabbed her cup and took three gulps of the deep-red liquid.

He laughed a bit. "You might want to slow down. You haven't eaten since breakfast."

She set the cup on the table. "I thought you said it wasn't strong."

"It isn't, but you've never had alcohol before, and you're drinking on an empty stomach. Who knows how little it will take to intoxicate you?"

"Fine. I'll have some bread." She grabbed a slice, dipped it in the olive oil, and took a bite. "Mm."

"Is it good?" He took a piece.

"Delicious."

They finished the bread before the server came back. When he did, they both ordered chicken and vegetables and requested more bread. He returned with another basket in no time.

As they waited for their meals, they finished their second basket. Karter sipped his wine, and Zoey guzzled down four cups. Her cheeks grew rosy, her shoulders relaxing, and she wouldn't stop smiling. Other than that, she didn't show signs of intoxication—at least, not severe intoxication.

"How are you feeling?" Karter asked.

She grinned. "Just wonderful."

Even in the dim light, her sky-blue eyes sparkled, and he couldn't help but smile back. "I'm glad you're enjoying yourself, despite the circumstances."

"Weirdly enough"—her words slurred together slightly now—"I'm finding out that I really like spending time with you."

"I like spending time with you too."

She frowned suddenly. "Man, if Andy were here, he would be *so* mad to hear me say that. You know, the night before we left for Aphrodite City, he accused me of basically being in love with you because I was mad at you when you picked the gods over us."

Karter coughed, nearly choking on his wine. "He accused you of—of what now?"

"Of having feelings for you."

Karter hacked some more, beating his chest. *What are the odds?* "Wow, that's crazy."

She looked away, and Karter wondered if he'd said the wrong thing. "Yeah, definitely. Anyway, I think he was just angry because I told him I don't have feelings for him. Why can't he understand I only see him as a friend? I still love him, just not in *that* way, you know?"

With this context, things were starting to make sense. Why Andy hadn't slept in the cabin the night before they went to Aphrodite City, why he'd had a sour attitude as they entered the *polis*, why Zoey had apologized to him before he touched the statue of Anteros. Something was going on between them, just as Karter had suspected, but that something was one-sided.

He cleared his throat. "Sorry, yes. I know exactly what you mean." Her smile returned. "I think when our meals arrive, I'll ask for water. Would you like some?"

She hiccupped. "Sounds good."

When the server came with their food, Karter requested water as well. The main course was as delectable as the bread had been, and the pair devoured the entirety of their plates.

Zoey did have water, but she also insisted on finishing the pitcher of wine. Karter knew that probably wasn't a good idea, but considering these could be some of her last days "alive," he didn't have the heart to stop her. Instead, he opted to help her finish it, and hopefully, she wouldn't get sick.

It took a while, but they finished the pitcher, and by the time they paid and made it up the stairs to the room, Karter's head was fuzzy, a blissful warmth in his belly, and Zoey could hardly walk.

Zoey leaned on Karter, giggling as he unlocked the door. It opened and she stumbled inside, snorting with laughter, and he tottered forward, the foggy feeling in his head almost forcing him to the floor. He caught himself, locked the door behind them, and tossed his cloak aside. Then he used electricity to light the sconces on both sides of the door so they could see.

He turned around to find Zoey sprawled on the ground. "I *cannot* walk anymore," she said. "It's like—like the room is tilting back and forth."

"Do you feel sick?"

"No. Just . . . funny."

"You must hold alcohol well. That was a lot of wine." If he'd drunk as much as she had, he would have already vomited. It had happened to him before—Spencer, Syrena, and he hadn't been strangers to parties. "I'll help you to bed, if you need me to."

"Please. I'm ready for sleep."

He scooped her up, and she threw her arms around him as if holding on for dear life. "You okay?" he asked.

She nuzzled her nose into his neck, and his heart skipped a beat. It took all his focus to stay upright. "Yes," she said, her breath hot on his skin. "Tired."

"Well, let's get you to bed. We have a long couple of days ahead of us." He carried her toward the nearest bed; he'd take the one by the window. However, when he was only a few paces away, the fuzziness in his head intensified. His legs gave out beneath him, and he staggered sideways onto the mattress, Zoey still in his arms.

They hit the bed. Zoey rolled out of his grasp and burst into a fit of giggles. "You're just as out of it as I am."

"I am not," he argued, laughing.

"You are too." Her giggling subsided, though she didn't stop grinning at him. He smiled back, their gazes locked, and for a short while, Karter forgot about their problems, about their horrible fates.

She reached toward him, toward the scarred side of his face, just as she had in Aphrodite City. But instead of jerking away this time, he sat still.

Gently, she brushed her fingers against the uneven flesh beneath his right eye. Tingling warmth spread through his body from the point of contact. "I didn't mean to embarrass you about this earlier today," she said. "It's not bad."

"You don't have to lie."

"I'm not lying." She moved the pads of her fingers down his face, along the lines of the scar, and as her thumb passed over his lips, he shivered. "I don't really notice it anymore, to be honest. It's just a part of you." Her fingers stopped at his jawline. She paused, her smile fading, and pulled her hand away. He wished she hadn't. "Can I tell you something?"

"Anything."

"You're my friend now, and if I'm going to be gone soon, I want another one of my friends to know about this. Andy does, but he—he doesn't get it. We love each other, but I don't feel like he completely *gets* me, you know? I was going to tell Diana about it at one point, but Kali walked in before I could, and I considered telling Spencer, but I never got the chance. I thought maybe you'd understand. I just want someone to understand."

"I'll do my best." He swallowed hard. "What is it?"

"Remember how I told you I have a horrible secret? And how, after I told my old boyfriend about it, he spread it around to everyone to get revenge on me, and it made me a 'disgrace' in my own time?"

"I remember."

Her eyes grew watery. "After my parents split up, times were tough." Her voice trembled, her words slurring together, but Karter listened closely so he wouldn't miss anything. "I was fourteen. My mom couldn't pay for our apartment, and they were gonna kick us out. I didn't know it at the time, but my dad had died. He obviously wouldn't answer my calls, and I had no other family.

"Anyway, my mom and I—we'd been homeless before. It was awful. I didn't wanna do it again. I was so scared. So I . . . I took matters into my own hands." Tears trickled from her eyes down onto the bed, and Karter dried her cheeks with his hands. "We had a week until they were gonna kick us out, and I went out every night that week, looking for men and—and asking them if they wanted to sleep with me in exchange for money. The money I needed to pay rent."

He wiped more of her tears away. "What happened next?"

She sucked in a long, shuddering breath. "I found two guys. They were friends. Much older than me. They—they gave me what I asked for." Her face crumpled, and her body racked with sobs.

At Zoey's anguish, Karter's chest ached so badly it was as if he were bruised from the inside and someone was battering the contusions. He took her hand in one of his and gave it a squeeze.

Several minutes passed before her cries subsided slightly. "I've regretted what I did ever since. It kept me and my mom off the streets, yeah, but sometimes . . . it makes me feel like I'm less. Like I'm tainted, spoiled. Ruined."

"You might regret what you did, but it doesn't make you any of those things."

She sniffled. "It's the biggest mistake I've ever made."

"You were young, scared." He let go of her and dried her face again. "You felt trapped, like you had no other choice, like you were alone.

You did what you could to survive. I understand what that's like. I've experienced it many times in my life. But you're here now, and you're not alone anymore. It's okay."

A peaceful, contented expression came over her face. She broke their eye contact, her gaze falling to his mouth.

She inched toward him, closed her eyes, and pressed her lips against his.

The kiss was so light, so tender, and such a surprise that for a second, Karter could only lay there in fuzzy-headed shock.

But then he registered what was happening. This girl—this strong, beautiful, amazing girl—was kissing him. She smelled and tasted of sweet red wine, her lips pillowy soft.

Closing his eyes, he deepened the kiss, and she grabbed a fistful of his hair. Heart pounding, breaths quickening, he circled his arms around her waist and pulled her body against his.

Karter couldn't say for sure how long they remained kissing like that. All he knew was one moment they lay on their sides, mouth to mouth and chest to chest. The next, he was on top of her and she was wrapping her legs around him and—

No, wait, he thought. *We have to stop.* He tore away from her.

"What's wrong?" she asked, sitting up.

Her speech was still slurred, and he thanked the Fates they hadn't taken this any further. "We're drunk," he said. "And whatever is happening between us—whatever this feeling is—what if it's gone by morning? What if we had done something that can't be taken back? Something you'll regret?"

She looked away. "You're right. I'm—I'm sorry."

"No, *I'm* sorry." He shook his head. "I got so caught up in the moment, I just kept kissing you."

"It's okay. So did I."

"Are you all right?"

She brushed some hair behind her ear. "Yeah. Are you?"

"Yes."

"Should we . . . should we try and sleep this off?"

He wasn't sure whether she meant the wine or what had just happened. "I think so," he said.

Slowly, she crawled around him, pulled up one of the blankets, and rested her head against her pillow. "Okay. Umm . . . good night, I guess."

"Good night." He stood, stumbled toward the sconces, and snuffed out the lights, then teetered to his own bed and yanked the blankets over himself.

"Hey, Karter?" she said.

"Yes?"

"Thank you."

He didn't know what she was thanking him for. Still, he replied, "Of course."

Her breathing slowed, and he guessed she'd gone to sleep, but he knew it would take an eternity before he'd manage to drift off. He couldn't stop thinking about everything that had happened this evening, about everything that had happened over the past several days, about everything that had happened since he'd met Zoey and Andy. And the more he thought, the more he came to understand something.

His feelings for Zoey were strong. Stronger than he could have ever imagined.

He didn't know when they'd begun to develop, only that he'd become fully aware of them within the past few days. If he had to guess, he'd say they'd started up in Hephaestus City, but romance had been the last thing on his mind then, so he couldn't be sure.

All he could be sure of was that he might be falling in love.

It was a terrifying realization—especially because he knew they could never be.

He was destined to die. She was destined to converge with Calliope.

If only he could shield her from what was to come, if only he could save her from her cruel fate. Maybe then he'd be able to rest.

CHAPTER SIXTEEN

READ

Persephone marched through miles of forest, the sky black in the night as she led the army of nymphs to Olympus and contemplated how absurd her situation had become.

She'd never imagined that a mortal child-of-Apollo would be giving her orders. More than that, she'd never imagined that she'd be *following* such orders.

Yet Diana, the insufferable waif of a girl, had told Persephone that she was going to leave camp with Zoey and Karter, and that Persephone was not to follow them—that she was to help the nymphs save Andy from Ares. Diana had also told Persephone to lie to the nymphs by saying she couldn't access Zoey, Diana, and Karter's location after they left so that the nymphs wouldn't try to follow them.

And Persephone had done just as Diana demanded.

Despite the fact that Persephone agreed with Zoey's strategy of independently reconnecting with Calliope, it had taken everything in her to not argue with the Daughter of Apollo, to not follow them out of spite. Because what Diana had said to Persephone—about how she was just as self-serving as the Olympians—had infuriated her.

Not because it wasn't true.

But because deep down, Persephone knew it was true.

No, she'd never participated in the Storm. She'd never helped in decimating humanity. But she hadn't tried to stop the Olympians from doing so either. *Just like when they cast Prometheus into the pit*, she thought. *I did nothing to stop them.*

Persephone had also exercised wickedness on mortals more than once, just like the Olympians, and although she'd believed she was justified in her actions, she was starting to wonder if perhaps she'd been wrong.

She was starting to wonder if perhaps she'd put just as much misery into the world as they had.

She chuckled and shook her head. What a strange, cruel thing fate was.

Zoey awoke with a throbbing headache.

Sunlight spilled from the window into their room in the inn. She blinked and groaned, taking in her surroundings.

The room looked just as it had yesterday. Small, no bathroom—the innkeeper had notified them that there was only one bathroom per floor, and that all the guests shared it.

She rolled over to face Karter, her headache fading a bit, and the moment she caught sight of him sleeping, she began to recall what had happened last night, the events storming through her mind like a raging hurricane.

Oh my God, she thought, her cheeks practically lighting on fire as she imagined what might have occurred if Karter hadn't stopped their make-out session. She covered her face with her hand. What the hell had she been thinking? Why in the world had she kissed him in the first place?

Andy's words from their fight the other day echoed in her mind, and guilt crept through her. *"It's not Spencer, is it? You couldn't have him, so you decided on the next best thing. His closest friend. Karter."*

No way. It's not like that.

What was it like, then? Was she falling for Karter? Did she have legitimate feelings for him?

She'd contemplated the possibility the night before last, during their long conversation by the campfire, but it didn't seem likely. She'd hated him a week ago.

Did I really hate him, or was I just hurt?

She lowered her hand from her face so she could see him, so she could really look at him. As he slept his expression was tranquil. His hair stuck out in every direction, his arms up and around his head at weird angles.

The more she studied him—his wild hair, his full lips, his strong jawline—the more she noticed how handsome he was. Well, she'd noticed it back in Hephaestus City, back when he'd told her the story of how he got his scar. But after he'd betrayed her, she'd disregarded any sort of desirability he might have possessed.

Why am I even thinking about this? Any day now, we're going to have to sacrifice ourselves to save the world. We'll both be gone, and none of this will matter anymore.

Except thoughts like that made her feel worse. She was resigned to her fate, but not to his. She wanted him to get through this. To live a life free of his father, one full of love and happiness.

Shit.

I am falling for him, aren't I?

As though Karter sensed she was thinking about him, he woke up. Her stomach did a flip. He yawned, stretched, and smiled at her. "Hey."

"Hey," she said back. "Do you, umm—do you by chance remember anything from last night? After we got back to the room?"

His smile disappeared, his cheeks flushing pink. "Oh, gods . . . Yes, I do. Do you?"

"Yeah." She buried her face in her blanket. "Crap. Crap crap *crap*. I'm so sorry."

"Don't apologize," he replied quickly. "Maybe there was an aphrodisiac in the wine, or something. Besides, it didn't bother me. I mean, I'm—I'm no stranger to, uh, kissing."

She shot him a glare. "Oh, really?"

He cursed, pinching the bridge of his nose. "Sorry. I didn't mean it like that."

"Sure you didn't." She rolled over so she wouldn't have to look at him for a bit.

"Zoey." Her heart fluttered as he said her name. "I'm serious. I didn't mean for it to sound that way. I'm not always the best at talking to people, and it doesn't help that you, um ... make me nervous. You don't all the time, but sometimes. Like right now."

She huffed. "I don't see why I'd make you nervous."

A long pause before he spoke again. "Listen. About last night. It's all right. What I was trying to say before is, well ... I didn't exactly pull away from you, did I?"

"Why would you have, if there was an aphrodisiac in the wine?"

He groaned. "I only said that to explain why you kissed me in the first place—not why I kissed you back. I just don't want you to feel bad about any of it. It was my fault it went as far as it did. I should be the one apologizing. I would never want to—to take advantage of you, especially when you were in such a vulnerable state."

"I appreciate that," she said, and she meant it. "To be fair, though, you were in a vulnerable state too."

"That's true, I suppose."

She grunted in pain, pressing her hand against her forehead. "I think I'm hungover."

"You're not feeling well?"

"No, not at all."

There was a sound like blankets rustling, then footfalls, and Karter appeared in her peripheral. He grabbed his cloak up off the floor and pulled it over his head. "I'll get you some water. That should help." He exited the room, and a little while later he returned with two cups of water. He plopped down onto the foot of her bed and offered her one of them.

She sat up to take it. "Thank you."

"My pleasure."

She gulped down the drink. When she finished it, he handed her the other cup. "Isn't that one for you?" she asked.

"I'll have some at breakfast." She raised a brow at him, but he just stared hard at her with those golden eyes of his, insisting she drink it. "You need it more than I do. We have a long day ahead of us."

She relented, taking the glass. But even after chugging both cups, she still didn't feel great.

He must have suspected it hadn't helped much. "Why don't we eat something?" he suggested. "If water doesn't work, food is usually the next thing I try after a night of drinking."

"Okay." She climbed out of bed, then ran her fingers through the tangles in her hair and straightened the wrinkles in her dress as best she could. "Do I look all right? All right enough to go out into the city, I mean. So that I don't stand out to the citizens?"

"You always stand out." Her heart skipped, and he swallowed hard. "Sorry. I'm sure you'll blend in. Well, you'll blend in as much as you can, considering . . ." He gestured up and down at her awkwardly.

He wasn't kidding when he said I make him nervous sometimes. It's kind of cute. She reached out, took one of his hands in hers, and gave it a reassuring squeeze. "You stand out, too. Let's go." He blushed, but before he had a chance to reply she dragged him into the hall, and they headed downstairs.

After returning their key to the innkeeper, Zoey and Karter went over to the inn's built-in restaurant and sat down at the same table as last night. The first thing their server brought them was a pitcher of wine. They refused it, asking for water instead. The server gave them an odd look, took the pitcher away, and returned with their drink of choice.

Breakfast consisted of bread and porridge,

which Zoey was grateful for. It was easy on her stomach, and coupled with the water, it helped her headache subside. Once finished, they paid for their meal, exited the building, and started back toward the library.

"After today, we only have three days left before Andy is supposed to be discovered," Karter said as they traversed the crowded paths.

"I know," Zoey replied. "We have to find something with Calliope, like, now."

It wasn't long before they reached the library. They hurried inside and found the spot they'd stopped at in the epics section yesterday, then began pulling new books from the shelves and scanning them for any sign of the Goddess of Eloquence.

As they continued their search, there were a few instances in which Zoey thought she saw other people in the library looking at her and Karter and whispering to each other. Whenever it happened, Karter stepped in front of Zoey and told her to keep her head down. "It'll be fine," he kept saying. "We just have to be quick."

However, it was impossible to be quick. Hours passed before they made it through every English-translation poem, and they still hadn't found anything.

Zoey hung her head. "I'm starting to wonder if this was a mistake. Maybe the nymphs were right, and the only way to reconnect with Calliope is by touching Andy. Maybe I shouldn't have asked you to bring me here. Maybe I shouldn't have left the nymph camp at all."

"No, you should have." He rested a hand on her shoulder. To her surprise, the touch relaxed her a bit. "You were right. What if Zeus discovers Andy prematurely, and he's—he's put in Tartarus? I pray that doesn't happen, but if it does, and if you haven't reconnected with Calliope on your own, how would you then? How would you—you know, converge with her? Allow her to become a full avatar?"

She smiled sadly. "You're going to let me do that now, huh?"

"It wasn't my choice to begin with. I just . . . I didn't want you to."

"I know you didn't, but there isn't another way. There never was."

He dropped his hand to his side. "We have to keep searching. Let's try the history section next."

"Wouldn't the old poems we already looked through technically be a part of history, since a lot of the things the authors describe actually happened?" Zoey asked.

"Yes and no. At times, the poems contradict one another because every writer interprets the gods a little differently, but the books in the history section were written by the gods themselves."

"If the history books were written by the gods, then who's to say they didn't erase Calliope from history altogether? Or, at least, that Zeus didn't, since this is *his* library?"

"It's a possibility," Karter replied. "But that doesn't mean we shouldn't look while we're here, just to be certain."

It turned out that the history section was organized by centuries, and that it hogged the entire second and third levels of the building. Zoey and Karter climbed one of the winding staircases that led up to the second and got straight to work, but even after sifting through hundreds of more books, Zoey didn't feel a buzzing in her chest. No crazy pull like Andy had had with the statue of Anteros, either.

Well into the afternoon, as Zoey put away one tome and prepared to grab another, a noise like hooves clopping echoed from the library entrance. Her stomach dropped, and she and Karter shared a panicked glance. They raced toward the nearest edge of the second level to look out at the first floor.

Just as she'd suspected, *astynomia* had entered the library. Four satyrs and two centaurs trotted across the tiled floor, weapons in hand. The citizens browsing the shelves and reading at the tables below cried out, tossing books aside and dashing toward the entrance.

"Nobody move!" a dark-skinned centaur with braids falling down his back barked at the citizens. They froze in place.

"Thank you for following the instructions of your local *astynomia*," the cold, regal voice of a woman sounded from outside the entryway. Zoey couldn't see her, but if she had to guess, she'd say the woman was a goddess.

Beside Zoey, Karter sucked in a sharp breath. He stepped closer to her, shielding her with his arm.

"I received word that Karter, Son of Zeus might have been spotted here this morning," the woman—or goddess, she was still outside—went on. "I need to speak with everyone present. I'd like to locate him if he's somewhere in the city, you see."

"It's Hera, my father's wife," Karter whispered to Zoey. He seized her hand and hurried back, tugging her along with him. "We have to find something that mentions Calliope, and we have to get out of here. *Now.*"

Thankfully, the only other people they could see on the second level stood all the way on the balcony across from them, and those citizens' terrified stares remained fixed on the *astynomia* below.

A noise like hundreds of blades dragging across stone sounded from outside the building, and Zoey winced. It was the most horrible thing she'd ever heard, and her ears rang after it stopped. Had it come from a god, a monster? Some kind of weapon?

She looked to Karter, hoping he'd have an explanation, but he didn't say anything. His face went pale, and he yanked Zoey behind a shelf. His breaths grew fast and shallow, his body shaking.

Hera and the *astynomia* kept talking, probably ordering around the citizens or something, but Zoey didn't process their words. She was too focused on Karter as he panicked before her. "What is it?" she asked.

He grasped her by the shoulders, his expression more fearful than ever before. "That sound—I'd recognize it anywhere. Ladon is here. He's the hundred-headed dragon. Hera sent him after me and my mother when I was a child, and he killed my mother, but I escaped. He might know my smell. If he does, he could find me in minutes. He could break down the walls, come running in here—"

"Then we'll just have to fight him," she interjected. "We'll do it together. I only brought a dagger, but—"

"No." Determination overcame the fear on his face. "I'll fight Ladon. I'll fight Hera, and the *astynomia* too. I'll lead them outside and do whatever it takes to distract them, to get them away from you. While I do that, you'll find the book you need, and then you'll escape. You'll get out of the city as fast as you can. Find Diana and Kali. If I make it out of here alive, I'll catch up with you."

She shook her head. "No, no. Absolutely not. You're the one who agreed to come with me on this mission in the first place. I'm not leaving you to fight alone."

"You have to. You can't worry about me. Not anymore."

"How can you ask that of me?" She tried to keep her voice low, but it was difficult. She swallowed down the lump in her throat. "And how are Andy and I supposed to defeat the gods if you don't survive? Asteria said you'd probably be the one to put Zeus in Tartarus. If you're gone, who's going to do that?"

"You will, with Calliope's voice-powers."

Hands shaking, he brushed some hair behind her ears and cupped her cheeks. "Listen, I don't see any other way out of this, so I need you to swear you'll reconnect with Calliope and finish saving the world, no matter what happens next. Please, promise me you'll do it."

Outside, there was that horrible noise again, like a bunch of knives dragging against rock.

When the noise faded, Zoey said, "I'll reconnect with Calliope. I'll finish saving the world. I promise, okay?"

He smiled, sucked in a shuddering breath, and pressed his lips against hers.

Zoey stood there, heart in her throat and rigid with surprise. But then she closed her eyes and kissed him back. Fiercely, as if this was the last time they'd see each other. Because it very well could be.

For just a few moments, it was her and him and no one else, and in that short time, she wasn't scared anymore. She thought that maybe everything would be okay in the end.

Almost as quickly as the kiss began, it ended. Karter enveloped her in a tight embrace. "Be careful," he whispered in her ear.

She hugged him back, burying her face in his shoulder. "You, too."

He pulled away and tugged off his cloak, then

leapt into the air, conjured peridot electricity in his hands, and soared toward the danger below.

"It's him!" someone shouted.

"He's here!" another yelled.

"There he is!" a third screamed.

Arrows *whoosh*ed, surely straight at Karter. Ladon screeched, and Zoey's chest grew tight as she thought about Karter fighting the creature that had killed his mother all by himself. But no matter how much she wanted to go after him, no matter how much she wanted to help him, she couldn't.

She had to restore her connection with Calliope.

Ignoring the commotion below, she turned to the shelf she and Karter had been hiding behind and began tearing books from it. She ripped through their pages, barely skimming the words. There wasn't time to go through them carefully, and reading bits and pieces of them hadn't been working anyway.

Andy felt a buzzing in his chest when the statue of Anteros called to him, she thought. *In theory, the same thing should be happening to me. Sure, Karter said some people might not consider literature to be as strong of a form of worship as statues, but Calliope's a goddess of freaking epic poetry. The literature that mentions her would call to her, even if it's faint. It's only logical.*

The problem is none of the literature here mentions her.

At least, not what we could find.

Another shriek from Ladon. It sounded farther away this time, and Zoey wondered if Karter had flown outside. Instinctively, she almost turned around to go to him, but she stopped herself. *He said it himself: I can't worry about him. I have to stay focused and find something that calls to me like the statue of Anteros called to Andy.*

Just then, an idea came to her. What if, instead of combing through each book, or even skimming their pages, she sprinted through the library, along the bookshelves, and touched the books' spines until one of them demanded she stop to look at it?

She wouldn't have been able to do that earlier today or yesterday. Not without drawing unwanted attention to herself. But now that everyone was distracted . . .

Considering how little time she had to find what she needed, it didn't look as though she had any other choice.

Coursing with new determination, her blood pounding in her ears, Zoey sprinted from bookshelf to bookshelf. She ran her fingers across the tomes' spines, praying to whatever god was listening that one of them would contain a passage, *any* passage, to awaken Calliope.

The citizens' bloodcurdling screams filled the air, and green electricity blasted outside, the light it emitted flashing through the windows and illuminating the interior of the library. Ladon shrieked even more, and the building's walls tremored in sync with the monster's squalls.

It took around twenty minutes before Zoey had touched every spine of every book on the second level of the library. Gasping for air, sweat pouring from her skin, she barreled up the staircase leading to the third floor.

Halfway up, she thought she heard Karter crying out—as if in pain, as if he'd been injured—but she forced herself to press on.

She reached the third level and did just as she had on the second. *Please, let me find something!*

When she was midway through her sixth shelf, there was a strange thudding sensation in her chest, and it wasn't her heart. As quickly as the strange feeling came it disappeared, and she halted. She doubled back, slower this time.

She dragged her hand against one, two, three books. As she touched the third tome, there was another thud in her chest, then another. Again, they didn't come from her heart.

Zoey snatched the book and looked at it. It was a plain black hardcover, and on the front in big white letters it read *Humanity's Great Mistake: The End of the Before Time.*

That's weird. This shouldn't have anything to do with Calliope. Still, it was the only title she'd found that had any promise. She threw it onto the nearest table and began swiping through the pages. As she did so, the thumping in her chest grew faster, faster, faster. Soon it felt as though something was vibrating within her rib cage, as though something was trapped inside of her, trying to break free.

Close to a third of the way through the book, she stopped at something strange. It was a brittle, yellow, folded-up piece of paper. *This is it.*

She touched the paper, and the vibrating in her chest grew stronger. However, she didn't freeze up as Andy had, didn't receive visions as he had. *Maybe I have to read whatever's written on it?*

She unfolded the paper. At the very top, handwritten in black ink, was a letter in an ancient foreign language, and although Zoey only knew English, she could read exactly what it said.

READ

Then, below that, printed in English:

As Zoey scanned the last three lines, the vibrations in her chest reached a crescendo. They were so intense her whole body shook, her teeth chattering, but she hadn't frozen up as Andy had, hadn't connected with Calliope as he'd connected with Anteros. She wondered if perhaps the words must be read aloud. *"And Calliope, who is the chiefest of them all, for she attends on worshipful princes."*

An electric shock jolted through her body. The hairs on her arms and legs stood up straight. Goose bumps prickled her skin.

She tried jerking her hand from the page and found she couldn't move. Her body was still, perfectly petrified.

Satisfaction coursed through her as black smoke invaded the corners of her vision and swallowed her whole. *I did it*, she thought. *I reconnected with Calliope.*

CHAPTER SEVENTEEN

PROGRESSION

Andy wasn't sure how long he'd been locked up with Layla in Ares's bedroom on New Mount Olympus. All he knew was last night, as Layla had been helping him escape, Ares and Aphrodite had captured them, and they'd been trapped here since.

When Ares and Aphrodite had first brought Andy and Layla here, Andy had done his best to explain to the gods everything he knew about him and Anteros and Zoey and Calliope. About how Anteros and Calliope were avatars, about how they were supposed to take over Andy's and Zoey's bodies, about how they were destined to rule the world in Zeus's place.

He'd hoped this would be enough to convince Ares and Aphrodite to let him go so that he could get back to Zoey—after all, he'd emphasized to them that he needed to help her reconnect with Calliope—but he'd had no such luck. Instead, they'd been so pleased with the prospect of their "beloved, long-lost son" taking Zeus's place, they'd seemed to forget about everything else he'd said.

"This is perfect!" Aphrodite had exclaimed. *"When we tell the other gods what Zeus did to Anteros and Calliope, they'll be furious he lied. Surely, many will side with us. We can rally together and overthrow Zeus and those who stand with him. Then Anteros will rule the pantheon, and we'll have even more power, even more worshippers!"*

"Indeed," Ares had agreed. *"This is a most fortuitous turn of events."*

At least they'd given Andy food and water (although he'd had to remind them that Layla needed some too), but after that, they'd left the pair here, saying something about gathering Anteros's "full-siblings." With thick iron chains, they'd secured Andy and Layla to columns on opposite sides of the room.

Andy struggled against his bindings, doing everything he could to free himself. So far, all he'd done was rub his skin raw and soak himself with sweat. On the bright side, though, Anteros was leaving him alone. He hadn't heard from the god since Ares and Aphrodite had captured him and Layla.

"It's no use," Layla said. "You won't be able to get free. I have the gift of super-strength, and even I can't break these chains."

"Wait a second, what about the columns?" Andy cried. "You could break those, and we could escape that way."

"I could try. The issue is, if I manage to break the pillars, I run the risk of caving in the ceiling. It could kill us."

Andy cursed, gritting his teeth. "What the hell is wrong with those assholes? Didn't they listen to a word I said? Zoey needs me!"

"Diana needs you as well." Layla's voice quivered. "In all honesty, she needs me too. I see that now more than ever. I was one of her best friends, but I let her down. I should have never pulled away from her after Pearl's death."

"That's no kidding," Andy blurted out before thinking, anger coursing through his body as he continued struggling against his bonds. "I'm sure Syrena had just as many daddy issues as you, and I'm sure Diana does too, but they didn't let that stop them from avenging Pearl." As soon as he finished his sentence, he regretted every word. He stopped struggling. "I— I'm— *Crap*. What is *wrong* with me? I know you're trying to help. I—I shouldn't have said that. I'm sorry."

"Don't apologize," she replied. "It's time someone made me face the truth. About everything."

"Wait, what?"

Layla shook her head. "My father has hurt me in the past, but my fear of him isn't the only reason I pulled away from Diana. It isn't the only reason I stayed here after she asked me to leave with her either."

Andy had an idea of where this was going, but he wanted to let Layla say it on her own. He didn't know her well—he didn't know her at all, actually—but he had a feeling admitting this was a big deal for her. "What's the other reason for it, then? Or the other reasons, I guess."

"Love," Layla said. "That's it. That's the reason. I'm in love with Diana, and I always have been, but she doesn't love me back, and she never will. I'm only a friend to her, while she's everything to me."

Andy was quiet as he processed Layla's words. They made him think of Zoey, of his feelings for her. Of how she didn't feel the same.

"When Pearl was still alive," Layla went on, "and she and Diana were together, we were all on a team. I had to stand back and watch them be happy. It killed me inside. Still, Pearl became my best friend over the years, and when she died, I was devastated. I even asked my father to consider resurrecting her. Sure, it would have made her an immortal god, and Diana and I would have remained mortal, but at least Diana would have been happy again, and I would have had my best friend back. He said 'no,' of course, and it was painful, but . . ."

"But?"

She let out a shaky sigh. "But a part of me hoped that with Pearl gone, I could have Diana for myself."

Andy's lips parted. "O-oh."

"When I told Diana how I felt about her, she let me know right away that she didn't feel the same. She said she only wanted to be friends. That I'd always been her friend, that I always would be. Afterward, she and Syrena became obsessed with avenging Pearl, and I used their behavior as an excuse to pull away from her. Even as she pointed out all the ways in which the gods were corrupt, I acted like I didn't see things her way. I ruined our friendship because I thought it would be easier to remain a pawn of the gods than to stay close to her and, inevitably, watch her find and fall for someone else."

Andy was at a loss for words. He rested the back of his head against the pillar he was bound to, thinking of the fight he'd had with Zoey the night before they'd headed into Aphrodite City.

"You know, I've had my heart broken too," he said. "I've pushed away the person I'm in love with because she hurt me, even though she didn't mean to. I understand what you're going through, and maybe—maybe it's not too late for you and Diana." Layla glanced up at him in confusion. "Maybe the two of you will get out of this alive, and maybe you can repair your friendship. Or maybe you can make a new one."

A noise like snakes slithering through grass sounded from the window on the far-left side of the bedroom. Andy and Layla looked that way, and Andy spotted long, twisting vines creeping in through the window, the greenery carrying a familiar goddess.

Although Andy had considered Persephone an enemy since she'd betrayed the group in Hades—although he wasn't sure he'd ever trust that she was truly on their side—his heart leapt with joy at the sight of her. "Persephone!" he cried. "You found me!"

Narcissa, Harmony, Chloe, and three Naiads—all wearing similar armor to Persephone—appeared next, carried by the vines. Persephone manipulated the plants to lower the seven of them onto the floor. "Actually, Asteria is the one who found you," she said. "I couldn't access your location, as Ares cast a cloaking spell on you. But Asteria sacrificed herself to travel to the lair of the Fates, touch your life thread, and see where Ares had brought you."

Andy's stomach sank. "Asteria is— She's gone? She faded away?"

"I'm afraid so, yes," Persephone said, and Andy thought he saw genuine sadness in her expression. "She turned to stardust when she returned from the Fates' lair, right after she notified us of your location."

Andy tried to imagine what it would be like to exist one moment and to not the next. If Asteria had known what would happen to her after getting Andy's location, she'd been very brave to go through with it.

Narcissa and Harmony stepped forward, two big black sacks full of gear slung over each of their shoulders. "We need to find a way to get

Andy out of those chains," Narcissa said.

"I might be able to do it," Layla piped up. "If Persephone supports the ceiling with her plants, I won't have to worry about causing a cave-in. I can put everything I have into breaking the pillars."

Harmony raised a brow at Layla. "We don't even know who you are, let alone whether you can be trusted."

"I'm Layla, Daughter of Ares, and I—"

"Layla?" Harmony barked. Andy had never heard such a hostile tone in her voice. "Aren't you one of the demigod warriors that destroyed Alikan Village?"

Layla hung her head in shame. "Yes."

"We're some of the nymphs who helped *astynomia* reach that village." Harmony jutted a finger in Layla's direction. "And you *slaughtered* them, all of them. How could we ever trust you? You're a murderer, a monster!"

"I am," Layla agreed with a heavy sigh. "And a coward, too."

"Then why would we ever want you to fight alongside us?"

Before Layla could reply, Andy spoke up. "Because she's one of Diana's longtime friends," he blurted out. "And because she tried helping me escape Olympus. That's why she's chained up too. Ares and Aphrodite caught us. Long story short, Layla's made mistakes. Big ones—just like Karter and Persephone have. But just like them, she's turned her back on the gods. She's set aside her own personal hang-ups to finally do the right thing, and she's—she's with us now."

He looked over at Layla. Her hard expression had softened.

"How would Darko feel about this?" Harmony asked. "He was traveling to Alikan Village with his brother before you met him, wasn't he?"

Sharp pain seared through Andy's chest at the mention of Darko. "I . . . I don't know how Darko would feel about it. I wish I could ask him, but I can't."

Narcissa stepped up beside Harmony and rested a hand on her shoulder. "Darko was a special young satyr, Harmony. Sensitive, caring, selfless—his life cut far too short." A few tears escaped Harmony's eyes as Narcissa spoke. "But this isn't about him, and this isn't about you. We can't allow our personal feelings to cloud our judgment. If the Daughter of Ares truly wishes to help us, we must accept it, as we've accepted the help of Karter and Persephone."

Harmony wiped her face with the back of her hand, her bottom lip quivering. "Fine. We need to hurry out of here anyway. The others can't hide in the garden forever."

"That's where Zoey is, right?" Andy asked, and Persephone began conjuring more vines from her hands, presumably to hold up the ceiling so Layla could break the columns. "I still have to help her reconnect with Calliope."

Narcissa frowned. "No, she's not in the garden. She left on her own to reconnect with Calliope. She worried that if we couldn't reach you before Zeus discovered you, her chance at contacting the goddess would be lost, and there would be no one to cast the Descent Spell. It's our understanding that she plans to reconvene with us after she awakens Calliope."

"That's what Troy and Marina said, at least," Chloe added.

Andy's pulse quickened. "When you say Zoey left on her own, you don't mean she's all by herself, do you?"

"Of course not," Narcissa said. "Diana, Kali, and Karter went with her."

Andy relaxed at these words. "Thank God. They'll keep her safe."

"Let's hope so," Chloe remarked. "Because she took the Helm, Trident, and Lightning Bolt with her."

By now, most of Persephone's vines were fashioned into a sort of net up against the ceiling, while the rest were wrapped around Andy's and Layla's pillars. If there was a cave-in, the plants would surely catch most of the debris. "Do it, Layla," Persephone said. "Free yourself."

Layla strained against the metal links. It wasn't long before her brown skin turned as red as her coil-y hair, the veins in her neck and forehead popping out.

It took a minute, but there was a loud *craaack*, fractures traveling up the column Layla was secured to. She clamped her eyes shut and screamed in effort.

The column began to crumble. Persephone used her vegetation to bat rubble away from Layla as it fell.

Layla's chains clanked to the floor.

Layla ran to Andy and worked on his column. By the time she'd freed him, she was gasping for breath, beads of sweat rolling down her forehead.

"Before we leave, there's something else you'll need, Andy," Narcissa said. She shared a glance with Harmony, and the two of them dumped out the contents of their bags to reveal armor nearly identical to theirs, a shield, and a sword.

Before Andy could pick up the gear, the Dryads did so, then helped him into it. It was heavy, and he felt awkward and clunky in it, but he was sure once Anteros took over his body, it would be like a second skin. "Is there anything Layla could use to protect herself with too?" he asked as Harmony handed him the sword.

"We weren't expecting to rescue two people," Narcissa replied. "We'll retrieve supplies for Layla at a later time."

"Be quiet, all of you!" Persephone suddenly ordered, and they turned to her in surprise. She had her eyes closed and seemed deep in concentration. "The nymph recruits in the Garden of Olympus are in danger. Zeus is back, and he's discovered them. If we don't reach them quickly—"

"Let's go, then!" Harmony cried, gesturing at the window she and the others had climbed in through.

Persephone shook her head. "There isn't time to go back the way we came. I have to teleport us there. Come, everyone. We have to be touching so no one is left behind."

They rushed to Persephone, and once she confirmed they were all holding hands, she lit up with white light, just as Ares had when he'd transported Andy and himself here. Andy shut his eyes tight so the flare wouldn't fry them.

Sorry, Anteros, he thought. *I know you wanted me to stay here, but for now I'm still in control of my body. Until I give it to you, I'm going to do what I think is best.*

"I'm starting to wonder if perhaps you might be right about a few things," Anteros said in Andy's mind.

Andy flinched in surprise at Anteros's voice. *Whoa, dude. Haven't heard from you in a while. Wasn't expecting you to say anything to me about that.*

"Apologies for my absence," Anteros replied. *"I've been listening. Thinking. Especially about what Mother and Father said—you know, regarding their motivations for helping us."*

Before Andy could respond, the earsplitting shrieks of young women sounded in the distance. *Oh no.*

Releasing Harmony's hand, Andy snapped open his eyes and found himself in the Garden of Olympus once more. As he processed the carnage before him, he wished he'd kept them shut.

Around a dozen nymph recruits—dead ones—lay in front of the group. Some had stab wounds, some had silver arrows stuck in them, and some were burned to a crisp. The scent of blood and scorched flesh assaulted Andy's nostrils, and he held his breath, trying not to gag.

Harmony, Chloe, and the three Naiads who'd come for Andy released a volley of anguished cries as they looked upon the bodies.

More yells sounded from behind them, farther in the trees. Andy tightened his grip on his sword, raised his shield, and swung around—only to spot something even more horrible than the fresh corpses of his allies.

There were stone statues of young women everywhere, more than he could count, and he suspected they hadn't been here before because they didn't look like any of the other statues in the garden. The ones he'd seen had been sensual in nature, but the girls depicted here could have been characters in the chase scenes of a slasher flick. Their eyes were wide with dread, their mouths hanging open in silent, eternal screams.

They reminded Andy of the statues created by Medusa.

Worse than that, they reminded him of the nymph recruits.

Harmony and the others gaped at the statues. "Did the gods track down Medusa's head?" Harmony cried.

"Even if they did, it was lost in a wildfire," Narcissa pointed out. "No one should be able to utilize it, not unless they expend a great deal of magical energy."

Persephone waved her hands, manipulating the greenery around them into a dome-like shield. "Unless the head was reduced to ashes, Athena could have used a minimal amount of magic to restore it to a functional state."

"What are we going to do?" Chloe asked.

"Give me time to gather my strength, and I'll teleport us out of here," Persephone said.

"No, we can't leave the others," Harmony argued. "We left over three hundred nymph recruits in the garden, and I don't see all of them among the bodies here. Not everyone has been killed!"

A silver projectile pierced through the barrier of vegetation—an arrow. It speared Chloe's bare calf, and she cried out and collapsed. Harmony and the Naiads raced to Chloe, yelping her name.

Something else broke through their shield. This time, it was a spear, and it sank into the ground at Persephone's feet. Wide-eyed, she stared at the weapon and stepped back.

Through the gaps in the vines, Andy could see everything go dark outside. Rain began to pour from the sky, green light flashing. A bang of thunder followed, and then a voice that Andy recognized as the King of the Gods' boomed. "Come out, come out, little Chosen One. Stop hiding behind your companions and face me like the god you claim to be."

When the haze cleared from Zoey's vision, she found herself no longer in the library of Zeus City.

She stood in a garden, and it looked eerily similar to the one where Calliope had chased her in a dream.

Cypress trees reached hundreds of feet into a dark, boundless galaxy dotted with vibrantly colored planets and twinkling stars. Golden paths twisted and curled along the terrain around her, and bushes full of fragrant, exotic flowers grew at every corner, water flowing from marble fountains into glittering ponds.

There was a woman's muffled voice, then a man's. Zoey guessed the voices belonged to Calliope and Anteros because when Andy had connected with Anteros, he'd received visions of them.

Zoey ran along a path toward the voices.

Soon she reached a gazebo hidden within bushes and trees, and sure enough, two gods that could only be Calliope and Anteros stood hand in hand beneath it. They were similar in appearance to Zoey and Andy, although taller, more muscular, and more conventionally good-looking.

Zoey stepped closer to them, trying to hear their words. "—ou really mean to tell me you're not afraid of fading away?" Anteros asked.

"I really do," Calliope replied. "Of course, I'm not ready to go now. But someday, after I've gotten to spend several more millennia with you—after my powers have dwindled to almost nothing—would it really be so bad?"

"Do you realize how crazy you sound?"

"I know how I sound, but I remain firm in my stance."

Anteros pulled her closer. "Then enlighten me. Teach me a new perspective, as you always do."

"If you insist." Calliope smiled at him so sweetly it almost gave Zoey a toothache, but before she could hear more of their conversation, her surroundings began to disintegrate. They fragmented into tiny pieces of matter, then reshaped themselves into clouds of dark fog. The clouds submerged her, just as before, and she was transported to another scene.

Zoey stood in an empty, dimly lit hall on what could only be Olympus; it looked just as it had when she and her companions had been there a short while back. Up ahead, Calliope walked down the hall, her turquoise dress billowing out behind her, a tablet in hand. As the goddess reached the end of the passageway, a massive, muscular god with silver hair and a matching beard—Zoey recognized him as Zeus—lunged out from the shadows.

Zeus seized Calliope by the wrists. She cried out in surprise, her tablet clattering to the floor. "Father, what are you—"

"The next time you speak out against me," Zeus hissed, glaring down at her, "you will regret it. This I promise."

Calliope wriggled free of his grasp and bent down to pick up her tablet. "You cannot expect me to sit idly by as you propose such foolish plans to the rest of the pantheon. They crave humanity's adoration and worship, but the mortals will never see us as they once did, and it's wrong to try and force them to do so. They've developed their own miracles and magic, and many even follow new deities. We are the old gods now, destined to fade with time, but we are not alone. This has happened to pantheons before, and it's happening to pantheons today. It's all right."

"I won't allow you to kill us all," Zeus snarled. "You might wish to fade away into nothingness, but the rest of us would prefer to keep on existing."

Calliope waved her tablet in exasperation. "Is that really what dying is? A state of no longer existing? Or could dying be something else? Could it be the first step of something new, of our next great adventure?" Zeus's frown deepened, and Calliope went on. "Don't you see? This is the natural progression of all living things. They are born, they live, they die. But I believe they're never really gone. I believe their essences are transferred from one state to another, forever progressing through the universe in a cosmic dance.

"In fact, the more I deliberate upon the subject, the more I've begun to believe you're not afraid of fading away, Father. You're afraid of change. Of losing your power, your control. This pantheon has bent to your whims for thousands of years, fearing your wrath, and you would do anything to keep it that way. You would even destroy the world, all the progress humanity has made on its own."

Zeus clenched his jaw. "This is your last warning, daughter. Back down, or else."

"Or else what? You'll put me in Tartarus? Good luck doing so without a vote from the rest of the Olympians. I'll convince them to side with me, no matter what kind of threats you make against them. You can be sure of that." He sneered, but it didn't intimidate Calliope. She stood prouder than ever. "Now, if you'll excuse me, I'm going to bed. Good night." She stomped out of sight, Zeus watching her as she left.

The hall disintegrated, just like the garden before it had. Black smoke engulfed Zoey, and when the mist cleared, a third scene appeared before her.

This time, she was in a place she'd never visited before, although it was oddly familiar. It was a temple, dark and cold. It was also vacant, save for Calliope and Anteros as they stood before a statue of Calliope herself. The pair was huddled together, whispering over a massive stone tablet they were holding. The tablet had foreign, ancient-looking words carved into it, and Zoey stepped forward, trying to hear what they were saying. *Are these the words to the Descent Spell?*

"—efore I return the tablet to its hiding spot,

we must memorize the spell engraved upon its stone," Calliope murmured. "Those words are of the greatest importance. They could be the only leverage we'll ever have over my father."

"Are you sure about this, my love?" Anteros asked. "What if he finds out?"

"Even if he finds out, the worst he can do is put us in Tartarus."

"Right, right." He nodded. "And he can't banish us there because he'll need the vote of the rest of the Olympians to do so. My parents are both Olympians, and you have strong powers of persuasion, so he won't be able to convince everyone to agree to it, no matter how hard he tries."

"I've discovered something else about Tartarus as well: how to open a portal there. It's how Zeus, Poseidon, and Hades banished Kronos and his followers. Apparently, my father and uncles are the only ones who know how to open the portal. Well, I suppose that's not true—I know how to, now that I've obtained the words to the spell. It's called the Descent."

Anteros gasped. "What? But—but how? How did you find . . ." He trailed off, glancing down at the tablet.

She smirked. "Like I told you before, my powers of persuasion are *very* strong."

As Calliope finished speaking, the vision dissolved, and black smoke engulfed Zoey again. However, rather than transporting her to another vision, the haze grew thicker, darker, and electrifying pain unlike anything she'd experienced before shot up and down her throat. It felt as if a thunderstorm were ripping through her vocal cords.

Within moments the pain grew so great her head began to spin. She fell to the ground, onto her side, and clamped her eyes shut. If she could have screamed, she would have. But all she could do was writhe in agony. *Stay strong,* she told herself. *This is part of the process, remember? Andy had pains in his back before Anteros's wings came in.*

It seemed like an eternity before the torture finally relented, and she opened her eyes to find herself lying on the floor of the third level of the library in Zeus City. There was a scratchy sensation in her throat, as if she were having severe allergies, and when she tried to speak, her voice came out in a raspy whisper.

Outside, Ladon's shrieking had grown even louder. Zoey thought she heard the squawks of birds, and blasts of green electricity continued flashing through the windows.

At the sight of the lightning, Zoey sighed in

relief. Karter must still be alive. *I know he said I have to leave him behind, but . . .*

No, as much as she wanted to, she couldn't try to help him. Not only had she promised him that she'd escape, that she'd allow him to face Hera and Ladon by himself, but if she was captured by the gods and something happened to Andy, they'd lose the war for sure. She had to leave now. If Karter survived, he'd find her later.

Groggily, she climbed to her feet, then hastened down to the bottom level of the library. It wouldn't be smart to go through the entrance in case Hera was right outside and noticed her, so she'd better bust out one of the windows instead.

Once downstairs, she grabbed an iron statuette from one of the tables and raced to a window on the side of the building. She rammed the object against the bottom right corner of the glass, again and again until it fractured and, eventually, shattered.

Tiny pieces of glass spiraled through the air and tinkled as they hit the ground. Some of the fragments nipped Zoey's hand, but she paid them no mind. She tossed the statuette aside and clambered through the broken window, the smell of smoke hitting her. Then she bolted down the grassy hill the library stood upon, toward the now debris-riddled streets of Zeus City. *I'll have to go around the fight so Hera doesn't see me.*

When she neared the bottom of the hill, she leapt onto the closest path and started toward a row of buildings beside the library. However, she couldn't help but halt when she caught sight of the scene in her peripheral.

Most of Karter's fight with Hera, Ladon, and the *astynomia* must have taken place in front of the library because everything there was in disarray. Chariots had been overturned, all the buildings knocked down. Lightning craters, the bloodied corpses of citizens and animals, and an insane amount of vegetation peppered the paths and streets; there were flowers, vines, bushes, and trees that hadn't been there before, and Zoey realized the plants must be the remains of satyrs and centaurs who'd been killed in the conflict.

From somewhere within the hills of rubble, a young man's cry echoed. The flares of peridot light ceased, and Zoey's stomach plunged to her feet. There was no doubt in her mind that the yell belonged to Karter. Had he been injured? Would he be okay?

He cried out again, and Zoey fought the urge to go find him, to try and save him. Tears stinging her eyes, she sprinted across the side street toward the buildings beside the library.

Rumbling sounds came from the ruins, like debris plummeting to the ground. In the corner of her vision there was a glint of green and blue. She reached the edge of the road and dashed along the paths between structures.

The squawks of birds sounded. The sky above her darkened. Still running, she glanced up.

A chariot pulled by four peacocks the size of Artemis's stags, with iridescent green-and-blue feathers, soared after Karter. Steam curled off his skin as he flew from them, and he clutched a bleeding gash in his side.

His gaze met Zoey's, his eyes going wide. He reached out and shot toward her, but the peacocks flapped in front of him, swiping at him with their talons. They dug their nails into his arms and dragged him toward the sidewalk below.

Ladon's shrieking sounded behind her. She looked back to see a monster that could have only been him barreling after her.

Larger than a horse, Ladon was covered in shining black scales, clusters of long, sharp claws extending from his massive feet. It was no wonder why Karter had called him the hundred-headed dragon, too—the creature had so many snakelike heads coiling from his neck he would have had to be lying dead for Zoey to properly count them.

Heart hammering in her chest, Zoey snatched the dagger from her robes and picked up the pace. The monster had already seen her, possibly even smelled her. She couldn't hide. All she could do was run.

Boom boom boom.

Boom boom boom.

BOOM BOOM BOOM.

Ladon's swift, heavy footfalls sent tremors through the ground as he got closer. She stumbled to the side. As she regained her footing, something sharp slashed across the back of her thighs.

There was burning, blinding pain. Zoey opened her mouth to yell, but all that came out was a weak croak. She fell face-first to the ground.

Another stab of pain, this time in the back of her right arm. Something flipped her around, onto her spine. She looked up to see Ladon looming over her.

His heads hissed, twisting and curling around her. Some of them were so close their forked tongues brushed against her cheeks and throat.

The stench of death assaulted her nostrils.

Mustering all her strength, she stabbed at the creature's closest neck with her dagger, but the blade bounced off his scales as if they were an impenetrable suit of armor. Was that why Karter hadn't managed to slay him yet, even with the ability to conjure green lightning?

Ladon raised a claw. It dripped with blood, *her* blood. *He's going to kill me.*

Something *whoosh*ed to the left. Ladon shrieked and somersaulted through the air away from Zoey. She rolled over to see who had saved her, although she already knew who it was.

Karter and Ladon smashed into a building fifty feet from her. They tumbled onto the sidewalk, wood and bricks showering them, and Ladon swiped his claws and clacked his fangs at Karter. Karter conjured peridot electricity in his hands, but it was no use. It ricocheted off Ladon's scales as Zoey's knife had and dissolved into thin air.

Someone seized Zoey by the arm and yanked her to her feet. She thrashed against her attacker—a tall, inhumanly beautiful woman wearing a deep-blue silk gown, her long brown hair hanging in a braid over her shoulder. *Hera.* The golden chariot was overturned far behind

Hera, the peacocks who had been pulling it strewn dead on the ground. Green lightning still crackled along the birds' scorched bodies.

Hera pulled Zoey close and pressed a dagger against her throat. The sharp, cold metal nicked her, and she stopped struggling. She could hear Karter and Ladon grappling behind her.

"For some reason, my husband claims you can't be killed." Hera sneered at Zoey. "Time and time again, he's been adamant that you must be banished to Tartarus, and I don't understand it. You're so small, so breakable. What secrets lie beneath your fragile flesh?"

The goddess chuckled and dug her blade deeper into Zoey's skin. *What am I supposed to do?*

"Channel my magic," a familiar voice said in her head, so faint she almost didn't register it. *"I grow stronger with each passing moment. I believe I can save you, and the Son of Zeus too."*

Calliope? she thought. *Is that you?*

"Yes, child. Find me in the labyrinth of your mind. I still wait for you at the entrance."

Zoey didn't hesitate to follow Calliope's instructions. She closed her eyes and searched the darkness of her mind.

She found Calliope quickly. The goddess stood at the entrance of a cave-like structure, and she looked just as Zoey remembered.

Similar to Zoey, but more classically beautiful. They ran toward each other.

When they reached one another, Calliope grabbed her by the arms. A buzzing sensation hummed in Zoey's chest. The feeling grew stronger, stronger, stronger, spreading through the rest of her body . . .

In a brilliant flash of blue light, Zoey became one with Calliope.

CHAPTER EIGHTEEN

ELOQUENCE

After a cyclone of Calliope's memories whirled through Zoey's mind, she opened her eyes against her will.

Just as before, she was in the *Agora* in Zeus City, surrounded by the buildings beside the library. Hera, who towered over her, held her up by the arm. With a dagger the goddess sliced the outermost flesh of Zoey's neck. Warm blood dribbled from the cut.

Involuntarily, Zoey cleared her throat. It felt

scratchy, as if it were coated with phlegm, but even so, her vocal cords began vibrating in a familiar manner.

Hera paused, lowering the dagger. "What . . . ?"

Not of her own accord, Zoey cleared her throat again—more forcefully this time. The scratchy feeling evaporated, and the tingling in her vocal cords slithered out into the rest of her body. It was as though the energy had been blocked before, trapped in one spot. But whatever had been obstructing it had shattered, and now it charged through her from head to toe.

Soon all of Zoey thrummed with power, and she knew Calliope had taken over.

"Release me, Hera." Her newly regal voice reverberated over Karter's and Ladon's shrieks behind her, clear and melodious and commanding. She sounded every bit like a great goddess—she sounded every bit like Calliope— and it was as terrifying as it was comforting. "Release me and stand down."

For the moment, Hera obeyed the command. She let go of Zoey.

Despite the pain in Zoey's neck, arm, and legs, Calliope made her turn and stalk boldly, fearlessly, toward Karter and Ladon as they fought. "Ladon, *stop*."

The monster paused. He had a claw raised as if about to slash Karter with it. Karter scrambled backward, out from under Ladon.

Calliope forced Zoey to step toward Ladon. "Why are you, the guardian of the golden apples, here? Why are you rampaging through this *polis*, murdering innocent people, when you should be hunting Heracles?" The creature's serpentine heads cocked this way and that, many of his glowing red eyes narrowing in puzzlement. "Don't you remember? The hulking brute stole the apples from the Garden of Hesperides. It was his eleventh labor, and to this day he roams free, a god among the rest. Now go, hunt him down! Make him pay for what he did!"

Ladon seemed to consider Calliope's words. Dozens of his eyes blinked, and he dragged his front claws along the ground, leaving gouges in the sidewalk.

A few more moments passed like this before the monster swung around and trotted away, presumably to go find Heracles.

Karter stumbled to his feet, staring at Zoey with bewilderment, his body even more bruised and bloodied than before. "Zoey?" he called out hesitantly. "Are you still there?"

The mixture of fear and grief in his voice

made Zoey's heart hurt. She wanted to tell him that yes, she was still here. She wanted to rush toward him, to hug him and never let go. But when she tried opening her mouth to speak, she couldn't, and when she tried running in his direction, she couldn't.

Calliope wouldn't allow it.

Please, let me go to him, Zoey thought. *Give me time to be with him for just a little while longer, and to make up with Andy, too. I promise to give you my body for good afterward.*

"I have to finish something first," Calliope replied.

As if on cue, the furious, earsplitting screech of a woman sounded behind Zoey. She knew right away it was Hera. *Oh no. The persuasion magic wore off.*

Calliope forced Zoey to pivot toward Hera. The Queen of the Gods charged for Zoey, her dagger raised. "Demon!" she screamed. "Wretched, conniving thing! Ladon was finally about to gut that filthy ingrate, and you—"

"Have you learned nothing after all these years, Hera?" Despite the calm tone in Calliope's voice, Zoey's vocal cords hummed like mad.

Hera stopped in her tracks. "How? How can this be? When I saw you last, you were merely mortal. Minutes ago, you were mortal too." She looked Zoey up and down. "But now your divine essence is unmistakable. It's growing inside you at a rapid pace. What's happening?"

"Don't you see, great Queen of the Gods?" Calliope went on, ignoring Hera's questions. "Killing Zeus's mistresses and illegitimate children solves nothing. It doesn't change the fact that Zeus was unfaithful to you, and it certainly doesn't alleviate the pain caused by his betrayal."

"How could you possibly know what does and does not alleviate my pain?"

"I've watched you weep because of Zeus time and time again, even after you've managed to enact vengeance upon his lovers and bastard children." Against her will, Zoey reached out, as if beckoning Hera to come closer. "I know it's painful, Hera. I can't imagine what it's been like to endure such a union for all these centuries. But killing Karter won't bring you peace."

Hera released a cry of indignation. "What *will* bring me peace, then? Hm? What would you have me do, Goddess of Eloquence? My only option is to punish them because I can't punish my half-wit husband. Not only am I bound to him by law, but I swore to never try to usurp him again."

"Just as he swore to gain control over his

wandering eye and no longer commit adultery? Tell me, has Zeus ever honored his word? Has he ever kept a promise to you?" As Calliope continued, Hera's nostrils flared. "Before you try killing Karter again, you must know something. He's no ordinary demigod. He's the prophesied Son of Zeus and Metis."

"*Metis?*" Hera's cheeks flushed with fury.

"Yes, Metis," Calliope repeated. "She escaped Zeus when Athena burst from his head. Asteria kept her hidden until the time was right, until she was ready to be reborn into an avatar— the spirit of a god confined within a mortal body. Zeus impregnated her with Karter, just as he was always meant to, and now Karter will cast Zeus into Tartarus. I saw it myself, when my own mortal vessel touched Karter's life thread in the lair of the Fates." She paused for dramatic effect. "You can finally punish Zeus, Hera. Let Karter go, and he'll destroy your king. That monster won't be able to control you or the rest of us any longer. You'll be free of him, and you'll be at peace."

Hera glared at Zoey, her breaths growing quicker as the seconds passed. Eventually, she tossed the knife aside, and tears streamed from her eyes, black makeup running down her face. She let out an agonized wail—a howl that reminded Zoey of a wild animal trapped inside a cage, lamenting for its long-lost freedom. "That's what—you are—isn't it?" the goddess choked out between sobs. "An—avatar?"

Calliope made Zoey nod. "Yes, I am. As is Anteros."

"Asteria—created—you? Both of—you?"

"No, Asteria only made Metis into an avatar. It's Zeus who did this to Anteros and me, years before the Storm."

Hera was still crying, but she seemed to understand what Calliope was saying. "Because you—discovered the—Descent Spell. And he feared—you would reveal—his secrets—and stop him from—decimating humanity."

"Correct."

It took what felt like forever for Hera to somewhat compose herself, and even then, she trembled so violently she could barely stand up. She sniffled and used her dress to wipe the snot and makeup from her face.

"What say you, great Queen of the Gods?" Calliope asked. "Will you stand aside and allow your unfaithful husband to be destroyed? Or will you keep him in power by murdering the one fated to overthrow him?"

Hera dropped the fabric of her skirt, setting her jaw. "I will do neither. Instead, I will cast the adulterous rat into the flames of Tartarus myself."

White light flared from Hera's body. When it faded, she was gone.

Even though Hera had disappeared, Zoey's pulse raced, her palm growing slick with sweat, and soon she noticed strange sensations in her body. There was a vibrating in her chest, like earlier when she'd discovered the passage referencing Calliope. It grew stronger, and a burning feeling accompanied it, like fire raging inside of her.

Clutching her chest, Zoey spun around toward Karter—this time all of her own accord. He was standing now, a hand extended in her direction. "Zoey?"

"Karter, I . . ."

She wasn't sure of what to say, but she never finished the sentence anyway. She felt as if the ground were shifting beneath her, and then everything was spinning. She staggered sideways and collapsed.

"*Zoey!*"

In seconds Karter was at her side, and the last thing she saw before her vision went dark was him, black and red from bruises and blood, as he pulled her into his arms and took flight.

Andy's heart hammered against his rib cage as more of Zeus's thunder roared, rain teeming from the sky and pounding against the dome-like shield of vines protecting him and his companions. *What do I do?* he thought at Anteros. *Should I let you take over? Can you fight Zeus?*

"*No,*" Anteros replied. "*Without the gods' objects of power, we cannot overpower him.*"

You'd at least have a better chance at beating him than I do, right?

"*At this point, our only chance is to escape and return later, properly equipped.*"

"I said come out, little Chosen One!" Zeus bellowed. Golden electricity hissed along the vines surrounding them. "If you want my throne so much, why don't you try and take it?"

Persephone waved her arms frantically,

keeping the plants from turning black and shriveling up. "Don't leave this barrier," she said.

"Wasn't planning on it," Andy replied.

Chloe groaned in pain. The three Naiads who'd helped save Andy were already stabilizing the arrow in her leg with strips of cloth. Layla watched them; she looked as though she wanted to help but wasn't sure whether she should. "I think Persephone is right," Chloe said to Harmony. "We need to teleport out of here. No one wants to leave the others behind, but we arrived too late. Andy must be protected at all costs."

"There are others?" a woman's voice asked from just outside the vines, so formidable it had to belong to an Olympian goddess. "Ah, yes. Of course. They must be hiding in the trees and ponds."

"That sounds like Athena!" Anteros cried.

"How fun it will be to track the rest," a second goddess added. "They might have escaped me before, but the hunt isn't over yet."

And I'm pretty sure that's Artemis, Andy thought back, his blood turning cold.

A pair of pale hands burst through the dome and seized one of the Naiads by the hair. She screamed, grappling against her captor as they dragged her backward.

Andy leapt forward. He slashed his sword through the wrists of the pale hands. The blow separated them from the rest of their body, and a wail pierced the air, golden fluid spraying from the stumps. The Naiad tumbled to the grass beside Andy and scrambled toward the others, the severed hands dangling from her hair.

Another spear pierced through the vegetation. Narcissa lunged to the side, barely avoiding the attack. The weapon sank into the soil. "There isn't time to retrieve the others," Narcissa said. "Persephone, teleport us out of here." Harmony's face tightened with grief, but she didn't argue with Narcissa.

Just then, a white glow spilled in through the tiny gaps in the shield, and Andy cursed under his breath. Which immortal had transported here now?

A few moments later, he got his answer. "Stand down, Zeus!" Aphrodite shouted. "It's over. We know what really happened to Anteros."

"What you did to our son is unforgivable," Ares added. "And unless you surrender now, there will be war."

"What's the meaning of this?" Artemis cried. Zeus and Athena yelled different things at the same time, and a flurry of other voices Andy didn't recognize joined the mix too.

"Let's go," Persephone said. They all grabbed onto each other, and she transported them away.

Zoey stood in the garden full of cypress trees, marble fountains, golden paths, and bushes of flowers. A fantastical view of space shone above her, the stars and planets levitating so closely it was as though she could reach up and touch them.

A twig snapped behind her, and she swung around to see Calliope stepping out of the trees toward her. Heart in her throat, she prepared to run away, thinking, I'm not ready for this! I need more time—just a little more time!

"You have nothing to fear, child," Calliope said. "I have no intention of stealing your body from you."

Zoey paused. "You don't?"

"No, not at all."

"But this is where you chased me before to do exactly that."

"Yes, because I thought I was doing the right thing— for both of us. Please, let me explain."

"Okay." Zoey crossed her arms. "Go ahead, I guess."

Calliope sighed, tucking some hair behind her ears. "Before Asteria spoke to you and showed you your potential futures, she spoke to me in dreams. She told me that you and I were one and the same, and it made me believe that you were me, that I was you. That Zeus had split my spirit to lock me in this mortal form, that the convergence was simply the two becoming one. But now I'm not so sure anymore. There's no way I can be certain whether anything Asteria told us is true.

"However, if she told you the truth, then you'll be making the ultimate sacrifice to liberate humanity. So, when you're ready, come to me. Then, and only then, is when we will complete the convergence."

Calliope disappeared, and then Zoey awoke in Karter's arms. Like before, he was covered in blood and bruises, and steam curled up from his skin. The sun, high in the sky, blazed behind him as he soared through the air.

"You're awake!" Karter exclaimed. "Are you okay? What happened?"

She reached up to cup his cheek. To make sure that this was real, that she wasn't dreaming. "Yeah," she started. "I—I'm okay. I channeled Calliope after reconnecting with her, and she used her voice-powers to rescue us. She and I haven't fully converged yet, so I think using all that energy exhausted my body." She recalled everything that had happened after she'd left the library. "I'm so sorry. I tried to go around the fight so Hera and Ladon wouldn't see me. I swear I planned to keep my promise and escape while you held them off. I don't think Hera told Ladon about how Andy and I aren't supposed to be killed. Seriously, you . . . you saved my life."

"No, you saved mine." His gaze softened. "All I did was buy you time." She rested her head on his shoulder and her hand on his chest. He hugged her a bit tighter.

She looked down to see they were flying above Zeus City toward the forest where they'd left Diana and Kali. Below, citizens and even a few *astynomia* watched them as though in awe, and surprisingly, no one seemed as if they planned to attack. *They must be hoping for our victory*, she thought. *We can't let them down.*

It took the pair about an hour to fly out of the city and into the forest. During that time, they shared more of their favorite memories with each other. Karter spoke of reading stories with his mother, of training with Syrena and Spencer. Zoey talked about going on car rides with her father, about laughing with Andy, Diana, Kali, and Darko.

In a short while Zoey had learned a lot about Karter, and he had learned a lot about her. How much more would they have discovered if given the chance?

When they reached Diana and Kali, Zoey spotted a bunch of red-clothed, spear-wielding men and women standing in the trees with the girls, along with a ton of pegasi. Karter, who was hot to the touch, sweat pouring from his skin, tensed at the sight.

"Wait a second." Zoey peered down at the men and women. "They look familiar, and they have pegasi. I think they're from Kali's village!"

Karter didn't say anything. He could barely breathe. He landed on the forest floor before Diana, set Zoey down, and collapsed.

Diana knelt before Zoey, presumably to heal her. "Heal Karter first," Zoey said. "He's burning up."

Trembling, Karter reached over and took Zoey's hand. "No, I'm—I'm fine," he wheezed. "But Hera—and Ladon—wounded you." The men and women Zoey guessed were from Deltama Village gasped at the mention of the Queen of the Gods and the hundred-headed dragon.

Diana raised a brow at Zoey and Karter. Her body lit up, and she began to heal Zoey. The throbbing pain in Zoey's neck, arm, and thighs dissipated, and although she wished Diana had healed Karter first, she sighed in relief.

Diana worked on Karter next, and Zoey held his hand the whole time. Diana glanced between them but didn't make a comment.

Kali stepped forward. "So, you were attacked by Hera and Ladon. Did you defeat them, or do we need to hurry out of here because they're on their way?"

"We didn't beat them, but we tricked them," Zoey said. "Well, kind of."

Diana finished healing Karter, and he sat up. "How?" Diana asked. "Is that the reason it took you so long? Did you at least reconnect with Calliope?"

Zoey and Karter explained what had happened and why they'd had to stay overnight in the city, although they left out the kisses and private conversations they'd shared. *Those details aren't relevant to the mission anyway*, Zoey thought.

"I'm glad you both made it out alive," Diana said. "Our time here was also . . . eventful, to say the least."

Karter gestured at the men and women around them. "We gathered that. Are these people from your village, Kali?"

"Yes. They're warriors." Kali seemed to

carefully consider her words. "Apparently, all seventy-one of them have been searching for me ever since I ran away."

An older guy with dark skin, a thick beard, and dreads like Chief Agni's trudged ahead of the rest of the Deltama Village warriors. "We are here to help in the battle against the gods."

"We must ensure Kali survives the conflict," a woman said. Tall and muscular, she had to be around forty years old, with brown skin and shoulder-length black hair. "After she ran away, Chief Agni prayed to our gods for guidance and received visions of the future from Kali, Goddess of Destruction. According to the Mother Goddess, Kali is destined to return safely to the village, marry the suitor Chief Agni has selected for her, and become our new chief early. She will be the greatest leader the village has ever seen. She will lead Deltama Village into a new era—one of great fortune and prosperity, where we will no longer require walls to protect us."

Zoey's stomach twisted and turned. She faced Diana and Kali. They shifted uncomfortably, not looking at each other.

"Why would Kali *have* to do any of that?" Zoey asked, letting go of Karter's hand. She climbed to her feet, and he followed suit. "If she's going to be the leader of the village," Zoey continued, "she shouldn't be forced to step into the role prematurely. She should also get to decide who she marries, or whether she marries at all."

"The Mother Goddess told Chief Agni that this is Kali's destiny, and so it shall be," the man from before insisted.

Zoey balled her fist at her side. "But fate isn't a fixed thing. Nothing is truly predetermined."

"If fate isn't a fixed thing, then why hasn't Kali managed to come up with another way to cast the Descent Spell?" a second woman, a younger one, countered, and Zoey paused. "Yes, she told us all about how you and the boy are being forced to sacrifice yourselves to save the world. How she's afraid there's no way to save you."

Zoey glanced back at Kali; Kali glared at the ground.

Zoey turned to the warriors. "My and Andy's situation is different from Kali's. Even if we no longer get to choose how our lives play out, she still does."

"No, she doesn't," another man from farther in the back piped up. "When we return to the village, she'll become our new chief."

"Oh my God, okay." Zoey shook her head.

"Say Kali agrees to become chief early. She shouldn't also have to get married, especially to someone she hasn't picked."

"Kali is Chief Agni's only child," the first woman explained. "She must marry a worthy suitor so she can produce a worthy heir. This is the way things have been done since the village's conception. It has helped our leaders maintain order, and it has ensured that we have only ever had the strongest of chiefs. If not for the tradition, Kali would not be the woman she is today. She would not have accompanied all of you on your journey."

Zoey groaned in frustration. "You realize Chief Agni tried keeping Kali from coming with us, right? She had to sneak away to do it. It seems to me she's become an amazing person on her own, not because of her heritage or some outdated tradition."

The warriors made sounds of outrage, and Diana shot to her feet and grabbed Zoey by the wrist. "Stop," she whispered. "Andy only has two days left, and we're in desperate need of help. I agree with everything you're saying, but we can't put a strain on this alliance."

Zoey glanced between Diana and Kali some more. Diana wore a sad, pleading expression, and Kali refused to look at anyone.

"Fine," Zoey said. Begrudgingly, she apologized to the warriors for any offense she might have caused, and after a quick conversation among themselves, they pardoned her "outburst."

Kali walked to Zoey's side, still scowling. "Like Diana said, Andy only has two days left. We need to make a sacrifice to Persephone and ask whether she and the nymphs have rescued him yet. If not, we need to head his way immediately. I won't be able to live with myself if he gets locked up in Tartarus."

"Neither will I," Zoey replied.

Together, they dug up the Helm, Trident, and Lightning Bolt and started to gather supplies for a sacrifice to Persephone. As they did so, Zoey couldn't stop thinking about what was to come, couldn't shake the sick, anxious feeling in her stomach. *Please*, she thought, *to whatever god is listening and willing to help, keep Andy safe. Keep him safe, let him still be* him *when I see him next, and make him stop being so mad at me. I can't be trapped in the "labyrinth of my mind" for the rest of my life knowing that the last time we were together, all we did was fight.*

"My power is limited—for obvious reasons." Calliope's voice echoed in Zoey's head, and Zoey flinched in surprise. She hadn't heard from the goddess since her most recent dream in the

garden. *"But I'll do what I can."*

Thanks, Calliope. I appreciate that. Zoey glanced over at Karter, Diana, and Kali as they set down their finds and built a pit for a bonfire. *While you're at it, can you protect the rest of my friends too? Keep them alive? Help them follow their own paths, not the ones everyone else has decided for them?*

"I'll try my best."

Awesome.

Karter blasted red electricity into the bonfire pit, and crackling flames erupted from it. "Gather around with your offerings, everybody," he shouted. "It's time to call on Persephone."

CHAPTER NINETEEN

CONVERGENCE

When Persephone's white light dwindled, Andy found himself and his companions standing below the massive floating boulder holding Zeus's palace, and they fled into the forest immediately. Everyone except for Chloe ran, as Harmony and Narcissa carried her with vines.

After racing through the trees for what felt like hours, they stopped to contact the other groups of nymphs. Apparently, while one team had been saving Andy, the other two had been either guarding Artemis's Huntresses or gathering more recruits to help fight the gods.

To contact the others and get their locations, the group had to burn some of the nymphs' orange daylilies, just as Andy and his friends had done before traveling into the Labyrinth and infiltrating Poseidon's palace. Once Persephone knew where the other teams were, she teleported herself to them, then transported them back to where Andy, Narcissa, Harmony, Layla, Chloe, and the others were.

By the time Persephone finished bringing all three groups to one location, she was incredibly taxed from using so much power. She panted, beads of sweat rolling down her face, steam curling from her skin. Andy hoped she wasn't burning herself up and making herself fade away.

"Andy!" the familiar voices of Troy and Marina shouted in unison over the chatter of the crowd around him.

He pivoted to see the twins wheeling toward him through the horde, surprise setting in when he spotted the brand-new chairs they were using to get around. Rather than wood, these ones had been crafted from pure metal, the handlebars covered in an array of shining buttons, switches, and levers.

"Whoa, those look great," Andy said, gesturing at the wheelchairs as the twins slowed to a stop in front of him. "Did you take these from one of the cities and add on to them? Or did you make them from scratch in the past couple of days?"

"We fashioned them ourselves, naturally," Marina replied with a shrug. "Wood was too limiting for the kind of modifications we wanted to make. We stole some metal while passing through Ares's and Hera's cities and finished constructing these this morning."

Andy let out a low whistle. "Jeez. You guys really are master blacksmiths."

"You're damn right we are." Troy grinned, patting the tiny area on his right-side handlebar that wasn't riddled with contraptions. "Just wait until you see everything we came up with, too. Unlike with the Pocket-Sized Submarines, we could test these out and fix the bugs ahead of time, so there shouldn't be many malfunctions."

"So long as our calculations are correct, there shouldn't be *any* malfunctions," Marina corrected him.

"But best of all," Troy continued, "we managed to gather almost a hundred new recruits to fight with us."

Marina nodded excitedly. "Nymphs, centaurs, satyrs, regular mortals, and even a few descendants of immortals who, like Troy and me, didn't have enough divine blood to live on Olympus."

Troy pumped a fist in the air. "The gods won't know what hit them when we finally attack!"

Andy wanted to be as enthusiastic as the twins were about all of this, but he couldn't even bring himself to smile. Over three hundred recruits had already infiltrated Olympus to rescue him, and only six plus Persephone had made it out. The rest had been slaughtered, turned to stone, or had hidden in the Garden of Olympus. *Even with all this extra help, the odds don't look good*, Andy thought.

Someone with brown skin and burgundy hair suddenly stepped up beside him, and he turned to see Layla. Troy's and Marina's smiles faded. "What's she doing here?" Troy asked.

Andy put up a hand in defense; he understood why Troy and Marina would be confused about Layla hanging around. She was one of the demigods who'd carted the twins to Zeus's palace to be executed. "It's okay," Andy said. "She's on our side now. She's here to help, just like our new recruits."

Before Troy and Marina could respond, Narcissa's voice sounded from high above them. "Hear me, everyone." A hush fell over the crowd. Andy looked up to see the Dryad manipulating vines to suspend herself near the tips of the trees. "It appears many more recruits have been gathered for our final stand against the gods, and for that I am eternally grateful. Now that we are all together—prepared to lay down our lives for freedom—we must search for the other Chosen One, the girl named Zoey. She left on her own with the gods' objects of power, as she believed she needed to reconnect with the goddess trapped inside of her all on her own. Until we retrieve her and the Helm, Trident, and Lightning Bolt, we cannot—"

"Wait!" Persephone interrupted, and Andy glanced over at the goddess. She wasn't sweaty or out of breath anymore, and her skin was no longer smoking. In fact, she looked more radiant than ever. It was as if she was glowing from the inside out, her hair floating in the air around her head. "Zoey—she's made a sacrifice to me. She's reconnected with Calliope, has the objects of power, and is ready to join us once more."

Another white flare, and Persephone disappeared. Andy held his breath.

Agonizing minutes passed before

Persephone returned. And, when she did, not only had she brought back Andy's friends, but she'd also brought back a bunch of pegasi and dozens of spear-wielding people clad in red.

However, Andy couldn't focus on anyone but the girl he'd argued with only a few days ago. The girl he'd seriously hurt twice now, the girl he needed to apologize to and make up with once and for all.

"Andy!" Zoey grinned ear to ear. "You're okay!" She barreled toward him, and he her, tears blurring his vision.

She threw her arms around his neck. To his surprise, an electrifying sensation—like tiny lightning bolts frying his insides—rushed through his body.

He yelped in surprise and drew back. Not that the feeling was unbearable; it hurt, but it wasn't the worst pain ever. Zoey must have experienced it too because she flinched and pulled away. "Oh," she said. "It's the shock again."

"The shock?" he asked. "Wait, do you mean the shock you felt when I touched you after connecting with Anteros the first time? And when—when Anteros and Calliope made us kiss?"

"Yes and yes. We should be good now,

though." She tackled him in a bear hug, and he embraced her as well.

As they hugged, his tears from earlier returned, his throat closing up. Not caring that they were surrounded by tons of people, he choked out the words he needed to say. "Zoey, I've been a real asshole."

She made a sound like a laugh mixed with a sob. "You're right. You *have* been a real asshole. But in your defense, you've been through a lot lately."

"Yeah, I have, but so have you. It's no excuse for the messed-up stuff I've said to you. You don't deserve to be made to feel like crap."

"No, I don't."

"I'm so, *so* sorry."

She gave him a squeeze. "I forgive you."

"Layla?" Diana called. Andy pulled out of the hug with Zoey to see Diana as she stepped toward Layla, her eyes round with disbelief. "You're really here?"

"I am . . ." Layla watched Diana with a fearful expression. "And I apologize for taking so long to come."

Diana ran to Layla and hugged her, and Andy smiled a little.

"God, I'm glad you're all right," Zoey said, and Andy turned back to her. Kali and Karter were walking up toward her, although Kali was staring at Layla with a hint of suspicion. "I didn't know if we were going to make it to you in time."

"In time for what?" Andy asked.

"After Ares took you, Asteria told us you had six days," Karter said. "We assumed that meant six days before Zeus discovered you and threw you in Tartarus."

"Well, you weren't wrong to assume that. Zeus did discover me, and if Persephone hadn't teleported us away, he *definitely* would've put me in Tartarus after he got ahold of me."

Karter reached Zoey's side, standing so close to her that a sick feeling settled in Andy's stomach. Had his suspicions about them been right all along? *Gotta let it go*, he thought. *There're more important things to worry about. Besides, she's not into me anyway.*

Kali stopped on Zoey's other side. Andy faced Kali, intending on asking her if the spear-wielding people in red were from her village since they looked like it, but before he could she threw her arms around him. "We were so worried about you, Bird-Boy," she said.

"Bird-Boy?" Andy chuckled, hugging her back. "Only Prometheus has ever called me that."

"Yeah, well, I'm coming up with nicknames for everyone now, and I couldn't think of something better than the one he gave you. Why mess with perfection, you know?"

Diana and Layla approached them. "At least it's better than Princess," Diana said.

"And Sweet Stuff," Zoey chimed in.

Andy pulled away from Kali and embraced Diana next.

Narcissa and Harmony hurried over to the group. Harmony was carrying Chloe with her vines, and right after Diana noticed Chloe's injury, she healed it. "As heartwarming as this reunion is," Narcissa began, "there isn't time to relish it." She recounted what had happened for Zoey, Diana, Kali, and Karter—how Persephone and the nymphs had rescued Andy and Layla from Ares's bedchamber, then discovered the other nymphs on their team had been attacked in the Garden of Olympus, and ultimately how they'd had to leave behind a ton of recruits to escape Zeus.

Zoey covered her face with her hand. "I can't believe they found Medusa's head. I thought it wouldn't be an issue after we lost it in the fire."

"We'll have to warn the recruits to remain vigilant," Karter said. He pinched the bridge of his nose. "I'm guessing Athena reattached it to the aegis. Only Zeus and Athena use the aegis, so we'll need to find them and destroy it as soon as possible."

"Thankfully, we won't be fighting *all* the gods," Andy said. "Ares and Aphrodite showed up and started fighting Zeus right before Persephone whisked us away. While they had me and Layla chained up, I told them what's going on with the Anteros-Calliope stuff in the hopes that they'd let me go. They concluded that if they help Anteros win the war, they'll get more power out of it. Instead of setting me free, they kept me locked up while they went to get Anteros's 'full-siblings' to help them, but yeah."

"Oh! Eros, the God of Carnal Love; Deimos and Phobos, the Gods of Fear; and Harmonia, the Goddess of Concord," Diana said. "Those are the other children Ares and Aphrodite have together. Anteros's full-siblings."

Sometime during the discussion, Persephone had made her way over to the crew. "We have no time to waste," she said. "Ares, Aphrodite, and their children will be a great help in battling Zeus, but if we don't reach them soon, they could be annihilated. Now is the time for us to take our final stand against the gods."

The color drained from Zoey's face. "If we plan on leaving soon, that means Andy and I will have to converge with Calliope and Anteros right now."

"It does," Persephone confirmed. "Unless you retrieve the words from Anteros and Calliope and ask another god to cast the Descent Spell for you."

Andy's gut ached as realization set in. "No. That's out of the question. None of the gods who have helped us have done so purely out of the goodness of their hearts—even if they came around eventually, like I think Prometheus did. I guess I don't know what Asteria's motivation for helping us was, but I'd bet part of it was because, at some point or another, one of the gods pissed her off.

"What I'm trying to say is that most, if not all, of the immortals are too selfish for this. We can't trust them to give back the objects of power after they finish casting the Descent Spell. No offense, Persephone."

She shrugged. "None taken. Your conclusions are understandable."

"I'm not sure I agree with you about Asteria," Karter said. "If she were here, and if she were powerful enough to cast the spell, I believe she'd give the objects of power back afterward."

"Maybe she would, but in the end, it doesn't matter," Andy replied. "She's not here. She can't cast the spell. Only Zoey and I—er, Calliope and Anteros—can do it while also *not* going power-hungry and ruling the world with an iron fist."

Diana sighed. "I hate to say this, but I think you're right, Andy. While I'm grateful that my father helped us before, I know he didn't do it to save anyone but me. If he'd genuinely cared about humanity, he would have never shot arrows from the sky during the Storm. He would have never murdered all those people the way he did. Maybe someday he could have learned the error of his ways and become a better person, but I don't think it would have happened anytime soon."

"Asteria was right this whole time, despite how badly I wanted her not to be," Kali said, despair lacing her tone. "The era of the avatars has to happen for real change to be made."

Karter snapped his fingers. "Wait a moment. Andy, you keep saying the gods are selfish and Anteros and Calliope aren't, but they're getting something out of this, aren't they? They get to take over your and Zoey's bodies and be together for the rest of your lives. They get to be heroes held in the highest regard, while the two of you will be forced to suffer until death. Doesn't that make them selfish? Doesn't that make them unfit to cast the spell?"

"I don't think it makes them unfit to cast the spell," Zoey said. "Like Asteria mentioned before, they were forced out of stagnation because of what Zeus did to them. Also, I think it helps that they'll die one day rather than live for thousands of years. They won't be relying on worship to keep them from fading away, so they won't have as much of an incentive to act like tyrants."

Narcissa cut into the conversation. "I'm sorry, but we don't have time to continue discussing this. If we want to reach the gods helping Anteros before Zeus overpowers them, we need to leave."

Andy's chest tightened with anxiety. He turned to Zoey. She looked as scared as he felt. "I guess it's time," she said.

"Seems like it," he replied. "I'll go first. I wanna get this over with."

He bid farewell to Luna, Ajax, Aladdin, Troy, Marina, Layla, Narcissa, Harmony, Chloe, and even Persephone, then hugged Zoey, Diana, and Kali one last time. "We'll take good care of Darko's flower," Kali said.

"I know. I wasn't worried." Andy faced Karter, and before Karter could object, Andy hugged him. "Good luck, man."

Karter reciprocated the embrace. "I hope to

see you again."

"You, too." Andy stepped back to look at Zoey, Diana, Kali, and Karter. He offered them a wave. "See you on the other side." They waved back, their faces scrunching up with grief.

Not wanting to see them cry, he closed his eyes. *Hey, Anteros. You ready to finish the convergence?*

"Absolutely," Anteros replied in Andy's head. *"And rest assured, I'm still certain you and I are one and the same, and Zoey and Calliope are too. There's nothing to fear or be upset about. She* does *love you the way you love her. She must, because you're destined for each other, just as Calliope and I are destined for each other. You'll see. Everything will turn out in the end."*

As much as Andy wished Anteros were right—as much as he wanted Zoey to return his feelings and for them to be together—he knew it wasn't the case. Worse than that, they wouldn't even get to start over and rebuild their friendship, as he hoped Diana and Layla would. At least he could take solace in the fact that he'd been able to apologize to her, and that she'd forgiven him.

Whatever you say, he thought at Anteros. *Now, how are we supposed to do this?*

"Search for me in your mind. I'll take you to the

garden."

Andy focused on finding Anteros and spotted him right away. Anteros stood at the mouth of a cave-like structure, just like every other time Andy had purposely connected with him. Like times before, Andy also didn't have wings here, so he ran toward Anteros, and Anteros flew toward him. They reached each other, and Anteros grabbed Andy by the wrists.

A familiar buzzing sensation started up in Andy's chest. The feeling grew stronger, spreading through his whole body, until there was a blast of silver light.

It didn't take long for the beam to wane. When it did, Andy *found himself in the Garden of Olympus, except unlike when he'd been here in person, the sky was made up of a colorful galaxy.*

At first, Andy had the strong urge to run. Anteros was after him. He knew it. But then he remembered: he was supposed to get caught.

So he stood there, heart in his throat as he waited for Anteros to seize him, to trap him in the labyrinth of his mind, to take over his body and fulfill the destiny laid out for them by the threads of fate.

It happened fast. Anteros grasped Andy by the shoulder and spun him around.

An electric shock jolted through Andy, the hairs on his arms and legs standing straight, goose bumps rising on his skin. He tried to pull away, but he was petrified. What the hell? He tried opening his mouth to yell. His lips wouldn't budge.

He looked at Anteros as best he could. Anteros was frozen too, as still as Medusa's statues. The god grunted several times. It was as though he wanted to speak but couldn't, and his eyes bugged out with terror.

Andy's heart pounded as he realized he couldn't feel his feet anymore. He did his best to look down and saw black smoke pooling around him, around Anteros.

Out of nowhere, the voice of his mother echoed in his mind. "We're proud of you, sweetheart."

His father's voice came next. "You're so brave. Braver than anyone I've ever met."

The mist traveled up his legs, and the limbs went numb.

"We love you," Mel-Mel said.

"More than you can imagine," Mark added.

The smoke reached his waist, his hands, his arms, his shoulders. Those parts of him fell senseless too.

Spencer's voice sounded in his head last. "Goodbye, Andy. I'm grateful to have known you."

What do you mean, goodbye? *Andy wanted to* scream. What do you mean, you're grateful to have known me?

But he only realized what Spencer meant when the mist finished devouring him and he was no more.

Zoey watched in anguish as Andy sacrificed himself. She leaned on Karter, Diana, and Kali for support, certain that without them, she wouldn't have stayed upright.

At first, the only thing that happened was Andy's eyes snapped open, glowing the same all-consuming silver as they had in the past when his connection to Anteros grew stronger.

But then there was a *craaack*ing from inside of him, as if someone were breaking his bones and putting them back together. Seconds later he shot up, growing entire inches taller.

A wet squishing noise came next, and a jiggly, fat-like substance appeared beneath his skin. It wriggled down his arms and legs, then settled on his muscles and hardened like magma cooling to rock.

Finally, the illumination in his eyes declined. He blinked, gazing around like a newborn baby seeing the world for the first time.

As Zoey studied him, she noticed the structure of his face had changed slightly. His cheekbones were higher, his jawline sharper. It was as though he'd transformed into someone new, someone perfectly balanced between Andy and Anteros.

Persephone stepped toward him. "Anteros? Is that you? Your divine essence is . . . different. At least from what I remember."

"I . . ." Even his voice sounded weird. It certainly didn't belong to Andy, but it wasn't deep enough to belong to Anteros. "I don't know."

"Are you still Andy?" Diana tried.

". . . I don't know."

"Is there anything you *do* know?" Kali asked.

He knit his brow and blinked some more, contemplating the question, and Zoey wondered if perhaps Asteria had been wrong about what she'd believed the convergence to be. *Maybe it's a process beyond anyone's understanding,* she thought. *Until you experience it yourself.* That notion terrified her more than dying or being trapped in her mind.

"I'm not Anteros, and I'm not Andy," he eventually stated. "Yet at the same time, I'm both of them. I'm Andy-Anteros, and I know what I have to do next. I have to end the era of the gods."

"That's what's most important." Persephone gestured at Zoey. "Are you ready?"

What kind of a question was that? How would she ever be ready to do what Andy had just done? Especially when he was saying crazy stuff like he wasn't Anteros, and he wasn't Andy, yet at the same time he was both of them?

Still, it's not like I have a choice. I have to go through with the convergence, or else all of this will have been for nothing.

"As ready as I'll ever be," she replied.

Zoey said goodbye to everyone as Andy had before merging with Anteros, and although Kali and Diana had already assured her that they'd plant Darko's flower somewhere beautiful, and although Kali had just promised Andy that she'd take care of the poppy too, Zoey asked them to reaffirm that they'd keep it safe.

"We swear to you," Diana whispered.

Kali forced a smile. "You can count on us."

Together, they hugged Zoey for the last time.

After the embrace ended, there was only one more person to say goodbye to.

Zoey walked over to Karter, grasped one of his hands, and stared into his golden eyes. "Will you do something for me?"

"What is it?"

She swallowed hard. "Even though I can't escape my fate, I want you to try and escape yours. I want you to live."

His gaze softened. "I'll try my best, but what's most important is that you and Andy don't sacrifice yourselves in vain. If I have to die to make that happen, it will be more than worth it."

Right then and there, she didn't care whether the two of them were surrounded by people, or whether those people were watching them. If she didn't kiss him before leaving, she was going to regret it.

And so she did just that.

After the kiss ended, Karter hugged her tighter than ever. "I wish you didn't have to go," he whispered.

"Maybe we'll meet in the next life," she whispered back.

"I certainly hope so."

She pulled away from him, trying not to cry, and just as she was about to call on Calliope, her eyes locked on Andy's—no, on Andy-Anteros's—her stomach sinking with guilt. *Crap.* He appeared stung as he stared back at her, but he didn't seem mad. Just surprised and hurt.

I'm sorry, she thought. *I never meant to do this to you.* Unable to look at him any longer—unable to look at any of them, lest she lose her resolve—she closed her eyes, going into her mind to search for Calliope. *Calliope, are you there? I'm ready to complete the convergence.*

"I'm here, child."

A second later Calliope appeared, standing at the mouth of a dark cavern in Zoey's mind. They stepped toward each other, and Calliope gently took Zoey's hand. *There's that buzzing feeling again.* The sensation flooded Zoey's body, and a blue glare blinded her.

Soon the brilliance dwindled, and Zoey was *in a garden, the same one she'd seen in visions, the same one Calliope had chased her through.* I have to run, *she thought.* I have to get away!

Wait, no. She needed to stay put. She needed Calliope to capture her. She needed to finish this.

Someone tapped her on the shoulder, but before she could turn around to confirm it was Calliope, electricity arced through her. Her hair stood on end. Goose bumps prickled her skin. She tried to move but couldn't, just like when she'd reconnected with Calliope in the Zeus City library. It's happening.

Black smoke billowed in the bottom corners of her vision, and she realized with a pang of dread that a numbing sensation was spreading through her feet. Instinctively, she tried to scream. All she could manage was a muffled yelp.

"You're amazing, hon." Her father's voice echoed in her head as the numbness infected her legs. *"Courageous. Kind. Selfless. I couldn't love you more, and I'm going to miss you so much."* You'll miss me so much? What's that supposed to mean?

A young woman spoke next—Syrena—as Zoey lost feeling in her torso and arms. "If you and Andy hadn't gone through with this, the gods might have never been stopped. Not until they'd faded away completely. Thank you for your sacrifice."

"Thank you for helping push Karter onto a better path as well," Spencer said, Zoey's shoulders and neck falling senseless. "And, of course, goodbye. I'm grateful to have known you, Zoey."

Why are they talking as if they're never going to see me again? Isn't my soul supposed to be set free after my body dies? Won't I have the chance to be reunited with everyone someday?

It wasn't until after the black smoke engulfed her entirely—it wasn't until she ceased to exist—that she received the answers to her questions.

Zoey-Calliope gazed out at the world for the first time.

Well, not *quite* for the first time.

She possessed thousands of years of memories from Calliope, and eighteen years of memories from Zoey. Because of their experiences, she knew what the world looked like. She knew its smells and tastes, its sounds and textures. She knew pleasure and suffering and everything in between.

But here and now belonged to her. It was hers and hers alone, as Zoey and Calliope no longer existed. Their souls had merged to create Zoey-Calliope; she was someone different, someone new.

She recalled the way Asteria had described the convergence to Zoey and Andy a short while ago—after they'd concluded that they were, in fact, *not* Calliope and Anteros. Asteria had told them a convergence was the process of someone handing over their mortal shell to a god, akin to a willing possession.

Zoey-Calliope also remembered how, in dreams both in the Before Time and After Storm, Asteria had come to Calliope and (presumably) Anteros to explain what a convergence was—and that her descriptions then were far different from what she'd eventually relayed to Zoey and Andy.

The Titan goddess had told Calliope that

Calliope and Zoey were one and the same, that Anteros and Andy were one and the same. That the gods' spirits had been split and reincarnated into human forms. That the convergence was simply the two parts of them merging once more: a transformation to help them become their most powerful selves.

Zoey-Calliope realized then that Asteria had been lying to everyone. She'd manipulated Zoey, Calliope, Andy, Anteros, and the people around them so that they'd agree to this.

But why lie? The humans and deities had wanted some of the same things. Especially when it came to ending Zeus's tyranny. If melding souls was the best way to complete that daunting task, Zoey-Calliope was sure the two halves of herself would have eventually agreed to it, even knowing that once it was over, they'd cease to exist.

So why had Asteria done so much to first make Zoey and Calliope believe that they were one and the same, that Andy and Anteros were one and the same? Then that they were all separate, that Calliope and Anteros would need to possess Zoey and Andy to liberate humanity?

Zoey-Calliope could only think of one reason. *"The gods are selfish, selfish creatures,"* Asteria had said. *"Unable to think of anyone but themselves.*"

Asteria had never believed Calliope and Anteros had gone through a personal transformation because of what Zeus had done to them, as she'd argued before. She'd always believed they were too selfish to do what was right. She'd convinced herself there had to be something in it for a god if they were to agree to something like a convergence.

At least in Calliope's case, Asteria had been wrong.

Thoughts racing, Zoey-Calliope looked down at her hands. Yes, *hands*, plural. This body had lost its right one a short while back, but now it had two again.

"Zoey-Calliope?" Andy-Anteros said. "Is that you?"

She looked to him and a flurry of burning pain and clashing emotions struck her. Her body jolted one way, then the other, and sky-blue light overtook her vision.

As quickly as the pain and emotions came, they vanished, her sight returning to normal, but the voices of two young women reverberated over one another in her head.

"*Finally, we—*"
"*No, I won't—*"
"*—can be together—*"

"—be with him—"
"—when all of—"
"—even when all—"
"—this is over."
"—of this has ended."

The voices abruptly stopped.

"Yes, it's me," Zoey-Calliope answered, and gasped at the way she sounded. It was as if the women in her head were speaking through her at once, as if their vocalizations were layered on top of each other.

Andy-Anteros rushed to her side. "Are you all right? You had some kind of seizure, and your voice . . ."

"Is strange," she finished for him. "Still, I'm sure I'm Zoey-Calliope. I'm sure I completed the convergence."

Andy-Anteros smiled at her. "If you're sure of it, then so am I."

Zoey-Calliope opened her mouth to tell him she loved him—that she was in love with him—because she did, she was. Calliope's memories of Anteros made it so.

However, something compelled her to stop, to glance at Karter instead. Karter stared back at her, a mixture of confusion and sorrow etched on his features, and another gust of searing sensations and conflicting emotions hit her. She started to shake, a glare of sky-blue light overtaking her sight.

When her vision came back, the voices echoed again.

"What am—"

"I can't say that—"

"—I doing?"

"—to Andy-Anteros."

"I don't—"

"I fell for Karter and—"

"—love him."

"—he fell for me too."

"I don't care—"

"I can't bear—"

"—if I hurt him."

"—to hurt him."

Finally, the voices stopped.

Zoey-Calliope shook her head and turned away from Karter and Andy-Anteros, afraid to look them in the eye for fear of the pain, tremors, and voices returning.

Narcissa stepped forward. "Please, we're running out of time. We *must* leave."

"If I'm going to transport everyone to Olympus, I'll need more sacrifices," Persephone said.

Andy-Anteros put up a hand. "Wait. We shouldn't go until we make sure that Zoey-

Calliope and I can open a portal to Tartarus."

"He's right," Zoey-Calliope said. "What good would teleporting there do if we arrived and weren't able to take down the gods?"

Narcissa cupped her chin. "A fair point. We need to rid ourselves of Artemis's Huntresses anyway, so the recruits guarding them can help us fight."

With that, they set to the task of gathering the Helm, the Trident, the Bolt, and Artemis's "dead" Huntresses, then cleared the recruits out of the surrounding area so that no one would be sucked into the pit of Tartarus if they managed to open a portal there. All the while, Zoey-Calliope did everything she could to avoid facing Andy-Anteros and Karter.

Once the area was clear and Zoey-Calliope and Andy-Anteros had the objects of power in hand, the lifeless Huntresses piled in a heap twenty feet ahead of them, they began to chant the ancient words of the Descent Spell, and the memory of Calliope obtaining the words rushed through Zoey-Calliope's mind. How the goddess had used her persuasion powers to trick Hades into giving her the spell's location, how she'd utilized his jealousy of his more powerful brothers to coax it out of him.

That's the only way her abilities worked on

beings more powerful than her—she had to strike a nerve. She had to suggest something they already wanted to do, deep down. Otherwise, she could only sway them into doing as she proposed for a short while, or sometimes not at all.

Zoey-Calliope also recalled how Calliope had covered her tracks by convincing Hades that their encounter had been a nightmare, that it hadn't really happened, that it was so insignificant he'd forget about it altogether. Calliope had known his fear of Zeus and Poseidon was as great as his jealousy of them, and she'd used that to her advantage.

"If Zeus and Poseidon ever had reason to believe you'd betrayed them, the consequences would be dire," Calliope had whispered in his ear as he slept. She'd traveled to the Underworld herself, and Eris had helped her escape it. *"That's why you know this was only a nightmare, a figment of your overactive imagination. You'd* never *give away the Descent Spell's location. By morning, you'll forget you even had this dream."*

At least for a while, Calliope's secret had been safe, but Zeus had still discovered what she'd been up to, and Zoey-Calliope couldn't help but wonder how. She was sure it couldn't have been Hades remembering his "dream." Maybe it had been Eris, but the Goddess of Chaos had seemed so eager to help Calliope in her plot against the gods that Zoey-Calliope didn't think she would have sabotaged it like that.

Perhaps someday Zoey-Calliope would discover who'd revealed her plans. For now, though, she needed to focus on casting this spell.

As Zoey-Calliope and Andy-Anteros progressed with the Descent, the forest floor tremored. The shaking grew so violent that cracks split the ground, the earth breaking off and plummeting into the fissures. Soon the crevices had fractured enough that they'd formed a pit so endless Zoey-Calliope couldn't see the bottom of it.

Dirt continued to cascade into the cavity, and cerulean flames crawled up out of it. Gales blew into it, as if it were taking a deep, violent breath. The winds picked up Artemis's Huntresses, and they swirled down, down, down. After they disappeared, Zoey-Calliope and Andy-Anteros closed the portal.

Sweat seeped from Zoey-Calliope's skin, her breaths shallow, a fiery sensation spreading from her chest through the rest of her form. She recognized the feeling as a divine essence overheating after one uses an immense amount of energy, but strangely enough, she hadn't overtaxed herself, and she knew she hadn't because she recalled memories of Calliope's in which the goddess *had*.

When Calliope strained herself in the past, it hadn't felt like this. The goddess had experienced the burning, yes, but she'd also become exhausted. However, Zoey-Calliope wasn't tired. She felt better than ever. The word "exhilarated" came to mind, and she thought that perhaps Asteria had at least been honest about one thing: that the convergence would transform her and Andy-Anteros into more powerful beings than Zoey, Calliope, Andy, and Anteros could have ever been.

"Did it work?" Harmony asked, and Zoey-Calliope and Andy-Anteros turned toward her and the rest of their companions. "Was that actually a portal there, or—"

"Yes, it was," Persephone interjected. "Those were the blue flames of the deepest pit of Tartarus."

Silence blanketed everyone as they allowed the reality of the situation to sink in.

Eventually, Diana broke the quiet. "In that case, it's time for us to take our final stand against the gods. Let's armor up and leave."

"Like I mentioned before, I'll need more

sacrifices to transport all of us to Olympus," Persephone said.

Andy-Anteros wiped the sweat from his brow. "Actually, I don't think you'll need to worry about doing that anymore."

Persephone raised a brow at him. "Oh? And why not?"

"Because we're going to do it," Andy-Anteros replied. "Aren't we, Zoey-Calliope?"

She blinked, facing him, and thankfully, she didn't spasm or hear voices this time. "You think we're strong enough?"

"I do."

And, as they discovered about a half hour later, he was right. When they worked together, they *were* strong enough to transport everyone to the forest outside of Olympus, and it didn't seem to exhaust them like teleporting exhausted Persephone. In fact, it was easy. They simply pictured the place they were now, then imagined the atoms making up their bodies peeling apart, dissolving into light, and re-manifesting in the place they wanted to be.

Hopefully, Zoey-Calliope thought as she and the others donned their armor and formulated a plan of attack, *we're also strong enough to win this war once and for all.*

CHAPTER TWENTY

PREDETERMINED

*W*hen the world is taken back, and monsters rule the trees, blood of a demigod will spill.

Karter thought of the Dreaded Prophecy as he directed the gray pegasus he'd stolen toward New Mount Olympus, cold rain pelting him in the face and soaking him from head to toe. Layla sat behind him, her arms tight around his waist so she wouldn't fall.

Two mortals will rise, two from the Before, reborn from sacrifice.

Up ahead, Zoey and Andy—no, Zoey-Calliope and Andy-Anteros, wearing armor that the nymphs had stolen, like everyone else—directed their own pegasi toward the massive hunk of rock.

And when the sky is black and green, and the heavens cry, they will lead a war. A war on the gods.

The black clouds above the Garden of Olympus flared with green lightning, the sounds of thunder and screams ripping across the stormy sky. *This is it. I pray Zoey and Andy's sacrifice wasn't in vain.*

He recalled the glow in their eyes as they'd gone through with the convergences, recalled the way their bodies had been reconstructed, remolded into different people. They didn't look like themselves anymore; they looked like beings stuck between human and deity, which he supposed they were, since they were mortal but had teleported everyone here in a way only the gods could.

A lump formed in Karter's throat. Were Zoey and Andy trapped in the labyrinth of their minds, as Asteria had asserted they would be? Or had their spirits fused with Calliope's and Anteros's, creating new entities altogether?

Karter guessed the latter, considering Andy-Anteros had said that he was neither Andy nor

Anteros, but that he was also both. It made Karter wonder about the future of their souls, about whether he'd ever see Zoey and Andy— the *real* Zoey and Andy—again.

He gulped, blinking back tears. *I can't think about this right now. I have to put it out of my head. I have to focus.*

To the right, Kali directed a pegasus, Diana holding onto her. To the left, Troy and Marina, secured in metal wheelchairs with buckles and belts, steered the mechanisms through the sky with some attached levers. One of the modifications they'd made to the chairs was adding engines to them, like the engines used in automobiles in Hephaestus City. They'd also installed mechanical wings that unfolded from the sides with the push of a few buttons. The contraptions reminded Karter of Daedalus's wings, despite being made of metal rather than feathers and wax.

Behind the group, the warriors of Deltama Village each rode their own pegasus. They'd insisted on remaining close, not only to help Zoey-Calliope and Andy-Anteros, but also to protect their "future chief." Karter prayed that if Kali and Diana got out of this alive, they'd find a way to stay together, and Kali wouldn't be forced to marry and take over her village.

As they neared New Mount Olympus, Zoey-Calliope steered her pegasus ahead of Andy-Anteros. She raised Poseidon's Trident and let out a war cry, her strange, two-person voice making it sound as if a pair of young women were bellowing rather than one, then brought down the Trident as though she were slamming it against the ground.

The boulder holding Olympus rocked from side to side, rumbling louder than the thunder. Then it plunged downward and crashed to the forest floor.

Andy-Anteros was next to steer ahead. He raised the Lightning Bolt and howled like a beast. The weapon squealed in response to his fury, and the most massive golden bolt yet shot from the clouds. The lightning exploded a section of the palace. It sent debris flying, left craters in its wake.

Specks that Karter knew were Persephone, the nymphs, and the rest of the recruits rushed out of the forest, onto Olympus, and into the garden. Zoey-Calliope and Andy-Anteros swooped down after them, and Karter, Layla, Diana, Kali, and the Deltama Village warriors followed suit. "Remember, the gods have

Medusa's head," Diana yelled. "Watch out for the aegis, and if you see Zeus or Athena, shield your eyes."

They landed in the thick of destruction, gods, demigods, nymphs, *astynomia*, humans, Harpies, and Cyclopes clashing in a battle unlike anything Karter had seen. Everywhere he turned there were toppled trees, overturned statues, and trampled vegetation, and where the ground wasn't covered with bodies and debris, it was slick with rain and ichor and blood.

Karter, his friends, and the Deltama Village warriors strapped their shields to their arms. Zoey-Calliope donned the Helm of Darkness, she and Poseidon's Trident disappearing with it, and Andy-Anteros readied the Master Lightning Bolt, his hands big enough to grip it properly, unlike Andy's. At the same time, Karter conjured green electricity, Diana summoned a sphere of sunlight, Layla unsheathed her sword, and Kali and the Deltama Village warriors brandished their spears. Troy and Marina had already explained that to fight, they'd be using the fireball and cannon mechanisms they'd added to their wheelchairs. They kept their wings deployed, their free hands hovering over levers and buttons.

The crew had barely assessed their surroundings before a beast's roar reverberated from behind them. Karter swung around to find his half-brother Heracles riding through the chaos toward them on the back of a male lion with shimmering golden fur.

"The Nemean Lion!" Diana shouted. "His hide can't be penetrated with any weapon, and he has claws strong enough to tear through our shields!"

Andy-Anteros screamed, "*Scatter!*"

No one argued. The group split up, dashing out of the lion's way, but two of the Deltama Village warriors weren't quick enough. The beast slashed his claws through one of them, splitting her body in half at the waist. He sank his teeth into the other's throat and ripped the man's head from his neck.

What was left of the warriors tumbled to the ground. Blood and entrails spewed from their mutilated figures. The monster slid to a stop in the muck, gathered his bearings, and stalked back toward the group.

As quickly as he could, Karter moved the shield from his arm to his back and allowed his green bolt to disintegrate.

"What are you doing?" Kali cried from behind him.

"In the old days, slaying the Nemean Lion was Heracles's first labor," Karter replied. "Heracles has super-strength, so he managed to kill the creature via strangulation. I have to do the same before anyone else is slaughtered."

"No," Zoey-Calliope said. "I have a better plan. Andy-Anteros, use the Bolt to knock Heracles from the Nemean Lion and get me on the creature's back. I'll turn him against his 'master.'"

Andy-Anteros raised the Lightning Bolt and released a furious yell. The Bolt wailed, and lightning zapped from the sky toward Heracles, who still rode the Nemean Lion.

Heracles seemed to anticipate Andy-Anteros's attack. He deflected it with his arm cuff, just as Ares had done in Aphrodite City. But the force of the lightning was enough to knock Heracles off the lion. He flew backward and crashed to the ground.

Andy-Anteros disappeared. Karter assumed that he'd grabbed Zoey-Calliope, that they'd gone after the Nemean Lion.

There was a blur of movement in Karter's peripheral. Something smacked into him at lightspeed. He flew sideways and rammed shoulder-first into mud. Head spinning, pain arcing through his shoulder, he looked up and found he'd been separated from the others.

One hundred feet away, Andy-Anteros reappeared, the Nemean Lion vanishing as Heracles climbed to his feet. Three squawking Harpies and four grumbling Cyclopes went after the others, and Troy and Marina streaked into the sky. They pressed buttons and pulled levers, and cannonballs and streams of fire shot out from compartments in their wheelchairs at the monsters. Kali, Layla, and the Deltama Village warriors mounted pegasi and joined Troy and Marina in fighting the creatures, while Diana sprinted in Karter's direction.

Another blur. Stabbing pain in Karter's palms.

Hermes, Messenger of the Gods appeared before Karter, his eyes glinting with malice. His usually slicked-back hair was a mess of black, and he had his golden sword in hand. Blood dripped from the blade.

Hermes leapt into the air, the wings on his sandals flittering. "You murdered my son. I'm going to gut you like a pig."

Something hot and sticky oozed from Karter's hands. He glanced down to see deep, bloody gashes. *Hermes wounded me at super-speed.*

Karter tried to stand. A third blur, and there was more of the stabbing pain, this time behind his knees. He fell onto his back.

One last blur. Hermes appeared in the air above Karter, sword raised.

A sphere of sunlight blasted Hermes. The god spiraled to the left and nose-dived into a pile of rubble.

"It's okay, I'll heal you," Diana said, suddenly hovering over Karter. She lit her hands and placed them over him. Soothing warmth flooded his body, the hurt evaporating.

Although Diana had healed him, his relief didn't last. Over in the wreckage, Hermes groaned and climbed to his feet, and a screech like hundreds of knives dragging across stone pierced the air, the ground quaking with booming footfalls. *No*, Karter thought, his heart leaping into his throat. *Calliope's trick wore off!*

Hera and Ladon have come to kill us all!

Sure enough, the hundred-headed dragon barreled into Karter's line of sight. Hera rode on his back. With one hand she grasped his closest neck; with the other she held her battle scepter.

Karter and Diana jumped to their feet and conjured their respective attacks, but Ladon paid them no mind. He seemed most interested in Hermes. He trotted that way, his hungry stares fixed on the god.

Hermes grimaced and rubbed his nose. "What are you doing? Karter and the Daughter of Apollo are right *there*." He jutted a finger in their direction.

Hera tilted her head slightly. Her eyes briefly met Karter's. "So they are." She hopped off Ladon's back as the monster approached Hermes. "Go ahead, my pet."

Ladon was upon Hermes before the god could realize he'd been betrayed. Fangs sank into every inch of his flesh, and he screamed. The shriek was soon replaced with wet ripping noises, with the sickening sounds of skin and muscle tearing, of bones and tendons snapping. Ichor pooled beneath Ladon's front claws.

Hera hurried toward Karter and Diana. "Karter, are you all right? Is your injury healed entirely?" He opened and closed his mouth, stunned. Hera was only concerned because she wanted him to be able to defeat Zeus, but her reaction still jarred him. "Has the storm deafened you? I asked you a question."

He never had the chance to reply. Peridot lightning struck the space between Karter and Hera. They cried out, falling back, and Karter re-strapped his shield to his arm and used the reflective interior to gaze at their attacker.

Just as Karter had suspected, it was Zeus. The god didn't have the aegis, but he was rearing back another green bolt. He aimed it for Diana.

"*Look out!*" Karter screamed.

Diana somersaulted to the left. The lightning struck the ground beside her.

Zeus summoned another bolt. It fizzled out when an arrow pierced his right shoulder. He whirled around, and Karter saw Ares directing his war chariot drawn by his four immortal pegasi through the sky toward the King of the Gods. Phobos and Deimos, who looked like Ares but with wavy golden locks, stood in the chariot beside Ares with their blades drawn. The dark-haired winged god Eros fluttered beside the chariot, his bow and arrow ready.

Eros sent another projectile toward Zeus. Zeus veered sideways, his attention on Ares, Phobos, Deimos, and Eros for the moment.

Still, Karter, Diana, and Hera had other opponents to worry about. There was a rumbling behind them, the ground shaking so violently they stumbled to the side. At first, Karter thought the quakes came from Zoey-Calliope using the Trident. But when he turned around, he realized they came from the blue-skinned Lord of the Seas himself.

Down on one knee, Poseidon rammed his fists against the ground. Cracks split down it toward Karter, Diana, and Hera, making deep trenches Karter couldn't see the bottom of. He grabbed Diana and jumped into the air.

"Ladon," Hera barked, "feast on Poseidon's flesh!" The monster stopped devouring what was left of Hermes—which wasn't much—and bounded over the trenches toward Poseidon. In seconds Ladon was upon the Lord of the Seas, and Hera was gathering up Hermes's carcass.

White flashed behind Karter and Diana. Karter swung around midair to see Hades, pale and lanky as ever, materialize not far from them. Hades raised his arms and chanted something, his words incoherent because of the rain.

While Hades chanted, the corpses of the people and monsters around him began to stir. *Oh no*, Karter thought. *He's going to raise the dead, just as he did to terrorize humanity after the Storm.*

If he does so to all the corpses, we'll be horribly outnumbered!

The bodies continued to stir, but before they could rise, before they could join the battle moaning and groaning in a macabre choir, hundreds of thorned vines snaked toward them from every direction at a rapid pace.

The plants rammed into the corpses, slithered inside of them through their wide eye sockets and gaping mouths. The vegetation wormed down into their arms, their legs, making the appendages twitch. Hades snarled, moving his hands frantically, but it seemed he no longer had control of the carcasses. The vegetation inside them forced them to stand and march stiffly toward the god, and then Persephone, Demeter, and some of Demeter's other immortal children—Despoina, Plutus, and Philomelus, all of whom closely resembled Persephone, their older half-sister—vaulted out from a pile of rubble. The gods waved their arms, directing the corpses with their greenery.

Hades flashed white. Persephone did too. They reappeared in the same spot outside of the horde of walking dead, and Hades summoned his black metal bident while Persephone conjured more vines. Teeth bared, they began the struggle against each other.

Demeter, Despoina, Plutus, and Philomelus transported themselves and the vine-infested corpses to Persephone's side and, all together, they fought Hades.

The sight of them working as a team made Karter briefly wonder where Corinna, Daughter of Demeter was. *Perhaps Demeter has hidden her somewhere. It's likely the goddess doesn't want her mortal child involved in this.*

Taking a deep breath, Karter turned his attention to where the rest of the group was located. Kali, Troy, Marina, Layla, and the Deltama Village warriors had killed some of the Harpies and Cyclopes that had come after them, the monsters' unmoving forms strewn about the ruins of the garden, but now more of the creatures were approaching, along with several demigods. Thankfully, many nymph recruits had arrived to help, including Narcissa and Harmony, but Zoey-Calliope and Andy-Anteros were nowhere to be seen, and Heracles was still alive, wrestling the Nemean Lion.

Karter soared toward the group with Diana in his arms, wind and rain assailing them, but before they could reach their companions, something looped around Karter's ankles. He looked down to see grapevines coiling up his body and Diana's. The vines pulled them to the ground. They slammed face-first into trampled bushes and flowers, and then they were twirling up, up, up.

"It's such a shame the two of you have forced our hands like this," Karter's half-brother Dionysus said. Stomach churning, Karter caught an upside-down glimpse of the god's fiery red curls as he stood in the grass below, using his grapevines to rotate Karter and Diana around and around. "At least you'll make good snacks for my Cyclops friends."

As if on cue, two of the one-eyed giants stomped into view. The first reached for Diana, while the second extended a hand toward Karter.

The roar of a cannon assaulted Karter's eardrums, then another and another and another. Four iron orbs bigger even than Karter's head shot toward the Cyclopes from the right. The missiles crashed into the sides of the Cyclopes' skulls, and chunks of bone and brain exploded everywhere. What remained of the monsters toppled over.

The attack granted Karter time to gain his bearings. He channeled his strength and ripped through Dionysus's grapevines, then flew to Diana's side and freed her as well.

From where the cannonballs had appeared, Troy and Marina glided through the air. They switched directions and circled Dionysus. The god launched plants at them, but with the push of some buttons they sent streams of orange fire blazing. The flames burned through Dionysus's vegetation.

Dionysus moved frantically to conjure more greenery. Karter, Diana, Troy, and Marina landed and charged at him. His vines careened toward them. The plants coiled around Karter's and Diana's limbs, around Troy's and Marina's chairs, but that didn't stop them. Karter tore apart the vegetation, Diana used spheres of sunlight to reduce it to ash, and Troy and Marina burned it with fire they shot from their chairs.

Dionysus cast out more vines, which Karter, Diana, Troy, and Marina demolished as they pressed on toward the god. It wasn't long before they reached him. However, he lit up with white and disappeared before they could fight him up close. "Coward!" Marina snarled.

The ground shuddered from where Heracles had been wrestling the Nemean Lion. Karter glanced that way to find a cavernous portal to Tartarus opening. Zoey-Calliope must have been wearing the Helm because Karter couldn't see her anywhere, but Andy-Anteros stood at a distance from the expanding cavity, the Bolt in his hands. A dead Nemean Lion and the crumpled, ichor-covered corpse of Heracles lay at Andy-Anteros's feet.

Andy-Anteros kicked Heracles and the Lion. The winds of Tartarus picked them up, and they vanished into the fiery pit.

There was a white glare fifty feet to the left of Andy-Anteros, and Karter's gut clenched. Was it Dionysus? Was that where the god had teleported to? Was he planning on trying to banish Zoey-Calliope and Andy-Anteros to Tartarus himself? Karter jumped into the air and flew toward Andy-Anteros, intending on protecting him and Zoey-Calliope.

In the end, Karter didn't have to protect either of them; it wasn't Dionysus who manifested. It was Hera, with Hermes's mutilated remains in tow. She hurled the god's broken form into the flames.

A second white light, this time directly behind Hera. Silver-haired Athena manifested. The Goddess of Wisdom had the aegis strapped to her arm, a spear in hand. As fast as she appeared she plunged the spear through Hera's back, then wrenched the weapon out of Hera and shoved her toward the pit. The Queen of the Gods howled in rage, Tartarus sucking her in.

Karter almost cried out for Andy-Anteros, to warn him that Athena had appeared with the aegis, but the avatar had already vanished. He and Zoey-Calliope were hopefully high in the sky, the Helm cloaking them with invisibility.

Athena disappeared. A moment later light gleamed in the distance from where the rest of Karter's allies were fighting demigods and monsters, and bloodcurdling screams pierced the air.

Karter landed in the muck and used the reflection in his shield to gaze that way, afraid he already knew what had happened. His heart sank, his suspicions confirmed.

Athena stood among Karter's companions. She raised the aegis, the emerald-scaled head of Medusa mounted upon the shield. Medusa's snake-hair dangled limply around her stiff face.

Narcissa, a dozen other nymph recruits, and a handful of Deltama Village warriors seized up. Karter thought that as Medusa's head turned them to stone her dead eyes would have shone with brilliance, but they didn't. They remained dull as ever while rock climbed up their victims' figures like a second skin. It happened quickly, though not so quickly the soldiers didn't realize their time was up. The horror in their expressions showed that they'd registered their fates.

Harmony wailed something incomprehensible. She cupped Narcissa's cheek as the other Dryad became a statue. When Narcissa's transformation was complete, Harmony fell to her knees, shaking with sobs, and Kali and two Naiads rushed to her side, raising their shields to protect her and themselves from Medusa's gaze. Kali and the Naiads pulled Harmony to her feet and yanked her away from Narcissa.

More screams. The demigods and monsters closest to Athena dispersed as she spun every which way, brandishing the aegis with reckless abandon, but they couldn't all escape. Four Cyclopes and two demigods—who Karter assumed had been fighting for the gods—turned to stone as well.

Meanwhile, Layla and the remaining warriors and recruits turned their backs on Athena. They used the reflections in their shields to track her movements. The Dryads sent plants twisting around her limbs, the Naiads slapped her with whips of freshwater, and five of the Deltama Village warriors closed their eyes and charged blindly at her, spears in hand. One managed to stab her in the leg, but she impaled him with her own spear, surely killing him.

I have to get over there, Karter thought. *I have to destroy Medusa's head!*

Green arced in the corner of Karter's shield. Breath catching, he dove to the side. A peridot bolt exploded in the space where he'd been standing seconds before.

He jumped to his feet and swung around. Zeus stalked toward him, green crackling up and down the god's form. Behind Zeus marched Artemis, Hestia, and Dionysus. Artemis nocked a silver arrow, Hestia summoned fire in her palms, and Dionysus manipulated vines around himself.

Ares's pegasi and chariot soared down from the clouds at high speed and landed in front of Zeus and the other immortals. Ares, Phobos, and Deimos vaulted out of the chariot and sprinted toward Zeus. When they reached him, they brawled against him together.

Eros swooped down next. He sent arrow after arrow toward Artemis and Hestia. Artemis turned her attention to Eros and shot her projectiles at him instead of Karter. Hestia did the same, hurling her flames Eros's way.

There were more flashes of white, and the nearly identical mother-daughter duo of Aphrodite and Harmonia manifested before Dionysus, looped a rope around his neck, and started strangling him.

Karter didn't stay to watch how events would unfold. His allies needed him. He leapt into the air and flew in Athena's direction, using his shield to protect his eyes from Medusa's stare in case the goddess directed it at him.

Before he could reach her, he spotted Diana, Troy, and Marina in one of the now-ravaged courtyards of Olympus. Hephaestus, Blacksmith of the Gods hobbled after Diana through the ruins, swinging his massive hammer through every sphere of sunlight she threw at him. Troy and Marina streaked through the air behind Hephaestus, sending fire and cannonballs at him as well, but he dodged the assaults. *They must have been going to help Kali and the others, and then he showed up.*

Karter veered toward them. He needed to stop Athena quickly, but he stood a better chance against her with Diana and the twins at his side. Hephaestus seemed to be avoiding attacking Troy and Marina too, so maybe they could convince him to help.

"You know better than this," Hephaestus said as Karter landed ten feet from Diana. "All of you were taught to serve the gods." Hephaestus swung his hammer at Diana. She barely somersaulted out of the way in time to avoid it.

"The gods aren't worth serving." Troy pressed buttons on his chair, shooting another cannonball at Hephaestus.

Hephaestus swerved to the side. The cannonball exploded into the wreckage behind him. "All your lives, I did what I could to protect you. Believe it or not, I care for you. Both of you."

"Stop lying." Marina sent a stream of fire toward Hephaestus. He ducked, and the flames blasted into mud and grass. "If you really cared about us, you wouldn't have ratted out our father!"

Troy circled the space above Hephaestus's head. "And you'd be helping us now."

"Wrong again." Hephaestus's deformed face sagged with something that looked like torment. "I never lied when I said I loved you, my grandson. But I am an eternal being, and your life is finite. You have forced my hand."

Before anyone had time to react, Hephaestus swung his hammer at Troy. The tool slammed sideways into Troy's helmet. The metal *cruuunch*ed inward, bodily liquid and tissue splattering out from the openings in the helmet, onto Hephaestus's face. Troy's helmet—and what remained of his head—flew off his shoulders.

Karter watched in horror as a headless Troy, still strapped into the wheelchair, crashed to the ground. Hephaestus stared down at the body as if he couldn't believe what he'd just done.

Marina screamed. She descended to Troy's side and began working at his chair to free him. Karter and Diana rushed in front of her to protect her from Hephaestus.

"Zeus suspected me of treachery," Hephaestus said, limping forward. He slipped in the muck and fell. If Karter didn't know any better, he'd say the god was whimpering. "They forced my hand, don't you see?"

Karter shook his head, pointed at Hephaestus, and shot the god with deadly lightning.

He turned around. Marina sobbed, cradling what was left of Troy in her arms, and the sight gutted Karter. If there weren't so much going on, he might have allowed himself to weep. *Later*, he thought. *If I make it out of this alive like Zoey wanted me to.*

Diana grabbed Karter's arm. "Athena. We— we have to stop her."

"G-g-go," Marina said. "G-go w-without me."

Karter and Diana didn't argue with Marina. There wasn't time. Diana flung her arms around Karter's neck, and Karter jumped into the air.

They soared out of the ruined courtyard, and Karter saw Athena in the distance. She ripped her spear through three charging Naiads in rapid succession. Heaps of corpses lay before her, the statues of her other victims, piles of debris, and fallen vegetation surrounding her like thick woodland. If Kali, Layla, Harmony, and many of the others who'd been fighting her earlier were still around, Karter couldn't see them, nor could he see the demigods and monsters who'd been in the area either. Had they all been slaughtered?

He stayed low to keep Athena from spotting them. Finally, he landed on the outskirts of the carnage and set Diana down. They crouched behind a mound of rubble. "Stay hidden," Diana said. "If we're going to beat her, we have to use the element of surprise. You attack from the left, me the right. We'll go at the same time—I'll use my light to signal you. Above everything else, we have to destroy that head."

"Agreed." He offered his hand to her. She clasped it, shook it as though to say farewell. They parted ways.

Karter crept behind statues and debris, making his way toward Athena. *"Who dares challenge me next?*" Athena roared into the rain. Heart pounding, Karter darted behind the stone calf of a Cyclops. "*Come out, come out!*" Karter used the reflection in his shield to peek past the Cyclops. He had to be around fifty feet away from Athena now.

A Dryad and a Deltama Village warrior leapt out from behind some of their frozen comrades diagonal to Athena, holding their shields in front of their faces. They lunged for Athena, but the goddess easily sidestepped them, then speared them through their throats. They dropped their weapons and collapsed. Choking noises escaped their lips. Blood spilled from their wounds and pooled around them.

They stilled, their unblinking eyes staring at nothing. Athena kicked them aside. "*You can do better than that!*"

A sphere of sunlight shot into the sky. *The signal.* Karter sucked in a sharp breath, stepped out from behind the Cyclops, and—

Someone grabbed his wrist and pulled him back. He turned to see Zoey-Calliope. She had the Trident. "Wait," she said in her two-person voice. "Let us destroy the head, and then we'll all fight her together." Karter furrowed his brow. Was Andy-Anteros here too?

"There you are," Athena said. Karter checked his shield's reflection. Athena was striding in the direction Diana's signal had come from. He couldn't see Diana, but Athena reared back her spear.

A familiar squealing noise pierced the air, and a giant gold bolt shot from the clouds toward Athena. She raised the aegis to shield herself. The lightning hit the aegis and redirected into the sky.

Athena lowered the aegis. Relief flooded Karter; the bolt had incinerated Medusa's head, the rain washing away its ashes. "Dammit!" Athena snarled.

Karter swung around, unafraid to look at Athena now, and a noise like feathered wings flapping sounded beside him. He looked over, but no one was there. *Andy-Anteros?* he wondered, and it must have been, because there was another screech, and lightning arced toward Athena.

Zoey-Calliope let go of Karter and ran around him in front of the stone Cyclops. She slammed the Trident against the ground, and the force made Athena stumble a bit. Regaining her footing, Athena launched her spear at Zoey-Calliope. Zoey-Calliope hastened to the right.

The spear grazed the side of her armored shoulder and hit the Cyclops instead.

Karter sprinted out from behind the statue and hurled green electricity at Athena. Diana appeared across from him, throwing spheres of sunlight at the goddess. Athena easily blocked Karter's assaults with the aegis, but one of Diana's attacks blasted her in the back, sending her face-first into the muck.

A third screech. Athena rolled over and raised the aegis just in time to deflect Andy-Anteros's lightning. She started climbing to her feet.

An arrow *whoosh*ed past Karter's head from behind, missing him by the narrowest of margins. He glanced over his shoulder and saw several familiar demigods—Ebony, Luca, Iro, Liam, Justine, and was that Violet?—darting between corpses, statues, and ruins toward him. "Scarface!" they screamed. "Traitor! Disgrace!"

Ebony, Daughter of Nyx shot a second arrow at Karter. He dodged it and released a volley of curses. He couldn't let them help Athena fight Zoey-Calliope and Andy-Anteros. He hurried toward them.

From the left, something solid collided with him. The force threw him off-balance, and a pair of arms latched onto him, pinning his hands at his sides. It was a young man—another demigod. Griffin, Son of Kratos was unmistakable. He was hugely muscular, his long brown hair clinging wetly to his face, neck, and shoulders.

Griffin adjusted his hold on Karter and squeezed with his super-strength. Karter grunted, grappling against him. "Let me go, or I'll be forced to kill you."

Griffin squeezed harder, and one of Karter's ribs popped. "It's time to die, deserter."

Has he forgotten what I'm capable of? Karter generated green electricity in his restricted hands and allowed it to crackle up his arms.

When the lightning touched Griffin, he froze. He yelled, his eyes bulging from their sockets, and went limp. Karter shoved him away, and he sank to the ground.

Just as Karter rid himself of Griffin, another demigod attacked him. Green-eyed, red-haired Liam, Son of Dionysus. Liam stood a short way from Karter, directing vines at him. "Stop this," Karter pleaded. He staggered backward, trying to ignore how badly his chest hurt and how hard it had become to breathe. "I'm not the enemy here. The gods are. Fight them with us so you can be free!"

"Free?" Liam said. "What honor is there in being free? I'd rather be rewarded by the gods."

"Please, I don't want to hurt you."

"Then don't." Liam flicked his wrists, making his plants wrap around Karter's ankles. "Just let me kill you."

Karter knelt, grabbed Liam's vines, and sent peridot electricity hissing up them. The currents hit Liam almost instantly, and he let out a yelp before falling dead.

Fierce battle cries sounded all around Karter, and suddenly he realized he wasn't alone in fighting the demigods. Kali and two Deltama Village warriors charged at Justine, Daughter of Nemesis, and Ebony with their spears. Luca, Son of Hemera sent beams of light at Diana, who retaliated with her own glittering attacks. Layla clashed swords with Iro, Daughter of Heracles, and Violet too—yes, it was Violet; she'd survived the encounter in Aphrodite City. Karter couldn't see her face, but he recognized her golden hair.

They must have been hiding in the wreckage because of Medusa's head, Karter realized. *But if they're helping me, who's helping Zoey-Calliope and Andy-Anteros?* He glanced back to see what had to be over forty nymph recruits swarming Athena. Far behind Athena stood Zoey-Calliope and Andy-

Anteros, and it appeared they'd begun to cast the Descent Spell again.

Kali's frantic shriek snapped Karter back to his immediate surroundings. "*Diana!*"

Heart in his throat, Karter looked to Diana. Her helmet had been knocked off, and she lay sprawled on the ground, her eyes clamped shut. Luca stalked toward her, summoning another beam of light. *He's going to kill her!*

On instinct, Karter shot a green bolt at Luca before he could finish off Diana. It hit the bare skin of his leg, and he crumpled into the mud.

Karter and Kali reached Diana's side at the same time. Kali leaned over Diana, cupping her cheek and stroking her hair, and Karter checked her pulse. It was faint, but it was there.

Something *ping*ed against the back of Karter's armor, sending ricochets of pain through his shoulder. He clambered around. Ebony approached them, bow and arrow ready. Behind her, Justine and the Deltama Village warriors lay bloody and motionless.

Karter cast peridot lightning at Ebony. She dodged it, but she wasn't fast enough. The bolt hit her on the breastplate, sending her careening back. She hit the ground headfirst, her neck twisting at an odd angle.

From the left, Iro rushed toward Karter, sword raised. He put up a hand. "Iro, stop, please!" To Karter's surprise, she hesitated. "We don't have to do this!"

"Of course we do," Violet interjected. She and Layla had paused their sword fight, and Karter could see her face now. Most of it was a mottled mess of flesh, the waxy, crater-ridden skin blotched pink and red and black. It looked worse than when Zeus had electrocuted Karter, and the sight of it made his scar throb with the memory of old pain. "Zeus commands it."

Karter's gaze darted between Iro and Violet. "Iro, your father is already gone. I saw the Chosen Two cast him into Tartarus. And Violet, your mother has switched sides. If you join us—"

"My 'mother,'" Violet interrupted, "doesn't even care that my face is ruined. I spent whole days in the healing shrine of her city, and she didn't visit me once. Apparently, she was too busy conspiring against the rest of the gods!"

Tremors rocked the earth beneath them. Karter looked back at where Zoey-Calliope and Andy-Anteros had been standing. They'd opened a second portal to Tartarus. The nymphs and warriors were still grappling with Athena, but Poseidon and Hades had shown up too. Poseidon wrestled several of Ladon's heads; it appeared he'd killed some of them already. If Ladon had managed to injure Poseidon, it didn't show. All the while, Hades skewered Philomelus with his bident and heaved the minor god in the direction of Tartarus. The winds picked up Philomelus and dragged him down, and Persephone, Demeter, Plutus, and Despoina howled in rage, making their horde of plant-infested corpses stampede toward Hades.

Peridot shone in Karter's peripheral. He swerved out of the way. Deadly lightning hit the grass beside him, and he glanced at where it had come from. Sure enough, Zeus soared toward them from hundreds of feet away. Behind Zeus—at the edge of the first portal to Tartarus—Artemis, Hestia, and Dionysus tossed a motionless Ares, Aphrodite, Eros, Phobos, Deimos, and Harmonia into the blue flames.

"Kali!" Karter cried. "Get Diana out of here! Hide until she wakes up! Layla and I will handle Zeus!"

Her dark eyes round with fear, Kali grabbed Diana under the armpits and started hauling her away.

Violet raced after Kali. "Get back here, peasant scum!" Karter raised a hand to kill Violet, but Layla intercepted her instead.

I don't want to accidentally hit Layla, he thought, and turned back to Iro, hoping to convince her to join him and Layla. However, he was met with Iro's silver blade speeding toward his throat. He staggered back. His foot skidded, and he tripped into muck. Iro stepped over him, weapon ready. She brought down her sword, giving him no other choice. He shot deadly electricity at her naked biceps.

Iro screamed as the lightning coursed through her. She dropped her sword. Karter raised his shield to stop the blade from landing on him, and it tumbled to the side. Iro's limp body fell on Karter next. He shoved it off.

Violet cackled from behind him. Who had she hurt? Was it Kali, Diana, Layla? He scrambled around to see.

Kali was on top of Diana, shielding the demigod with her own body as if braced for a killing blow. At the same time, Layla stood guard over Kali, Violet's sword lodged in her throat.

"You're pathetic." Violet jerked her sword out of Layla, and Layla fell to her knees. "At least now I think I know why my love spell doesn't work on you. It was Diana all along, wasn't it? Don't you know she never loved you back? That she never will?"

Layla nodded once, then toppled over.

Violet lifted her sword again, surely to attack Kali next. Kali jumped to her feet and drew a dagger.

Karter sent a green bolt at Violet. It hit the exposed part of her leg, and she cried out and fell dead.

"Go!" Karter shouted at Kali. "Get out of here before—"

Zeus rammed onto the ground ten feet in front of Karter, peridot in his palms. Zeus stalked forward. Karter scrambled back.

Karter hurled deadly lightning at his father. Zeus easily deflected the assault with his shield, pressing on. Karter shot another bolt, then a third and fourth, but it was no use.

Karter thought of Heracles and Hera and Aphrodite and Ares and everyone else who'd been sucked into Tartarus, and an idea struck him. *Zoey-Calliope and Andy-Anteros opened another portal nearby. The winds are strong. They'll drag Zeus into the pit if he's close enough.*

I just need to wound him so that he'll die down there after his powers are neutralized, and then . . .

Lightning flashed in the stormy sky above, illuminating Iro's silver sword in the corner of

Karter's vision. In that moment, he knew what to do.

As Zeus sent another assault, Karter hurtled over to the sword and grabbed it. *Even if it means I perish in Tartarus and my soul is trapped there forever, I have to go through with this. Once Zeus is gone, it will be easier for Zoey-Calliope and Andy-Anteros to get rid of the rest of the gods. They* have *to survive this.* His vision blurred with tears. *Otherwise, Zoey and Andy's sacrifice will amount to nothing.*

"You witless cockroach." Zeus pitched more peridot at Karter, and instead of running away this time, Karter raised his shield. As the lightning hissed toward him, he focused on the seething sky, on his divine abilities, and poured that energy into the metal. He imagined Zeus's attack bouncing off his shield, shooting toward the clouds instead.

The strike of the bolt sent him stumbling back in mire. Even so, he made the metal deflect the electricity.

With new resolve coursing through him, Karter streaked over corpses and statues and debris and nymphs and warriors and gods toward the second portal to Tartarus. Zeus leapt into the sky after him, launching green bolts at him. He redirected them all.

Nearing the portal, Karter plunged to the ground. Zeus landed a distance away. Karter turned to face his father.

Zeus sauntered toward Karter. "You're more of a fool than I initially thought. You'd have to be to trade blissful immortality for an eternity burning in Tartarus." He stopped, thinking. "I suppose you inherited such stupidity from your mother. You know, she really believed me when I lied to her about my identity. It was probably for the best that Hera had her killed, the idiotic thing."

Zeus's words struck a nerve with Karter. He was soaked from the rain and chilled to the bone, but his flesh grew hot with rage. "You're wrong about her. She knew who you were."

The god stroked his beard. "Oh? What makes you say that?"

"She had the memories of your first wife," Andy-Anteros suddenly said from above. Karter looked up to see him circling Zeus, the Master Lightning Bolt in hand. "What remained of Metis resided within her because she was Metis's avatar, just as Zoey-Calliope is Calliope's avatar, and just as I am Anteros's avatar."

Zeus squinted at Andy-Anteros. "Is that what the two of you are calling yourselves these days? Avatars? I must say, I derived inspiration from the Hindus when I trapped you in those mortal shells, but I didn't think you'd be clever enough to discover the name of the concept. And Katarina being one of you? An avatar of Metis?" He snorted. "Impossible. Metis has been trapped inside me for millennia, and even if she had escaped, I would have sensed her divine essence within Katarina."

"Really?" Andy-Anteros challenged. "Did any of the gods sense Anteros within Andy before their connection was made? Do you sense Anteros within me now that the convergence is complete?"

The questions gave Zeus pause. "No, I suppose I don't sense Anteros within you, which begs the question—who are you, exactly? Are you the human boy, but with godlike powers? Or are you just a watered-down version of Anteros?"

"No, I'm not Andy," he replied. "I'm not Anteros either. I'm someone new. Someone *you* created."

"You're an abomination," Zeus said plainly.

Andy-Anteros sneered. "Maybe. But I was also prophesied to be the pantheon's undoing"—he gestured at Karter—"just as he's prophesied to be yours."

Zeus's nostrils flared. "After I realized that the two of you were harboring Anteros and Calliope within your bodies—that Anteros and Calliope hadn't been *truly* reincarnated as I'd originally intended, and so possessed memories of their godly lives—I was determined to ensure neither of you were killed here in the world above. I wanted you both to die in the pit of Tartarus so your souls would be trapped and dormant there, so no one could ever discover what really happened to Anteros and Calliope. That was a mistake."

The King of the Gods summoned a green bolt and aimed it for Andy-Anteros. Karter vaulted toward his father to stop him.

A sickening *slice*. Zeus's electricity fizzled out. A choking noise escaped him, golden ichor trickling from three puncture wounds in his chest.

He removed his shield and used both hands to reach for his invisible attacker. He seized them, jerked them forward, and yanked something from them. Zoey-Calliope appeared, the Helm in Zeus's grasp.

Zeus lunged for the Trident next. Zoey-Calliope staggered back, barely out of reach. A high-pitched squealing sound—the sound the Master Lightning Bolt made when in use—filled the air, and golden electricity shot from the clouds.

Zeus raised the Helm above his head. The bolt Andy-Anteros summoned bounced off the object, but the force knocked it from Zeus's hands. It skidded to the side, toward the portal. Andy-Anteros flapped after it while Karter landed in front of Zoey-Calliope.

Zeus rushed at them with green crackling in his hands. Karter threw up his shield, focusing on his super-strength, on his child-of-Zeus powers, and charged forward.

Karter slammed the shield into Zeus. The god's lightning hissed around the metal, around Karter. Karter screamed, putting everything he had into pushing Zeus back, into deflecting the god's attack, into getting him far from Zoey-Calliope.

Zeus's lightning dissolved. He seized Karter by the shield and sped toward the clouds. Within seconds they were hovering high above the blue flames of Tartarus, wind tugging at Karter, threatening to pull him into the pit.

The King of the Gods positioned himself as though to toss Karter into Tartarus, the torn skin around his wounds knitting back together. "I've had enough of you, you worthless son of a whore."

Blood pounding in his ears, Karter wrenched his arm out of the shield straps and gashed his borrowed blade through Zeus's stomach. The god bellowed, still clutching the shield, and Karter ripped out the sword and flew upward. He stabbed the weapon through Zeus's neck, then twisted it up, down, and out.

Gurgling sounds escaped Zeus's lips as ichor spilled from his gaping throat. *If I banish him now, he'll die down there*, Karter thought. *He won't be able to regenerate.* Bracing himself against the gales, he kicked Zeus toward the portal. Tornadoes of wind dragged Zeus down, cerulean fire clawing up around the god. He dropped the shield. It was sucked into the pit almost instantly.

For a moment Karter wondered if he might make it through this, just as Zoey had wanted him to. Instinctively, he glanced in Zoey-Calliope's direction, his breaths heaving, his body burning.

Zoey-Calliope was facing him. He couldn't see her expression, but from so far away she looked like Zoey. It made his heart clench.

Andy-Anteros shrieked from above Karter. *"Karter, move!"*

White flashed beneath Karter. He looked down. Zeus materialized there, his throat still ripped open, his eyes growing glassy, dazed.

Karter tried to swerve away, but he was a second too slow. Zeus seized him by the ankle and held fast. *This is it*, Karter thought. *This is when he kills me.*

Karter conjured a green bolt and pitched it at Zeus. At the same time, peridot hissed from Zeus's fingers. The electricity arced up Karter's leg.

Searing pain lurched through every inch of Karter, and then his heart stopped.

CHAPTER TWENTY-ONE
PERSUASION

Zoey-Calliope watched helplessly as Karter plummeted alongside Zeus toward Tartarus. "*No!*" She dashed forward, reaching for him.

High in the sky above, Andy-Anteros donned the Helm and disappeared. Seconds later Karter vanished too. The wind and flames of Tartarus consumed Zeus's lifeless figure.

After the King of the Gods was gone, the storm ceased. The rain stopped, the thunder quieting. The sun peeked out from below the horizon, illuminating the gory wreckage of the once-beautiful garden. The only sounds now were those of war cries and clashing blades, of crackling fire and whistling gales.

Despite the shift around her, Zoey-Calliope couldn't focus on anything except for where Karter and Andy-Anteros had gone. Had Tartarus claimed them as it had claimed Zeus, or had they escaped before it could drag them down?

It took half a minute before she received her answer, before Karter's limp form landed at her feet. Andy-Anteros appeared behind him, breaths heaving.

Karter's unblinking eyes, once bright and gold, were dull and colorless. His mouth hung open, his expression contorted in a permanent grimace. His right leg had been reduced to smoking, blackened flesh.

Although the battle raged on around them, Zoey-Calliope crumpled to her knees beside Karter. She'd seen the green hit him, but a part of her had foolishly hoped he'd somehow deflected it, as he'd done with the shield. "No," she croaked. "Please, no."

She checked his pulse, hoping for the faintest of throbs.

Nothing.

She shoved a hand beneath his breastplate, hoping for the rise and fall of his chest.

Nothing.

She leaned over him, calling his name, hoping for him to wake, for him to return to her.

Nothing.

As reality washed over her, the breath escaped her lungs. Her sight flashed blue, then returned to normal, then switched through both again. A violent mixture of emotions stampeded through her, the two voices in her mind shouting over one another in rapid succession.

"I'm in love—"

"No, he's—"

"—with Andy-Anteros."

"—my friend."

"I'm indifferent—"

"No, I can't—"

"—toward Karter."

"—believe he's gone."

"He fulfilled—"

"He deserved to—"

"—his destiny."

"—live a long life."

"I'll be—"

"I'll never be—"

"—happier now."

"—happy again."

Once more she stared down at Karter, at his unmoving face.

On the one hand, she was in love with Andy-Anteros, and she felt *nothing* for Karter. She didn't care that he was gone. He'd completed his life purpose, achieved his destined greatness, and had no reason to still be alive.

On the other hand, she loved Andy-Anteros as a friend, and she felt *everything* for Karter. She cared very much that he was gone. He might have completed his life purpose, achieved his destined greatness, but he had every reason to still be alive.

Tears burned in her eyes, a lump in her throat and an ache in her chest. Her vision blazed blue.

The voices in her head went on. Pain and rage and confusion tore through her, body and soul. She began to tremble, to convulse. She slammed sideways into the ground.

As she continued to shudder and spasm, she had the distinct feeling that she was wrenching in half. It was as if she was two people and not one, as if the different parts of her were locked together in the prison of her mortal form, desperately trying to escape.

The familiar voice of a young man echoed above the others in her mind. "Zoey-Calliope!

What's happening to you?" She couldn't see him, but she could hear him, and she could feel him. He grasped her hands. At his touch, her convulsions subsided slightly. "What's going on? Please, I can't do this without you! You have to be okay!"

"The love—"

"The person I—"

"—of my life—"

"—share this burden with—"

Suddenly the voices came together, separate but synced, speaking in unison.

"One of my best friends."

The seizure stopped. Her vision returned to normal.

Terror warped Andy-Anteros's expression, his drenched brown hair clinging to his forehead. "Zoey-Calliope?"

Laughter and applause sounded in the air. "What an incredible display," hissed the familiar voice of a goddess. "I haven't had this much fun since the Trojan War."

Tendrils of black smoke began to curl up on Zoey-Calliope's right, and then a deity she'd met in both her past lives formed from it.

"What are you doing here?" Andy-Anteros asked Eris, Goddess of Chaos. "Have you come to help us finish off the gods, like when you helped Andy and Zoey escape Hades?"

Eris smoothed out an invisible wrinkle in her plum dress. "I've already done my fair share of helping you. If it weren't for me, Zoey wouldn't have managed to reconnect with Calliope. And I didn't even require payment for that gift, generous as it was."

"Wait," Zoey-Calliope started. "You're the one who left Calliope's relic in the library?"

Her forked tongue slithered in and out of her lips. "I am. Zeus removed as much evidence of Calliope's existence as he could long ago, after he told everyone he'd witnessed her fading away. It's part of the reason Anteros grew suspicious of the whole ordeal, you know. But there's no need to thank me. I assure you, I've done just as much to help the gods as I've done to help you."

Andy-Anteros raised a brow. "What are you talking about?"

Zoey-Calliope gasped as the realization hit her. "Oh my— It *was* you. You told Zeus that Calliope tricked Hades into giving her the location of the Descent Spell."

"I did." Eris smiled wickedly.

Zoey-Calliope grabbed the Trident, leapt to her feet, and brandished it at Eris. "Why? If you'd never exposed Calliope, she might have been able to rally the minor gods against the Olympians and stop them from decimating humanity!"

"And what fun would that have been? I might have never witnessed the Storm, might have never seen the strife that came after. This war on the gods might have never happened. Don't you see? I despise the Olympians, but I never wanted to take a side. I only wanted to watch."

Zoey-Calliope lunged forward, intent on skewering the Goddess of Chaos, but Andy-Anteros put a hand on her shoulder and pulled her back. "Why tell us this?" he said. "It sounds to me like you've already had your fun. Why go to the trouble of manifesting before us and relaying what you did?"

Eris snorted. "You can't honestly expect me to keep something so glorious to myself. *Someone* had to know how I contributed to this"—she gestured at their surroundings—"and who better than the Chosen Two of the Dreaded Prophecy themselves?"

Now it was Andy-Anteros's turn to get angry. He let go of Zoey-Calliope and stomped around her toward Eris. However, Eris was gone before he could do anything. She cackled maniacally and dissolved into black smoke.

White light flared around them. When it faded, three gods were left behind: Artemis, Hestia, and Dionysus. The deities panted, their forms sagging with exhaustion, their skin shiny with sweat.

Andy-Anteros raised the Bolt to attack, but Zoey-Calliope put up a hand to stop him, recalling something Karter had said to Athena back in Aphrodite City. *"I know you're the wisest god in the pantheon. Not Father, as he likes to believe. I know you'd make a far better leader than him, and I also know you crave his title, because you tried to overthrow him in the old days with some of the other Olympians. The only reason all of you didn't succeed is because Thetis overheard you arguing about who should rule in Zeus's place and summoned Briareus to save him."*

Then she remembered Athena's reply. *"I'd love to lead the pantheon. But what I'd love even more is to not succumb to eternal sleep."*

Zoey-Calliope had an idea. She prayed to the Fates it would work, because if anyone else dear to her died fighting today, she wouldn't be able to go on.

She focused on her powers of persuasion. Her vocal cords began to vibrate, and the sensation spread through the rest of her.

Artemis, Hestia, and Dionysus finished

catching their breath, and Artemis stepped forward, her curly red hair a nest of tangles upon her head, the slimy blood and innards coating her armor glistening in the early-morning sun. "So, the two of you successfully banished Zeus to Tartarus."

"Zeus is gone, it's true," Zoey-Calliope said. "Let me ask you something, Moon Goddess. What will all of you do in his absence?"

Dionysus narrowed his bright-green eyes at Zoey-Calliope. "First we'll banish *you* to Tartarus, and then we'll find a way to rescue him, of course."

"Oh?" The vibrating within Zoey-Calliope grew stronger. Her body thrummed with energy. "Are you sure?"

Hestia tucked some of her long brown hair behind her ears. "What else would we do, Chosen One? We have to keep the pantheon intact. We can't risk losing our worshippers and fading away."

"Why do you need Zeus to do that? Can't someone else take his place as the new, *rightful* ruler of the Greek pantheon? A god worthy of his vast number of worshippers, of his unimaginable power?"

The immortals perked up, their lips parting slightly. For several moments they simply stood there, stunned.

"The *rightful* ruler?" Artemis finally asked.

"Yes," Zoey-Calliope replied.

Dionysus licked his lips. "How would we determine who that is?"

"By fighting the other gods to the death." Zoey-Calliope said it as if the answer were obvious. "Whoever's left standing at the end can send the others to Tartarus to ensure there won't be any chance of rebellion. Really, it's the only reasonable way to handle this." She paused to let her words sink in before continuing. "Why don't the three of you go on, then? Kill each other, and kill every immortal who stands in your way. And then when it's over, when one of you rises victorious, cast your adversaries into the blue flames so you can rule over us all."

Artemis was first to attack. She shot Hestia in the throat. Dionysus directed vines Artemis's way, but Artemis sprang out of reach of his plants and sent an arrow through his left eye. With Hestia and Dionysus incapacitated, Artemis seized them by their hair and dragged them toward the portal to Tartarus.

Zoey-Calliope looked to Andy-Anteros. "Hide yourself and Karter with the Helm, and stay close but out of the way." She shoved the Trident into his hands. She wouldn't be needing it, but he would. "Don't attack the gods until I tell you to." Before he could argue with her, she focused on transporting herself to the closest conflict still unfolding.

A moment later she stood twenty feet away from Demeter, Persephone, Despoina, and Plutus as they fought Hades. "Zeus is gone! He's in Tartarus!" she yelled at the top of her lungs, her vocal cords vibrating like mad. "It's up to the most powerful of the gods to fight to the death and determine who will rule the pantheon in his place! Artemis has already slain Hestia and Dionysus and cast them into Tartarus, and now she comes for you!"

Just then, Artemis manifested in the middle of the five immortals. She and Hades snarled, lunging for each other, while Despoina and Plutus teleported away. Persephone stumbled toward Zoey-Calliope, but Demeter grabbed the Goddess of Spring by the hand. They both disappeared.

It's working, Zoey-Calliope thought. *But I'm not done yet.* She transported to Athena and Poseidon next.

It appeared Poseidon had won his wrestling match with Ladon; he'd joined Athena in fighting the nymph recruits. Half of the recruits who'd swarmed Athena earlier already lay dead, the rest of them struggling against the two gods. Athena used her spear on them, and Poseidon opened fissures in the earth beneath their feet.

"Athena!" Zoey-Calliope screamed. "Poseidon! *Stop!*" Everyone paused to look at her, and she relayed what she'd said to the other gods. The second she finished, Athena and Poseidon turned on one another, the nymphs scattering.

That just leaves Hephaestus to convince. The question is, where has he gone?

As if on cue, white light flashed behind Athena and Poseidon, and Hephaestus appeared. "What are you doing?" he cried, jumping between them. "Stop this! We have to work together, remember?" But they didn't listen. They tore the Blacksmith of the Gods to shreds, literally—they ripped his head and limbs from his torso, and his golden ichor spewed out in all directions.

It wasn't long before the gods made their way toward the portal to Tartarus, and Zoey-Calliope followed them, encouraging them to continue fighting. She couldn't loosen her hold on them, not for a moment.

Poseidon and Athena tossed Hephaestus's remains to the winds, then returned their attention to each other. At the same time, Hades stabbed Artemis in the armpit with his bident. He wrenched the weapon out of the Moon Goddess and kicked her toward the portal. Artemis screamed as the gales picked her up and dragged her down.

"That's it!" Zoey-Calliope shouted. "There're only three of you left! One of you will soon rise victorious, and the pantheon will be yours! The people of the world will be yours! Everlasting life will be yours!"

Poseidon and Athena still brawled. Hades charged toward them, but Athena was ready for the King of the Underworld. She swung around and speared him through the exposed part of his head, and he went limp. She ripped her weapon from his body and kicked him toward Tartarus.

Athena started turning back toward Poseidon, smirking as though she'd already won. But before she could face the Sea God again, he seized her by the neck, snapped it, and pitched her to the violent gusts.

Once Athena was gone, Poseidon the last immortal standing, he spun around to gaze at Zoey-Calliope. There was a crazed, murderous look in his eyes. A maniacal smile turned up his lips. "Thank you, Chosen One, for making that so easy. Unfortunately, I can't reward you for your help."

He stalked toward her, flexing his fingers as if preparing to strangle her. The sight should have scared her, but it didn't. Andy-Anteros was nowhere to be seen. That meant he'd followed her instructions.

"Andy-Anteros," she called, keeping her stare trained on Poseidon, "cast the Sea God into the flames with the others where he belongs." Poseidon paused and cocked his head. He glanced around. Andy-Anteros couldn't be seen.

There was the sound of prongs tearing into flesh, and Poseidon grunted. Golden ichor leaked from his neck. He choked and gasped. Another wet ripping sound, and his throat split open. Ichor sprayed from his wound like a fountain.

Andy-Anteros appeared ten feet before Poseidon with the Trident in hand, the Helm behind him. The avatar brought down the Trident once, twice, three times. The force sent massive quakes through the earth. Poseidon flew backward, and the winds of Tartarus picked him up and sucked him in.

Her heart suddenly racing, her chest suddenly burning, Zoey-Calliope looked around, desperately trying to spot Karter and the Bolt. She saw them far to the right, then teleported over, seized the Bolt, and teleported back.

"We just have to shut the portals," Andy-Anteros said.

"I—know," she replied between breaths. "Then—it's—done."

As they closed the portals, Zoey-Calliope was numb. She thought she should have been overjoyed, or at the very least relieved, but she couldn't bring herself to feel anything.

Even when it was over, when their enemies were vanquished, when the portals to Tartarus were gone, when Andy-Anteros smiled at her, she couldn't smile back. She could only think of the lives lost today, and especially of Karter as he battled his father in the sky, as his father electrocuted him with green.

And so she made her way back to him and collapsed beside him. Then, just as the threads of fate had predicted, she closed his eyes and propped his head in her lap.

Cradling his face in her hands, she wept.

CHAPTER TWENTY-TWO

SACRIFICE

It was soul-crushing for Andy-Anteros to watch Zoey-Calliope wail over Karter's body, her features contorted with anguish.

Andy-Anteros trudged over to her, knelt beside her, and wrapped an arm around her shoulders. She leaned into him, bawling still, the sorrow coming from her so palpable he found himself crying too. "Z-Zoey was wr-wrong," she managed to stammer out in her strange, two-person voice. "There r-really is n-no ch-

changing f-f-fate. Our d-destinies—they're tr-truly p-predetermined." It sounded difficult for her to speak.

Just as when they'd first completed their convergences, and then again when Karter had been killed, her eyes flared in and out with blue light. She doubled over in pain and howled like a wounded animal. Writhing and thrashing, she shoved Karter's head out of her lap and threw herself to the ground.

As she convulsed, the light of her eyes winking, flickering, Andy-Anteros set his jaw. *I don't know what's wrong with her*, he thought. *But I have to find out, and I have to fix it.* Calling on his divine powers, on his ability to teleport, he thought of a place he'd visited in his past lives: the lair of the Fates.

Light consumed him. Seconds later it faded away, revealing three bony old women with pupil-less, glowing blue eyes. The Fates stood in their cavern of greenery and threads as if awaiting his arrival.

He caught his breath, the scent of dewy grass filling his nostrils, and rushed toward Clotho, Lachesis, and Atropos. "Will you help me with something? Please, it's urgent!"

"Young avatar, you have new godlike powers," Lachesis said with a chuckle. "Why not help yourself?"

"It's about Zoey-Calliope. I don't know what's wrong with her. How am I supposed to fix her if I don't know what's wrong with her?"

Atropos clicked her tongue. "Isn't it obvious what's happening to her?"

He balled his fists, already losing patience. "No."

"The souls making her *her* have not fully merged because their feelings toward you and the late Son of Zeus are strong and conflicting," Atropos explained. "It is causing her great mental and physical pain as they battle within her."

"If you leave her as she is now, her suffering will someday pass," Clotho said. "It could take months, possibly even years, but her opposing sides will eventually come to grips with one another, and she will be happy. The part of her that is not in love with you, Andy-Anteros, will learn to love you. When that happens, her heart will belong to you, just as we always intended."

"Just as you always intended," he repeated. "So, Anteros was right. He and Calliope were destined for each other, and Andy and Zoey were too."

"Precisely," Clotho said. "It is why—when Zeus cast Calliope and Anteros from Olympus, intending on reincarnating them into human forms—we placed Calliope within Zoey and Anteros within Andy. Since Calliope and Anteros were already in love, we had hoped Zoey would fall for Andy, and Andy for Zoey."

"With Zoey and Andy in love, the convergence process would have been less difficult." Atropos pulled out a pair of scissors, knelt, and cut the threads closest to her. "It would have meant the desires of all four beings were aligned. They would have found comfort in each other and become 'something new' more easily."

Lachesis sighed, shaking her head. "But things did not go according to plan—that happens often, you know—and Zoey's feelings for Andy did not develop the way we had planned for them to."

"Why not?" Andy-Anteros asked, his chest tightening, bitterness lacing his tone. The fact that half of Zoey-Calliope didn't reciprocate his feelings for her was hard to accept. "You're the *Fates*. You're supposed to be even more powerful than the gods. Why didn't you make things unfold the way you wanted?"

The Fates narrowed their eyes at him in the same instance. "Because what fun would it be if we took humanity's choice and free will?" they replied in unison.

"Maybe things wouldn't be as fun for you, but they'd be a lot easier for the rest of us. If you'd have made events unfold exactly as you wanted them to, the person I love wouldn't be suffering right now."

"But then we would be no better than the Olympians forcing humanity to worship them," Atropos pointed out.

Clotho smiled with her crooked brown teeth. "Besides, there *is* a way to end Zoey-Calliope's suffering."

"Just as I mentioned before," Lachesis started, "you have new godlike powers. If you so choose, you can take away her pain."

"How?" he cried. "Tell me!"

"You will have to ask the threads." Lachesis reached into her robes and pulled out a tangle of white and blue strings. It was Andy-Anteros's, Zoey-Calliope's, and Karter's life threads snarled together. As she held the strands out to him, he could tell some of Karter's was missing. *Atropos cut it when he died.*

Andy-Anteros snatched the threads from Lachesis, preparing himself to witness potential futures, but none came. "Why aren't I seeing visions?"

"Now that you are a full avatar, you can 'will'

that sort of thing to happen rather than it being forced upon you," Clotho explained. "I suggest examining the threads more closely before plunging into visions of the future, though."

He did as she said and, upon an inspection of the strings, realized that his and Zoey-Calliope's weren't two threads but four: a pair of glowing white strands twined around a pair of regular blue ones.

That's how Zoey-Calliope and I came to be, Andy-Anteros realized. *When Calliope was placed within Zoey's body and Anteros into Andy's body, their immortal and mortal threads tangled.*

It was more than that, though. As he continued to stare at the white strands, he noticed them coiling tighter and tighter around their blue partners. It was as if the pairs were fusing together, melding into two strings instead of four.

"Now that you and Zoey-Calliope have completed your convergences, it will not take long for the separate life threads to merge," Clotho said. "When they do, your fates will be sealed. You will not be able to go back."

"Go back?"

"But of course. How else would Zoey-Calliope's suffering end?"

"I don't . . ." He trailed off.

"The threads," Lachesis said. "Ask them what must be done."

He brushed his fingers against the silky cords. *Threads of fate, how can I help Zoey-Calliope? I love her so much, I can't bear to see her like this. How can I take away her pain? Make her happy?*

In a blink he saw himself, here in the lair of the Fates, tying two halves of a blue string back together—Karter's life thread. He finished the knot, and the two halves fused, becoming one again. Karter's strand turned white and started to glow. Then he saw himself pulling apart his and Zoey-Calliope's cords, separating the white from the blue.

Another blink, and Andy-Anteros was transported again, this time to the ruins of New Mount Olympus. Karter was alive, as vibrant as a god. His once-golden irises had turned to peridot green. Andy and Zoey were there too, their mortal shells no longer resembling Andy-Anteros and Zoey-Calliope. Reunited, Zoey and Karter kissed. Andy stood a ways from them and hugged Diana and Kali.

The vision ended, and Andy-Anteros stared down at the threads. His hands had grown slick with sweat, his heart thudding against his rib cage. "If I do that, Zoey-Calliope and I won't exist anymore."

"No, you will not," Atropos replied. "But the four entities that comprise the two of you will be restored."

"While Zoey and Andy will be human, Anteros and Calliope will be ghosts," Lachesis said. "They will be dead, but they will be happy. They will be together."

A slightly wistful expression came over Clotho's features. "Zoey will be happy too. She will be herself again, capable of forging her own future."

Andy-Anteros licked his lips. They were suddenly very dry. "And Karter will be a god, because when someone is brought back to life, they're made immortal."

"Yes," Lachesis said. "It is important that if you choose this path, you truly believe Karter is worthy of being made immortal. You must believe he will put a great amount of good into the world."

Andy-Anteros considered their words. "Hmm. I think Karter *is* worthy of being made into a god, but so are the others who laid down their lives for the cause."

"You cannot bring back everyone." Lachesis's tone was grave. "You are a full avatar, yes, but you do not possess that kind of strength. Neither did the Olympians, even in their prime."

Clotho shrugged. "You could attempt it, I suppose, but your efforts would be useless. You would burn yourself up trying, and for what?"

"I was afraid you'd say something like that." Andy-Anteros deliberated a while longer, thinking about how if he did this, Anteros and Calliope would be reunited. How Zoey and Calliope would be happy, free of the agony plaguing Zoey-Calliope now.

At the same time, he thought of how Andy—an entire half of himself—*wouldn't* be happy. How his heart would break as he watched Zoey and Karter be together.

"Did you mean it when you said the part of Zoey-Calliope that doesn't love me now will learn to eventually?" he asked.

Clotho nodded. "As I told you, we always intended for the two of you to be together, and we *are* the Fates. Your union was destiny."

Andy-Anteros opened his mouth to reply—with what, he wasn't sure. Atropos stopped cutting threads and stood up. "You doubt our word," she said. "We have not lied, avatar." She pointed her scissors at the strings he was holding. "Ask them, and you will see."

He took a deep breath, then brushed his fingers against the cords again. *Threads of fate, is what they say true? Will Zoey-Calliope be happy with me someday if I allow you to fully merge?*

In an instant, the threads showed him a vision that had to take place years from now. It was nighttime, a crescent moon in the clear sky, and Andy-Anteros and Zoey-Calliope danced in a garden similar to the Garden of Olympus before it was demolished in the pair's battle against the gods. They looked older—the youthful chub of their cheeks gone, a bit of weight added to the rest of them—but they were together, and they were happy. They talked and laughed as they swayed back and forth, side to side, staring at each other with warmth and adoration.

Andy-Anteros blinked, and he was back in the lair of the Fates.

Atropos huffed, tucking her scissors into her robes. "What did we tell you? You and Zoey-Calliope will be together if that's what you want."

"Yeah, you were right," he replied, although for some reason that fact brought him no joy.

"Well?" Atropos snapped. "Do you know what you are going to do?"

Clotho clasped her bony, wrinkled hands. "There is not much time left."

"Soon, the life threads will finish melding,"

Lachesis said, "and you will not be able to separate them. You will not be able to go back. You must make a decision *now*."

Tears filled Andy-Anteros's eyes, a hollow feeling settling in his chest, his stomach. He gazed down at the fusing cords in his hands and thought of Zoey-Calliope, of her seizing and wailing as the two halves of her struggled against each other.

"This is wrong," he said, his voice breaking. "I love Zoey-Calliope. I want to be with her. But I won't allow her to suffer."

The Fates nodded in understanding, and Lachesis reached into her robes and pulled out another blue string: Karter's cut piece. She handed it to Andy-Anteros.

Andy-Anteros stuffed his and Zoey-Calliope's cords into his pocket, then raised the two halves of Karter's thread and tied them together. Once he finished, he pictured Karter's corpse in his mind's eye and focused on raising the demigod from the dead—on restarting his heart, on breathing new life into his lungs.

White-hot energy seared in Andy-Anteros's chest and spread through the rest of him, scorching his insides like a savage inferno. His vision faded between red and black, and he gritted his teeth, trying not to scream.

Minutes passed before the burning sensation subsided. His sight returned to normal, and he looked down at Karter's thread in his trembling hands. It was whole and white and glowing.

Suddenly Andy-Anteros sagged with exhaustion, short of breath and sapped of strength. His eyes drooped, his arms and legs heavy, but he handed Karter's string back to Lachesis. Then he called on his ability to teleport for the last time, thinking of the ruins of New Mount Olympus and imagining himself traveling back there.

White light overcame him. When it diminished, he found himself standing among the bloodshed and debris.

Limbs quivering and weak, he collapsed onto his back, but he couldn't give up. *I'm not done yet*, he thought. He snatched the cords from his pocket and started to untangle them, prying apart Zoey's and Calliope's threads first.

After finishing theirs he began on Andy's and Anteros's, and in the same moment he completed the task, he was no more.

CHAPTER TWENTY-THREE
IMMORTAL

Karter had been surrounded by death since childhood—quite recently, he'd even ventured into the Underworld to save his best friend's life—yet he'd had no idea what to expect when he finally met his demise.

Would his soul be forced to reside in Hades?

Since other pantheons of gods existed, would they take pity on him and offer him refuge in their underworlds?

Or would death be darkness, a black expanse

of nothing, of nonexistence?

These questions and more had rushed through Karter's mind in the milliseconds his father's peridot electricity scorched his flesh.

And then his heart had stopped.

When it did, his pain had evaporated, replaced with a feeling he could only describe as something deep within him being snipped, sliced, cut.

He soon realized the sensation had been his soul being severed from his body. He watched from high in the sky as his lifeless corpse tumbled toward the blue flames of Tartarus.

However, he hadn't been able to watch the rest of the scene unfold. He couldn't be sure of what had happened to his mortal shell, or whether Zoey-Calliope and Andy-Anteros had won their war on the gods.

Because the next thing he knew, he was *standing on the beach near New Mount Olympus, watching a sunset paint the sky with shades of yellow and orange and pink. Wind whipped his hair from side to side, and the waves before him crashed to shore. Their spray filled the air with the smell of the sea.*

"Hello, Karter," the familiar voice of a young woman said from behind him.

He whirled around to see the ghost. Although hazy and blue, Syrena was unmistakable.

Murmuring her name in disbelief, he reached toward her, his eyes widening when he saw that his hand—no, that the whole of him—was made of the same blue mist as her.

His surprise must have seemed foolish, because Syrena giggled and shook her head at him. "Yes, our appearances change when we die."

"So it's . . . it's really you?"

"It's really her," another familiar voice—this one a young man's—answered. A gust of wind swirled in the space beside Syrena, and a second spirit appeared. Spencer. "In case you were wondering, it's really me too."

Karter glanced between Spencer and Syrena. Taking them in, processing that they were here, that he was here. That at last, they were together again.

Finally, he faced Syrena. "I'm so sorry." His voice cracked, tears welling in his eyes. "For everything. I should have left with you from the beginning. I was a coward. I allowed my fear of my father to—"

"It's all right." Syrena took his hands in hers. "I wouldn't trade how the last days of my life unfolded for anything. In the end, I accomplished what I set out to do. I resurrected the Chosen Two from the Before Time."

"But you should have gotten to help Zoey and Andy train for war and fight the gods," Karter said. "You should have gotten to live a long, happy life. You didn't deserve to die."

She hugged him, and he couldn't stop himself from

crying. "You say that as if you think my death is all of me," she said. "But it's not. When and how I perished doesn't define the rest of my time spent breathing. My life was made of so many other moments, some very precious to me. Those are what make me me, not anything else."

"I'm still sorry," Karter whispered.

"Stop apologizing," Spencer said. "We've already forgiven you." He wrapped his arms around Karter and Syrena, and for a while they stood hugging like that, Karter weeping as his friends held him.

It felt like forever before Karter managed to quell his tears. "I'm so grateful to see you again. I've missed you so much. Are you here to help guide me to the next life? Do we have to go to Hades?"

"We don't reside in Hades," Spencer replied.

"We live in a better place," Syrena said. "A more merciful place."

Karter was relieved to hear that at least they hadn't been forced to suffer in the Greek Underworld for their crimes against the gods. But the relief was short lived.

His arms—once resting around Syrena's shoulders—fell through her as though her body had suddenly turned into thin air.

Gasping, Karter reached for Syrena again, but his hands passed straight through her foggy form. He reached for Spencer, but the same thing happened. "What's going on? You were solid before, but now . . ." He looked at his hands. The color seemed to be returning to his skin.

No! *he thought*. I've already lost them once. I can't lose them again!

Spencer's lips parted. "My gods, it's happening."

"What's happening?" Karter cried.

Syrena smiled. "It seems Andy-Anteros and Zoey-Calliope have defeated the gods, and they must have decided your time on Earth isn't over yet."

"There's more for you to do, my friend," Spencer said. "Perhaps you can work toward righting the wrongs of our parents."

"How can this be? Zeus killed me. There's no coming back from that, right? Only the gods can resurrect a mortal."

They gazed at him with something that looked like pride and told him they loved him. "We'll see you again," Syrena assured him. "So don't be sad, all right?"

He blinked in disbelief, and then he was lying on the ground among the rubble of New Mount Olympus, the morning sun rising in the distance. Not far from him, Zoey-Calliope wept and convulsed on the ground.

Suddenly she stopped tremoring, and her eyes glowed an all-consuming sky-blue as they had during the convergence. As the organs blazed, her body began to change. First her bones *craaac*ked, her right hand shriveling back into the wrist, her frame growing shorter and smaller, her facial features becoming delicate.

Then there was a noise like innards sloshing about, and the muscles of her body softened.

When it was over, she looked like Zoey, not Zoey-Calliope.

She stopped shaking, stopped crying. The illumination in her eyes subsided. She caught sight of Karter awake, watching her, and stared back at him in shock.

"Zoey?" he said hesitantly. "Is that you?"

"Yeah," she replied. Her voice was back to normal. "It's me."

He sat up, though he kept his gaze trained on her, feeling as if she were going to disappear at any moment. "Is this real, or am I dreaming?"

"I think it's real." She cocked her head, studying him. "But you . . . look different."

"Different how?"

She crawled over to him and cupped the scarred side of his face. He relaxed, leaning into her touch. "It's like you're glowing from the inside," she began. "And your irises . . . they're not gold anymore. They're green. The most beautiful peridot green."

Footsteps sounded on Karter's left, and he and Zoey turned that way. Andy—yes, it had to be Andy, because he looked like himself again—approached them. Somehow his wings were gone, and he squinted at them as though he was having trouble seeing.

Zoey dropped her hand to her side. She opened her mouth to speak, but Andy beat her to it. "Yeah, so, none of this is a dream," he stated simply. "It's one hundred percent real."

"What happened?" Zoey asked. "I mean, I remember Zoey-Calliope and Andy-Anteros defeating the gods. But how are the three of us, you know, *here*?"

"Well, Andy-Anteros resurrected Karter, and it made him immortal," Andy said. "Andy-Anteros also separated my and Anteros's and your and Calliope's life threads. Because Zoey-Calliope's desires weren't aligned—the two halves of her wanted different things—it was torturing her. Andy-Anteros did what he had to so her pain would go away. More than anything, he wanted her to be happy." He gave Zoey a measured look. "More than anything, *I* want *you* to be happy."

Zoey's bottom lip quivered. She leapt to her feet and threw her arms around Andy's neck.

As they hugged, Karter's breaths grew shallow. Surely, this wasn't happening. Andy-Anteros hadn't made him immortal. He couldn't have, he shouldn't have.

Karter stood and searched the surrounding debris for a weapon. Soon he found a sharp rock among chunks of rubble. He seized the stone and dragged it across his forearm.

Instead of red fluid trickling from the cut, golden ichor did. *The blood of the gods*, he thought, his breath catching in his throat. *If Andy is right— if this is real, and I'm a god now—what does this mean for me and Zoey?*

He knew he should have been worried about what it meant for the remainder of the pantheon, for humanity, for the universe. He should have been thinking about righting the wrongs of the gods, as Spencer had mentioned. Yet all he could concern himself with was how Zoey was going to die within the century, and how he was going to live on for thousands of years.

Unless she becomes immortal too. If I'm a strong enough god, I can find a way to grant her eternal life— if that's what she wants.

Except it was far too soon to be asking her about something so permanent. It was far too soon to even be *thinking* about something so permanent. Not only that, but making someone immortal was a serious matter, and it had to be done for the right reasons.

Shrieks of joy sounded from where Zoey and Andy stood, and Karter turned back to them. Diana, Kali, Marina, and Harmony were there, and it looked as though Andy was explaining something to them. When he finished talking, Diana and Kali shrieked again, then began crying and hugging Zoey and Andy. Marina and Harmony smiled slightly, but the expressions were pained, and Karter understood why. They'd lost people they loved.

Maybe for now, I won't worry about the future. I'll just be grateful that Zoey and Andy and I were given a second chance when so many others are gone.

He started toward his companions, hoping to cherish a few moments of victory with them before they'd likely take on the grueling task of counting the dead, when white flared in the corner of his sight. A goddess with long chestnut curls appeared, and she headed toward him.

On instinct, Karter conjured a green bolt. Now that the Olympians were defeated, what was Persephone's plan? Would she try to steal the Helm, Trident, and Bolt? Try to take over the world? *It's probably for the best I was made into an immortal. This way, I can easily put a stop to anything nefarious she might try.*

Persephone reached him and crossed her arms. "Calm yourself, little god. As much as I'd love to take the objects of power and rule the world, I've decided I'm not going to."

"What are you going to do, then?" he asked. "I'm assuming Demeter was lost to Tartarus."

She shook her head. "No, and you won't have to worry about her either. She knows that many hate her for what she did to humanity after the Storm, and she has no interest in ruling the world. For now, she just wants to protect her remaining children." Persephone's eyes grew watery. "Hades cast Philomelus into Tartarus, and she's not taking it very well. She wanted all of us to survive."

Karter allowed his electricity to dissolve. "Is that what you're going to do? Try to save your brother?"

A few tears trickled down her cheeks. She swiped them away and cleared her throat. "It pains me to say this, but retrieving the immortals who don't deserve to be locked in Tartarus is out of the question. Rescuing them would cause far too many problems in the future. It would give Zeus's loyal followers the idea to travel there and retrieve him and his cronies.

"Still, I must do something. I can't deny the great deal of ugliness I've put into the world since Spencer was born. Even before then, I did nothing to stop the gods from decimating humanity. If there's a way to make up for my crimes, to balance the horrors with something beautiful, I'd like to find it."

Karter thought for a while, considering her words. Finally, he said, "I know you hate the Underworld, but with Hades gone, it's going to need someone to care for it—at least for the time being. It will also need someone to guard Tartarus, to ensure none of the minor gods go into the pit after the Olympians."

"You're—you're right." Her expression brightened just a bit. "Until the future of the Underworld can be decided, it needs my help." She shone with white light and disappeared.

Karter sighed in relief. At least for now, it seemed Persephone wouldn't be an issue. *Thank the Fates.*

He pivoted to finish making his way over to his companions and was met with Zoey running toward him. "What are you doing all the way over here?" she asked.

"Making sure I'm really immortal."

She stopped in front of him. "And? What'd you find out?"

He held up his forearm to show her his injury, but the skin had already mended itself. "Oh, there was a cut there before. I was bleeding golden ichor, the blood of the gods."

"So you really are a god now."

"It seems that way."

"Do you feel different?"

"I don't think so." He ran a hand through his hair. "It's just hard to believe."

Zoey stared at him in a way that made his insides feel fuzzy. "I'm glad you're back. I wasn't *me* after the convergence, but a part of me was still in there, and when you died, I . . . Well, I wasn't sure whether I'd ever recover from that. The way I . . . I mean, I definitely have feelings for you, and I couldn't imagine . . ." She trailed off, as if afraid to continue.

He swept a stray curl from her face. "I understand. I felt the same way when you converged with Calliope." At this her anxiety seemed to dissipate, and he pulled her close and kissed her.

After the group took a bit more time to process and discuss everything that had happened, they took count of all who had died. They found the corpses of fifty-six Deltama Village warriors and determined that 2,001 recruits had been killed. None of the demigods who'd fought for the Olympians were still alive, and any monsters and minor gods who'd lasted through the conflict had already fled the area.

With grateful but heavy hearts, Karter, Zoey, Andy, and their surviving companions made plans for how they would honor those who had sacrificed themselves for the cause.

CHAPTER TWENTY-FOUR

FRIEND

A YEAR AND THREE MONTHS LATER . . .

Autumn, Year 501 AS

With the Trident in her hand, Zoey walked alongside Andy, Karter, Diana, Kali, Marina, Harmony, and Chloe through the bustling *Agora* of what had once been Aphrodite City. It was a cool, crisp autumn morning, the sun hidden behind gray clouds, a blanket of fog hovering above the cobblestone paths. The group had been here for two months, and today they'd be leaving, but they had some goodbyes to make and a few last-minute matters to wrap up with the stand-in city officials before going.

Since their final clash against the gods—the fight everyone called the Battle of the Avatars—so much had changed. While Zoey had become the guardian of the Trident, Andy had become the guardian of the Lightning Bolt and Kali of the Helm of Darkness. Initially, Zoey and Andy had wanted Karter to guard the Bolt and Andy the Helm, but Karter had insisted that although he was technically a god and could now touch the magical objects, he wasn't fit to oversee them.

"Considering the mistakes I've made in the past," he'd said, *"I don't want to be responsible for any of the gods' old weapons, or to step into any sort of leadership role. I only want to try righting the wrongs of the immortals who came before me and ensure nothing like this happens again."*

After that, Karter had teleported the group to the twelve cities on the east coast of what used to be the United States, and the group had informed the citizens that the Olympians were gone. They'd also overthrown the city governments and helped the people start building new, fair government systems. Aphrodite City had been the last one they'd helped begin reforming before they had to drop off Kali at Deltama Village. Once Kali was safely returned, Chief Agni and the villagers placated, the rest of the crew planned to travel to the other cities of the world and help them as well.

There had, of course, been some attacks against the group. Plenty of people, *astynomia*, and nymphs had remained loyal to the gods even after their defeat. But many more were in support of Zoey, Andy, and their friends, including the surviving fifteen Deltama Village warriors, who had been traveling with the crew and protecting Kali and everyone else since the Battle of the Avatars. Zoey had no doubt that there would be unrest for a while, but that with time things would improve.

Soon they reached a familiar shop in the *Agora*, a shop they'd already visited several times since coming to the city. Jasmine's bakery.

Beside Zoey, Andy adjusted the glasses he'd been prescribed by an optometrist in Hephaestus City, as the lenses of his old glasses were cracked (the new ones had thick, round black frames, almost like steampunk-styled goggles). He tucked the Master Lightning Bolt under his arm, stepped up to the door of the bakery, and tried opening it. It wouldn't budge.

"Oh no," Zoey said. "You don't think Jasmine decided to close shop for today, do you? I don't want to leave without saying goodbye."

"She knew we were coming." There was a hint of disappointment in Andy's tone. "She wouldn't bail on us, right?"

"I don't think so," Kali said on Zoey's other side, switching the bag she stored the Helm in from her right shoulder to her left.

As if on cue, the door swung open, and Jasmine burst outside. She wore a tattered cream-colored dress over her slim figure, her frizzy black hair swept into a braid and a pack slung over her back. "Hey there," she chirped. "You made it."

"Of course we did," Andy replied. "We wouldn't have skipped out on saying bye before we go." He gestured at her bag. "Are you planning a trip now that citizens are free to leave the cities?"

"Um, sort of."

"Where're you headed?"

She took a deep breath. "Ever since you all came here and told me about what happened to Prometheus, I've been thinking . . . Would it be possible for me to come with you? I—I have so many bad memories of this place, and I'm ready to leave them behind, to make new ones."

Diana stepped forward. "What about your bakery? Didn't your family own this? Don't *you* own it?"

"They did, and I do, but I plan to transfer ownership of it to the city. I'm ready to start a new life."

Zoey and Andy shared a knowing look. "You're Prometheus's great-great-granddaughter," Zoey started. "You're more than welcome to join us if that's what you want."

Andy shrugged. "Heck, if you'd wanted to help us fight the gods before, we would have let you."

"As a matter of fact, I *did* want to." Jasmine smiled sadly. "I tried to follow you, but Prometheus wouldn't let me leave the bakery. He said if anything bad happened to me, he'd never forgive himself."

Zoey's eyes filled with tears at the memory of Prometheus. "He really cared about you. He wanted to make the world a better place for you."

Jasmine sniffled. "Well, he succeeded. The gods are gone. I'm free."

"Even so, we can't guarantee your safety," Diana said. "There are still monsters loose in the world, and there will be more revolts by those loyal to Zeus. We'll do what we can to protect you, but before you leave everything behind, you need to understand that coming with us could be dangerous."

"I do understand," Jasmine replied. "But there's danger everywhere, even in the cities. I can't spend the rest of my life stuck here being afraid of what might happen."

With that, the group accompanied Jasmine while she transferred ownership of her bakery to the city, and then they finished wrapping up their last-minute matters with the stand-in government officials and left. Now it was time to return Kali to Deltama Village.

Karter told the Deltama Village warriors that he'd overused his powers and was too weak to simply transport them to the village. However, later that night, he explained to Zoey, Andy, Diana, and Kali that he'd lied to give Diana and Kali more time together before Chief Agni tore them apart. They'd been sneaking around since the Battle of the Avatars, but Zoey would be lying if she said she hadn't noticed things getting tense between them. They'd been bickering more and more, and not in their usual flirtatious manner. In fact, a few of their most recent interactions had resulted in bitter arguments, disagreements that ended with Zoey and Andy consoling one or both of them.

"You didn't have to do that," Diana said to Karter, her tone crestfallen, and Kali frowned deeply at Diana.

That night, the girls slept on opposite sides of the camp, and Andy told Zoey the next day that he'd woken up twice to hear Kali crying. He said he'd tried to comfort her and she'd shooed him away, refusing to talk about what was wrong but confirming it had to do with Diana. Later that afternoon Zoey asked Diana about it, but Diana wouldn't discuss what had happened between her and Kali either.

During the rest of the trip Diana and Kali barely spoke. Zoey, Andy, Karter, and even Marina, Harmony, Chloe, and Jasmine tried various methods to get them to make up because it was obvious they still cared about each other, but they refused.

"You and Kali won't get to see each other for much longer," Zoey whispered to Diana one night. "Why not spend some time together?"

Diana's face crumpled. "That's exactly why we shouldn't. It will only make things harder when we're forced to part ways."

It took a little over a week for the group to reach Deltama Village. They approached the settlement from above, and men in the watchtowers near the tall log gates at the entrance began shouting happily about Kali's return.

"Kali is back!"

"Finally, she's returned!"

"Everyone, come out and greet your future chief!"

The men sounded joyful, but their words made Zoey sick to her stomach. *I'm not ready to say goodbye to Kali, and I know no one else is either.*

The cheers of Kali's people roared through the air, many of them racing out of their gardens and cabins to watch the crew land near the entrance of the village. They swarmed Kali, buzzing with a million questions, yelling over and pushing each other for a chance to speak with her. It was so loud, and there were so many people talking at once, Zoey couldn't understand a word anyone was saying.

A red-clothed man wielding a spear—Zoey recognized him as one of Chief Agni's guards—shoved his way through the crowd. "Silence!" the guard yelled, and the throng quieted just enough so that he could speak in a regular voice as he went on. "Chief Agni is waiting for you at his cabin," he said to Kali. "He needs to see you immediately. Come with me."

Kali sighed in defeat. "Fine."

The guard led Kali away, and Zoey, Andy, Karter, Diana, Marina, Harmony, Chloe, and Jasmine followed while the warriors and pegasi stayed behind. *This is it*, Zoey thought, swallowing hard and trying not to cry. *We're really about to say goodbye to Kali.*

The group trudged down a winding path that Zoey recalled led to Chief Agni's giant four-story cabin, which was surrounded by its own fence. When they reached the cabin, it looked just as Zoey remembered, complete with fiery torches and more guards before its gates.

The guard who'd fetched Kali waved the others off, and they allowed the group to pass through the gates and up to the cabin. Kali inhaled sharply as the guard knocked on the door. The door creaked open, and Chief Agni— with his huge build and long dreaded hair— stepped outside.

For what felt like whole minutes, Kali and Chief Agni stared at each other. It was totally silent, as if everyone were holding their breath.

Finally, Chief Agni's eyes grew watery, and he broke the silence. "Daughter, is it really you?"

"It's really me, Father," Kali replied.

He practically lunged toward Kali and wrapped her in a hug that looked as though it would have squished her if she weren't so tough. "You did it," he said, tears rolling down his cheeks. He kissed the top of her head. "You helped vanquish the gods and returned safely to us as the Mother Goddess prophesied."

She hugged him back, although she wasn't as enthusiastic about it as he was. "Yes, I did."

"For that, I'm so grateful." The chief pulled away and wiped his face with the back of his hand. "All of you, come in. There's much we have to discuss." The group obliged to his request, although the guard who'd led them there remained outside.

Like the rest of Deltama Village, the interior of the chief's cabin appeared exactly as it had when Zoey had last been here. With woven rugs and fluffy couches and a fireplace crackling on the back wall, the first level felt homey. A servant girl was busy sweeping the floor when they walked in, and the chief told her to "run along." She did as he ordered.

"Please, make yourselves comfortable." Chief Agni gestured at the rugs and couches. "I imagine it will take a long while to relay everything that has happened since you left. I cannot wait to hear about your heroics."

Everyone except for Kali started searching for a spot to relax. Kali remained standing, her fists clenched at her sides.

Chief Agni raised a brow at her. "Is something wrong?"

"Yes," she replied. The group stopped what they were doing and turned to Kali. "Before we discuss my 'heroics,' there's something I'm going to tell you, Father. And even though you won't like it, you're not going to argue with me about it."

The chief seemed taken aback by her sudden ferocity, but he didn't say anything.

Kali glanced at Diana. "I know this isn't what we discussed, but I can't go through with what my people expect of me—no matter how much they sacrificed to help us."

Diana stepped forward. "Kali—"

"No." Kali shook her head. "It's *my* life."

"Daughter." There was genuine confusion in Chief Agni's voice. "What is the meaning of this?"

Kali puffed out her chest as if to make herself bigger. "You claim the Goddess of Destruction sent you visions about my future, about how I'm going to marry someone you pick for me and become the chief early. But I'm not going to do any of that."

The chief blinked. "What are you— This is your *destiny* prophesied by a true god, Kali. You cannot simply—"

"I already told you," Kali interrupted, "you're not going to argue with me. Let me finish." He crossed his arms and nodded reluctantly. She went on. "In the time since I left the village, I've learned a lot about 'destiny,' and I've realized something. Yes, there are things that happen to us that we can't control, but that doesn't mean our futures are locked into what the gods, or the universe, or anyone else has planned for us. There are choices we get to make for ourselves, and in my case, I choose to *not* become chief prematurely, and to spend my life with someone I love"—she faced Diana—"so long as she'll have me."

Diana rolled her eyes, but her bottom lip quivered. "I—I guess that doesn't sound *so* bad."

Kali let out a relieved laugh, and her shoulders relaxed. She rushed to Diana, grabbed her by the face, and kissed her.

After Kali and Diana pulled away from each other, flushed and grinning, Chief Agni pinched the bridge of his nose. "It's wonderful that you've found love, Daughter. It really is. But if you and this girl become lifelong partners, how will you produce an heir when you *do* become chief?"

"Maybe I won't need to," Kali said. "Maybe the village doesn't need to be so strict in following the old ways. We could try a different method of 'producing' an heir—that is, whoever's chief could choose a worthy successor and, when the time comes, teach them what they need to know for when they become the new leader."

Chief Agni mulled over Kali's suggestion. "Hmm. I must admit, I'm not enthusiastic about the idea. However, what you did to help the Chosen Two—and, in turn, our people—cannot be ignored. Your views on destiny are especially radical, but you do have some newfound worldly experience, so they might be worth considering."

"I'm glad you're willing to consider my 'radical' views," Kali replied. "But no matter what, I've made up my mind about what I'm going to do. Speaking of, I just decided something else. I'm leaving the village again."

"What?" the chief exclaimed. "You've been gone for over a year!"

"I have, but there are still cities around the world that need to be reformed, people who need help."

"But the village—"

"Will have a brighter future," Kali asserted.

"Because the rest of the world will too. Besides, I thought you were plenty capable of taking care of this place without me. You don't mean to tell me you're not, do you?"

Chief Agni couldn't argue with her there. In fact, her words even made him chuckle. They spent the rest of the afternoon catching up, Kali telling her father about the quest she'd embarked on, and Zoey's heart swelled with pride at the way Kali had handled herself.

"I have to admit," Zoey said to Karter and Andy later that evening, "I'm more than just a little excited we won't be leaving Kali behind."

Andy nodded. "I was hoping she'd stand up to her dad like that."

"Me too," Karter agreed. "Things wouldn't be the same without her around."

The group stayed in Deltama Village for the night, but the next day they ventured into the forest again, as they had one last stop to make before traveling to the other cities around the world.

Andy held Darko's red poppy close to his heart

as he walked through thick pines toward the spot where he and his friends were going to plant the flower. It was surprisingly warm for a fall day, the sun peeking through the gaps in the forest, and the air smelled of pine and fallen leaves.

"I think we're almost there," Zoey said from beside Andy. She carried the Trident and Bolt in a pack on her back so Andy could handle the poppy, Karter on her other side. They'd been inseparable since the Battle of the Avatars, constantly staring at each other like lovestruck dummies. Andy knew he used to look at Zoey like that all the time, but over the past year he'd found himself doing it less and less.

"You're sure you don't want to plant it someplace where it's warm year-round?" Diana asked. Behind Andy, she trod alongside Kali, Jasmine, Marina, Harmony, and Chloe, and Luna, Ajax, Aladdin, and a few other pegasi followed the six of them. "Someplace with a great view?"

Andy shook his head. "No way. This is where he'd want his flower to be. I know it."

They traveled for a short while longer before reaching a small clearing in the forest. Wilting periwinkle bellflowers stood between bushes and tall grass. In the shadows of the trees at the edge of the clearing, there was a dark, unmoving figure.

"Here it is," Andy said. He stopped to examine the clearing for a moment.

Harmony paused beside Andy. "So this is where Medusa turned his brother to stone." She pointed at the dark form. "Is that him? Phoenix?"

"Yes," Zoey confirmed. "We found Phoenix right before meeting Darko."

They crossed the clearing, and Andy gasped.

Cracks riddled Phoenix's statue, green vines breaking through and curling around the stone.

The sight made Andy recall a time before the group had stolen Poseidon's Trident, when they'd been in Aphrodite City and had just watched a bunch of *astynomia* transform into plants after being killed. Darko had explained that all satyrs, centaurs, nymphs, and the like "returned to nature" after dying.

"What about your brother?" Andy had asked. *"What about Phoenix? He was turned to stone. Will he ever return to nature?"*

"I'm not sure," Darko had replied. *"I don't know if Medusa trapped her victims or just killed them. I know his body won't change now, but I hope his spirit was able to escape at least."*

Andy and Zoey shared a tearful glance.

Over the next half hour, the group said prayers over Darko's poppy and bid it farewell. Karter blessed the flower, and then they planted it next to Phoenix's vines.

As Zoey patted down the soil around the poppy, Andy couldn't help but smile at her. No, they hadn't ended up together, but she was still one of the most important people in his life. Even if it was occasionally awkward between them because of everything that had happened, he refused to stop talking to her, to push her away.

No matter what, he thought, *she'll always be my friend.*

And that was enough.

THE END

A. P. Mobley is a dark fantasy author with an undying love for world mythologies and epic, magical tales. She grew up in Wyoming and currently lives in South Dakota. She considers herself a huge nerd, loves coffee a little too much, and can be found snuggling with one of her pets into late hours of the night.

Thank you for reading *The Threads of Fate*! If you enjoyed this book, please consider leaving it a review on Amazon, Goodreads, Bookbub, or wherever it is you like to get your books from.

I say this because reviews are the best way to thank authors for writing the books you love. The more positive reviews a book has, the more new readers websites show it to. I do not have a big publisher paying to promote my books, so reviews are the most important component in spreading the word about my stories.

A review doesn't have to be lengthy; just a few words or a sentence or two is amazing.

Thank you again for reading *The Threads of Fate*. It is an absolute dream come true to be able to publish my stories for you to read.

ALSO BY A. P. MOBLEY:

48972CB00001B/22